I0585941

# End of Morrow

## J.P. Manning

Guardians of the East – Book 3

First published in Australia in 2023 by J.P. Manning
Website: www.lostbookproductions.com
Email: lostbookproductions@gmail.com

Cover design and map by Daniel Greenup

Cover image: iStock.com/Lutz Berlemont-Bernard

The moral right of the author has been asserted.

ISBN 9780648737643 (paperback)

A catalogue record for this
book is available from the
National Library of Australia

NATIONAL
LIBRARY
OF AUSTRALIA

**Disclaimer**
This is a work of fiction. Names, characters, places, incidents and
events, other than those clearly in the public domain, are either the
product of the author's imagination or used fictitiously. Any resemblance to actual persons, living or dead, is entirely coincidental.

*For my father, David*

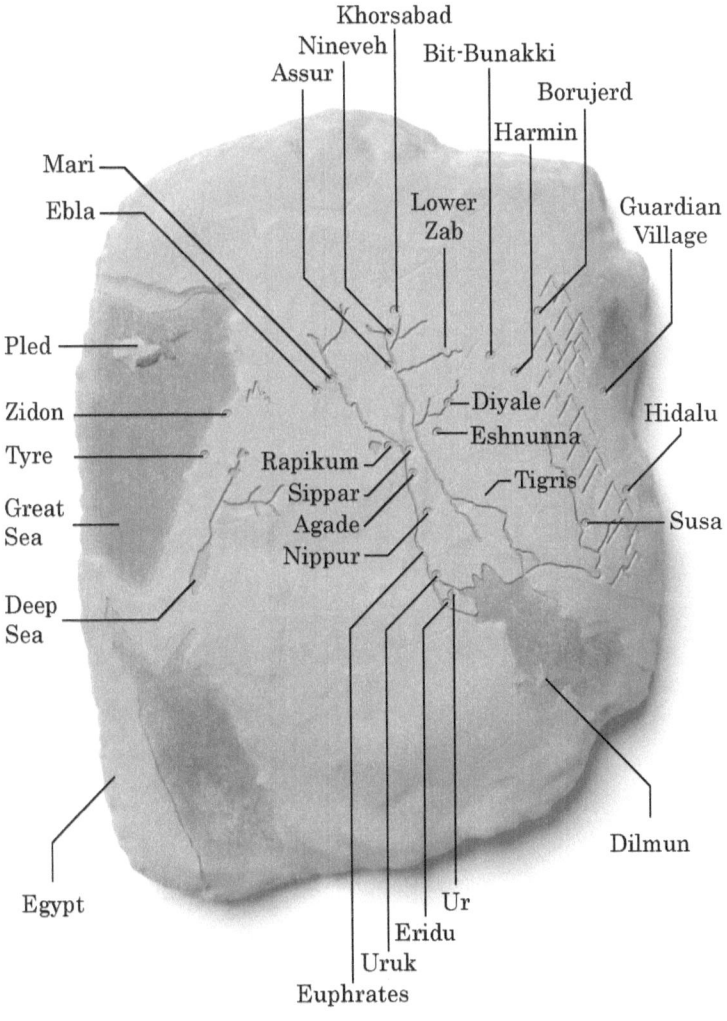

Khorsabad
Nineveh
Assur
Bit-Bunakki
Borujerd
Harmin
Mari
Ebla
Lower
Zab
Guardian
Village
Pled
Zidon
Diyale
Hidalu
Tyre
Eshnunna
Rapikum
Great
Sea
Sippar
Tigris
Agade
Susa
Nippur
Deep
Sea
Dilmun
Egypt
Ur
Eridu
Uruk
Euphrates

# CONTENTS

# 1

# The Archaeologist's Wager

*Frederick Baker's Journal, Cairo, Egypt,*
*15–19 November 1850.*

The Guardian manuscript had identified the location of a lost city. Thankfully, I'd had time to share this with the librarian, Babu, his assistant, Lateef, and my colleague, Victor, before our meeting was rudely interrupted. The main agenda of the meeting had been met and, whilst I can't say for certain what the other men were thinking as Babu locked his study and ushered us down the hall, I'm sure it wasn't about lunch.

Babu's English wife ensured we were always with drink as we sat in the library's parlour ahead of a meal in the next room. She stood by the liquor cabinet, surely listening to our stifled conversation but giving no indication. Her familiar perfume mixed with the library's scent of cedar wood and calmed my nerves.

The sudden interruption by embassy officials and

police officers almost seemed part of Babu's plan. He had remained calm and, in the presence of the intruders, referred to the confiscation of items as an opportunity to have our proposed dig lodged without fee. They had collected his maps of Mesopotamia and Persia, and my diary, but did not show interest in, or awareness of, the Guardian manuscript—the source behind our planned expedition. This suggested that their tip-off was ill informed or part of a larger scheme. My diary, mostly filled with appointment times and measurements from excavations, also included my hand-drawn map of the region and a distinctive triangle that represented the Port of Assur. The ink strokes that formed my triangle were twice as thick as any other marking. Whilst it might gain attention on the page, there was no explanation of its meaning. The Guardian manuscript and my journal is what anyone trying to thwart our plans required. My journal, in which I write now, describes all my noteworthy encounters and thoughts since our unearthing of the tomb outside of Cairo in May. I still had my journal and I did not need my map. It was based on the Guardian manuscript.

Babu did not seem ready to discuss the intrusion, so I tried to lighten the mood in view of a delayed explanation. 'Did you hear about the archaeologist who found an Egyptian mummy who had died of a heart attack?'

'Heart attack?' questioned Lateef from the deep-buttoned leather sofa opposite me. 'When did this happen?'

'It's a joke,' I explained.

'Oh, continue then.' The young researcher screwed up his face to his own interruption.

'In the mummy's hand was a crumpled bet slip and it read, 1000 shekels on Goliath.'

Babu released a short laugh followed by an extended groan, and Lateef looked to Victor for his reaction.

Victor, seated next to me, swayed his brandy and admired its dark colour. He spoke from beyond his tilted glass. 'Samuel 17:10, the Philistine said, "I defy the armies of Israel this day; give me a man, that we may fight together." And a young shepherd boy, David, accepted the giant's challenge.'

Lateef nodded slowly and smiled, his moustache lifting on his thin face. 'I understand the joke. Goliath was the favourite to win the fight.'

'He was described in the Book of Samuel as being six cubits and a span. That's over nine feet tall.' I sipped my warm ale and smacked my lips. 'A short-priced favourite.'

'Like Sargon,' added Lateef.

'I don't know.' The leather sofa squeaked as I sat upright. 'Was Sargon a giant? Did he fight Kar?'

'You have not finished reading, so I would not spoil this for you, Fred.' Lateef's tongue poked out momentarily before he bit his lip and turned his stare to the empty coffee table between us, acting distracted.

'Sargon?' Victor questioned himself. 'Sargon, Sargon?' he repeated.

'Ill luck comes from chanting the name of the dead,' warned Babu, adjusting his tailored pants in his lean to one side of his armchair.

Victor lowered his glass and raised an eyebrow as he wriggled his body loose of any demon that might have attached itself to his person.

13

Lateef was perplexed by his movement and almost stood to assist.

'Apologies,' said Victor. 'I have heard the name before. Maybe in Layard's book about Nineveh?'

'You have heard the name but not in reference to Sargon of Akkad,' said Babu, sitting upright in his chair and loosening his red tie. 'I have also read *Nineveh and Its Remains* and can confirm that Layard writes of a different Sargon. Twice he mentions the name. A common name among kings, for sure, as it means true king.' The librarian looked up at his wife. His nod was barely noticeable.

She walked to Babu's side, her step as proper as her light application of blush and controlled expression. 'Gentlemen, when you are ready, lunch is now prepared in the dining room.'

Victor stood promptly, swished his golden hair behind his shoulders and braced his hat under one arm. He led his walk with an extended grasp of his glass of brandy.

\*\*\*

In the dining room, Victor chose a seat to the left side of the twelve-foot table and I sat opposite. The large table sat neatly in the room, with comfortable space remaining between outdrawn chairs and the walls. There was an entrance from the parlour and the kitchen on the other side. With no windows, freestanding candelabrums provided the only light. Smoke from the candles wafted to wall vents above an empty picture rail. The cedar wood walls were a new addition and there were no paintings or wall hangings interrupting our timber slat enclosure. I had enjoyed a meal at this table only a few days ago. My entry to the room did not feel as pleasant this time. Too much had been left unsaid since our meeting in the drawing room had been interrupted.

Lateef sat at the table end closest the parlour and Babu rounded the table to sit near the door to the kitchen. His wife drew his chair and helped him shuffle it closer to the table. She then exited the dining room into the kitchen.

Victor winked at me from across the table.

'Don't do that,' I said. 'I'm still confused by today's happenings.'

'You could have signalled your response with a shrug,' said Victor.

'If I'm responsible for the need to shrug, I apologise,' said Babu. 'You're upfront, Fred. I like that.' He spread his arms and signalled his maids to serve us soup.

Silver bowls and spoons were already placed and the maids delicately ladled from their tureens, not spilling a drop on the pristine white tablecloth.

'Please stay,' said Babu as the maids returned across the room towards the kitchen. He pointed them towards the wall behind Victor.

The maids' eyes darted between the table, the soup served and each other.

Babu's wife re-entered the room from the kitchen and stood behind her husband, waiting for him to speak.

'I shall begin by saying, one of us in this room is a traitor.'

'A solid point to start with,' said Victor, thankfully winking at Babu this time. 'I can vouch for Fred. The only people he has had contact with are me and Hu, our host at the guesthouse.'

'Your thoughts, Fred?' asked Babu.

'I have not spoken of the manuscript since our meeting apart to say I am reading a book. This is all I revealed to Hu, my host, so that I might not be disturbed and Victor so that he would also allow me time to read before this meeting.'

Babu looked towards Lateef at the opposite end of the table.

The young researcher was trying to tame his hair by pushing it down with his palms. This never worked. His thick moustache gained my attention again as he stilled his hands and readied his response.

Victor gained Babu's attention first. 'Might I be bold in asking whether all is sound under this roof?'

Babu's head twisted like a bird judging the distance of its prey. 'Please tell me what you know before I insult those I know well.'

Victor shifted his chair back from the table, the screech hurting my ears. He held his stiff hat against his chest and drummed it with his fingers. It looked like a bowler hat but Victor was adamant that it was called a Coke. 'Three things have happened since I entered your library that weigh on my mind.' Victor stood and slowly slid his chair back to the table.

I was not sure if he was trying to emphasise the screeching sound of the chair's legs or soften it through a slow and jittered shift. I almost yelled for him to lift it.

He shoved the chair once more and stood next

to the two maids, in view of all. 'First there was the movement of the police officers,' said Victor. 'They did not follow the embassy officials into the drawing room.' He looked at Babu and pointed at the wall behind. 'Instead, they entered your private study from the hall. Considering that they did not take anything from your study, I find that peculiar.'

Babu leant his bearded chin on his clasped hands. 'I believe they thought to block our escape and prevent us from hiding anything.'

'And that is logical, so I'll continue with my second observation.' Victor hung his hat on one side of his chair's backrest and took a moment to sip his brandy.

I had seen Victor act this way before, when negotiating funding for a dig. He liked for each point of consideration to have time to settle before offering greater reason. He controlled the discussion with extended pause.

'Your reaction to the intrusion, Babu, was both reassuring and strange to me.'

'Please explain,' said Babu, leaning back in his chair and further loosening his tie. His wife offered to take his tie but Babu signalled her to stand back.

'Reassuring in that not for a moment did you see the intrusion as any sign of defeat or inconvenience. And strange in that you left the drawing room and reappeared seemingly unthreatened by their presence.' Victor raised his arms by his side, 'Honestly, Babu, I thought it all part of your plan in the moment. Your words, I think you said something like, "They will lodge our claim without fee," made sense at the time.'

'Do my words no longer make sense?'

'Your words still make sense because they will need to come to us for assistance. It was your calmness. I make no accusation. I'm just sharing my observations and seeking understanding.'

Babu flashed his teeth at Victor and turned to me with the same bemused look. 'I'm comforted to know that I'm not accused.' The librarian placed his hands on the table as he faced Victor. 'There was another happening that bothered you?'

'Yes, we can re-visit my second observation later. The third happening involves the ladies standing next to me.'

The younger maid braced her bosom and the older maid half raised a hand to her mouth. They were both dressed like English maids in black ankle length dresses with white aprons tied at their neck and waist. Stiff white bonnets adorned their faces.

Babu rolled his weight to one side of his chair and squinted as he focused his stare on the maids' faces. 'They have both been in my employ for five years. Akila is the daughter of a friend of mine. She also works in my library. I have been tutoring her in arithmetic, history, and English literature. For many Egyptian girls, writing and reciting verses from the Quran is the extent of their education. Chione ...' Babu paused and turned to look at his wife. 'Chione applied for the position, I think.'

'Yes,' replied Babu's wife.

'Her service has been without fault.'

Victor rotated his glass of brandy before taking his last sip. 'A superb drop,' he exclaimed. 'Unbranded, you say?'

'The cask would have been branded before I purchased it by the bottle. I thought you could tell me,' replied Babu, sitting up in his chair. His inquisitive look and the resemblance of a smile reminded me of the Babu I had met a few days earlier. His long beard without a moustache, had given him a jovial appearance. Today, instead of joking about coming to his desk in slippers, he complained about his formal attire.

Victor spiked a smile. 'One day I hope I can identify Cognac or brandy by its taste and qualities. This is still a new pursuit of mine.'

'A finer pursuit than mine, it is. I hope to dress like my professors in Oxford one day. The wearing of a tie during a single meeting, I find unbearable. My pants clutch me like foreign hands, always finding a new spot to fondle.'

'Might I suggest a blend of the lounge jacket and the high collar shirt,' said Victor, gesturing to me.

I tried to look down at my collar. 'I think you are both distracted.'

Victor winked at me. 'The distraction is purposeful, Fred.'

'Interesting,' said Babu, 'I think we are involved in a game of observation.'

Lateef pointed at my shirt. 'Fred has a short collar and wears a safari suit.'

Victor sighed at his empty glass and Babu turned promptly to excuse his wife for the errand.

I looked at the two maids standing next to Victor. The younger maid, Akila, had tears in her eyes, her shoulders shuddering as she tried to control her breathing and maintain her hold of a tureen. The older maid, probably in her early thirties, like me, did not know to whom she should look for understanding. Her eyes flickered around the room, never settling.

Victor walked towards the parlour door, behind Lateef's seat, and opened it for Babu's wife. After she had exited the room, he asked me to stand. 'I need you for this experiment, Fred' he said. 'Lateef and Babu, could I ask you to stand at the two exits?'

I stood behind my chair, opposite the frightened maids. I wanted to comfort the younger maid with some reassuring words. She looked no older than eighteen.

When Babu's wife entered the room with a new drink for Victor, she almost dropped it, surely startled by our movement in her short absence.

'I'll take that,' said Victor, clutching the glass as it wobbled in her hand. 'I'd hate for a drop to be spilt. Please stand here with Lateef, Ma'am.' He walked towards the maids and ushered them around the table until they stood in the corner of the room between Babu and me. 'I had to be sure,' said Victor, when he was standing next to Babu at the kitchen door. He took a sip of his new drink and tilted his glass to Babu. 'It's a Cognac, not a brandy.'

'Very good,' said Babu. The librarian gestured to the maids. 'You had another point to make.'

'Ah, yes, my third observation today concerned the maid standing closest to Fred.'

'Chione,' said Babu.

'Chione,' repeated Victor, 'if you don't mind, could you please disclose any weapon you might be concealing.'

The younger maid's head snapped sideways at the accused maid and she stepped away from her. Her back met the touch of the freestanding candelabrum and she yelped.

'*Ahmil hadha ana*,' yelled Chione, removing a corkscrew from her apron pocket.

'She carries this,' translated Lateef.

'Thank you, Lateef.' I looked at Victor.

He fluttered his spare hand. 'Take it from her please, Fred.'

I approached Chione and she handed me the corkscrew. I displayed it to Victor.

'Superb. Now, Chione,' continued Victor, 'is there anything else you carry that might be considered a weapon?' Victor patted his side and raised his hand in a questioning manner.

'No,' said Chione. She looked to Babu for sympathy.

'Mr Ascott?' inquired Babu.

'Let me explain my third observation.' Victor walked back to his chair at the table. 'Chione is the eldest of the two maids. Age is not always coupled with experience, yet today I encounter a maid whose service is described as "without fault." Your words, Babu,' said Victor as he placed his hands on the backrest of his chair that still hung his hat. 'Now consider that the customary service of soup is from the left. This is simply a custom and not an expectation in private service. I took no offence from being served soup from the right.' Victor paused and looked upon the table.

The soup had been served and in Victor's pause,

I think we all replayed our own recollection of the service. Chione had also served Lateef and the young researcher gave Victor an agreeable nod that sped up as his recollection became clearer.

'The serving of soup from the left is not only customary, Lateef,' continued Victor. 'It is usually beneficial for the server. They must hold a tureen and have a steady hand to ladle to the bowl. The exception would be if the server was left-handed or so inexperienced that they unintentionally performed the task in an ineffective manner.'

Babu looked to the maid in question. Her stare was locked on Victor. The younger maid, Akila, shared flighty glances with anyone who might rescue her from the situation.

'Therefore, I believe Chione had reason to serve Lateef and me from the right. She carries something to the left of her person that would have interfered with or have been noticed in her service.'

The room was silent for a moment as all eyes turned to Chione.

She looked down at her left side and then turned to Babu, her eyes wide.

'What has you acting this way?' Babu asked Chione.

'Notice the hand in which she now holds the tureen,' added Victor. 'It has changed since service.'

'Chione?' questioned Babu.

'*Ana sa'ashrah*,' she replied as she approached the table to set down the tureen she carried.

'What does she say?' asked Victor.

'She will explain,' Lateef translated.

'We have our traitor,' asserted Victor. 'Be ready, men. Her hands are free.'

'I'm not the traitor,' Chione shouted. 'Babu has turned English. He gives all to foreigners.'

'I would give you to anyone who would take you,' said Babu. 'Let me reprimand her insolence and treachery.'

Chione looked to the door to the parlour and tried to rush past me.

I held her back but she kept wriggling and screaming in my grasp. Her resistance became unbearable and I thrust her back into the corner.

'Stay calm and we can discuss your involvement,' Victor advised.

She slipped her hand through a tear in her dress behind her apron on her left side and drew a serrated kitchen knife. 'Stay back,' she threatened.

'Chione, sit so we can talk properly,' I said as she poked her knife at me and I defended myself by waving her corkscrew just as erratically.

Victor lifted his Coke hat from his chair's backrest and, from the opposite side of the table, he flung it at the maid.

The hat's stiff brim hit her in the side of the head and knocked her from her feet. As she stumbled, I removed the knife from her hand and placed it and the corkscrew on the table.

The librarian stepped towards the woman on the floor.

'Babu?' his wife's voice strained, giving him pause.

He looked back at her and exhaled audibly. 'Akila, clear the table. Prepare new meals for us all. Anything touched by Chione is to be tossed.'

Babu's wife picked up the tureen that Chione had been carrying and Akila waited for her to approach and escort her from the room.

'Help Chione to a seat, Fred,' said Victor.

It was a pleasantly stated order from Victor, not a request. I helped Chione to a chair and unpinned her bonnet that was flopping to one side since her fall. I placed it on the table in front of her, next to my un-touched bowl of soup.

'Remarkable observation,' Babu praised Victor.

'And we never had to delve into my second obser-vation,' he replied.

'Gentlemen,' I said, 'she is seated and cooperative. Do you have any questions for her?'

'I will keep my distance for fear of using my fist,' said Babu. 'You disgust me, Chione.'

I stood behind her. I was ready to keep her planted should she try to stand without invitation.

Babu sat and leant his arms on the table. 'Speak, woman, what have you told them?'

'You side with the English,' she said.

'And you told them this before or after they ar-rived with guns?' questioned Victor.

'No gun,' said Chione. 'Do you see a gun?'

I looked at Victor, 'I don't think she understands.'

'She understands English perfectly well. Why did you betray me?' asked Babu.

'*Akhbartuk*,' she shouted. Her lips trembled, want-ing to say more.

'I told you,' translated Lateef.

Victor looked at me and I shook my head. Her motivation was clear. Any further questioning would be as pointless as asking a thief why they stole. And Chione was not guilty of a crime, just a betrayal of trust. Our detainment and interrogation of the woman risked escalating to a crime.

'For five years I've trusted this woman with free wander of my house and allowed her to serve my wife and I meals. I offer her no further favour.'

Victor looked at me again.

I returned his look and said nothing. I had made my stance clear.

Victor placed his glass of Cognac with a sip still left. 'Remove your apron, Chione, and leave it on the table. I will escort you from the library in your dress.'

'Chione?' I tapped her gently on the shoulder.

She turned, her eyes and mouth braced like a frightened cat.

Her stare reminded me of someone whom in the moment I could not recall. I signalled to the door and stepped back to show her that her exit was unobstructed.

'Leave your apron,' repeated Victor.

Chione stood and removed her apron. She dumped it in my bowl of soup.

I grabbed her wrist as her fingers tightened around the bowl. 'Don't create more trouble.'

Victor straightened his arm in the direction of the door.

She released her hold on the bowl and Victor and I followed her out of the dining room, across the parlour and towards the main hall. She paused in the hall.

Victor paced towards her and pointed ahead, 'Go find a friend.'

She hurried through the main entrance and into the early afternoon light.

I followed her outside and down the first few steps, interested to see if she walked or ran. She ran and she did not look back.

Victor placed a hand on my shoulder. 'It's not our country, Fred. It won't be Babu's country either if we head east into the Ottoman Empire.'

'If we head east?' I questioned. 'If I do not see the moon tonight, can I still say it was splendid?'

'Don't make this decision beguiled by expected splendour or Layard's luck. It's a wager with even odds on us finding nothing because we are turned around before we can reach our site or complete an excavation,' said Victor. 'We may not see the moon tonight. We might be indoors or it be blocked by cloud. Account for what we have now.'

I took a moment to admire our position on the sandstone steps to the old library, with its Roman style façade. The hardened dirt road in front was occupied by a slow flow of camels and hand-drawn carts. Above the clay brick buildings opposite the library, a hot sun sat low in a dust-filled sky.

Victor pointed down the road. 'We saw the maid run for almost two hundred metres before entering the lane next to the tailor's shop. She did not look back because she did not fear pursuit.'

'She may not fear us but should we be worried about her?'

'Fred,' Victor chuckled. 'I met with English embassy officials yesterday. They know I have returned and that your work is ongoing. Life in Egypt is unchanged for us. As for a departure east, well, that I'm certain will meet resistance despite any explanation. Some fear is healthy.'

'Babu said—'

'Babu is a librarian,' interrupted Victor. 'Remember me, the British invader of foreign soil?' Victor adopted a victorious stance for a moment with his head turned to the sky. He sighed at his own antics. 'I need you to confirm Babu's investment in the venture and I'll use that to leverage British support. I might be able to secure us a retainer.'

I gave Victor a nod. 'I bet the moon is splendid tonight.'

'And I bet that when you discuss its splendour, you also talk of what it lights below, what we already have. Alone, the moon is just a reflection of light.'

I laughed and encouraged him back up the steps to the library. 'Let's finish this meeting so that we can talk properly.'

'Ah,' Victor raised a finger, 'your verbal confidentiality agreement. Always add a clause, Fred. Always add a discussion clause.'

\*\*\*

Babu met us as we entered the parlour. He held Victor's Coke hat like it was the only relic remaining from a devastating fire. 'There is a mark on its brim,' said Babu. His head lowered as he held it out to Victor with both hands.

'Not a mark, a scar,' said Victor, and he rapped the hat with his knuckles before tucking it under his arm.

'We thought you might have left with her,' said Babu. His voice was muffled by the sound of the heavy library door at the end of the hall being closed and bolted.

Lateef approached me from his seat in the parlour. 'I knew you would come back Mr Fred, I mean, Fred.'

'Hopefully, no more interruptions,' I said and I shook his hand when I noticed it half-raised and ready to recoil like a jilted lover.

He enjoyed the handshake. I know this because our hands were still shaking through his explanation of our last three meetings. '... And then I watched you throw her away. You could have hurt her much worse. I see this in your face.'

'You should see what he can do with a cricket bat,' said Victor, distracting Lateef and saving my hand.

I pointed to the wall behind the sofas and demonstrated a slog. 'I hit seven boundaries in my last match. Off stump bowls were my weakness.'

Lateef glanced at the wall and back to my hands. 'The off stump,' he said pointing at my hands.

I pointed to his seat as I found mine again.

Akila, the young maid, offered me a glass of ale and I graciously accepted. I assumed that Babu's wife was preparing a new meal. That was comforting.

Babu sat in the same armchair. 'I apologise for the interruptions. I'm sure—'

'Interruptions?' blurted Victor. 'No, these are dire warnings, Babu. Strict advice that your planned search for ancient treasure is known at a government level.'

'I sense fear of authority,' said Babu. The librarian looked at me when he did not get a response from

Victor.

I watched Victor being Victor.

With his usual casual control, he made his way around the parlour, studying more precisely the construction of new walls. I had not revealed to Victor that the new cedar-wood walls had changed the open plan of the library or that they allowed Babu to create secret chambers for the storing of special works.

Babu twisted in his chair to keep Victor always in sight.

Before seating himself next to me, Victor pointed to the wall next to the hall to Babu's study. 'Is there a second floor to this library?'

'The maids' closet,' replied Babu.

'And I'm the King of England,' laughed Victor, leaning back in the studded sofa. 'We need to be honest with each other.'

Babu stood, faster than I had seen him move before, 'Please demonstrate this honesty. What brings you back to Cairo, Mr Ascott, more than a desire to sample brandy and sport a new hat?'

'I can answer for him,' I said.

'That would be improper, Fred, because I am present and have a voice.' Victor slapped my thigh as he stood. 'I return because our fates have crossed.' He walked between Babu's armchair and the curled end of the sofa. 'Instead of crossing the English Channel and returning to my wife, I have the honour of your present company. You're not as attractive, mind you. Akila excluded,' he gave her a wink.

Misunderstanding his gesture, she approached with the bottle of Cognac.

Victor halted her with a raised palm before continuing. 'You talk my talk and play my game. Now, maybe you all know more about Layard than I do, but I just had to return when I learnt of the developments in Nineveh.' He took a sip of his Cognac and Babu eased himself back into his armchair, comfortable that his questions were being answered. 'The Egyptian influence in the carvings is not to be ignored. And I have learnt that Layard is now the Head of the British Archaeological Mission to Mesopotamia, backed by the British Museum. He continues to unearth clay tablets and another Brit, Rawlinson, has now decoded a second cuneiform script. Chances are, anything we unearth can be translated. This is monumental. There has never been a better time to dig a hole in old Persia.'

'He also asked you about the hat,' I said with mirth.

Victor lifted his arm and let it fall into his hand. 'It's a Coke, from Lock and Co., London. Spelt c, o, k, e but pronounced Cook, like the navigator who discovered New Holland. It's fashionable and useful, as I demonstrated earlier. Normally, a personal fitting is required. I purchased this hat from an English banker man for a pound and twelve shillings. I had to have it and it almost fits perfectly. Allows room for my head to grow, if you know what I mean? And if anyone tries to tell me it's a bowler hat, I'll ask, would you pay a pound and a half for a bowler hat?'

Babu clutched the armrests to his chair and eased himself to his feet, 'Thank you for sharing, Mr Ascott. I hope you can accept my behaviour today as being against my normal character.'

'A challenging day it has been for you,' said Victor

as he sat next to me on the leather sofa.

'Challenging, I like that word. I like you, Mr Ascott. You are upfront, like Fred.' Babu swayed his half-empty glass in the direction of Akila. 'And you are right, we must be honest with each other. There is more than a broom closet behind the wall you identified. There is more to everything than that which meets the eye at first glance.'

'Yes, there is,' said Victor.

'Babu?' I said, joining in the conversation. 'Are we ready to continue our discussion from the drawing room?'

'Certainly. Where would you like to start?'

'Assur,' I replied and went on to explain my observations, based on the text, that had led me to identify this city as the most profitable site for a dig. Assur was not beneath an existing city and, if required, evidence of its existence could be demonstrated through the description provided in select pages of the Guardian manuscript. All listened intently, nodding agreeably until I mentioned its proximity to Nineveh.

'Our claim would have to be approved by the Ottoman Sultan Abdulmejid I and his embassies in Baghdad and Constantinople,' said Victor.

'What about Layard's approach?' Babu inquired. 'Did he not transport massive three-metre high statues without permission?'

Victor nodded. 'He did and that is why the Sultan is less carefree now. The winged-bull statues have made it to the British Museum and there is no doubt that the Sultan has since heard of Layard's heroic welcome in London. There was no fanfare for the Sultan despite the hospitality he afforded Layard.'

'Remember the moon, Victor.' I added.

Lateef, seated opposite on an identical leather sofa, shifted closer, his head bridging the gap to the coffee table.

Victor leant back next to me and tilted his glass. 'You have the floor, Fred.'

I stayed seated. 'We might not see the moon to-night but we know it's there. It's a full moon too, with light enough to reveal things not looked to in the brightness of day.'

Victor assumed my analogy and nudged me with his elbow. His smile was too large for him to celebrate with a sip of Cognac.

'In the East,' I continued, 'there is a city lost to time. It was a great city that existed at the same time as Nineveh and was closer to the king's city, Sargon's city, Agade.' I looked at Babu, then Lateef and back to Babu. 'We can find it without lifting a spade. We don't need approval to travel. All we need is funding for the journey. I anticipate that we can identify the site and return in the space of two months.'

Victor cleared his throat. 'With your approval Babu, I could seek funding from the British Embassy in Cairo.'

'Not required,' said Babu, stroking his tie. 'Lateef can travel with you. Payment for an Ottoman guide will be necessary, camels to carry stores and, let me think ...'

'Fred and I would appreciate a retainer,' prompted Victor.

'Two pound upfront,' said Babu without pause.

'You work for me, Mr Ascott, not England.'

Victor raised his glass and took a sip. 'Bury that bitch, Chione, with good faith, I say. Tell your embassy more than she revealed. There is Egyptian interest in the digs to our east and we will find the evidence they require to delve deeper.'

'Thank you,' said Babu, removing his tie and stretching his body to the point that his top buttons popped on his ruffled shirt. His dark thicket of chest hair was visible and from this growth he withdrew the cross of Saint Helena, the patron saint of archaeologists. He raised the golden cross, embedded with blood red rubies. 'I pray for your safety on this journey, gentlemen, and express my thanks for meeting with you all this day.'

\*\*\*

Victor and I visited the English Embassy in Cairo early the next morning. It was a quick meeting because we did not need funding or support. We were simply advising them of our travel plans. The embassy knew vaguely where we were going and how long we would be away, should anyone need to contact us. Gloria, my ex-fiancé, had contacted the embassy before sending me her separation letter. Good news also arrived via the embassy, such as the publication of our previous find in *The Archaeologist's Companion*. In the event of us not returning as scheduled from this journey, not much could or would be done. Archaeologists often go missing in Egypt and beyond. I knew this more than I wanted to but as Chaucer wrote in *The Canterbury Tales*, 'Nothing ventured, nothing gained.' Victor was too right when he told me that I'd explode if I were contained to the monotony of a desk job in England. The whole world was calling to me from the texts I'd read and the Guardian manuscript did more than call to me. I felt summoned to find the Guardians or be buried like them in the folds of lost history. Being buried didn't strike me as a favourable conclusion, be it figuratively with work or physically with dirt.

*\*\**

Lateef proved his worth by recruiting an Ottoman guide and arranging for the purchase of camels. The guide was born in Mosul, an ancient city on the west bank of the Tigris River, opposite the site Layard had identified as Nineveh, on the east bank. His knowledge of the region would be fundamental to our success.

'I met Qasim on my first dig,' said Lateef, turning to face Victor and me as we followed him on foot towards a trade square. 'He was a fisherman on the Tigris before he started to dig.'

'And is he a trustworthy man?' asked Victor.

'I think so,' replied Lateef and he slowed his pace. 'Your observation skills will be important again at our meeting this noon.' Lateef resumed a fast trot.

I ran to catch up with him. 'Why camels?' I asked as we paced forwards.

'To carry our stores.'

'I get that. I mean, why not horses? The Guardians and the Akkadians rode horses in most accounts from the book.'

Lateef smiled at me and looked at me twice when he realised that it was an honest question. 'Camels require less water and are more resilient to travel. We won't use them to hunt for our food or fight battles.'

'Of course,' I said, my pace unconsciously slowed as I confronted my naivety.

'All good?' asked Victor as he strode past me.

Not all good. All my work until this point had been within a day's travel of a known city. I was not prepared for our planned journey. Lines from Robert Burn's poem, *To a Mouse*, repeated in my head. *The best-laid schemes of mice and men*. My suggested plan promised reward in two months. Victor predicted even odds of us being turned back before any claim had been made. I felt like the young Guardian Kar, vouching for a journey to a distant island despite my knowledge that the odds were against us.

'Catch up, Fred,' yelled Victor from the entrance to the square.

Victor waited for me and we followed Lateef through the ornament and food stalls to an area of the markets set aside for the sale of live animals. It was noisy here and wafting sand met your eyes no matter which way you looked. Fifty goats were bellowing from a crowded pen and nearby a trader was securing a sheet to the side of his stall to protect his caged exotic birds. In front of the caged birds, snakes were kept in clay pots. An Egyptian cobra lifted its head when the trader removed the lid to show a customer. It tried to escape and he shepherded it back with the lid as he kept talking. Past the pen of goats, a trader walked a striped hyena on a short lead. The hyena kept its large head hung as if embarrassed to be walking in the light of day.

Lateef ducked under a single rail fence and entered an arena where horses and camels were being paraded. He walked alongside a man leading a camel for a few steps before turning to us and pointing towards his exit in the eastern corner.

Victor and I squeezed our way between the men watching the parade of horses and camels. Behind the fenced arena, I watched Lateef decline the camel trader's first offer with a wave of his hands. He pointed at particular camels tied to posts in the neighbouring square.

The camel trader pointed at four of these camels and the one he was leading.

Lateef accepted his second offer.

***

Lateef tied the five camels to the rail above a trough in the courtyard behind Babu's library. 'I will see you inside, Fred?'

'You will.' I feigned a smile. In the centre of the courtyard was an olive tree with a slim trunk and even thinner branches that struggled to hold leaves. I thought, in the moment, that Babu should replace the tree with a statue as it was surrounded by hundred-year-old date palms and the fronds blocked most light even at noon. Ignoring the struggling olive tree, the back entrance to the library was as elegant as the Roman style frontage.

'They would not grow back home,' said Victor, noticing my skyward stare.

'I was wondering what it would be like to take shelter in a date palm grove.'

'I'm sure we will have to do that.'

'I'm not ready,' I admitted, showing Victor my eyes as a statement of fact. 'The success of our journey relies upon our guide.'

Victor ushered me inside, 'Rely on me.'

We walked past the privy and through an open door into a long corridor. The scent of cedar was strong in this passage and I wondered what was on the other side of the walls that confined our step.

Qasim was speaking with Lateef in the parlour when we entered. He ended the discussion promptly and walked our way. The first thing I noticed was his dress. Unlike Babu and Lateef, who had adopted European attire, Qasim wore a blue turban and a grey kaftan. A long dark beard covered his face and neck.

'I know you men from Lateef's description,' he said with a smile as he approached. His English seemed fluent, despite a heavy accent.

'Are you Babu's new maid?' asked Victor ahead of Qasim's asserted handshake.

Qasim paused for a moment. His eyes tightened as his half-extended hand hovered. 'Qasim is my name, Victor, and I hope to unearth a city with you.'

'Let's find one first,' said Victor. He shook hands with Qasim and Akila was ready with a Cognac. 'Impeccable.'

Akila curtsied before returning to the liquor cabinet.

I faced Qasim. Up close, he looked younger than me. He didn't have Victor's character wrinkles or my tired eyes. His eyes, however, masked deeper pain or anger. I could see the hurt even when he smiled. Victor was already engaging Babu and Lateef in a story, and less attention was paid to my introduction to the guide. 'Fred,' I said, extending my hand.

'Qasim,' said the guide as his hand met mine. 'Lateef speaks highly of you.' He shook my hand firmly and released without a long story or intense eye stare.

'I hear you know of the Tigris flow,' I said as I walked next to him towards the parlour's leather sofas.

'I can provide a meal each night if I'm allowed time.'

'By rod, hand reel or net?' I asked.

'I will bring my own supplies, do not be worried.'

'What type of fish swims the Tigris?'

Qasim looked at me and nodded.

I was unsettled by his vague response and choice, or inability, to maintain a conversation. Qasim stood at polite distance to the other men before being welcomed into the conversation as it ended.

'Please have a seat, gentlemen,' said Babu, gesturing to the leather sofas.

I felt like it was my last chance to raise any concerns. Victor sat first and Qasim sat next to him. I sat opposite them on the sofa with Lateef.

'Welcome gentlemen,' said Babu from his armchair. 'My father's library has hosted many esteemed guests but none more important than those gathered this afternoon.' Babu pointed to Qasim, 'We have a guest without drink, Akila.'

'I do not drink alcohol,' stated Qasim.

'Do you party?' asked Victor, smiling across the table at Lateef and me.

'I do not partake in reckless activity,' said Qasim.

Victor laughed and took a sip of his Cognac.

'Is there a problem, Mr Ascott?' asked Babu, his head cocked to one side.

Victor sucked in his bottom lip and then released it as he looked up at the hanging candelabrum. 'If one candle above was extinguished, light in the room would be affected. The conversation would go on. Qasim is not a candle in this journey. He is the rope that ties our light to Babu's roof.'

'Indeed,' said Babu, looking at Qasim. 'We are relying on you. How well do you know the road east?'

'I know my home,' said Qasim. 'I have been gone for many years but I have not abandoned my religion, language or family.'

'Have you heard of Assur?' I asked.

Qasim's head lifted on his neck. 'Qal'at Sherqat, Assur, the god of the Assyrians.'

The other men exchanged glances. I never took my eyes off Qasim. 'What do you know?'

'Qal'at Sherqat was the Assyrian's god.'

'A new god?' I questioned.

'An old god, he was the god of the sky and wind.' Qasim's eyes were wide and he sat high in his seat.

I remembered Samor, of the Harmin Village, speaking of the dead travelling by the winds and finding new life. In the desert, the Harmin did not have the water provided by Enki. The Harmin favoured another god. 'Do you mean, Enlil?'

Qasim sat back, his hand half raised, 'How do you know this?'

Victor shifted away from Qasim in his seat, so that he could face him easily. 'What do you know?'

Qasim huffed and shook his head. 'I think I just take you on a journey. Lateef,' he said, tipping his beard in Lateef's direction, 'never told me you looked for a god. He said you were looking for a city.'

'Say we look for both,' said Babu. 'What concerns you about the search for a god?'

'Do you try to prove something in the Christian holy book?'

'No, we care not.' Babu looked at Victor and then me. 'Do we?'

Victor chuckled. 'I think the only religious element in this proposed journey is Qasim.'

'Is my religion a problem for you, Mr Ascott?' asked Qasim. His eyes did not blink as he stared at Victor. There was only a foot of space between them on the shared sofa.

Victor pushed his unfastened golden hair behind one ear and stared back at Qasim.

From the sofa opposite, I answered for him. 'Victor has a problem with religion.' Both men turned to face me and I continued. 'He does not like what he cannot understand. He is a realist. Even if a god were to speak with him, it would be a debate rather than a divine intervention.'

Victor nodded. 'Well said, Fred.'

Qasim's nod was more like a bow. 'I understand.'

Babu cleared his throat. 'Lateef will pay for everything you require, Qasim. Bring my friends safely back to my library and the payment is one pound.'

'Should a candle be extinguished, what then?' asked Qasim.

'Do not anticipate death or it will find you,' advised Babu. 'I suggest you focus on all returning safely or expect reduced payment.'

Qasim turned to face Victor and Victor leant back

and gestured to Babu and the previous answer.

The payment message was clear and it seemed likely that Qasim knew the lands east but something from my first question, the one I asked as we entered the parlour, still bothered me. Victor stood to inspect the library again and Babu followed him. Lateef switched seats and engaged his friend in a discussion about their first dig. Alone on the sofa, I took a moment to question myself. I looked around the parlour and paused Akila's advance by mouthing, 'no', and then shaking my head when she looked confused. My glass was still half full. 'Qasim?' I said in a loud voice. I felt like Victor in bringing the whole room to a halt. 'I apologise for interrupting your conversation.' I leant towards Qasim who was seated opposite, next to Lateef. 'Earlier, I enquired about your favoured fishing method. The net maybe?'

'The spear,' he replied, his hand claiming Lateef's glass with a quick strike and raising it above his head before the young man could turn.

Babu began a slow clap.

Lateef got his drink back and placed it so that he could join in the clap.

Victor started tapping his hat, his Coke, faster and in time with the clapping.

Babu and Lateef clapped even louder and Victor winked at me.

This time, I did not object to his wink. When an opportunity allowed, I winked back. It was our silent agreement. We were heading east and things were not as proper as we would have liked them to be.

That's right, Gloria, my lost love, I am rushing

to discovery once more. Whilst this venture has no religious intentions, Saint Helena surely blesses the earnestness of our quest. And, on this journey, I have something rarely afforded to archaeologists, the accounts of ancient guides—the Guardians. We are set to walk in the Guardians' footsteps. Where I left off reading, Kar, Arman and Tuley, a distinctive band of Guardians, were heading west from Assur. Where will they be in their travels when we find the city from which they departed?

# 2

# Zidon

*Scribed by Kar.*

We had crossed harsh, barren lands, and climbed mountains as imposing as some of the Zagros's slopes. After breaching the maze of hinterland that followed, we shadowed the army's trail towards fresher tasting air. It was nearing high sun the day Arman, Tuley and I arrived in Zidon, a majestic city named after its founder, a great grandson of Utnapishtim. Utnapishtim was the man chosen by the God of fresh water, Enki, to gather the best men and women and save the animals that could not swim before Enlil subjected the earth to the Great Deluge. Utnapishtim's ark settled upon solid ground six days later when the water receded. The people of Elam believed Utnapishtim founded their capital, Susa. The Akkadians preached that he returned to Eridu to care for the city that Enki founded. In Zidon, they told the story differently again; they believed they were the true descendants of Utnapishtim. They lived where the sea first rose and they were once the people Enlil sought to wipe from the face of the earth. Zidon was now a peaceful city with one language and many gods. It was nestled between lush hills with fertile plains, and a tapestry of mud brick homes and white stone buildings covered the descent to the shimmering sea that expanded west to the end of the world.

Whilst we had not eaten for two days prior to our arrival, we had been blessed with an abundant supply of water. We sighted a safe place to camp on our ride into the city and continued in search of food. Tired after countless days of travel, we gathered most of our stores from the first stall we visited and raised little qualm over the price. Arman was tearing apart the flatbread and sharing it as we led our horses away. We chewed slowly as our mouths had been softened through unintentional fasting.

'Should we rest first or secure a boat for the morrow?' asked Arman.

'I think it is best if I go alone,' I advised. 'Best not to draw attention to our movements.' When we were lost in the hinterland, a day's ride east of Zidon, I had also offered my advice. After tripping and falling to my hands and knees, I had pointed Arman and Tuley south. They had walked that way without protest and my course led us back to the trail we had lost in the mountains. We had continued our journey to this city on the shores of the Great Sea in the hope of rescuing the people of Pled. My mother's mother, also named Kinsufa, had travelled from these shores and I believed Pledian blood flowed in me. Yet, as I stood overlooking the expanse of blue stretching to the next horizon, I felt no kindred sense of hope. Senea knew the Pledian's language and we had lost his company in Assur. Salarn had said that I must make this journey and then he had fallen silent. Was I falling into the Bull's burrow or nearing the King's nesting place? Elkin's advice became my assurance of purpose. I had promised Salarn's old friend that I would not be afraid to live or die, and he had told me to seek what is over the horizon and over everyone after that.

'Look for a stable boat, Kar, and, when I say stable, I do mean one made for horses.' Arman looked about. 'The people of Zidon are all strangers to me and I will not leave my mare behind.'

I nodded. 'I am sure that Senea is taking good care of my stallion, Har Man, so it is only right that I care for his mare. I will search for such a boat.'

Arman untied the pouch of silver from the saddle on Senea's mare. He removed three shekels and handed them to me. 'Know their worth, Kar. A farmer will work from the full moon to the next to earn one.'

I lifted my tunic and tucked the shekels behind my belt.

'Tuley and I will fetch more supplies while you're gone. We'll wait in the fuller's yard that we passed on the ride in. There is always a place to camp near a fuller.'

'You taking your weapon?' asked Tuley.

'I thought to.'

Tuley extended his arm and opened his hand to accept my weapon. 'Word from Assur of a young man with such a weapon will soon be shared. There are many young men but few, if any, weapons like yours.'

I left my staff behind and began the ride down to the port alone on Senea's mare. I had not yet made sense of my sudden change of mind since falling during our climb of the densely forested mountains east of Zidon. I had fallen upon a sharp stake remaining from a snapped tree root. When I looked down, I saw its tip pressing against my chest. My braced arms had saved me. In my mind's eye, I had seen the stake go through me. Everything was new to me now: the faces, the view and a feeling I could not place. I looked at those I passed, smiling peacefully as if from a separate world. The women who dyed cloth, the men struggling to lift a heavy chest of drawers to a balcony and the maidens dressed for offering also seemed carefree in their duties. Was this why I told Arman and Tuley that I wanted to ride alone? My eyes were drawn to the little things, like the subtle expressions on the people's faces, white paint peeling from stone and sea birds soaring low in the sky. Lost in my own thoughts that beat to the steady sound of my horse's hooves on cobble, I did not realise for a long while that my hand was resting on my shoulder.

Water rushed over me and I startled, like I was waking from a dream. Sitting upright in my mount, I patted my waist to check I was still carrying the three shekels nestled behind my belt. The rush of water had hit me with the force of that which flows through the Karun Gorge but I was dry and I had come to no harm through my period of distraction. Senea's mare had carried me safely to Zidon's port. Eight wharves, each a hundred steps long, extended out into the sea. The four wharves to the north harboured only ten vessels. Every mooring post on the four wharves to the south secured an Akkadian vessel. The sails on the Akkadian vessels were down and red flags rippled in the wind atop of each mast.

I raised my hand to my shoulder again and caressed

my tattoo through the cloth that had left it covered since my journey downriver from Nineveh. It could not have been a vision I had experienced because I had only seen what I passed on the way down. Maybe, I had closed my eyes for a moment, my dream beginning and ending with a surge of water. I twisted my hand holding the reins and stilled Senea's mare. Along the beach leading to the wharves were three watchtowers. A stone sea wall separated the southern stretch of the beach from the Akkadian soldiers' encampment on the inland side. It was the largest army I had seen and they had made the beach a temporary home like the traders' camp outside the walls of Bit-Bunakki. I forced myself to look away before the force of their numbers deterred me from my mission. To the north, there was no need for a sea wall. The ground between the beach and the top of the next rise was the height of two horses. Wooden huts were perched along this rise that spread north from the road I had ridden to the port. Around me, the Zidonians were packing their goods from the markets. Those not loading carts and baskets were dismantling their shelters. There was no talk or festivity among the people. They packed their stores hastily as if a storm were approaching. The sky was cloudless and the sea's breeze was gentle.

Senea's mare lifted her head and turned without my command when a man carting a long bundle of reeds passed too close to her snout.

'Sorry, girl, walk on.' I trotted her from the end of the road and into the sand. The beach between the occupied watchtowers was empty. I looked north at the limited offering of vessels. Only two looked capable of transporting horses or more than ten men. With not a single man or beast on the shore beyond me, I decided it best to approach the wharves from the north. Despite my fear of failing to save the Pledians or ever finding King Sargon, I was enjoying this journey.

'Looking for fish? Need a boat? I know everyone here.'

I looked down at the young boy tapping my leg and smiled courteously.

'Welcome to Zidon. My name is Hevtoakobias. Most choose to call me Bias.' His hair was brown like mine and tied back, apart from a fringe that covered his forehead. 'I can help you find anything you are looking for,' he said excitedly.

'I am in search of a stable boat and, when I say stable, I do mean one that will transport horses.'

'That is not going to be easy to find unless you gain a position on an Akkadian vessel.' He squinted as he stared at the wharves. The sun sat low above the sea behind. 'I don't think you want to go where they're going.'

'Where are they going?' I asked, looking at the boats occupying every mooring post on the four wharves to our south.

'To the Island of Trees they go. I think they will build a statue there too.' He pointed to the soldier's encampment.

A hundred small fires burned in the encampment and, as I peered through the drifting smoke, a glint of light caught my eye. I recognised the plaited chin beard from the face on the back of the silver shekels I carried. Cast in bronze, the statue was twice the height of a man and showed the King pinning a giant cat to the ground with his foot. His sword was raised to the sky.

Bias acted out what the statue was depicting using an imaginary sword to cut the cat's head from its body.

'Maybe his next statue will have him holding the cat's head,' I replied, assuming that Bias must have heard many stories about the King since his city had been occupied.

He dropped his imaginary sword. 'I could help you trade your horse and you could get a new one wherever you are going. Where are you going?'

The boy's large, brown eyes hid nothing and his bare feet signalled that he had not walked far this day and was most probably a citizen of Zidon. Still, I thought it best not to divulge our true plans. I climbed down from my mount. 'There is a place I have heard of beyond Kush. So far away by land yet only ten days by boat,' I chose to tell him. 'Though please tell me more about this Island of Trees. Have the soldiers been there before?'

'Not many people have been to the island. I know it is beautiful. My mother tells me that Zidon once looked the same. The trees,' he said, pointing at the spreading branches of a massive cedar tree amongst the white stone buildings, 'run all the way to the shore, and smaller islands, some no bigger than a boat, circle it like the stars circle Earth.' The boy reached to the sky with his tanned slender arms and demonstrated circling motions. He then spoke in a lowered voice, drawing his face closer to mine, and articulating each word with great importance, almost as if he were disclosing to me the secrets of life itself. 'We have a painting of the island hanging in our home that my mother traded for with five fish. She tells me that if we ever find ourselves without food we can look at that painting and fall asleep dreaming of better days.'

'She sounds very wise. I would love to see the painting.'

'She does not allow strangers in our home. She does not like the soldiers coming here or even travellers or traders.' He shook his head vehemently and scowled.

'I understand. One must protect the sanctuary of their home or it will become no different to any other place.'

'That is what she says,' exclaimed Bias, swiping his fringe, sticky from salty air, back from his forehead. 'Do you know my mother?'

I shook my head. 'This is my first time in Zidon. Should I know her?'

'Everyone here does, only because she talks to no one else apart from Father and me. They think she is weird. She knows things. She probably knows of your arrival. She knew the soldiers were coming.' Bias looked towards the white stone buildings that sat highest on the hill, overlooking the sea. 'My father does not mind what people think of her because our garden grows all the vegetables we need and she takes care of it while he is out fishing and I am out playing. I do not play all the time though. Sometimes, when I meet my father at the end of the day I am able to show him how much silver I have earned and we buy bread or a present for my mother on the walk home.'

'How do you earn your silver?'

'By helping people like you find what they are

looking for. Some of the rich travellers throw silver away like it is too heavy for them to carry. Do not worry though, I would not ask for much from you.'

'Why not?'

'You are young and tired from your journey. And, my father will be back soon. I have already earned a half-shekel and a meal this morn.'

'Then maybe it is a lucky day for you. I would appreciate your help finding a boatman not afraid of travelling far from shore.'

The boy's eyes widened. 'I know a man. Follow me.'

He skipped his way through the sand and I followed, leading Senea's mare. The mare was not used to the soft ground, or maybe it reminded her of the foul alley we rode through in Assur. As we headed north towards a wharf that was almost empty with only three boats tied, I looked up at the wooden huts overlooking this stretch of the beach. The first hut was perched on a rock outcrop closest to the most northern watchtower. I could hear the men talking in the watchtower above as we passed beneath. Between the first hut and the next, a wide path led down to the beach, atop of which were boats undergoing repair and construction. Some of the boats were lifted in wooden frames and others appeared abandoned, grass growing around and through their reed hulls. From a road behind the boats on the hill, a procession of men pulled carts loaded with baskets our way.

Bias waved for me to follow him onto the wharf. 'They come to load the day's catch,' he said. 'Look, you can see them already.' Fishing boats were returning from every direction in unison and each vessel's sail cast a hazy shadow on the reflective sea. 'You have chosen a good time,' said Bias. 'Unless Gibantis has secured work already, he should eagerly accept your offer. He tells me that he has also seen the Island of Trees on many a voyage. Once he even saw people on the shore and tells me that it is not the safe haven my mother dreams it to be. He might even know of the place you are going.'

We approached the boat owned by Gibantis and I tied the mare to a mooring post that would soon be required by one of the returning fishing boats.

Bias boarded the boat without invitation and began calling out to the owner. 'Gibantis. Gibantis. Bias brings you a visitor.'

A man with dark, sun-drenched skin, wearing a tunic that barely reached his thighs, appeared on deck, turning his face from the low sun. 'I hear you Bias. I hear you too well. I would swear you were calling me in from sea with a voice so loud.'

'I bring work for you,' said Bias.

Gibantis stepped towards me with his hand held to the side of his forehead, shielding his face from the sun. 'Come aboard, friend,' he said in greeting, looking beyond at the horse I had tied to a mooring post.

His boat had a thick, bundled-reed side—a thicker hull than the boat we had occupied to travel to Assur. I jumped aboard his vessel and crossed the deck to meet him. He held his arms back from courteous greeting and I was immediately reminded of the way Delari had negotiated with the boatman in Nineveh. I hoped this deal would be exchanged with both our interests in mind.

'No need to brace arms yet, we have not formed an agreement,' he said with a smile.

I saw how Bias mixed work with playtime as he explored the bow of the boat, leaning out over the water and hanging on as he grappled between ropes fastened to the mast.

'Do not mind him. He can swim if he falls. His patter on deck does not even wake me now.'

I looked back at Gibantis and took a moment to study his face. Most importantly, I looked at his eyes that were blue like the sea and shone brightly set against his dark complexion. His brown hair with streaks of grey was mostly tied back leaving only stray locks to flick about in the sea breeze.

'I apologise if my voice sounds gruff. I have been sleeping all afternoon,' he explained. 'Or maybe you are just taking a moment to judge my character.'

That was exactly what I was doing and, though his stare was sharp, it seemed peaceful and his smile was honest, if not playful. 'I wish to travel to an island, two nights away, northwest.'

'The Island of Trees?'

I nodded. 'I have heard it called another name.'

He huffed. 'I'd call it the land of lost souls. Not a place many travel to.' He walked away from me and found shade behind his mast. 'Why do you want to go there?'

'I have met a woman from those shores and I return for her family who was unable to travel with her. I have come alone to meet you but two others travel with me.'

'Have you been to the island before?' queried Gibantis. 'Did you tell Bias where you wanted to go?'

'I have not been there and I told Bias another story about my travels.'

'I see,' pondered Gibantis. 'Three to the island and possibly four or more on the return?'

'If more want to come back, we will offer accordingly.' I walked towards him. 'How many can your boat carry?'

'Leave your horse behind and my boat can carry twelve.'

'If we were to take our horses?'

'Then I would not leave dock.' Gibantis left his shaded spot behind the mast and walked past me to where I had been standing. 'Horses are not only the first to fall, they are the first to topple a vessel in heavy seas.'

'I understand.'

'Do you?' He pointed at Senea's mare. 'I see that you have never been to sea before. Bias should have told you to tie your horse at the end of the wharf and your friends should be there waiting. I do not see them.'

'They are not far away. What can I offer you now that will ensure you wait for us until morning?'

Gibantis pointed at me like I had been spotted in hiding. 'You've been there before.'

'I have never travelled this far west. We came when we heard that the Pledians needed to be rescued. More would have travelled with me if our homeland were safe. '

He opened his mouth to speak and then snapped it shut. Only his hair moved in the sea's breeze as he stared at me. 'A shekel now and another two upon our return.'

'Can I trust you will wait for us when we go ashore?'

He sighed. 'I will be honest with you, young man. My heart tells me ... No, I was convinced that only savages reside on those shores, though should your word be true then rescue these people we must. I will give you two days ashore and bring back up to ten people, counting your own.'

'We would not be so long ashore if we could take our horses.'

'You do not know the sea. No horses. Trust me.'

'Do you know when the Akkadians plan to sail?'

'If I told you, would it change your plans?'

I shook my head.

'They sail on the morrow.' He watched me for a reaction. 'You never told me your name?'

'I am Kar, son of Unbetum and Kinsufa.' I lifted my tunic to reach my belt and gave Gibantis a silver shekel. We braced arms.

'I am thankful for your arrival this day,' he explained, pointing south at a leafless forest of masts. 'You have decided for me where I'll be when that fleet of boats sails northwest on the morrow. Half the crews are made up of would-be fishermen and farmers, who have finally got the chance to sail to an unknown shore. I thought to sail at a distance to bear witness and maybe complete another painting.' Gibantis faced me, his sea-blue eyes revealing a hidden pain that I had not noticed before. 'The shame is that the people who really care for the island, people like Bias's mother, will be the last to know of the imminent plunder.' Gibantis turned to face the boy and we watched him talking to himself on the boat's bow. 'When he was still a baby, his mother walked with him resting in a sling from the other side of the city and paid for a painting I once did with five fish. That is why I never painted another. I get to see the island often and, in her possession, my painted memory is more than treasured; it is held sacred.' His voice dropped to almost a whisper and, staring straight into the sun, his gaze fixed on the boats returning from sea. 'Sacred things are rare these days.'

Looking at the Akkadian boats that would sail on the morrow, I envisaged a way that Tuley, Arman and I could make a greater difference without even leaving the shore. As the Akkadians slept, we could sabotage their boats and be the first to leave. It would be a risky undertaking beneath the three watchtowers standing vigil over the port, though what counts as a risk when valued against the lives that would be taken should the vessels sail unhindered? Whilst I had not met Bias's mother, her sheltered ideals seemed on par with those of the Pledians and our quest seemed even more necessary. 'We will deal with our horses and be back before dawn,' I told Gibantis.

'My ship is fast yet the sea cannot be taken for granted,' he warned. 'Waste no time in returning, Kar, or your time ashore will be pointless.'

'I will return soon.'

'Bias,' Gibantis called out. 'I have work for you now.'

Bias leapt to the wharf from where he was and ran to meet me.

'He was the sailor you needed, yes?' the boy questioned.

'He was,' I replied.

'Tell me how I can help you more? Need to sell your horse? Want fish?' he asked, as he walked backwards down the wharf in front of me. 'Wait a little longer and you can trade for fish fresh off the boats.'

'Where is your home?' I asked before he presented me with another question.

For a moment, Bias avoided replying, his mind set on the next trade agreement he would help secure. We walked past the men unloading empty baskets from their carts at the end of the wharf. They greeted Bias and stared at me. Eventually and with much reluctance, he raised his arm and pointed with loosely held fingers to the hills, north of the road I had ridden down to the port.

'Allow me to explain why I ask. I have enough fish already and I do not want to sell this mare. It belongs to a good friend of mine and he has my stallion, Har Man. If I leave it with my other friends then I would have to travel alone,' I told Bias, still masking our true plans. Bias had been accommodating, even wise to stay at the end of the boat whilst I spoke with Gibantis, and I felt wrong for misleading him further.

'Best not to go to sea without a friend,' he agreed, as we walked up the wide path towards boats propped up for repair. 'My father jokes with mother that she must have spent her last life alone at sea.'

I stopped walking and Senea's mare nuzzled my shoulder and ear. 'I do not understand.'

'My father tells me that the sea can be a lonely place and those who spend too long out there are changed men when they return. They seek solitude like my mother.'

'You seem to know everything, Bias,' I said, as I led the mare onto the road behind the wooden huts on the rise.

'I only know what others tell me, Kar.'

'Did I tell you my name?'

'You must have,' he said as he kept walking. 'I have never caught a fish or left the dock on a boat. As soon as I am old enough or strong enough to pull a net, I will spend my waking life at sea. That is why my mother wants me to play now and why my father asks that I give him everything I earn before we go home.'

I slipped a shekel from my belt and handed it to him. 'You earned this.'

'A whole shekel.' He turned it in his hands. 'It shows the King's face.'

'Show me.'

Bias turned the shekel and displayed the faced side.

'How do you know that's the King?'

Bias laughed. 'Who else could it be?' He scuffed the ground with his foot to expose rock. 'Lean close.'

I leant close as he dropped the coin.

'Did you hear that?' He gathered the shekel and dropped it again. 'It rings in your ear. Everyone hears a silver shekel when it drops or jingles in a pouch.'

'Did you hear the silver I carried before approaching me?'

Bias shook his head. He was about to drop the shekel again. Instead, he raised it to me. 'I would not take your last shekel.'

'It is yours.' I walked on, leading the mare along the road back to the port.

He ran after me. 'What do you want me to do, Kar?'

'Does your mother know where the soldier's boats are going?'

'I swore to my father that I would never tell her.'

'That's a problem, Bias.' I looked down at him walking next to me. 'One day she may discover what happened without her knowing and realise that you knew all along.'

'I know that.' He stopped near to where I had first met him and stared out to sea, surely hoping his father would arrive soon.

I let him be alone with his thoughts for a moment, for what I was about to suggest was reliant on his father's consideration as well. I understood his disposition. It hurts not to share knowledge and whilst a returning boat or, in my case, a Guardian spotted on the horizon can lift your spirits, it is not until you see the person's face and are sharing their embrace that you feel at peace again. 'I do not want to sell our mares. I want to leave them in your care.'

Bias turned from the sea to face me, his contorted face suggesting the absurdity of my request.

'Horses are like people to us,' I explained, 'so we cannot sell them and Gibantis will not allow them aboard.'

'I know how to sell a horse. I have never taken care of one before.'

'They are well trained,' I added, giving Senea's

mare the signal to walk away. 'Try to approach her,' I suggested.

Bias stepped closer to the mare and with each step he took, the horse trotted away an equal distance.

'I told you; I do not know horses.'

'Try again,' I requested. 'Stanf.' Salarn had taught the Guardians the stanf command. It meant be still.

Bias glanced back at me as I called the command and then turned to see the horse waiting in view of his advance. He approached her coyly and gently stroked her flank with his fingertips. 'Now what?' he questioned.

'If it were your horse, what would you do first when you saw her every morning?'

Bias walked in front of the mare and tried to look at her in the eye. He stroked the mare's nose and even her lips. Smiling at the mare, he then proceeded to nuzzle her mouth like his head was a snout.

She snorted and his fringe lifted with the gust of air.

'It likes me,' he exclaimed.

I wanted for him to be happy with the suggested duty as much as I wanted this solution to work in our favour. 'Do you know anyone else that could be trusted with their care?'

'You don't think I can look after a horse?'

'We leave at first light on the morrow, Bias. I have to find our horses a place to stay tonight.'

'Come on then,' he said with a waving glance to the mare and walked it back to me.

I looked at the mare and watched it nuzzle Bias. He was disappointed and Senea's mare sensed his sorrow.

'Maybe I was wrong. She seems to have taken a sudden fondness to you.'

'So you think I could look after her?' he perked up.

'She would have to stay at your home. You could not bring her to the port with you each day.'

'I do not know, Kar. My father arrives and I will have to ask him.' He pointed to the fishing boats returning to the empty wharves.

'I will wait for his answer.'

'I hope he agrees.' Bias stroked the mare's nose once more and she attempted to nuzzle him as he sprinted into the sand. He ran between the most northern watchtower and the hut on the rock outcrop towards the most northern wharf.

Bias's father, a tall, thin man, strode past the other weary fishermen. Lifting Bias above his shoulders, he carried him for three paces before kneeling and placing him back on his feet. The fisherman stayed knelt as he listened to his son's recount of the day. I think Bias started at the beginning and told him everything because it was a long while before his father looked to me. He gave Bias an answer. I could not tell if it was favourable or not. After hugging his son once more, he headed back to his boat and Bias returned my way with his head hung.

Senea's mare pranced by my side.

I reached up and stroked her mane. There was a knot in her hair and when I separated it, a foul odour was released. It was another remnant from our passage through the vile alley in Assur. The Caverns of Ersetu,

Arman had named the alley, a dreary underworld where lost souls dwelled without chance of rebirth, drinking dust. I took a handful of sand and rubbed it through the soiled part of her mane and rubbed my own fingers with the grit. 'We might have to smell this way until the journey is completed,' I told her. I looked for a well. Closer to the Akkadian encampment, beneath a tall, wide-limbed cedar tree, there was a clay water trough. It was not close enough. I had to wait for Bias and show him that I was not prepared to move on until I had a response from his father. The Zidonians who were packing their market stalls and stores had moved on. Their next day would be similar on the morrow. 'What did he say?' I asked Bias, as he approached from the beach.

'He does not believe your story. If you wait for him, he will let you explain. He has to offload the catch before he is allowed to leave.'

'I understand. Get to know her,' I said handing Bias the mare's rein.

'You will wait?'

'I believe your father will understand.'

Bias spotted where a feeder or stall had been located and led the mare closer to inspect the remaining offerings of grain and vegetable stalks.

Once more, I was convinced that Bias could be trusted with care of the mares. I looked at the city climbing the hills towards the eastern sky. I had been gone a while and was hopeful that Arman and Tuley were resting in my absence. If I did not return before dark, one of them was sure to leave in search of my whereabouts. Finding a home for the two mares, and possibly the Akkadian steed, was compromising our imminent departure aboard a boat I was certain was the right one—the only one. I had to see this plan through and I prayed for Arman and Tuley whilst I waited. *I pray their worry be silenced. Offer them rest in my absence. I will return safely.* My silent prayer was directed at Enki. He was the God of Fresh Water that quenched our thirst in the hinterlands and he was the pattern maker who made the stoned roads, the buildings and the people of Zidon one combined work. I held my shoulder as I prayed, conscious of doing so for I wanted my prayer to touch every Guardian. We needed all the help we could gather to be successful in our quest. Senea and the others we had left in Assur also had a long journey ahead of them and the Guardians at the tower were sure to be anxious without news. I prayed that the Guardians had already arrived in the Harmin Village and that Uk-Ban was engaged in the duty that would see him return home with water from the God's Garden. I did not allow any of these uncertain thoughts time to weigh too heavily on my mind. I just remembered the people who had helped me get this far and counted myself as a lucky man to still be alive and on such a journey.

'Kar, is that your name? I am Bias's father, Wevan.'

I was watching Bias feed the mare and did not expect his father to arrive without him noticing first. Words left my lips before I even turned to face him. 'I know this is an odd request to make of a stranger. I trust you from merely making acquaintance with your son.'

The tall, thin fisherman was barefooted like Bias and his skin was as dark as his eyes and long beard.

He took a moment to study my dress, face and stance before addressing me again. 'I spoke to Gibantis and he told me nothing. He would not even tell me when he planned to set sail. I already know when you plan to depart because you want to find a home for your horses this night,' Wevan admitted. 'If you really planned to sail to a land beyond Kush, I would not have been allowed a chance to talk with Gibantis. He would have been fetching stores adequate for the time at sea.'

'We sail to the Island of Trees to rescue a people.'

Wevan stepped away from me and held his hand out, signalling me not to encroach.

Bias was oblivious to our meeting, unable to see beyond the mare's engaging allure.

'We can offer you more silver,' I added to his thoughts.

'Now you have distracted me,' Wevan complained. 'Kar? Is that your true name?' he questioned, not allowing me time to answer. 'I know what that name means. No one on these shores would name their son such. Gibantis normally tells me everything yet to you he remains faithful. That concerns me. If I take these horses home, I will not sleep tonight. I will be asked to whom they belong, how long we must care for them, where you are going and why you go there? If I have the answer to any of these questions, then my wife will ask more in view of such knowledge. There will be no dinner for me, no sleep and I will not be able to leave her alone on the morrow for fear she might venture to the port alone to discover what was not told. Thus, I will lose my work, my family will go hungry and gods forbid she should ever hear of the army sailing to the island ...'

I stepped slowly towards Wevan and placed my hand on his shoulder. His whole body shuddered. 'I will return with you to your home,' I told him.

'You will not go near her.' He struck my hand away.

'Listen to me, Wevan. I am not a man to be feared. I will explain to my friends why I must go alone to your home and they will understand. They let me ride to the port alone today without question just as you trust that your son can take care of himself when you are at sea. I will help you settle the horses before leaving. I will not say anything to your wife if—'

'You do not know my wife, Kar.'

'I wish I did know her. Both Gibantis and Bias told me about the painting she traded five fish for, and how Zidon was once as beautiful. My closest friend has married the princess of the island, Yanereu. I believe the most sacred souls in the world live there and such it is our duty to see that their way of life is protected. Yanereu's father's dying wish was that the others join us and together we form a new people. Many would doubt our quest. Let your wife turn me away. Allow her the chance to bless or end our voyage.'

'Who are your people, Kar?'

'We are the Guardians of the East. We live beyond the Zagros Mountains.'

'And where are your friends?'

'Camped next to the road into the city, near the fuller's home.'

'Bias,' he called out, 'we are leaving.'

'You have not given me an answer, Wevan.'

'I will keep your horses at my home and my son

will watch them like a shepherd his flock.'

'May I ask what gave your mind rest?'

'You. You will answer all my wife's questions while Bias and I bathe our feet and eat.'

Wevan and Bias accompanied me as I led the mare back up the road that I had ridden to the port. The last light of the setting sun reflected off the sky and the white stone buildings. Many others, mostly fishermen, were returning home at the same time. They walked slowly and, like my present company, shared few words.

Near the top of the hill, I pointed beyond the larger white stone buildings and told Wevan where my friends were camped.

'Walk ahead and meet them,' said Wevan.

I shared a confused look, thinking it best if we all arrived together.

'We will wait at a distance. That is what one should do,' he told Bias, 'when meeting strangers alone or at night.'

'I understand,' I said to them both and walked on, leading the mare. At the top of the hill, overlooking the sea, were the largest of all the homes. Like Salarn's tower, each home only had one or two windows. From the ground, I could not tell if there was access to their roofs. They probably belonged to wealthy merchants or the founding farmers and fishermen of Zidon. Beyond these buildings, on the eastern side of the hill, were smaller buildings crafted from both timber and mud brick. The fuller had a hut the size of a stable that would shelter twenty horses, and surrounding the building were stomping racks and cloth hanging lines strung between thick posts. Work for the fuller and his workers had finished for the day and the racks and lines were cleared. There was vacant space between them and the next buildings and that is where I spotted the other Guardians.

Arman appeared to be sleeping and Tuley was standing watch. He spotted me at the same time I sighted him.

Tuley tapped Arman with his foot and the older Guardian stretched before getting to his feet.

I looked over my shoulder, hoping to see Wevan and Bias waiting near the road. It was dark on the eastern side of the city and, if they were nearby, I could not see them. I approached Arman and Tuley. The smell of the fuller's wash, human piss used to clean and whiten cloth, lingered in the still evening air. It was mild compared to the vile stenches we had encountered in our escape from Assur. 'The vessel I have secured will carry twelve men. It is the largest boat.'

'I trust you told him where we are going and judged his character wisely?' questioned Arman.

'I trust the boatman like he were a Guardian himself.'

'And he was happy to take the horses.'

'Horses will be the first to tip a vessel on open sea,' I recounted. 'He will not take them.'

'So what did you say to this?' asked Arman.

'I have made other arrangements. There is a fisherman and his boy waiting nearby. They are going to look after them.'

'And you trust them too?' further questioned Arman, a frown tightening on his forehead.

'I had more trouble convincing them that we could be trusted,' I explained. 'You are welcome to meet them, Arman. I must go alone to their home.'

'Why?'

'The man's wife is a quiet woman and she is not welcoming of visitors.'

'It sounds like a trap, Kar.'

'Did you see many soldiers?' asked Tuley.

'More than I have ever seen and they plan to set sail on the morrow.'

'Then we must leave before dawn,' insisted Tuley.

'No, we must leave now or never,' said Arman. 'Not every boatman is dutiful to Sargon. What if he did not need them to be? What if he rewarded citizens for acting as spies?'

'He is cunning,' supported Tuley.

'You have not even met these men. Do you really think they could be spies without looking into their eyes?'

'There is a chance they are, Kar, and you must always think the worst to avoid suffering the result of blind faith.'

'I would trust your judgment, Arman, if I hadn't already trusted mine. They wait for me. They are not running to sound a bell.' I turned and looked for Wevan and Bias. The moon had settled on our walk home from the port and now strangely shaped shadows lurked near every building, post and rack. Light from a small torch glowed at the entrance to the fuller's hut, suggesting someone was home.

'Kar, I am losing faith in you,' called Wevan from somewhere near the road.

I could not see him and so I answered in the direction of his voice. 'My friends have lost faith in me too. Like your wife, they are sceptical of all others.'

Wevan stepped out from the shadow of a drying line post and Bias ran from his side towards the closest building, the fuller's hut.

'Bias, wait,' I yelled, fearing he was about to prove Arman right.

The young boy stopped in the glow of the torch at the door to the fuller's hut.

Arman noted the positions of the father and son with a flick of his eyes.

'They told me they would wait at a distance.'

'Quiet, Kar,' said Wevan, walking towards us. 'I know a better way to discover true intentions.'

'Already, I do not trust him,' whispered Arman.

'Kar has told me your plans and now I want to hear them fresh from your mouth,' Wevan said to Arman. 'You are sceptical just like I was and am once more.'

I nodded at Arman, encouraging him to talk.

'Where or with who should I begin?' pondered Arman aloud. 'My friend, Delari, is also a Guardian now. He told me all I needed to know about the people of Pled and how long their princess waited for his arrival in Ebla. They believe the Guardians are gods thanks to the reputation instilled by our elder. I know we are not of such breed though I do believe the Pledians are a godlike people. They need nothing apart from what their hearts and souls condemn them to see as destined placement. I have only met the princess once, though what I have heard from the mouths of her husband, Kar who stands before you and my best friend, whom

I parted company with to fulfil this quest, assures me that they are not to be left wanting.'

Wevan opened his mouth to speak. He sighed and signalled his son away from the bell. 'I am not sorry for questioning your motive,' said Wevan as he braced arms with Arman. 'I now wish my wife could meet you as well.'

'She can.'

'My wish is not a want this eve,' said Wevan. 'You call yourself Guardians and I know why they think of you as gods. Only gods can defy a god like Sargon.'

'I am nothing like a god,' said Tuley. He brushed his hands down his sides like he was still wiping away the mess of the alley. 'Without forgetting any of the lessons I learnt as a child, I could have quite easily been among the men boarding the Akkadian vessels.'

'Yet you are not,' Arman reminded him.

'We should keep moving, Kar,' said Wevan. 'My wife will be starting to worry.'

'I will follow,' said Arman. 'Your wife never has to see me or I can wait visible in the distance if you would prefer. I will not let Kar go alone.'

'If you must,' surrendered Wevan, 'though it will be my wife not me who has the final say over whether we keep the horses and your presence may turn her favour.'

I had heard Bias speak of his mother's ways but Arman was still at a loss to understand how a quiet woman could hold such sway. It was not worth further delay to explain now. Waste no time was Gibantis's final instruction before I left his boat and in view of leaving tonight we were already behind schedule.

Tuley approached Arman as he was saddling his mare. 'What about the Akkadian steed? It bears the mark of Sargon on its hide.'

'We should keep it for the ride to the port and then free its walk.'

'I will be ready when you return,' assured Tuley.

'How far away is your home?' Arman asked Wevan.

'Not far though, should my wife take a liking to Kar, she may keep him talking till the sun rises.'

'Do not let that happen, Kar,' instructed Arman. 'We board our vessel tonight.'

I waved Bias close and lifted him onto the mount of Senea's mare.

His legs kicked about and thumped the mare's chest and flank.

Senea's mare walked when I instructed her to. A pat on her foreleg was required.

***

We walked the crest road north past the temples and larger homes before descending towards the valley on the north-eastern side. Even at a distance, I could tell which was Bias's home. It was the only property with furrows dug to ensure easy pickings and the maximum retention of soil and water on the steep slopes. His mother had surely spent many days tending to the cultivation of vegetables and herbs. 'I should go on alone from here, Arman,' I advised.

'I think it is best that I stand visible, so as not to alarm her.' He looked back at the full moon gracing the sky above the sea on the other side of the hill and then at his shadow that stretched the lay of the land across the first three rows of the garden. 'I do not like being excluded from an agreement that involves my mare.' He handed his lead to Wevan but held on with his own hand until I moved on down the steep path.

Bias dismounted with the assistance of a branch from an old olive tree. He landed nimbly on his hardened bare feet and ran ahead to prepare his mother for the first guest she had visit in a long while.

'Be yourself, Kar,' Wevan advised me from behind. 'Answer her truthfully and do your best to leave Bias and me out of your explanations. I understand why you hurry but I warn you that she senses these things. If you are in a hurry, she will be too. Haste brings out the worst in her. When I tell her about my day, I talk of the waves rippling by the boat's side and the fish that nip my hook before swimming away. I finish every recount with a story of a fisherman who caught nothing. I have never disclosed that most of our catch comes from the nets we cast and she never grows tired of the same, long story.' Wevan handed me the reins to Arman's mare. He parted a thin cloth to enter the hut.

I did not follow them in and there was no need to because I could hear too many a word clearly from where I stood. The entire city was quiet tonight. Silence hung like death on this side of the hill amongst the homes of fishermen and miners, and Bias's mother was surely not to like being the loudest on such a still night.

'He is only a boy and his elder waits for him,' I heard Wevan say.

'Do not remove your sandals. Go tell him to leave.'

'I thought you liked horses.'

I did not hear her reply or what Wevan said after. Once again the hillside was gripped in an unsettling silence. Also silent and unwavering was Arman, standing sentinel on the downward path above the stepped rows of vegetables and herbs. Senea's mare snorted. I had the attention of the woman I had to convince.

# 3

# The Weird Woman

*Scribed by Kar.*

She smelt like her garden and approached as quietly as her garden grew.

'My name is Kar,' I said without turning to face her. I pointed across her garden and up the hill at Arman. 'We plan to sail to the Island of Trees.'

'Say nothing else,' she ordered, her voice soft yet commanding. 'Walk to my side.'

I left the horses untied and followed her command.

She did not look at me. Instead, she held her hands out and told me when to stop. Her grey hair shined like silver in the moonlight and draped over her shoulders covering much of her face. Small seashells and dried herbs were tied delicately in place around her neck with woven strands of what looked to be her own silver hair. 'No need to step any closer. I can feel you now.' With her head downcast, she held the face of her palms towards me like they were her eyes and manoeuvred them over my body without ever touching me. 'Why do you travel to the Island of Trees?'

'To rescue a people,' I answered.

'And what if they do not want to be rescued?'

'I never thought of that,' I replied honestly. 'Though, should that be their will, we will return home and tell Yanereu why. I will struggle in this task for I do not know their language. My friend Senea was destined for this journey and I planned to walk by his side.'

'I know what it is like to be reliant on another.' Her hands moved in front of my face. 'You do not need to know their language to understand them. You have been blessed with sight and it will answer what your ears cannot interpret. The Pledians may have called for you. Do not take this as their final word. I have called for help more times than I can remember. It is not a man I call for. Man is the curse of this world for he changes what was right and salutes too readily what is wrong.' She placed a hand on my shoulder and looked up at me for the first time. Her eyes were vacant, blank like a dead man's stare. 'Tell me about the horses,' she whispered, her hand gliding down my arm until she found my hand.

'One mare belongs to my friend, Senea. He is the man who wed the island's Princess.'

'And you met her?' The woman tilted her head to the sky. 'What did she say?'

'In my people's language, she told me that Pled is a beautiful place, much like my home in the East.'

'What did she say in her tongue?'

'Senea interpreted her words. She said we are considered gods and that her people want to live with us.'

'In the East?'

'That is what I understood.'

'Tell me about the other horse.'

'She's an old mare with a brown coat and the only horse that Arman has ever called his own. Arman is the oldest on our journey and without his help we would not have escaped Assur. We would not have made it this far.' I stopped for a moment, shocked by my candidness with her. It was as if words were tumbling out of my mouth without any thought of control. There was something about her though that made me trust her instinctively.

Letting go of my hand, she turned to face Arman. He was silent in the distance and she was blind. Even so, they seemed to share a distant stare. 'I will take care of them until you return, though it is not too late for you to stay.'

'No doubt you can sense my longing to be home,' I confessed. I felt unusually warm in her company and restricted rather than benefited by sight not shared.

'I hear this desire in your voice, Kar. You are young and wise for your age. Do not convince yourself of this strength or you will rush through life defiant of purpose. Time will allow for the best decision to be made. Wait for the offerings that time makes available. Listen and you will hear. Look carefully and you will find what is often hidden at first glance.'

'I will,' I said, realising as I spoke that I did not even know her name.

'Laures,' she answered before I asked, 'And you may tell the Pledians that I am happy in my new life.'

'I will make every attempt to share your words.' Her words of wisdom were like those a Guardian would share with one about to embark on their first journey.

I could have spoken to her all night and I am sure she would have obliged. Arman had warned me against this. Our journey had to continue without delay, if only so that Gibantis could paint another picture before the Island of Trees was forever changed. Equipped with Laures's insight, our quest was no longer a rescue mission. It was a journey of discovery, its true purpose not yet born.

*** 

Arman found my recount of the exchange confusing, though he thanked me for not lingering to ask for even a simple explanation of her bestowed insight. He looked for movement inside each lit home we passed. 'Have you noticed how quiet the city is tonight?' he asked, as we approached Tuley waiting for us on the road down to the port.

'I have,' I whispered, not wanting to break the silence. I thought of the Zidonians hastily packing after the markets. 'Do you think it is because the soldiers are here?'

'It could be that many children of Zidon have been recruited. They could all be inside sharing a last meal with their families before the voyage on the morrow.'

'I think the people are scared.'

'Scared of the Akkadians?' he asked as he inspected the load Tuley had secured to the Akkadian steed. 'Maybe they have heard of another arriving—a boy who brings the wrath of gods with him.'

I grimaced and looked about again, noticing that the windows and doors to many homes were shut. For all I knew, these homes were deserted.

'It is time for Tuley and I to dress as Akkadians

once more,' said Arman. 'I trust your judgement of the boatman's character but we must leave tonight and I see no other way to board without notice.'

'I am not even sure that soldiers will be allowed near the boats,' said Tuley. 'We will stand a greater chance under the cover of darkness.'

'Did you both rest while I was at the port earlier?' I asked.

'We did, Kar,' answered Arman, 'and you can sleep while Tuley and I sail through the night. I feel like we are outwitting the Akkadians and that gives me strength.'

\*\*\*

Tuley looked the part, wearing an officer's bronze breastplate on top of a supportive uniform. Arman's long, scruffy beard and hair made him less suited to the role, though surely only a senior officer would reprimand him for his grooming. Other soldiers might view him as impudent and hopefully be distracted by thoughts of why they were not allowed such laxness in appearance. Accompanied by my costumed friends, I felt less afraid as we headed down the cobble road to the Port of Zidon.

Unlike the other cities I had walked at night, the roads were empty of people. There was no movement to or from a local drinking hut and the sound of music was absent. The only sound came from atop the white stone buildings overlooking the southern stretch of the shore where the soldiers camped behind the sea wall. Laughter and merry cheers mixed with the silent rising smoke of a hundred campfires below. Many of the soldiers who rested around the fires on the shore would not have encountered the sea before and others had probably heard stories, stories like the one Arman shared with Tuley and I.

'My father was sunk deep into the sea and was pulled from it by the weight of the boat, a tremendous weight that no ordinary man could bear,' said Arman. 'This plunging motion repeated itself until the winds calmed and the sea settled. Was my father scared? Of course he was. Did he ever let go? No. The Akkadians speak of gods and wraths I can hardly imagine; gods who make your world turn upside down. Yet look to Nammu: she has devastated fleets of ships; she has pre-treated bottomless holes in the ocean and raised waves as tall as mountains. The sea is her dominion and no Akkadian God would dare challenge her at home. She is on our side and my tattoo vouches for that.'

'I still think a prayer may be in order.'

'Not a prayer, Kar, homage to her strength is what will make safe our voyage.'

'How do we pay her homage?' asked Tuley.

'We sail silently out to sea and wait until all trace of land is void from sight. Then we sing her song.'

I looked at Tuley and he smiled back.

'Smile all you like now,' said Arman. 'When we enter her realm, forget yourselves. The last thing you want to do is amuse yourself in her presence. She is an old god, a prevailing god and not one to appreciate humour. Our undivided attention must go to her.'

'You have not sailed the Great Sea before, have you Arman?' inquired Tuley.

'I have not and I would prefer it if this were not my first and last opportunity.'

# 4

# The Fish Trader

*Scribed by Kar.*

I led Arman and Tuley along the road from the port to the hut on the rock outcrop. It was crafted from split timber and light escaped from wooden shutters that were tied open on the north-facing wall. It was the closest building to the wharf where Gibantis's boat was docked and the closest building to the northernmost watchtower. The wide path to the beach was before us. Beyond the beach, light from the full moon reflected off the sea, silhouetting the gently swaying masts of the docked fishing vessels.

We rested in the grass between the hut and the boats hauled from the sea to be repaired or slowly rot. Inside the hut, I could hear the occupants quarrelling. As Arman pointed out the watchtower that would notice our approach to the beach, I listened in on the heated conversation. Every harsh word was projected through the open window.

'No, you listen to me, Imbrut,' yelled a woman. Her voice was deep and her words seemed to gargle like she had too much spittle in her mouth. 'You have let yourself be known as a weak man in all your dealings with the Akkadians.'

'Raise your voice more and a brave Akkadian might come to your rescue,' said a man I assumed to be a fish trader or boat owner.

The sound of flesh slapping against flesh drew Arman's attention. Still holding the Akkadian steed by its rein, he crouched next to Tuley and me and questioned our distraction with a cocked head.

Tuley pointed to the open window and cupped his ear.

'You did the same thing last time,' furthered the woman inside. 'They were in need of our service and would have paid handsomely yet you fed them all for a smile and a few lonely shekels.'

'What about the statue?' the man argued.

'What of it? Will you melt a statue of a god into something that can be traded? It is no use to us. When do you ever make a trade worthy of mention? I married you, Imbrut, because you convinced me that you were the greatest fisherman on these shores and that soon all would work for you.'

'I can offer the statue to the holy men and they will bless our boats with fortunate catches and steady seas.'

'Did your little head ever tell you that the proceeds from these blessed catches could already be ours? We should be celebrating the army's arrival.'

'We should,' agreed Imbrut.

All was silent for a while and outside I braced in anticipation of the sound of another slap.

'I assure you, I did bargain with the soldiers,' added Imbrut.

'Bargain,' laughed his wife. 'Hesun would have kept working and ignored them until they made a proper offering.'

Again the room fell silent and outside Arman signalled us to retreat to another place of concealment. He pointed to one of the boats propped up for repair.

I held my hand out to him, requesting that he wait a while longer.

He reluctantly agreed and settled the steed that had already begun to walk away.

Silence prevailed inside the hut until the woman settled herself at the open window. Her enormous bosom rested on the window's sill and protruded further outside, via her shadow.

'No more will I let you treat me this way,' challenged the man. 'Your favourite young fisherman was there with me today and I tell you that he will not be with me on the morrow.'

His wife stepped from the window allowing the light from inside to escape unhindered. It reached in grasp of Tuley who had edged his way closer to the hut through the grass.

'You are listening to me now,' I heard Imbrut tell his wife. 'On the morrow, Hesun can look for work on one of Mabis's boats. He needs to learn that it's hard work under my direction, not flirtation with you, that will see him commanding a fleet one day.'

'You'll say nothing to Hesun,' the woman bellowed, stepping heavily across the raised floorboards of the hut.

Arman took the opportune chance to pull me

aside. 'Why do you and Tuley delay? We could be on the boat by now.'

'I am still thinking about what you said earlier. What if the city is silent because they wait for us? Listen.'

Arman listened and all that could be heard was the yelling coming from inside the fish trader's humble hut, perched above the beach.

'They are too quiet,' I explained, pointing south in the direction of the soldiers' encampment. 'The night should be awoken by an assembly so large.'

'Many would be sleeping—' began Arman before Imbrut, the fish trader, released a pain-filled shrill. Imbrut's wail was followed by the sound of snapping wood and the solid thump of flesh meeting the floor. Arman waited for the quarrel to resume before addressing me again. 'The soldiers' silence is not reason enough to linger.'

'It is, Arman.' My voice was raised for a moment. I took pause, reminding myself how close we were to the hut, the watchtower on the beach and how far sound travels at night. 'The guards watching over the port are protecting all vessels from seizure. If it is not viewed as a seized vessel, its departure will not cause alarm.'

'That is why we wear the soldiers' uniform,' said Arman. 'I will play along if you have a better plan. Remember my reason for joining you on this journey. I'm here to stop you acting without a plan.'

I suggested a retreat to the boat undergoing repair and Arman stilled me with a firm arm. His strong grip on my shoulder almost made me crumple but my resolve saw me bear the pain and grip his arm equally tight in response. At the same time, the fish trader was pushed backwards and almost fell out of the window before being caught and drawn back inside by his wife. Tuley was crouching for cover beneath the sill and the shove and recoil saw their heads clash. Arman clenched his teeth.

What seemed like an evenly matched fight continued inside. We had not been noticed.

'Will you hear my new plan?' I asked Arman.

He released his hold on my shoulder and beckoned Tuley away from the hut. 'Speak while they quarrel.'

'The fish trader can help us. Accompany me to the door with Tuley and act as Akkadian soldiers. I think I can appease him and his wife and gain their favour. Promise them wealth should our venture prove fruitful and hopefully he will escort us to the boat. We are sure to be noticed departing. The fish trader can do all the explaining.'

'And what venture do you intend to disclose?'

'One that would appeal to all fishermen, the promise of a bountiful catch in a secret fishing destination.'

The brawl between the fish trader and his wife raged on like the day Gilgamesh fought the wild man Enkidu in the streets of Uruk.

Tuley was smiling at their antics as he crawled back towards us from beneath the window. 'I think she's going to kill him. Do we have a plan?'

Arman gestured at me.

I pointed to the long stretch of moonlit beach we would have to cross to reach the wharf. 'I want the fish trader to escort us to the boat. The guards in the watchtower will not be alarmed if we make our departure obvious.'

'Let's move before he can no longer walk,' said Tuley. 'We have to leave before dawn and this fish trader would be a known face should there be guards we have not sighted.'

Arman was not convinced. 'Do not see the compromise that had you play god in Assur as testimony that this ploy will also prove successful, Kar.'

'I will not,' I promised, 'though once more I plan to act as one I am not.' My words, or maybe it was my scheming smile, appeased Arman.

He grabbed my tattooed shoulder but held it gently this time before releasing me.

'Help me lie again, for I will not be able to deceive them alone.'

'I will help how I can,' said Arman. 'If we encounter Akkadian resistance and cannot board the vessel, I want you and Tuley to ride away. Double on the same mount, retrieve your mare and escape the city. Do not wait for me. Trust I will find you in the mountains east of Zidon or the desert beyond. I'm a Guardian for Guardians on this journey. I will not rest in the West until you are no longer in my care.'

I braced arms with Arman.

Tuley slapped his tattooed shoulder, covered by his Akkadian uniform. 'We are three with the strength of seven. Our fathers and Arcobon are with us.'

Arman nodded. He secured the Akkadian steed to a support post beneath a boat undergoing repairs as Tuley and I walked from the northern side of the fish trader's hut towards the door on the seaside.

As soon as we stepped from the shadows, the guards

in the closest watchtower were drawn to our presence. They moved to the eastern side of the tower. I counted three guards before I looked away. We were at the same height as them above the beach and within reach of a loosed arrow. I laughed loudly at a joke not told and Tuley followed my act.

He drummed his fists against his breastplate and proceeded to finish the telling of a story in a slightly raised voice accustomed to one who is not afraid of attention. 'And he turned to me flapping his arms like a bird,' laughed Tuley as he acted out a routine unfamiliar to me. 'The man had never seen a fish out of water.'

I stepped up to the door and knocked against it with my staff. The ensuing fight inside muffled the sound. A bronze hand bell sat on a shelf next to the door and, considering the guards in the watchtower had already noticed us, I gave it a shake. The bell rang louder than I imagined it would and we easily gained the attention we sought. The sullen thump of a body hitting the floor reverberated off the walls and a moment later the door was unlatched and opened.

'What now?' yelled the fish trader's wife, raising a candelabrum to see our faces. The breeze made the light of the three candles dance and she lowered it to her side. 'Come to get more fish have you?' she snuffed. 'Do you think Imbrut might offer you a place to stay as well?' Sweat beaded on her upper lip and stuck strands of hair to her reddened face. Her breasts drooped to her belly and her dark nipples pointed in opposite directions, visible through the thin, sweat-coated cloth of her nightdress.

Tuley stepped up next to me at the door. 'There was no such offer, kind woman, though your generosity will be remembered.' He pushed me upwards from the landing, into the doorway. The woman did not accommodate my entrance.

I raised my hand to halt my advance and found myself touching one of her dangling breasts. It felt like my water bladder when it was almost empty.

She held my hand in place with her sweaty palms. 'Men have touched me like this before and had their hands cut at the wrist.'

'This man is the reason we are here,' continued Tuley. She let go of my hand when he pushed past me to enter.

The hut was not built for someone of his height and girth. Looking as uncomfortable as a horse in a chicken coop, Tuley stooped his head beneath the roof's thatch.

I followed him inside and stood behind one of the posts supporting the roof. The fish trader's wife might have thought I was hiding from her. I wiped sweat from my assaulted palm on the wood. 'I'm here to consult with Imbrut.'

'My husband has spoken enough today,' said Imbrut's wife. She shut the door. 'I will hear you.'

Tuley stood in the centre of the room where the roof was highest. A lit candelabrum balanced on the edge of the table at his side. Toppled and broken chairs lay at his feet. 'Imbrut is required. Where is your husband?'

I could not sight the fish trader on my darkened side of the hut. 'You might be able to help me,' I said to the large woman. 'I plan to leave tonight in search of the catch of a lifetime and I was told that if Imbrut does not understand, you would.'

Her mouth sagged open. I was not sure if it was an attempt to breathe or an expression of interest.

Tuley pointed to a split in her skin beneath her eye that tracked a steady flow of blood to her lips.

'Imbrut,' she yelled, unsettling the gathered blood at her mouth. It spluttered onto the floor as she stepped to the side. 'Be quick with your tale. I am hungry and have fish to gut.'

I stepped closer to the table where Tuley stood and looked through the flickering light of the candelabrum. 'Imbrut?' I asked the battered and bruised man collapsed in the far corner, near a stone fireplace, 'are you able to speak with me?'

He looked up at me, his hand pressed firmly against his forehead.

When he did not reply, his wife paced towards him, kicked a chair from her path and hoisted him to his feet, pulling his hand free from a split in his head that he had kept clamped. As wide as a finger, the deep gouge was white and yet to bleed. As she planted him on the only upright chair, gore surfaced from his fresh wound.

I cringed at the sight, feeling his pain.

'Have you never seen blood before, skinny man?' questioned the large woman. She reached across the table and picked up a dirty rag. 'Fine fisherman you would make.' She placed her candelabrum next to the other and tore the cloth into strips.

There was a knock at the door.

'I should have left it open,' she said, 'and invited all the soldiers inside.' Her laugh sounded like an old man clearing his throat.

Arman entered. He looked at Tuley and I before closing the door behind.

'Approach,' said Tuley to Arman. 'Tell these good people why I offer you leave and forego greater pleasures to visit them this eve.'

Arman nodded. 'I was the one who stopped this boy from talking to anyone else at the port today,' he told the fish trader and his wife. A toppled chair lay in his path to the table and when he tried to stand it, he realised one of its legs were broken. He tried to balance it on three legs.

The woman folded a piece of cloth and pressed it to her husband's head. Raising his arm, she told him to hold it in place. 'I can hear you. Speak before I lose interest or are there more of you waiting outside?' She wrapped another piece of torn cloth around Imbrut's head to secure her first dressing.

Arman let the chair fall and stepped closer to Imbrut and the light of the candelabrums on the tabletop. 'I heard this boy mention a secret fishing destination to a deck scrubber and warned him to keep such knowledge to himself lest it be fair game to all. I used to string nets on the Euphrates before I was a soldier. I always dreamed of what it would be like to cast one in the open sea.'

I listened to Arman's tale, seemingly more curious than the fish trader and his wife of its end. The fish trader's eyes were clenched and his wife had only faced Arman once since he'd entered her hut.

'Isvah is the only officer I trust,' Arman continued, facing Tuley, who was wearing the breastplate of an officer, 'and he was noble enough to allow me leave to pursue this venture.'

'What do you—' Imbrut began to speak before his wife clenched his shoulders and forced more blood to his head.

'My husband has taken part in enough foolish ventures. If you are here to negotiate a trade agreement, I expect to see your silver on the table. Otherwise, you are wasting our time and I ask that you leave.'

Continuing with my charade, I turned to leave.

Tuley halted my progress to the door. 'You need to stay.' He grabbed my arm and slung me back to the table, with the ease that he used to throw our little friend, Jas, around.

I turned on him, stopping short of rotating my staff.

Arman placed a hand on my shoulder. 'He would not tell us where it was or how he gained the knowledge,' he told the woman. 'He only revealed that he would find the secret site by the light of full moon.' Arman looked at Imbrut. 'It is a full moon this eve and so set sail we must with or without your assistance.'

'You see this man?' said the woman, staring down at her husband. 'He is the best fisherman to ever chart the Great Sea and when I met him he was a boy like this one.' She pointed at me. 'Scared, alone and useless they are without the insight of a real woman.' She wiped strands of hair from her face with her forearm. Her hands were coated in her husband's blood. 'I can tell you how we can help you if you can tell me what fish you search for,' she told us. 'We always set sail before or after the other vessels, never at the same time.

We often have many idle ships at sea to misdirect our competition from where the fish are most abundant. Every boat has its secret destination and I will not lose control of one of mine.'

'She means mine,' challenged Imbrut.

'Ours,' she asserted with a forced smile, 'I will not lose control of one vessel unless I know it will return with a greater catch. Our lead boats join the others early in the day, already loaded, and even our decoy vessels yield more than a shy return. My husband—'

'I must interrupt,' said Arman. 'We have already secured a vessel. It is merely nets and rope we require. If this boy speaks the truth, I will be able to guide you to the same destination after we return. I tell you this now in the presence of an Akkadian officer.'

The fish trader's wife and Arman stared at each other—not blinking. I wanted to see who would divert their eyes first, but I could not wait. 'I need the strongest rods and spears you have, for some of these fish are half the length of my walking stick.'

'A walking stick?' mused the fish trader's wife. 'I thought you might at least say it was a fishing spear.'

'It is also useful for spearing fish,' I added and I thought I saw a sympathetic side to the gruff, buxom woman when she ignored me for a moment to wipe blood that had flowed into her husband's eye with her sleeve.

When I paused, her dark eyes sprung upon me like I had performed an unforgettable wrong and I quickly continued with my deceitful tale.

'The stars that adorn the sky during the nights of full moon can lead me to a place in the water that has not been visited since my father's father fished there as a young man. Tied to the walls of his hut are the skeletal remains of sword shaped fish with teeth as large as a man's. It is a fish as large as a man. When my people asked him where they came from, he told them that each had bitten into a different limb, each arm and leg, and he had to swim from horizon to shore with the attached fish acting as paddles.'

'And then the sea swallowed the sky,' laughed the woman, something certainly loose in her throat begging for escape.

'Hear him,' Arman advised her. 'Tell her the real story.'

'No one believed him,' I continued, before she had a chance to object or mock me again. 'My elders laughed louder than you when they heard the tale. So, when my grandfather stopped talking and could only move his head, I snuck into his hut in search of proof. I found a map that showed two shores and the placing of five stars at dawn. And now, no one else knows of the map.'

The fish trader's wife paced towards me and I readied to duck or deflect a slap to the face. 'You disturb me at night to tell me you are a thief and think that I would want to help you?' She looked up at Tuley and smiled before she turned to face Arman. 'You look like you wandered from the Army's course last harvest.'

'This soldier,' I said, stepping between Arman and Tuley, 'is the only reason I am here. The man I was talking to earlier may have been a deck scrubber, but he did help me acquire a boat. The truth is, I do not need your help. Only Imbrut can help me.'

'Imbrut? He is—'

'Ready to speak for himself.' Imbrut grabbed hold of the table and stood. 'Stand aside woman or I'll order one of these men to take you with them when they set sail.' She leant backwards as he walked towards me. 'I can offer you the fishing equipment you require, though I cannot have you sailing to any other port if you find what you are looking for. Who is the boatman you have persuaded to take you from shore?'

'Gibantis,' I answered. 'He has offered us six days at sea.'

'Six days, you say.'

'We do not need six days. I can find the big fish before dawn if we sail now.'

'Or not find them again until the stars align once more.' Imbrut looked at Arman and up at Tuley. 'I know Gibantis like a lost toy. Every time I see him, he is a little more broken. Eventually, I told myself, I don't want to play with that toy anymore.'

'We have to sail tonight,' I said.

Imbrut nodded.

His wife stepped to his side. 'Gibantis enjoys long departures from dock and, if he is first to hear of such a location, we will never hear from these men again. I think we should offer them a boat,' she said, prompting her husband to agree by squeezing his hand.

Imbrut pulled his hand free of her clutch. 'The young man has chosen well,' he declared and walked clear of her control. 'Fish that large will break a net when you try to lift them. What you need is a barbed spear.' He asked for my staff to demonstrate and I obliged. 'Pull them close to the surface with the net and then spear them before they break free.' Imbrut leant on his table like it was the side of a boat. 'Lift them from the water with your own weight on the far end of the spear,' he demonstrated.

I did not like my staff being in another's hands and I was quick to reach for it as soon as he held it idle.

Arman stepped in front of me and bent to look at the fish trader in the eye. 'We must trade for a net and some spears without further delay. Tell us your offer.'

'Follow me,' he instructed, walking to the door.

'You can find your own meal and place to sleep tonight,' his wife shouted as he led us from the hut.

\*\*\*

We waited for Arman to untie the Akkadian steed before heading down the wide path to the beach.

'Do you always let your wife treat you that way?' Tuley asked Imbrut.

I looked back and saw her silhouette filling the doorway to the hut.

'She has her offerings,' said Imbrut, 'and who are you to ask? I see you are an officer yet you look younger than my son. Was it noble duty or the house of your father that gained you such title?'

'He is more worthy of authority than any other officer I know,' praised Arman as he approached with the steed.

'More worthy than you?' asked Imbrut, looking upon Arman, an older soldier, leading the horse.

'He is the only one who has been rewarded for acting against order,' replied Arman, speaking of Tuley.

'Isvah is his own man. He is not a common disciple of Sargon seeking wealth and land for service. He proved that in Assur by putting his own life before those of pilgrims to your land.'

'I do like that,' said Imbrut, smiling at Tuley. 'You might be the first officer the people of Zidon speak well of if you return from this voyage with Gibantis.' Imbrut's praising smile disappeared the moment he turned from facing Tuley.

'Keep moving, men,' said Tuley. 'I care not for your early praise.'

Imbrut did not seem convinced by my story and, as he watched us, I looked beyond him at the commotion atop the closest watchtower. They no longer stood on one side, quietly observing our progress. A torch had been lit and one guard had descended the watchtower's ladder to the beach.

When we reached the wharf that secured Gibantis's vessel, Arman began unloading our stores from the steed. Imbrut walked on and stepped onto the first of his swaying vessels. Our approach had gained notice and, as the fish trader began tossing the nets, spears and ropes we may need onto the wharf, four soldiers advanced on foot from the neighbouring wharf, fifty paces away.

'That should be all you need,' assured Imbrut, admiring his selection of select fishing equipment. 'I will speak with Gibantis personally though before you leave.'

I gathered together what I could carry and Imbrut helped with the rest. He lifted a lengthy coil of rope with ease and hoisted it onto his shoulder. The fish trader moved like the fight inside his hut had never happened. He seemed to have forgotten his bandaged head and bleeding mouth, or maybe he was distracting himself from his wife's instruction to find another place to sleep.

Arman carried our stores from the Akkadian steed and Tuley hesitated at the end of the wharf.

'Have a safe voyage,' said Tuley. 'It was good to see you both again.'

'Lift your pack and follow us,' Arman called back, risking alerting Imbrut to some form of deceit through his casual address of a senior officer.

'My place is here,' confirmed Tuley. 'I will make sure you are not missed on the count tomorrow. I expect you back in six days.'

The four soldiers from the neighbouring wharf arrived behind Tuley and Arman walked on.

I had stopped on the wharf ahead of Arman. 'We should wait for him,' I said as he approached.

'Keep moving,' he instructed, 'or nobody will be going anywhere.'

I reluctantly kept walking along the wharf, unable to resist looking back. Tuley seemed to have convinced the soldiers all was in order and he waited with them, like he was intent on staying.

'You arrive earlier than expected. Did you sell your horse?' Gibantis questioned me, ignoring Arman and Imbrut.

'No horses to tip your vessel,' I answered.

Gibantis pointed at Arman and Imbrut. 'Are these the friends you spoke of?'

'A six-day voyage, Gibantis?' inquired Imbrut before I had a chance to reply.

'If it takes so many days it will be. I did not expect to see you tonight.'

'I felt like a walk,' said Imbrut. He smirked and glanced at the sky.

'Been making love again I see,' mused Gibantis, gesturing to his own head.

Imbrut touched his bandaged head gingerly. 'This is only part of the reason I am here. I want you to know, Gibantis, that these nets and spears are only on loan. My wife will be stupefied if I return without silver, so that is exactly what I am planning to do. I am doing right by you tonight and I hope you will compliment my offering by bringing these men back safely with a catch. If you haul in one of those big ones, please keep it fresh so I can share its taste. Big is not always better.'

'What we bring back is up to these men to share. My only taking will be silver,' Gibantis assured him before turning to Arman. 'What about you? Are you not meant to be sailing on a narrow boat on the morrow?'

'I will be shackled or upright on a stake if we do not leave soon,' said Arman. 'I have been granted leave by an officer, though, he would appreciate that the other soldiers did not hear of this favour.' He looked towards Tuley at the end of the wharf.

Gibantis extended his arm towards me. 'Come aboard.'

I clutched Gibantis's arm and stepped aboard with my load of nets.

'Six days, no more,' insisted Imbrut as he handed

Arman the heavy coil of rope.

I nodded in agreement.

Imbrut untied the boat before walking back to the end of the wharf to where the soldiers waited with Tuley.

'Ignore them,' ordered Arman, 'and help Gibantis with the sail.'

'You two are both very good at lying,' said Gibantis. 'I would advise you to be more truthful with me from now on.'

'The city feels deserted,' I tried to explain. 'We thought the soldiers might stop us from boarding.'

'So you had one escort you.'

'Arman's not a soldier. He is my friend.'

'I know he is not a soldier,' admitted Gibantis, 'I am talking about the one you arrived with.'

'Imbrut?'

'Imbrut and I have known each other since our fathers ruled the sea. I speak of the officer waiting at the end of the wharf.'

'He is a friend too. He is not a soldier anymore.'

'And you are leaving him behind?'

'It was his choice,' said Arman, stepping between Gibantis and me. 'I do not like parting. What say do I have? Spoil not our advantage boatman. There will be time to talk at sea.'

I looked back at Tuley again, 'I did not farewell him. Do you think he will wait for us?'

'I hope not,' replied Arman. 'I'm quite sure I made the departure plan clear to both of you.'

The turn of the sea at the shore had already floated

the boat clear of the wharf.

'Hoist the sail, Gibantis, an island awaits,' Arman said like one born to the sea.

'Wait,' I pleaded, seeing Tuley standing alone. 'The soldiers have moved on. He is waiting for us.'

Arman returned to my side and looked across lapping water and the length of the wharf between the docked fishing boats towards Tuley. 'He is not waiting, Kar. He is saying a silent farewell. Tuley has chosen to travel a different path to us. He's out of my care now.'

I raised my hand high for Tuley to see and he signalled that he had seen this by placing his hand on his tattooed shoulder as we drifted away.

***

When the last trace of land had slipped out of sight beyond the moonlit horizon, Arman began to sing a sombre ballad to an old God. I fell asleep to his raspy, deep voice and the gently rolling sea knocking against the bow of the boat.

It was to morning light that I awoke. After taking a moment to envisage the day ahead, I slipped back into another deep sleep. When I woke for the second time, Arman was sitting by my side. He was no longer wearing the uniform of a soldier and looked comfortable in a tunic and his well-tread sandals.

'I am impressed by how soundly you sleep at sea.'

I stood and stretched in the mid-morning sun gracing the deck. 'Your song must have worked.' The clear skies above were one with the blue plains of sea expanding in all directions.

'I am going to teach you the song today and you

can sing with me tonight.'

'I think I remember the words, Arman. I can still hear your voice repeating in my head.'

'Nammu hears it too. I am going to rest now. Wake me if I look like sleeping through the night.'

'I will. I will wake you to the song.'

'Sing deep, Kar, and be sure to learn the sails. Gibantis will also need rest soon.'

'Sleep well, Arman.'

'I have been anticipating rest on a boat since I learnt my father was a man of the sea.' Arman lay down in the sail's shadow and rested his arm over his face.

I walked to the bow and shared Gibantis's view of the sea ahead.

'You are strange men,' he said.

I touched my fastened hair with one hand and held my coverall from flapping in the wind with the other. 'I have tried to dress like the men in the west.'

Gibantis smirked. 'I say you are strange because you don't feel like strangers. Your friend sang a song to the sea and you slept as soundly as my boat through surging waves. With the wind and Nammu on our side, we will reach the Island of Trees by morn.'

'I slept like I was at home.'

'You did,' said Gibantis. His eye twitched before he turned his stare to the horizon.

I wandered the deck, observing his adjustments of the sail and watching how they caught the wind. All the while, I was thinking of the island.

Our first task, when we reached the island, would be to convince the tribesmen who protected the Pledi-ans that we also had honest intentions. We would need to borrow horses from them in order to find the Pledians before the soldiers arrived or Gibantis abandoned his wait at shore. It seemed like everything was against us on this journey and I needed to consider all our options. We could not lie to the tribesmen. They needed to see us as Guardians. I planned to address them as I had Laures. No more lies, I silently vowed.

# 5

# Mayhem at First Light

*Scribed by Enheduanna, Priestess of Ur,*
*Sargon's Palace, Agade.*

W*ith my humility masked by stateliness, I introduce myself as Enheduanna, Priestess of Ur. My temple in Ur is devoted to Nanna, the God of the Moon. Nanna's pale face has comforted me often with silent counsel and given strength to my judgement. It is not, ashamedly, through counsel with any god that I find myself writing of the happenings in Zidon. Later, I would meet Derahmus, an Akkadian soldier respected for his battles in the name of Akkadia, and learn more about the three men entering Zidon the day before my story begins. This is one of my stories that will not be sung or preached from the high steps of ziggurats across our land. It will not find a place on a shelf amongst the songs of my people. Yet, should I not scribe this story, reported by the separate accounts of two tablet bearers, what really happened in the west would be determined solely by the Court of Agade. It begins in a city near the sea ...*

The sleeping city of Zidon was awoken to a state of mayhem at the port. Horns were sounded in the first light of dawn and the Akkadian soldiers assembled on the shore. Three of the army's vessels were floating near the horizon and the officers did not even know if these vessels were manned. Another two boats sat low, filling fast with water and beyond repair. Derahmus, the first liege officer and Commander of the North-eastern Frontier, had left his post in search of men who had evaded capture in Assur. Stories detrimental to his authority had begun to circulate and he was certain the same men were responsible for the sabotage overnight.

As Derahmus's horse trotted the final length of the cobble stone path that three men of interest had ridden the evening prior, he gained his first sight of another port in a state of chaos.

'Much damage has been done, my liege. We are lucky more boats did not float away during the night,' reported his most respected soldier, Izdubar.

'I want all the guards who were on duty in front of me now,' ordered Derahmus, holding his long, dark hair back from the sea breeze as he slid on his bronze helmet. The officers by his side also donned their helmets.

'Most are dead, my liege,' replied Izdubar. He kept his head stooped. Only his eyes were raised to his commander on horseback.

'What about those posted to the watchtowers?'

Izdubar's head remain tipped to the ground as he pointed to a group of guards mingling nervously at a distance. 'That would be those men. They were in the southern tower.'

'Three soldiers? Where are the others?'

'They are dead, my liege.'

'Derahmus,' bellowed Ratuun, the officer in charge

of the western assault. 'Is this the work of the men who evaded you in Assur?' Ratuun made this call from a distance so that the assembled soldiers overheard. As he marched towards Derahmus on foot, with a large, spear-wielding soldier by his side, he turned his head from side-to-side as if expecting to see soldiers welcoming his arrival. Ratuun removed his helmet as he neared Derahmus and wiped sweat from his brow with his sleeve.

'Be careful what you say,' warned Derahmus. 'This is your mess and I will happily leave you to deal with it alone.'

Ratuun was clad ready for war, though his pungent scent and bulging eyes suggested that he was still drunk from the night before. 'Do you think this is the work of the men you let escape in Assur?' he asked again, smirking.

'No, I do not,' answered Derahmus, even though he was almost convinced it was. 'The men in Assur—'

'The boy,' corrected Ratuun, smiling at the large soldier who accompanied him. 'People are saying it was a boy.'

'There was a boy involved,' Derahmus agreed. 'He only killed one of my officers and an Assurian officer who challenged him died in a duel. Even though he was trying to escape, it is a great leap in judgement to assume that he is part of a rebellion.'

'What makes you speak with such surety?' inquired Ratuun.

'I think it laughable that he carried the wrath of the gods,' explained Derahmus. 'He was a frightened pilgrim, not a cult leader or a tattoo-bearing enemy of the throne. These are nothing more than hysteric rumours. Even so, he must pay for his actions. I am here to find him in hiding, not fight your battles nor answer to you.'

Derahmus's loyal soldier, Izdubar, led the surviving watchtower guards across the beach to meet the officers.

Derahmus appeared in control with an officer either side of him and eight mounted soldiers assembled behind in two rows, four abreast. He looked down on Ratuun from his mounted position. 'Ask questions of your men, Ratuun,' he advised. 'Have them tell you who was seen near the boats or absent from camp during the night. The prosperous North-eastern Frontier will need me to return soon.'

'Do not be too quick to leave,' Ratuun said threateningly. 'Your frontier is subject to mine and we are both subject to Sargon.'

One of the tablets sent south-east from Zidon told that Ratuun had been drinking the local beer and readily accepting introductions to Zidonian maidens into the early hours. He was not prepared for such a hold-up.

'My plan for the day was to dress, count the soldiers aboard and already be asleep below deck when they set sail,' Ratuun told Derahmus. Instead he was faced with thirty dead soldiers, two sinking ships and three floating out at sea. 'What did you see?' Ratuun asked the guards posted to the southern watchtower.

'We only saw soldiers at the boats,' replied one.

Ratuun extended his arm towards the sea and jiggled his hand. 'Did you notice the boats floating away?'

'Their sails were at full mast,' said another guard. 'We did not think they had been cut loose. Guards from the other towers were investigating.'

'Why was this not reported to an officer?' yelled Ratuun.

'It was, my liege … to you personally. Do you not remember?' replied the third watchtower guard, bravely stepping forwards. 'You were—'

'I was what?' Ratuun questioned him.

'You were about to feed your fish to a whale, is your response that was shared with us.'

'Doing what?' exclaimed Izdubar, forgetting his place. He stooped his head and stepped back.

Ratuun shook his head vehemently.

Derahmus advised the reporting guard to distance himself from Ratuun with a tilt of his chin. 'Based on the reports from your own guards, I can confidently state it is all your responsibility now, Ratuun. You are lucky I only report to Sargon what happens on my frontier. Drunkenness and officers being deprived of breath, for game and on the night before a major expedition, is unacceptable.'

'Apologies for interrupting, my liege,' said the tower guard who had made the report. He stepped forwards again. 'I think the fish was Ratuun's manhood, his flesh rod, and the whale was a hefty maiden.'

Derahmus's head twisted sideways, looking for confirmation from his officers. He then looked to Izdubar and tilted his chin, prompting his response.

'That makes more sense,' Izdubar confirmed.

'Forget the confused message,' snapped Ratuun. 'Have you not heard the most important detail. My guards only saw soldiers. Did not soldiers turn against your rule in Assur, Derahmus?'

'Not my Akkadian soldiers, they were Assurians; a weak-minded breed, dutiful to the high priest.'

'Even so …' said Ratuun, pausing to dismiss the watchtower guards, 'my report to Sargon will mention your name. Shall I have it scribed that you were present and did nothing to help the greater good of our King's empire?'

'You do not want to do that.'

'No, I do not. I will though, unless you stay until we find those responsible.' Turning to the soldier by his side, Ratuun continued, 'Jemat, tell the officers to count the soldiers aboard. Down thirty men we may still have enough boats. Explain that it is preparation for a departure before dawn on the morrow.'

'Yes, my liege,' said the strong soldier, Jemat. He bellowed the command as he paced through the sand towards the shore.

\*\*\*

Derahmus and Ratuun rode along a road north from the port towards the fish trader's huts above the beach. They received polite greetings from the locals, only to hear them laugh as they walked away. The people of Zidon had no choice but to welcome the soldiers for they did not have an army of their own. When fate stepped in and disrupted Akkadian control, they quietly rejoiced. Zidon was under Akkadian rule only when the army was present. Quashing this propensity for rebellion in the outer states of the empire was an Akkadian imperative.

'We will be the only ones laughing after we sack

Mari,' said Ratuun.

'*If* you sack Mari, Ratuun,' replied Derahmus. 'I worry about your impetuous carousing. If you neglect vital reports like a ship sailing in the night without crew, maybe you also voice plans best left privy.'

'Even my drunkard self remembers what is secret, I assure you.' Ratuun spoke boastfully and smiled nervously at the same time.

Derahmus frowned. He could smell Ratuun's rich odour despite the scent of fish guts rotting in the sun.

Most of the fishing boats had set sail by the time the Akkadian officers reached the hut closest the most northern watchtower.

Derahmus knocked loudly before seeing a bell on a wall-mounted shelf. 'You ask the first question, Ratuun. You know more about the damage done last night.'

'What do you mean, I know more?'

'You have been down to the wharves. Surely you have seen how the soldiers were killed and if anything was taken.'

A fish trader opened the door with his wife leaning over his shoulder. 'How can I help?'

'Last night—' said Ratuun before Derahmus spoke over him.

'May we enter?'

'Do you need to ask?' questioned the fish trader's wife. 'You go where you please and bid entry at any time.'

'Thank you,' said Derahmus, ignoring her sarcastic tone.

'What happened to your chairs?' asked Ratuun.

'That is firewood,' replied the lady. 'If you want a

chair there is one there at the table.'

'Lady, we have some questions to ask of this man, so if you do not mind.'

'I do mind,' she yelled. 'Anything my husband—'

Ratuun pressed his finger to her lips. 'Shh,' he said.

Her eyes narrowed as she stepped away from him and wiped her mouth.

Ratuun sat down at the table and faced her husband. 'I have some questions for you.'

'If it is about those boats at sea, I believe they are unmanned and sailing loose of control.'

'They are our boats,' confirmed Ratuun, 'and they were cut loose with their sails drawn mast during the night.'

'Who would do this? Why raise a sail and go nowhere?' inquired Imbrut.

'That is why we are here. Who looks after your boats during the night?'

'No one would dare touch one of my boats lest they never work the sea again.'

Derahmus chuckled and decided to leave before embarrassing Ratuun further. Ratuun, however, did not gather insult from the fish trader's words and stood in a state of bemusement. Derahmus nodded politely at the fish trader and his wife, and walked towards the door.

Ratuun followed him to the door. 'Did you hear something I did not?' he asked Derahmus. Ratuun was not prepared to let anyone interfere with what he saw as God-given orders from Sargon himself to stake claim on the Island of Trees, sack and garrison Mari, and maintain rule in Zidon. 'From what I am told you were not laughing in Assur,' insinuated Ratuun. 'What has changed?'

Derahmus paused in the doorway. 'The fish trader demeaned you, Ratuun, without intention though right to your unshielded face.' Derahmus stepped outside and light from the morning sun glinted on his helmet. 'No one would touch one of his unguarded boats. They damaged your fleet under the watch of three towers.'

Ratuun glared at the fish trader before following Derahmus outside. 'My greatest concern is now you,' he decided. 'The loss of five boats is negligible. I call you to duel in the presence of this humble merchant.'

Derahmus spread his arms. 'I would defeat you before he even had chance to cheer.'

'I offer you control of my frontier if you strike me down with your blade,' declared Ratuun, removing his leather gloves and signalling the fish trader to follow them outside. 'Let us resolve our differences in sight of all.'

Derahmus was happy to stand against the younger officer until he sensed an ulterior motive. A duel between officers was news destined for Sargon's ears and he was not even meant to be in Zidon. 'You raise a pleasing offer but I will not draw on you, Ratuun,' he said as he stepped away from the hut and peered over the drop, the height of two horses, to the beach below.

'Then return east and await judgement sure to follow when Sargon hears of the folly that led to our meeting.'

Derahmus removed his gloves and tossed them

sideways before drawing his sword. 'I will bring you nigh to death,' he declared. 'Your last words of regret will reach my ears alone and then I will silence you and appoint a new officer in your stead.'

'There is another way to resolve this dispute,' appealed Ratuun, drawing his sword ready. 'We find those responsible and share drink tonight, united to the cause.'

'You should be sailing from these shores today, Ratuun. Already I count your words as dishonest.'

'We sail only when I give the order. Under the same authority beset upon you, I repeat to your face that no man, no magic or a god has authority greater than that of Sharru-Kin. We could duel today though that would only necessitate an explanation. Why are you so far from your frontier, Derahmus? Do you think Sharru-Kin would be interested in your explanation? Ensuring that the campaign continues despite what has happened is what will gain his approval. He cares not if ten of my officers bed the same big, beautiful woman. My drinking and other indulgences matter not when I report of lands claimed in the name of Akkadia and you know but few of my accomplishments. Thus I ask, have you travelled from your frontier to help or hinder?'

The fish trader had picked up Derahmus's gloves and was about to side with the officer until he witnessed how easily Derahmus was swayed by talk of Sharru-Kin. 'You men cannot even maintain order amongst your own ranks,' he told them. He placed Derahmus's gloves on his doorstep and turned towards the shore.

Ratuun halted the fish trader's next step by raising

his short sword to his throat.

Derahmus drew his long sword. 'He demeaned us both. Let him live and I will comply.'

A thin smile spread on Ratuun's face. 'See how I helped you understand we are in agreement.' He sheathed his sword. 'Let us share the burden of finding those responsible. Regardless of whether they are the same men who escaped your control in Assur, we will meet as comrades in view of a greater conquest this eve and share only our victorious tales.'

'Hopefully, come tonight, we will have found those responsible and a timely victorious tale to celebrate. Either way, I will still take pleasure in drinking you under the table,' boasted Derahmus.

'I welcome your challenge. I will have my representative in Zidon ready a selection of maidens for our pleasure.'

The officers braced their gloveless arms in front of the fish trader's home.

'You are too forgiving, Derahmus,' Ratuun told him as he watched the fish trader walk away without being reprimanded for his insults.

'No, Ratuun, I only give what I hope to receive.'

'That man's catch will feed us regardless.'

'And who will feed us on the morrow. Compliant the people of Zidon may be yet always foe to our rule.'

'Authority is instilled by action, Derahmus. Letting him walk only weakened our governance.'

'I hear you, so hear this. Relinquishing control over another is proper if you only hold him for personal gain. You would be best to learn from this lesson before we meet tonight.'

*Ratuun and Derahmus never met that night. The conflicting tales shared by tablet bearers appointed by each officer were read in the King's court, in Agade. After which, it was decided that they should be put aside until confirmed reports regarding Sharru-Kin's campaign were received. The court officials wanted to hear of the army's return from the island in the Great Sea before a final decision on the officers' standing was decided. The officials had forgotten that I was Enheduanna, the scriber of songs. My stories do not wait for new day. I write at night under the watchful eye of my god, Nanna. But I fancied this tale for godless reasons. If Derahmus's account was honest, I had found a man who, despite his power, sought to protect the meek. A silent trembling within me was awoken.*

Jemat, described as a strong soldier, and one of Ratuun's new recruits from Mari, reported all happenings of the previous night to Derahmus later that same day. He requested that in gratitude he be allowed to join Derahmus in his return to the East. According to Jemat, a tall officer, a man even larger than him, had ordered the men down from the towers and sent the guards from one tower to notify the other officers of the sinking vessels.

Derahmus agreed to Jemat's request. Jemat rode with a new accompaniment of soldiers back to Mari without informing Ratuun of their departure. Derahmus might have thought he was outwitting Ratuun. As it was, the tablet bearers, reporting conflicting sides of the same story, arrived in Agade at the same time and on the same boat. Ratuun and Derahmus had both attempted to be the first to tell their version of the incident in Zidon. The court officials did not look upon

Derahmus's account as favourably, as he had departed from his place of duty on the North-eastern Frontier.

In Mari, Derahmus appointed Izdubar Commander of the North-eastern Frontier, disappointing many first liege officers. He explained to the newly appointed officer that only Sharru-Kin himself could challenge such an offering of duty. 'You are responsible for the lives of your soldiers and the giving of orders that result in the taking of life and defence of the empire,' he told Izdubar, as he handed him a red brooch, shaped like a bull's head. 'So long as you wear this, you are a first liege officer to Sargon.'

Derahmus boarded a vessel on the Euphrates and travelled south to the capital, Agade. He arrived five days after his tablet bearer.

# 6

# Plea of a Priestess

*Scribed by Enheduanna, Priestess of Ur,*
*Sargon's Palace, Agade.*

If I had to name the greatest want of man and woman alike, I would say it is immortality. This gift of the gods, if one believes the epic tale of the God-King Gilgamesh of Uruk, has only been shared with one man and it was not Gilgamesh. Long before my father united the Sumerian states into the Akkadian Empire, rising waters buried the land, animals and people. Enki, the God of Freshwater, warned a man named Utnapishtim of the flood and instructed him to dismantle his house and build a boat. Only Utnapishtim and the people and animals aboard his boat survived. When Enlil, the God of Air, and the other conspiring gods who had created the flood inspected their work and found survivors, they were enraged. Enki sent Utnapishtim south to his temple in Eridu and shared the god's gift of immortality with him.

Siding with Enlil and the other gods, my father holds little respect for Utnapishtim, a man who should have been killed with all of mankind in the great deluge. Nor does he care for the people who exonerate him every time they read aloud the epic poem of Gilgamesh. According to my father, Enki defied the other gods when he warned Utnapishtim of the approaching deluge, and the children Utnapishtim beget, made my father's rise to power all the more difficult. To my father, the city of Zidon is a portal city to the Great Sea. Nothing great ever happened there before his time. Had my father been present in Agade when a first liege officer arrived after abandoning his post in the north, I would not be scribing this story. My father viewed Utnapishtim as a deserter, not a hero worthy of the greatest favour. King Sargon, my father, would have surely killed Derahmus for his desertion and paraded his body around the city like he would a lion—a trophy of strength.

Whilst I understood why Derahmus was not welcomed by my father's court in Agade, I could not condone their bigotry. The officials, in their matching white robes, remained seated. They released a deep chorus of unsettling moans. Despite the lack of respect Derahmus was afforded, he stood with pride and explained with conviction what happened in Assur and his reasons for riding west. When he told the court what happened in Zidon, the officials blasphemed and roused debate concerning his punishment. They had received his account of events and Ratuun's account at the same time and had already formed an opinion of the man's character.

I favoured Derahmus' decision to re-appoint duty and travel to the King's court to receive judgement. Not wanting to exceed my welcome, I stood quietly in protest. When I stood, so did my four maidens.

'Is she leaving?' I heard one of the officials ask.

I met eyes with Derahmus for the first time. He looked up at me questioningly from the floor, his eyes as dark and as commanding as I had imagined them to be. His arms, held straight by his side, were like the front legs of a stallion. 'I stand because it seems a decision has been made. Maybe the court made their decision before his hearing.'

The High Priest of Anu, Amar Sudra, allowed my interjection, if only for the knowledge that my word would make it to my father's ears. He requested silence and questioned my presence via discernible eye contact with my personal servants prior to announcing his verdict. His body looked feeble, yet there was power in the white-haired man's old voice that frightened me.

'Derahmus,' he announced, 'your failure to administer proper justice in Assur is disconcerting yet your objective of administering prompt response must be held notable. The happenings in Zidon and the governance administered by Ratuun is also questionable; however, until he is before my court, it is your actions alone that must be judged. Ratuun, despite his failings as a man, continues to fight with undisputable allegiance to the Empire. You have failed the King and are no longer fit to wear a soldier's uniform. Land already signed to your name shall remain the property of your family. For your failure, Derahmus, you are now deemed a servant of Akkadia and will work for food, without right to personal possessions, till the day you die.'

I turned to my maidens and the empty stone benches reserved for my brothers and their servants and advisors. Never had we all been present at the same time. Even my presence in this court that decided the fate of men was rare. 'Most noble servant of Anu, please forgive my interference in a matter beyond my control,' I requested of the High Priest, silencing the court officials' growing applause to a verdict already voiced.

'You are free to speak, daughter of Sharru-Kin.'

'I agree that Derahmus is no longer worthy to command a fight for my father. Your stance on desertion is not to be questioned though surely he is still of use to the Empire and should not be discarded so readily. His knowledge, that your representatives chose ready to waste, is all that separates us from the lands which in his absence, and with due privilege appointed by him, are now governed by a man who was once a stable keeper.'

'There are many shades to correct judgement, Enheduanna. Might I correct your view in saying that no man is born to a god? We cannot argue the placement of a man. The newly appointed Commander of the North-eastern Frontier might also make ill judgement. It is by deed and trial every day that one holds position and authority. If he, like Derahmus who is before us, abandons his post, the court's vote will again be unanimous.'

'Your stance is noteworthy, High Priest,' I replied and signalled my servants to bow with me in respect before I voiced my demands. 'I ask, therefore, that you post Derahmus to my personal service so that I might learn of the eastern conquests. I would be able to share both his knowledge and your wisdom with my father when we meet next. Whilst I have not seen my father for many a dark moon, we are soon to be reunited come the Feast of Ishtar. The festivities on such a day are certain to have us standing side by side. You will be there and together we can explain why such a dutiful and honest man was considered suitable for my service. After all, he was a first liege officer. My father did approve of his character prior to handing him control of such a vast frontier.'

'I understand your woes in subjecting this man to more simple duties yet I cannot help concerning myself with thoughts of distrust that could put the first-born daughter of the true King in jeopardy.'

'I understand why you have reached such a conclusion.' One of my servants aided me as I stepped down to the floor. 'You are a Priest of Anu, the Father God and share his strength and duty to family. I hear your woes and still believe that if my mother were here she would support me in my personal confirmation of this man's character. My father adversely, I am sure, would side with you. He is not here and if he were, my presence would not have been allowed long enough for me to raise such a qualm. If for no other reason, consider that my compromise.'

Amar Sudra always had an answer and that is why he was not a simple statesman or an officer of the court. He was the High Priest of Agade because he had held authority in the Ziggurat of Anu longer than my father had been King. The decisions of his court were final. My last statement, however, left the white-haired man silent and the court officials grew restless.

'Sharru-kin is privy to his daughter's words,' he eventually proclaimed, silencing the idle chatter. 'I have a new name for you, Enheduanna, one that cannot be disclosed until your father returns to Agade. Derahmus, you are forgiven for your inability to control such a threat to our land and rewarded by the forgiving hand of the King's daughter. Pledge your allegiance to me, the High Priest of Anu and to Sharru-Kin, and vow to be dutiful to every request of his daughter, Enheduanna, and she shall be given the key to your shackles.'

'I pledge that my allegiance to you and the crown never faltered,' voiced Derahmus. 'I vow to serve Priestess Enheduanna, The Singer of Songs, until the day I die.' He removed his bronze breastplate and gold signet ring that signed him as an officer of Sargon. With respect he bowed to the High Priest and in reverence, prostrated himself on the floor at my feet.

# 7

# The Island of Trees

*Scribed by Kar.*

The island was just how Bias had described, though it was hard to believe that Zidon had ever looked this way. The trees spread out into the blue sea and those on the fringe fought to hold their ground against strong winds and a lapping tide.

Gibantis lowered the sails as we cruised past a breaching surface of rock no larger than the vessel we occupied. He pointed ahead. 'You will have to signal me of your return. I will drop anchor at a distance so that I and my vessel are safe.'

'Will you be safe from this storm?' asked Arman, looking upon darkening skies in the east that shielded the light of the rising sun. The sky above the island was cloudless and the green of the trees endless.

'I may have to move the boat to shelter in a cove or sail further north if the army arrives. My yellow flag will always fly high on the mast. You should not have trouble sighting me.'

I watched and listened to the flag whipping side-to-side, 'I think the storm has come for the Akkadians.'

'Let Nammu fight that war alone, Kar,' instructed Arman.

I trusted his judgement. We were close to land though it was not too late to insult one of the oldest gods. Nammu did not want to hear from me what she would or would not do. Instead, I chose to place faith in our own actions.

A heavy frown weighed on Gibantis's face as we sailed closer to the island's shore. It was not until we stepped from the deck and climbed down into the shallows that he revealed the source of his anguish. 'Take this,' he said removing his necklace and handing it to Arman. 'It belonged to Laures.'

Arman turned the shell necklace in his palm, contemplating its meaning. The reflective underside to each shell shimmered green and blue as he turned it in his palm and he felt the horsehair that strung the shells together.

'You may already know, Kar, that Laures, Bias's mother, is native to this island. I confess it was I who stole her.' He raised his hands defensively. 'I was painting the island from a distance when I spotted her alone on the beach collecting shells. For my tired hands, she was too beautiful. My guilt made me set her free the moment I docked back in Zidon. She has forgiven me. That I learned the day she returned to my boat and offered me fish for my painting. Her forgiveness is not enough. I have not forgiven myself. I pray you are successful in your quest and what was done long ago will find purpose in my return to these shores.'

'Give us a day and night ashore and you will receive an answer,' said Arman. 'Let me also confess that I do not trust you to wait for us. I hope and pray that you prove me wrong.'

I looked concernedly back at Gibantis as we crossed the lapping water to the beach with our stores held high.

'I will be waiting,' he called out. His frown had faded after finally voicing his confession.

\*\*\*

With long cuts of intertwined hide, we tied our fur-wrapped belongings tight to our backs and ventured inland. I carried my staff in my hand and used it as a walking stick, like Samor did when he navigated steep dunes in the desert. The beach soon gave way to dense forest that only offered clearings where salt water from the sea had been trapped in gullies and formed small lagoons. We walked silently until we reached a fresh-water creek.

'Fill your water skin, Kar. I do not know the lay of this land.'

'I do not think we will find ourselves short of water on the Island of Trees.'

Arman laughed, 'I said the same thing once, only to see the Euphrates River turn red overnight.'

'With blood?' I exclaimed.

Arman stamped his foot on the dried-mud bank of the creek, between exposed tree roots. 'A riverbank collapsed outside of Sippar where they were digging irrigation channels. You could not drink the water for two days. It tasted like clay and sat like clay in your gut.'

The trees hung low across the creek's breadth. In the dappled light, rarely tread resting places were revealed, marked only by stolen growth amongst the thicket of branches. Animals could have created these clearings but I suspected the Pledians or the island's mountain tribe had created them. They looked like nice places to rest with sheltered views of the sea.

Not far from where we filled our water skins, we found a natural stone crossing. I stepped cautiously, not wanting to be soaked through before we even knew how far we had to travel. On the northern side, we climbed a steep muddy slope and arrived in a wide field of grass bordered by cedar trees. Like the grass that surrounded my village after rain, it seemed to flow like a green stream in the wind.

'Beautiful,' exclaimed Arman. 'It reminds me of our home in the East.'

'Like the Guardians, I don't think the Pledians want to leave their home.' I pointed north to the hills peaking above the cedar trees. 'Senea spoke of the Pledians moving inland after the Akkadian's failed attempt to take the island. We have a long way to go.'

'What if we stayed here?' he asked, reminding me of the morning I had spent at the Karun Gorge—Salarn's heaven.

I stopped walking and looked back at Arman. He stood knee deep in lush grass with a content smile relaxing his face. I was not sure if he was admiring the enclosed beauty of the land bordered by cedar forests or entertaining the idea of standing against the raiding Akkadians. Through gaps in the foliage, the Great Sea reflected a trickery of light. I tried to imagine what view Gibantis would be painting from offshore and I twisted my head to see if his yellow flag was visible through the trees.

'Do not move,' Arman warned.

'What have you seen?'

'We are being watched.'

'It must be the mountain tribe, the island's barbarians,' I assumed and I slowly extended my staff towards Arman. Its hide sheath covered its bladed tip. 'Tie the necklace Gibantis gave you to its end. We must gain their trust.'

Arman looped the necklace around the end of my staff. He then drew his sword and placed it on the ground at his feet and unfastened his pack. 'If they are savages, my sword or pack won't save me. It could all end for us here.'

I also untied and dropped my pack before I held the necklace high with my staff.

Arman spread his arms and turned to show he was unarmed.

'Let's hope they recognise the necklace or the few Pledian phrases I know.' I had not sighted the tribesmen yet but I could tell where they were because their crawl interrupted the green stream of grass. 'If they protect the Pledians, they should know their language.'

'Teach me some Pledian words while we wait,' said Arman, his head remained still as his eyes flickered in every direction.

'*An gamahn toppe.*'

'And what does that mean?' he asked.

'It is a long story.'

'Give me a quick explanation.'

'No, that is what it means. *An gamahn toppe* means long story.'

'How about friend? Do you know how to say

friend?' asked Arman.

'I know how to say love.'

'Oh, that will be helpful,' he sighed. 'Tell the first savage to wield a blade on you that it is a long story, love.'

'What if ... I know. I should draw a map like Salarn did.'

'Do not make any sudden moves, Kar.'

The island's tribesmen appeared from their concealment in the grass. Even though they were not covered in war paint or adorned in animal bones like the valley bandits, this tribe still incited fear. Almost naked, and with skin darker than ours, they had silently surrounded us in the long grass. They brandished long, barbed spears and they were pointed at Arman and me.

'I think you should lower your staff now,' suggested Arman as they edged closer.

'And surrender it?'

'Never. Keep hold of it and the necklace by your other hand. They need to fear us though not feel threatened until they learn meaning for our presence.'

I understood Arman's concern. We were here to rescue the Pledians and, if the tribesmen saw us as weak, our plight would not be respected. '*An gamahn toppe*,' I said, holding the necklace high in one hand and my staff upright in the other. I voiced the Pledian names I knew. 'Yanereu, Laures, Janke.'

My words halted their progress and they spoke amongst each other in a similar tongue. Their spears remained pointed at us.

I handed my staff to Arman and he accepted it cautiously, leaving his other hand suspended in a display of submission. Holding only the necklace, I took a step towards those gathered in front of me, to the north.

'*Un mas vert tahmas,*' yelled one from the horde gathered behind.

'*Vern sepp palage,*' I said, turning in the direction of the voice with the necklace dangling from my palm as an intended offering. I did not know what I was saying though I was sure they were kind words considering that they had been exchanged at Senea's union. 'Laures,' I repeated holding the necklace higher. I then tried to repeat the words one of the tribesmen had used. '*Umas vert ahmas.*' Still there was little response from the savage looking men who stood almost naked, covered only by loincloths. I wanted to hand the necklace to one of them yet each time I approached, they drew back, seemingly fearful of the object.

The circle of spear wielding men closed around us, as more appeared from the grass. Unless we could find a way to communicate with these people, we were sure never to reach the Pledians or leave the island.

'Kar?' Arman only turned slightly to address me. 'Find the Akkadian helmet in my pack. You have their attention; it is your words they do not understand.'

I kept the necklace held high as I untied Arman's fur and removed the helmet. There was not a visible leader amongst the men and they surrounded us in a circle, so I decided to place the helmet in front of us, to the north. It needed to be on display and north was the direction we planned to travel. I stepped back to Arman's side. 'Can I have my staff?'

'I'll swap you for that necklace,' he compromised.

I held the staff flat across my palms as I stepped towards the helmet. 'Akkadian,' I said, gripping my staff and pointing it at the helmet on the ground. I rotated my weapon and thrust the blunt end at the helmet.

The circle of spear wielding men parted as the rattle of my staff connecting with bronze echoed. Behind the spear bearers a row of bowmen stood and flexed their weapons. The hand of one of the bowmen shook.

I ducked as a loosed arrow cut the air above my head.

'*Gamahn toppe, gamahn toppe*,' yelled Arman, turning and waving the necklace in all directions.

Slowly I rested the end of my staff against the ground and, with my free hand, I pointed at the helmet. 'Akkadian,' I said again, dipping my head in the direction of my pointed finger.

Those with bows relaxed their applied tension, and those with spears shifted their aim upwards. One of the tribesmen boldly walked towards me and struck the helmet himself with his spear. An ear-shattering holler was sounded from the strange men's mouths in unison and the circle of dark-skinned men closed in on us. Arman prompted them to take the necklace from him but he was allowed to keep it. We were not ready for what ensued. They stole quick touches towards our bodies, revelling when they touched skin and hollering when they discovered that we had the same parts as most men.

'If they were women, I would not be troubled,' joked Arman. His grin disappeared when a spear cut his arm. He reefed it from the man and snapped it on his knee. 'Look at what I hold,' he told them, shaking the shell necklace.

I held one of my arms wide and let them inspect me in the same fashion but whenever they reached for my staff, I shook it and warned them not to touch. 'Pledians? Pled? Janke?' I repeated. They were either ignoring our words or did not know the words we spoke.

Their approach to touch our skin, at first playful, had become a mockery. Even if we were speaking the Pledian words correctly, they had become hard to hear over the tribe's excited hollers.

One of the men knocked the side of my head with the blunt end of his spear. I turned on him and blocked the strike of another spear driven towards my chest. From behind, a spear was prodded into my buttocks. My hide shorts did not stop the tip from penetrating my flesh. I felt blood running down the back of my leg.

'They do not fear us, Kar,' yelled Arman. 'We have lost control of this meet.'

'What can I do?'

'Stand back,' Arman yelled. He shook the necklace vigorously and parted the strange men until he was standing with his back to mine. Plunging his hand into the grass, he re-gathered his sword.

'Pledians, Pled,' I yelled.

They stopped reaching for us and pointed their spears. I knew that if I did not perform another marvelling spectacle soon, the curious men would dominate us. They pointed at Arman's sword and a slow gurgle of disdain was cued.

'Pledians?' requested Arman, jiggling the necklace in one hand and swaying his sword in his other.

The barbarians' deep-throated gurgle intensified.

I placed my staff on the trampled grass at my feet and pulled my cover-all over my head. Blinded for a moment, I was thankful that I did not receive another sneaky jab from a spear. I lifted my staff from the grass with my foot and flipped it into my hands. The leather sheath covering its blade was still tied. I needed it now. My fingers fumbled as I untied the sheath. One strand of leather laced the sheath together. It caught when I tried to pull it free. I looked beyond my focused stare as the tip of a spear was lunged at my exposed chest. I knocked it to the side and Arman struck upwards with his heavy sword, snapping the weapon beneath its barbs.

'Stand back,' he yelled with his sword raised. Arman turned on his feet, doing his best to address the threat from all sides.

I retied the leather sheath beneath its bladed end and twirled my staff above our heads. Beams of light crossed the faces of the horde and, for a moment, their disconcerting moan was silenced. Taking advantage of their pause, I used my staff's blade to reflect light onto my shoulder and display my tattoo. 'We are Guardians of the East.'

'Keep telling them, Kar,' said Arman as he pulled his tunic taught at his shoulder and cut the cloth. He tore his sleeve loose.

'We are Guardians of the East. Until all our people are safe, we will not rest in the West.' Signalling with one finger, I requested a sole barbarian to approach.

'See my tattoo. I am a Guardian.' I allowed those closest to me to lean forwards to inspect my tattoo and Arman's. When they stepped too close, I turned on them and twisted my staff's blade to reflect light in their eyes.

'Watch this one,' said Arman.

A skinny man, with his spear held close to his chest, was encouraged forwards by his tribesmen. He stole a few more cautious steps closer to Arman.

Arman, also with great caution, turned his shoulder to the man and let him look upon his tattoo.

The tribesmen closest to me had begun to talk amongst themselves and I listened closely. It seemed their native tongue was different to that of the Pledians. They used words that could not be sung as sweetly. Even so, I was convinced that they were the part of the mountain tribe who protected the Pledians and, until we gained their support, we were useless on these shores.

'There he is,' declared Arman, startling the skinny man into a quick retreat. 'Behind those with bows is the man who spoke Pledian words. They are keeping him sheltered.'

The few Pledian words and names I knew had failed to gather the attention we required and our audience was so loud now that to repeat them seemed pointless. Though I did not understand their language, I could tell from just watching them converse that, when they finished talking, negotiations would be over. Our fate was soon to be decided. 'Stanf,' I yelled, blocking a spear jabbed towards my chest from the side.

Those closest to me fell silent.

'Stanf,' repeated Arman in his deeper and louder voice.

It was the command we gave our horses when we wanted their attention though some sort of meaning now resonated amongst the tribesmen. They were still.

'We are Guardians of the East, sent your way by Salarn,' I announced, relishing the chance to be heard once more. 'We need to find the Pledians. Someone here must know the names I speak. Janke? Yanereu? Laures? Salarn?'

'Forget names, Kar. It is like talking to wild horses. It is easy to gain the attention of ears. Their minds are lost to our words. They will kill us out of fear.'

'Salarn?' sounded a voice from the crowd.

'Am I hearing right?' questioned Arman.

'Yes, Salarn.' I raised my staff above my head. 'Salarn,' I repeated.

'That's the one they've kept sheltered,' whispered Arman as the men armed with spears turned their weapons skyward and a hairless, heavily tattooed man parted their defence.

'Not belong here,' the man said, his eyes wide and wild. 'Return to far shore.'

'Are you a man of Pled?' I asked him, noticing that his skin was even darker than that of the tribesmen.

'Pled no more,' he told me, waving a short paddle-shaped weapon.

'I do not believe you. Yanereu made it safely to the East and the Akkadian boats are yet to arrive.'

'Why you here?' he asked with broken phrase.

Arman tapped my arm and bid me to remain silent for a moment. 'How is it you speak our tongue?'

The man held his arms wide and yelled unfamiliar words to his kinsmen. '*Iliar Vunde.*' His words made the tribesmen laugh.

'So you speak their tongue too?' said Arman, unimpressed. 'We are here to rescue the Pledians. Was it a false request?'

The dark-skinned man, with coloured tattoos coursing his entire body and a tapestry of seashells dangling from his neck, pointed east. 'Only Salarn is welcome.'

'When the boats arrive from Zidon, you may change your mind,' rebuked Arman.

I took one step closer to the man. 'Yanereu, a Pledian Princess, told us that the Pledians wanted to be at one with the Guardians. She said her people wanted to travel east to our home.' The tribe's spokesman did not reply and so I began describing Yanereu, using my hands and words. 'She has straight hair that reaches her hips. Her skin ...' I saw a man with skin slightly lighter than the others and pointed at him, 'is like his.'

'Yanereu is not Pledian Princess. She your Princess now,' he said and signalled the man I had pointed out to approach. 'This is son of Pled. You see he is Stanf Warrior now.'

'Stanf Warrior,' repeated Arman as he turned to me. 'The tribe do not protect the Pledians. They have taken over the island. Salarn has always played his own game. We have no place here.'

My mouth was agape. I could not believe that Salarn would send me without reason.

The son of Pled gripped his spear with tensed muscles. His skin was lighter than the rest of the tribe and similar to our skin in colour. The bald man who spoke our tongue had noticeably darker skin and was also the only man with tattoos decorating every part of his exposed body. His coloured inscriptions depicted animals of the land and markings of the moon and sun. Across his chest, beneath his seashell necklace, was a picture of significant detail. It showed an assembly of people queuing and holding gifts of offering for a man with a cat-like face. Salarn had never mentioned this man when he had spoken of Pled, yet there was something about him that seemed familiar.

'How do you know Salarn?' Arman asked him.

'Salarn ... friend,' the man grasped his paddle-shaped weapon with both hands and tapped it against the shells on his necklace. 'My brother.' He again gestured emphatically, this time holding one hand above him, signifying what we could only assume meant older brother, taller brother or one who had died.

Arman looked at me confused, 'Salarn is Verian's older brother. What is he trying to say?'

'Elkin?' I asked the man, drawing meaning from the colour of his skin.

'Elkin and Salarn ... go ...' and he pointed his paddle in an eastward direction, 'across the sea ... long ago.'

Finally, we had a connection with the men who surrounded us and I trusted again that Salarn had not sent us on a pointless quest. 'Salarn told me his story of leaving your island. I stayed with your brother, Elkin, for eight nights in his mountain home,' I told him, trying to emulate his very efficient signings and all the while sensing I was failing.

'Mountain?'

'Elkin lives in the Zagros Mountains.'

The man was quiet until Arman asked for his name.

'Ronses,' he answered promptly and, pointing to the young man standing next to him, 'Pontare.'

'My name is Arman and this is Kar.'

'Where Salarn?' he asked, the tattoos on his face changing shape as his eyes squinted.

'Salarn is old now,' answered Arman. 'He sent Kar in his place.'

'You come to take people away.' He pointed east with his short paddle.

'Only those who want to travel,' said Arman. 'It is a dangerous voyage and the East is not safe from the Akkadians.'

Ronses shook his head. 'Boats will find and fight Stanf Warriors.'

Arman nodded and pointed at the sky. 'They could be here even before the moon rises.'

Pontare, who I believed to be a Pledian, leant close and tapped me on the chest with a stiff finger. He then pointed the same finger east and signalled me to walk that direction by jabbing his spear towards me and hollering words I did not understand.

I stepped back defensively.

Ronses raised his voice in my defence. 'Pontare, *un mea danasai.*'

Arman sighed. 'They do not understand, Kar, and I will not avert from using my sword for the word of one girl, princess or not. There might be no escape for me but I will swing my sword again. That is the last thing I want to do.'

I knelt in the grass.

Arman rocked his head back and groaned, 'Please do not beg, Kar.'

I started to roll out my pack. It was Senea's sleeping fur but it had replaced mine since we left Assur. I did not want anything from the pack. The hide of the fur formed a level surface and I did not have a beach like Salarn did to draw on. I dug my fingers into the ground to find dirt to draw with. When I looked up, Ronses was leaning close, holding his shell necklace back with one hand. 'This is Arman and Kar,' I told Ronses and repeated my gestures towards each of us and back to my drawing. 'Stanf Warriors surround us.' I pointed to his men and circled my hand above my head. I then sprinkled more soil and shaped a small boat near the edge of the island. It became hard to see my picture when the shadows of encroaching spears blocked the light.

Ronses ordered his men back, pointing at the sun, '*Anu divid arnmes uf.*'

I looked at the sun also. It was high in the sky and we still had far to travel if any Pledians were to be returning with us. 'One boat,' I said and raised my smallest finger and displayed it to Ronses and Pontare. I drew bigger boats at a greater distance. 'Akkadians.' Repetitively sprinkling more dirt on to the hide in different spots, I tried to show that there were many vessels on their way. I drew an arrow to the Island through the sprinkled soil. 'An army of boats,' I yelled. I raised and lowered all my fingers many times and kept looking for signs that Ronses, or his tribesmen, understood. I scampered across the ground a few paces to where I had placed the helmet, and the warriors in that direction shuffled backwards to give me space. 'An army of boats,' I yelled again and when I looked up I was glad to see that Ronses had followed me. I picked up the helmet and pointed at it and then towards the east. Throwing it on the ground I tried my best to show my dislike for what it resembled. I hit it with my fist so hard that my skin broke. I hit it again and was about to draw my throwing blade and stab it when I felt a hand rest on my head. I looked up and Ronses pointed in a circling motion to the tribe who surrounded us.

'Boats fight Stanf Warriors,' he said.

'You tried, Kar.' Arman squeezed between Pontare and many more inquisitive Stanf Warriors. 'It is not our fight, Kar,' he said, offering me his hand. 'Salarn should have never sent you here. I helped you arrive and now it's my duty to get you home. I think they will let us leave. Let's leave.' He nodded to his own suggestion.

I wanted to agree with Arman; however, since arriving in Zidon, I had begun to question life's greater plan. My father had taught me to not predict life but Salarn had shown me the real world—a reason to stand still when everything moves. I looked up at Arman. 'Laures told me that the Pledians might not want to be rescued. She questioned our quest, Arman. What if our true purpose is to protect them and their homeland? We could make sure life for them does not change by fighting on their shore.'

'I questioned you and Senea about this quest in Nineveh. It never seemed right. Salarn might have turned mad with age but what of your father? Tell me again why Unbetum agreed to send you west.'

'The tree,' I murmured.

Arman turned to Ronses and apologised for our deliberation with a raised hand.

Elkin's brother, Ronses, nodded, 'I show you Pled ... you see ...' He shrugged and looked at me like all I had explained meant nothing.

'How far to Pled?' asked Arman.

Already Ronses was distracted as he relayed orders to his people.

Pontare, the son of Pled, walked closer to Arman to inspect more closely the necklace he held. Arman offered it but he declined and stepped away waving his spear.

I shook dirt from Senea's fur, still not sure if my drawing had helped me explain the Akkadian threat. Maybe we needed to see the Pledians with our own eyes to understand why they would not leave.

Ronses returned. 'Keep the necklace,' he told Arman. 'It tells that she who wore, no longer lives.'

'Wait,' I yelled, dropping the fur. 'You understand our language.' I pointed at him with a stiff arm. 'You understood all our words, didn't you? Do you understand the danger you face when the boats arrive? Yanereu sent us here to rescue her people. Why would you turn us away?'

Ronses raised his paddle above his head with both arms. His eyes were closed and he only opened them when he spoke. 'Salarn and Elkin vowed that they would never return. They, unlike the people of Pled, want more. Kinsufa want more. Yanereu want more. They are not part of the Pledian circle anymore.'

'Kinsufa was my mother.'

Ronses lowered his paddle. 'Stay and be Stanf Warrior, son of Pled.'

Arman distracted me by handing me the shell necklace. He was humoured by my anxiousness as I considered what to do with it. 'A death necklace it is,' laughed Arman. 'Remind me to thank your friendly boatman, Gibantis.'

'Laures still lives.' I turned to explain this to Ronses but he was already at a distance. The Stanf Warriors, bar Ronses and Pontare, had vanished amongst the grass and into the tree growth as quickly as they had appeared.

Arman knelt next to me and lifted Senea's fur. 'Do you want me to have a look at that?'

I went to hand him the necklace before I realised he was looking at my leg. Blood had trickled from beneath my shorts to my ankle. 'When we have time to rest,' I said. 'Now's not the time to be taking off my pants.'

He smirked as he started rolling Senea's fur. 'We have been attended to with great leniency by the gods, Kar, and are lucky to have made it this far.' He placed Senea's belongings—a spare bladder, five sticks of dried meat and the pouch of shekels—before he continued rolling the fur. 'From now on, we must be more deliberate in our actions. The Pledians have their own guardians. We have warned Ronses of the threat and we both know that they are less vulnerable than our own people.' Arman folded the rolled fur and tied it taught with a strip of leather. 'The Akkadians will be at a disadvantage on these shores. They will not succeed, yet here we find ourselves, never further from the threat to our own home.'

On my first journey to the Desert City, Bit-Bunakki, after our village was sacked, Salarn thought this way too. 'Maybe the Guardians have no place in the west.'

Arman closed an eye to the light of the sun as he watched Ronses and Pontare leading horses our way. 'We do not belong here though that is not to say that we were without reason for coming. In our quest, we have freed another Guardian and recovered stolen tablets. Lingering too long in search of greater purpose will be our downfall.'

'Do you remember when I fell on the path to Zidon?'

'You fell on your face and,' Arman cocked his head, 'then you pointed to the army's trail.'

'Only now am I making sense of what has been allowed. My chest should have been staked in that fall. I fell and landed on it and then, when I fell again, I braced myself in time.'

'We'd escaped a city and crossed a desert. You were tired.'

'It wasn't just my fall that made me think differently. In that moment I felt as if an even greater responsibility—a heavy load—had been transferred to my shoulders.'

'Then I will help you carry it,' vowed Arman. 'We must return east. Such a feeling of incumbent burden can only mean that a Guardian has made passage. We are connected through our tattoos. Your father taught me that.'

'You ride?' yelled Ronses, returning on a horse and leading two more.

Pontare, the Pledian turned Stanf Warrior, sat high in his mount as he trotted around us.

'We ride,' replied Arman. 'The gods are on our side, Kar.'

*** 

It seemed Pontare knew the path best for he led the ride. Even Ronses, who rode in front of us, struggled to keep up. Ronses was more wary of the unseen rises and falls of the land beneath the tall grass. I looked more closely at the tattoo on his back when he slowed his horse's canter. The tattoo was a depiction of the sun and from each side of the sun spread feathered wings that extended across his shoulders. When he raised his arms, the wings lifted on his shoulder muscles.

We entered the cedar forests to the north and trotted along a narrow, straight path through the trees. When we breached the woodlands, we were met with rolling hills leading to barren cliffs masked by tree growth on both sides. Pontare turned his mare westward before we had climbed the first hill and we trotted down a well-used track to the marsh at the bottom. The horses trudged forwards, knee deep in the sludge, until we reached the next hill.

Pontare and Ronses slapped their horses' sides and left us behind on their climb up a steep winding track.

I looked at Arman before encouraging my loaned mare to follow with a heel to its flank. We cantered towards the rise but our pace soon slowed to a scramble. Halfway up the climb, where there was level ground, I offered my mare rest. We were on one of the hills I had spotted from the grass field. I could see the Great Sea expanding to the horizon.

'Don't look for his boat,' yelled Arman as he rode by. 'We will ride to the shore regardless.'

I tapped the mare's side and we followed Arman up and along the narrow trail to the hill's peak.

Ronses and Pontare were waiting.

In the valley on the other side of the hill, I could count at least fifty people and they were either young or old. There was no one my age, nobody the age of Yanereu or Pontare. The children looked to be playing a game and the elders sat like they were in counsel. Both the children's game and the elder's counsel were staged in perfect circles and no Pledian sat between. There was stillness in their activity like that experienced in the real world that Salarn had shown me. 'The Pledians are Stanf,' I said half to myself.

'Where is their shelter?' Arman asked Ronses, encouraging his mare to keep trotting after the steep climb.

'This is home,' Ronses replied pointing to the sky and then sweeping his arm to the tree-lined hills on each side. 'When the boats come, long ago, they live at water's edge,' he continued, pointing towards the shore. 'I tell them come here.'

He did not speak with the candour of Guardians but Ronses did know our language well. I needed to trust that the Pledians were safe in his care. 'Where is your home, Ronses?'

'This is home,' he said, looking wistful as he stared past me towards the eastern shore of the island. 'My brother knows many lands and chose a mountain. We have mountains here.' He pointed north-east at a distant mountain. 'Yanereu choose to find Guardian Warriors' home. We have Stanf Warriors here.'

I wanted to still my voice and appreciate my surreal surroundings for what they were but knowing that we would never see such a sight again had me question Ronses further. What I had learned from Salarn and Elkin seemed vague, if not deceitful, considering that they had never mentioned Ronses or their vow to never return to the island. Neither of the wise, old men spoke of their reasons for leaving the island, more than a quest to go further. And I believed from Salarn's stories that the Pledians did live in huts because Janke farewelled Salarn from his balcony overlooking the sea. I raised my hands to the sky. 'Elkin tells me that heaven knows my story already. He told me to cross horizons and I have crossed many to be here.'

'Here is heaven. Pled finished. Pled is complete.' He looked at me and pointed his paddle east. 'Your fight is not here.'

'I met you and found you not in need of our help, Ronses,' said Arman, dismissing himself with a nod of gratitude, followed by a slight pause of discernment at my delay.

I watched Arman trot away a few paces before I turned back to face Ronses and Pontare.

Ronses's lips thinned into a half smile just like Elkin's did when he farewelled Salarn at the edge of the desert. 'I was birthed in the city where the sun first rises,' he said, pointing east and then south over the treetops to a place I had never heard of. 'There ...' and he thought hard to find the right words, 'beginning and end are strangers. Heaven knows no story where beginning and end meet unchanged.'

'Laures is alive. She lives in Zidon,' I told him. 'Take her necklace.'

Pontare circled his mare and snatched the necklace from my hands.

Ronses chuckled and Pontare smiled at him. 'Leave the horses where we find you.'

Arman nodded and began his return down the steep hill.

I faced Ronses. 'The sun rises first in the east. You pointed south when you told me where you were from.'

Ronses pointed south-east. 'Elkin and I were born on a far island in another sea.' His jaw tightened and his teeth scraped together. 'Our island became home to many kings.' He shook his head and turned his view to the Pledians. 'There are no kings in Pled. This is the way it must stay.'

I looked at the tattoo on Ronses's back and shared his tranquil view of the Pledian's home before I rode away. I wished that I could share Arman's conviction. I wanted his ability to retire without regret to a homeward course. As my horse trudged through the marsh, I looked back. I could no longer see Ronses or Pontare and I wondered how often they exchanged words with the Pledians. Maybe they were speaking to them now. Whatever was happening on the far side of the hill was no longer my story. A new destination was now calling my name. On an island in another sea, where the sun first rises, the beginning and end of my tale would meet. Elkin had told me to cross horizons to find heaven. Instead of heaven, I found his brother and his brother, Ronses, named an island that was home to many kings. Everything happens for a reason. I believed the island he spoke of to be the end of the Bull's Burrow, the nesting place of King Sargon. First, I had to see Arman safely to the East, to the Guardian Tower. It was so far away that I could not imagine myself ever stepping through its door again.

# 8

# Guard Duty

*Scribed by Lagesh.*

For nine days, I had waited for something to happen. I sat on the same stool at the tower door. There I watched the sun rise above the trees and set on the other side of the clearing. Nine days ago, it was Naten sneaking from the company of the other women that had made me think I had purpose. She had crouched next to me, where I sat on my stool, to rest her slender arm against mine.

'I will have skin like yours soon,' were her proudly spoken words and she stayed crouched in my shadow whilst she fanned her pale skin that was flushed pink from bucketing water to the crop.

Though short-lived, even a similar visit would start my count again. Life as a sentry was not getting any livelier. I mused in my dullest moments over my early days, when even Naten had ridden away during the day and I had counted myself lucky to have her nearby. I counted the birds in the sky, the number of times Unbetum called out to me from the roof of the tower and how often Karun, Salarn's black bird, swooped to

146

pluck a worm from the grass in my view. Everything can be counted when time moves slowly, and there is little to talk about when one day mirrors the last. Then life all happens at once and the count is forgotten in view of a surprise event.

An eagle beat its wings once and soared around the tower gracefully. I drew my eyes back to the tree it had launched from and readied my bow. Shadows from the pines stretched halfway across the clearing to the tower as the sun lowered in the west.

'Horses approach,' Unbetum called from the roof.

The women and children rushed to my side from where they had been tending to the crops.

'Inside and out of sight,' I told them but, when Jamine stayed, so did the rest. Why would they listen to me, a boy? And maybe she had sensed something I had not. I kept my bow raised as we waited for the horses to breach the woods. They were approaching from the southwest. Please don't be Senea and Kar, I prayed. I had received a vision of Kar returning to my completed tower in the plains where I was born. If he returned now, the vision I had experienced at the tree would mean nothing. The tower I envisioned might never be completed and I might never grow closer to Naten.

'It's Senea,' said Fankisi, gripping my arm and trying to look into my eyes for an explanation.

'And he rides Kar's stallion.' I glanced at Fankisi.

My brother stopped at the edge of the woods, and I lowered my aim when Cihnah and her younger sister, Meera, ran past me. The rest of us waited to see who followed. Fankisi saw her husband, Tahnas, and I saw my whole family. My mother shared my father's mount.

A wheezing sound, like wind between stone blocks of the tower, escaped my mouth. My hand reached for Fankisi's as she stepped past me. I wanted her or anyone to tell me they saw my mother too.

The trader, Delari, and two I did not recognise completed the group. Kar and Arman were not with them. I hoped Unbetum had known this before he had left the roof expecting to reunite with his son.

Senea and I only smiled at each other as we crossed paths near the stable. I thought of the quest he and Kar had explained before their departure and, for that reason, I was not joyous in his return. So many questions were left unanswered as he walked past me to hold himself against Yanereu's growing belly. I walked on towards my mother. It hurt to think what must have happened to her after being gone so long and now, finally, returning with deep scars on both cheeks. I dropped my bow and my father and I helped her down from the mount. Only her face was clean. The rest of her skin and clothes were covered in dust, mud and dried blood. She used to brush her long, brown hair every morning and braid it while we sat by the fire. Now, it was heavily knotted and cut to an uneven shoulder length. The skin under her eyes was dark like she had not slept in days or maybe it was because of the scars on her cheeks. When she smiled at me, I almost cried. That one smile reminded me of every other time I had seen her smile. My mother was alive and I wanted to fall asleep in her arms. I tried to speak.

'I am alive, my youngest man. That I know because you still recognise me.' She kissed me a hundred times though I was no longer counting. Each press of her lips was a new sensation. 'I am home, Lagesh, and

I am never leaving you again.'

For the first time, I felt at home at the tower. I even found the strength to untangle myself from her warm embrace to greet my father and the other arrivals.

After meeting my mother's new friend, Messim, and the skinny, old man they called Uk-Ban, all hands were called on to help offload the horses. Tahnas asked me to carry his fur. Standing in the shade of the tower, he shared only a few words to quell our fears for Arman and Kar. He told us that they parted company in Assur and held hope after seeing the battalion of soldiers grow furious with a hold up in the lane towards the city. Unbetum told those who had returned that Salarn had shared a more vivid sense of hope in the form of a painting inside the tower. Even those who had seen the crude image before, already cracking where the paint was applied thickly, eagerly headed inside for another shared viewing.

*** 

Tahnas, like me, saw Kar in the painting immediately.

'It's Kar. Could this be what happened in Assur?' Tahnas groaned when he turned to face Unbetum.

Unbetum shrugged but I knew he agreed. As the others examined the painting, Unbetum watched his friend, sensing Tahnas was hiding an injury beneath his loose-fitting tunic.

Lan held a torch closer to the wall. 'This is what concerned me,' he explained, pointing beyond the torch's flame to the shoulder of the man receiving the sword. 'Fankisi thinks it may be the run of the paint but I see the mark of Akkadia.'

'Did anyone see Salarn paint this?' asked my father, Gentuk. 'Did he speak to anyone?'

'Unbetum has been asked too many times these same questions,' answered Lan, moving the torch to the other side of the painting. 'This is what settled all my woes, Gentuk,' he told my father. 'Do you see this? Kar is smiling. There is no mistake made. Paint sliding down the wall here could have only saddened his face.'

'I will welcome Kar telling me himself what happened that day,' decided Tahnas. 'I agree with Lan and I will sleep well until Kar and Arman return with great tales.'

My father looked around at those gathered. 'I would have liked for Salarn to see Belline again.' He ran his fingers through his hair. It was longer than I had seen it before and he had grown a thin beard. 'Tell me more of what we have missed. Any visits from Boroe or news from the South?'

'Apart from Lan's surprise return and Salarn's sudden departure, life in the woods has been quite uneventful,' replied Unbetum.

Fankisi cleared her throat.

'Uneventful in comparison,' Unbetum corrected. 'Lagesh's appointment to tower guard was necessary and Jamine's successful harvest will see us through the season.' Unbetum glanced at Fankisi to judge by her facial expression whether he had spoken of everything. She was looking at Senea and his Princess from the West. 'And in your absence, Senea's wife has also been blessed with child, and I must say that I welcome new arrivals to our new Guardian home.' Unbetum nodded respectfully towards Belline, Delari, and the strangers,

Uk-Ban and Messim.

Tahnas stepped away from those gathered around the painting and stood near the giant's fur. 'It was a long journey home, Unbetum. Many of us are in need of rest.'

Fankisi whispered instructions to Naten and the Borujerdian girl lifted Parbi and called for the young girls to follow her outside.

Naten looked back from the tower's door to see if I was following.

I smiled at her and lifted my bow. 'I'll return to my watch soon.' I watched her walk outside. For a moment, her slender figure was silhouetted through the thin cloth of her dress.

Jamine took her husband, Lan, by the hand, 'Early rest will be good for us too. We will prepare bedding for all on the top floor.'

'I would like bedding,' Uk-Ban excitedly told everyone and looked around as his voice echoed in the confines of the tower.

Delari laughed as he watched the bony, old man follow Lan and Jamine to the stairs. 'You should wash first, Uk-Ban.'

The stairs had distracted Uk-Ban. He held the railing tightly as he ascended, comfortable with Jamine's amble.

'There is bread and broth if you're hungry?' Fankisi offered Delari, when she saw him linger.

'Do not worry about me, Fankisi,' said Delari. 'Tend to your husband. I have treated his shoulder wound many times. It needs a woman's care.'

'What have you done?' Unbetum asked Tahnas,

hesitant to approach his friend, as if afraid of the response.

'I turned my back in retreat,' said Tahnas.

'No,' said my father, 'you put your life before your horse.'

Fankisi directed Tahnas towards the giant's fur. 'I know my husband well. He will tell me it does not pain him until no one else can hear him.'

Tahnas shook his head slowly. 'This wound hurts to my bones. Like my friend, Unbetum, I won't be leaving the tower for a while.' He smiled at me. 'I might have to join you at the door, Lagesh.'

I was still standing with my mother beneath the stone arch near Salarn's painting.

'I'd like that,' I told Tahnas.

She held her arms around my chest and rested her head against mine.

'Kar might not return for a while,' I told her.

'Why not?' she asked, kissing my cheek and then staring into my eyes.

'His vision ended when he faced a sea and all turned white. In my vision, he returned to us to live in the village again.'

'Do you think we will live there again?'

'Yes, mother. It was a vision, not a dream.'

She hugged me tightly and I closed my eyes.

My father gained her attention. 'Belline, Senea would like to introduce you to Yanereu.'

She released her hold on me but reached for my hand. 'Do you know her, Lagesh? I'm not ready for this.'

my own mother was back, new fears began to grip me. A flock of birds flapped towards the wood's canopy as we approached the kill.

Unbetum asked me to withdraw the arrow and hold the bird. Placing his finger beneath its ruffled brown feathers, he gathered blood and painted a line on my cheek. 'This plump bird will feed you and your mother tonight. It is your reward for being dutiful and a welcoming present you can share with one who has been gone too long.'

I was happy in the moment for landing my first kill but, with blood now on my hands, sorrow for my mother became overwhelming. I felt, without knowing more than the scars on her cheeks, the pain she had suffered. 'Unbetum, I feel too much. How am I ever to be happy when so much pain is inflicted out of my control? Am I a coward to allow Kar to fight alone? Is it my place, like Senea, to remain in the East?'

Unbetum looked down at his finger and wiped the remaining blood on his own cheek. 'Learn acceptance, Lagesh. Accept your place more willingly than me. I had to be tortured by the Akkadians and admonished by women before I learnt that some things, even the most important, are out of my control.' He forced a smile that soon became a grimace when it pulled on his scarred face. 'You have read most of Salarn's tablets. There is only one I have kept separate.'

The weight of the bird slumped in my grip and I barely held it by one hand. 'Why did you hide a tablet from me?'

'The clay was still wet when I found it resting on wet cloth to dry. I am sure our Elder shared the tablet's story with Kar and, as you know, my son is not the most settled of men.' Unbetum tried again to smile.

'I believe in Kar. He told me that my dream was a truth not yet seen, a vision. I want it to come true. I only wish its slow birth would hurt less. When I am on guard duty, a duty you allowed, my mind is separate from my body. I long to fight even though I wish for peace to endure. When I start moving again or I am otherwise distracted, I fear every change. I want to live again in the plains. I want Kar to return safely and not leave again so soon. I want Naten to be happy whether or not she chooses to bear my child.'

Unbetum's eyes widened and then he tightened them and looked past me. 'It is the tree, Lagesh. Your soul, the only part of you that is different to all other men, knows things before its time. I have lived three-fold as long as you and I still spend nights pondering whether it would be better if I knew nothing.'

'If I could read Salarn's last tablet, it might help me understand my placement.'

Unbetum drew his stare back to me, troubled seemingly by his own ponderings kept silent.

'What does it say?' I asked. 'I must know and, if you give it to me to read myself, Fankisi is sure to read it too. Is it for all to read?'

'I see how you lead me with your words, Lagesh.' He knelt by the narrow stream and turned his hands in the water. 'Our elder understood your placement.' Unbetum shook his head. 'No, he accepted your placement. He accepted the placement of all Guardians, including himself. We can converse with gods, do the work of gods, or even think we understand their ways but we are not gods. His last tablet was more than a tribute to new passage. If a god dies on Earth then their strength is shared. This is what he chose to scribe on his last tablet.'

Unbetum stood from the stream and wiped his hands gently across his face. 'Salarn wrote, "I considered all the options and challenged the laws laid out, even the ones I had never questioned. My words, when spoken with conviction, are truth yet sometimes I just want to talk. In action, possibilities are tested; in thought, they are played out. I can never stand still. I can never listen without talking. I can never play without working. One moment leads to another. I write my own fate and change the destinies of others along the way. I am free to do this and regret not, for any response or the absence of, is in the wake of countless possibilities. That is my life and the burden I will share. Alone I am nothing but together we are the pattern maker. What has been started will play to an end. That is why I return. I too have much to learn and will not rest until every man, woman and child does first." Do you know now why I kept this tablet separate?' Unbetum looked at me and sighed. 'There is more to Salarn's story. It is not for me to recount and I could not remember it all if I tried,' he continued. 'I curse the gods every day for putting so many to trial whilst seemingly ignorant of the suffering involved in the part we play.' Unbetum looked upwards at the sky, mostly hidden by the interlocked branches of the pines. 'We should be getting home before dark.'

'Why, Unbetum? Why can you not tell me everything Salarn shared?'

'It is good for a boy to ponder questions.' He stood and wiped his hands dry on his hide skirt. 'The day you know your answers will come too soon and, if you are not happy with the answers, you will just reconsider them all over again. I have already said too much.'

'I am listening.'

'I know you are, Lagesh. That is why I have said too much. I don't have your answers. My words, like Salarn's, will only create more questions.'

'With the other Guardians back at the tower, I will have the time to visit the tree again,' I said, hoping to lead him into sharing more.

'You are free to do that, Lagesh, so let me reply in another way. Feeling too much concerns you because you understand that you have the power to change the world; yet, even this dead bird brings you sorrow. Think of your mother now. She may be resting, though, should she be awake, she may be feeling sorrow because your whereabouts are unknown. The first cure for your sorrow is to quell hers. That is already half done,' he said, smiling at the fat bird dangling from my grip. 'Let us return before they wake.'

I looked up from the bird and through the maze of pine trunks and branches that separated us from the tower. Like Kar, I now found the darkness of the woods comforting. Unbetum also seemed at peace as he watched the small stream of water trickle by near his toes, gathering pine needles and floating them like tiny boats. 'My father has not smiled since his return,' I said. 'My mother can and she was made a slave.'

Unbetum looked at me, his brow heavy on his eyes. 'Give him time. He will find himself again.' He tilted his chin in the direction of the tower and started walking.

I followed. 'My father's grey hair is longer, almost to his shoulders and his eyes are not focused on those present.'

'Did you expect your father to return unchanged?' said Unbetum, without turning or stopping.

'I wanted him to greet me with a smile. He does not seem happy in his return.'

'I'm sure he is not. Arman and Kar were left behind and this has never happened before without a plan. There should have been no rest in the West until the whereabouts of Kar and Arman were known.'

'Before my father left the village with Senea, I asked him what else I could do to show I was ready to be a Guardian. He told me that it was always a man's duty to empty the waste bucket.'

Unbetum glanced back at me and chuckled.

'Did he tell you this story?' I asked as Unbetum prepared to mount. 'The last time I saw my father smile was when he shared this advice.' I bent and allowed Unbetum to push off my shoulder with his foot as he mounted. 'Wanting to be a man, I waited for my mother to finish emptying herself and then went to collect the bucket. She yelled at me and told me to go away. She would not give me the bucket.'

'She didn't give you the bucket?' asked Unbetum, holding his bandaged arm still as he laughed.

'When I left our hut, I found my father laughing like you.'

Unbetum breathed heavily. 'Remind your father of that story and you'll see him smile again.'

# 9

# Princess of the Desert City

*Scribed by Arman,*
*The Always Travelling Guardian.*

Gibantis was waiting just offshore when we reached the beach. Kar waved his staff above his head to gain his attention. It did not take him long to spot us and he signalled this with a return wave. But he remained seated working on something before him on the deck. We had not even spent a full day on the Island and I had seen all I needed to see. Unlike Kar, I had no question that required answer. The dangers we had faced almost seemed pointless. The Pledians had their own Guardians and whatever would eventuate on these shores seemed destined, irrespective of our involvement.

Kar had been quiet since we departed the hilltop view of the Pledians. When I asked of his concern, he smiled promptly and explained that he was still thinking of Pled. I too was thinking of the Pledians, for what I had seen of their existence seemed unexplainable. Maybe they did have huts constructed in the trees behind where they gathered, or crops growing elsewhere on the island. According to Ronses, Commander of the Stanf Warriors, we had sighted them complete. The day's experience left me feeling incomplete yet satisfied at the same time. All Kar and I had to do now was return safely to the East and explain to the other Guardians why we deemed our quest successful—the Pledians were safer on their island than in the East. I hoped this plan would eventuate before Kar made sense of his latest revelation. I had promised that I would help Kar carry his new burden, whatever it may be. 'Do you want me to look at your rear now?' I asked him as we stood waiting on the shore.

He looked at me. His gaze did not find my eyes before he turned and untied his shorts, pulling them down below his buttocks.

I stepped closer and bent to inspect the spear wound. 'It is deep and still bleeds,' I told him. 'It needs to be washed with hot, salty water or it could get worse before it heals.'

Kar held onto his shorts with one hand as he stepped into the lapping water. When he was waist deep, he turned to me. 'Did we really see the Pledians?'

I looked beyond Kar and saw Gibantis working the sails. 'We saw enough.' I watched as Kar turned his hips in the folding waves close to shore, trying to cleanse his wound. A mark would remain on his buttocks, just like my illness as a child forever changed my face and voice. 'It will be a God's spear that takes you and me, Kar.'

Gibantis lowered the sail well before the shore and the turning waves soon had the vessel beached on a sand bank in the shallows.

'I had to be sure the tide was on the way out,' yelled Gibantis.

I hoisted my pack and Kar's onto my shoulders and stepped into the water. 'And your delay had nothing to do with your painting?' I called back.

'You saw that did you?' he asked as he knelt and helped lift my pack to deck.

'I could see that you were doing something. I thought of more reasons for your delay.'

Gibantis kept a watchful eye on the tree line behind us, 'I did not want to be stuck at shore too long. Did you encounter anyone?'

'Only the savages who occupy the island,' I replied, holding up Kar's pack to him.

Gibantis looked down at me from the deck as he lifted Kar's pack aboard. His eyes were the same shade of blue as the shallow water surrounding the island. 'Is that why you return so soon?'

'Kar's rear met with a spear. The Pledians are safe in their care.' I clasped my hands and Kar pushed off my grip and rolled over the reed edge of the vessel onto the deck. He returned the favour by offering me his arm as I leapt from the water.

Gibantis continued to inspect the tree line feverishly with his eyes.

'Calm yourself, Gibantis,' Kar told him. 'We returned the necklace. They know us now.'

I stood next to Kar and the boatman, watching the waves lapping on the shore and the trees behind that could hide many a man. I did not expect a farewell though I hoped the Stanf Warriors would be watching and ready when the boats arrived.

'Is anyone leaving with you?' asked Gibantis.

Kar lifted his pack to the centre of the deck. 'They thought Laures dead when they saw the necklace,' he replied. 'She is dead to them and she knows it. Laures knew we had no reason to travel to this shore.'

Gibantis shook his head. 'I don't understand some people.' He walked to the mast and hoisted the sail by heaving on a rope. The wind smacked against the cloth until it found its shape. 'Please tell Laures what I have done. She will understand and Wevan does not need to know that I was the one who found his wife before him. Blessed he was to encounter such a beautiful woman wandering lost without sight on his shore. My painting is for her also.'

Soon the boat lifted with the turning tide and, as Gibantis adjusted the sail, it began to move.

We had not seen his first painting that was worth a generous offer of five fish. His new painting was a true depiction of the island's grandeur. It was drying on the deck, weighted down with flat stones. Gibantis had put what his eyes saw to reed parchment and the only part I thought was out of shape was our size. The boatman had included Kar and me in the painting and we looked like giants standing on the strange shore.

The boat breached the island's shallows as the sun set across the water in the west. I did not wait to lose sight of the island before singing my song to Nammu. Kar joined in and, as the moon graced the sky to our south, Gibantis sung softly as well. When gentle rain began to fall, Gibantis offered us shelter beneath the deck. There was only room for two to lie and it smelt like fish had stowed away and not survived the crossing. It rained for most of the night and we took turns manning the sails.

I expected we would pass the Akkadian fleet on our return but we sailed alone across the sea until we crossed paths with fishing vessels near to the ports of Zidon the next morn. Gibantis sailed wide of them knowing not to interfere with their catch. Back and forth before my view, Kar paced the deck, mumbling to himself. As the white stone buildings of Zidon appeared in our view, he eased himself down next to me to ask what he should tell Imbrut, the fish trader.

I thought hard of a response that would settle my woes in the man's place. 'The fish you spoke of, did you imagine their existence?'

'Think of the fur on the floor of the tower. No animal is that large in the East or West, but it is real.'

'There once were animals as large, according to my father, Seeves. Of course he never saw one and I doubt Salarn did either. Salarn's father, Pardensai, once wrote that all the beasts were twice as large in the North and all wore thick coats of similar size. Your story of a fish with teeth as large as man is not too hard to fathom.'

'Then I will tell Imbrut I failed to find them and offer him silver regardless for the loan of his nets and spears.'

'I think it is best to tell him the truth. Tell him you found what you were looking for but they were not interested. Talk of the fish as we found the Pledians. They swim too deep for a net and they avoid bait because they already have enough to feed them. That's a story that will keep him happy. That's what keeps me happy.'

'Do I need to offer him silver?'

'A half shekel will help satisfy further questions.'

\*\*\*

The Akkadian boats were still tied at dock, as they were when we left for Pled. It seemed as if time had stood still since our departure. Akkadian soldiers still manned the watchtowers. Our arrival was noticed yet it did not seem to garnish any special attention.

'We owe Gibantis two shekels,' said Kar as Gibantis secured his boat to the wharf.

'Let me talk with him,' I replied, believing I could negotiate.

Kar lifted and tossed a large coil of rope onto the wharf.

'Leave the nets and spears, Kar,' said Gibantis from the wharf. 'Imbrut will know where to find them and I can tell your story better.'

I looked at Kar and then to the boatman. 'What story did Kar tell you?'

'He told me many stories, Arman. Fishermen can tell stories too. So long as you promise to take my painting to Laures before you depart Zidon our dealings are complete.'

Kar tossed his pack onto the wharf and then leapt after it, holding the rolled painting. He walked to Gibantis's side and they braced arms.

I stayed standing on the boat's deck. Never in my eight harvests spent travelling the land had I met a man who willingly turned his hand from an agreed offering. Maybe it was different for sea bearers. I wanted to believe Gibantis but Kar's pack had landed on the deck and the tinkle of silver was not right. 'Kar, check your pouch before we leave.'

Kar lifted his pack and turned it in his hands.

Gibantis picked up the coil of rope. 'I thank you for teaching me Nammu's song, Arman. Know that I will sing it every night and when the Akkadians sail for Pled, I will follow. I will tell the Zidonians what really happened on those shores.' The boatman went to walk on but was halted when the coil of rope snagged.

Kar had extended his staff between loops of the rope. 'Do I need to unwrap my fur and count my silver?' Kar asked Gibantis.

'Why do you ask me?' said Gibantis. He tried to lift the coil of rope over and away from Kar's staff.

I walked past Kar and Gibantis to the raised bow of the boat and slid over the edge onto the wharf.

Kar braced one end of his staff under his elbow and levered Gibantis and the coil of rope closer. 'Do you see this?' asked Kar, of the boatman. He showed him the knot that tied his pack. 'This is a fisherman's knot. I use a slip knot, so that I can unfasten my fur quickly.'

Gibantis released his hold of the rope and let it slump on the wharf. He turned and stepped into the fishing spear I held.

'Where did you store his silver?' I asked. The fishing spear was pressed to his chest.

Gibantis stared at me with his sharp blue eyes. His arms were held stiff by his side. Grey strands of his hair, loose from his mostly brown hair, lifted and flicked in the breeze.

'Where is his silver?' I asked again.

'You have enough silver,' he finally replied. 'I only took what I was owed.' He smiled. 'The guards in the watchtower are watching.'

'I'm watching you, Gibantis. The gods are watching you.'

His smile shook on his face. 'Look in my empty water pot if you must.'

I looked beyond Gibantis at Kar and tipped my chin towards the boat.

Kar climbed onto the boat and disappeared from sight.

'Will you kill me under the watch of the Akkadians?' asked Gibantis.

I withdrew the spear from his chest and cut my own hand with its tip. 'Do you think I fear another battle with the Akkadians?' I pushed the spear back to his chest. 'How many pieces of Kar's silver did you thieve?'

'I took two, as I was owed.'

'I ask again, how many—'

'Six. I took a handful.'

I wiped my bloodied hand across his cheek and nose. 'When we leave, you are to return to your boat and stay below deck. If I see you again, I will take your head, dunk it in the fuller's piss mix and stake it next to the road into Zidon.'

Kar stepped into view on the boat's deck. 'I found eight shekels.' He nursed them in a shared grip with his staff.

'Put them in a basket with some of Gibantis's dried fish,' I told Kar.

When Kar moved out of sight, Gibantis stepped away from the spear.

I grabbed him by the arm and forced his face into the coil of rope. 'Pick it up and load it on your boat. Our dealings are complete unless I see your face again.'

Kar climbed onto the wharf carrying his staff and a basket.

'Your blue eyes do not deserve the sight of sky,' I told Gibantis, lifting the rope onto his shoulder as he lay with his face to the wooden planks of the wharf and the water below. 'Wait for Imbrut, the fish trader to find you in your shelter.'

'Is that blood on his face?' asked Kar. He paused and showed concern.

'He can't show us his face anymore. I'll carry our packs. Secure your staff, Kar, and carry your basket of fish with pride. I'll follow you.' When Kar moved on, I instructed Gibantis to lift the rope and return to his boat.

I followed Kar to the end of the wharf. The moment he stepped from the last plank and onto the beach; an arrow was released from the most northern watchtower. The arrow dug into the sand, two paces in front of Kar.

'They want an offering,' I told Kar. 'Give them a dried fish.'

Kar opened his basket and placed a dried fish piece near the arrow dug into the sand.

Another arrow flew over our head. I looked back at Gibantis's boat. I could not see him. I looked at the guards in the watchtower. Another guard was taking aim. 'Hold a fish piece up and place it. Hold another up and lower it.' The guard still held his arrow taut. 'Show two pieces of fish and place them,' I told Kar.

The Guard lowered his aim.

'Keep walking, Kar.'

Kar walked briskly with the basket towards the ramp that led up to the boat repair yard.

I watched the guards in the watchtower as I followed. A guard took aim at Kar. 'Sharru Kin,' I yelled and pointed south. When the guard lowered his aim, I ran after Kar. I held our packs on my shoulders to protect my head. 'Keep moving to the shelter of the huts,' I told the young Guardian.

The watchtower guards did not release another arrow. They had gained an offering and I could hear their jovial response to the fear they had incited. The guards laughed as Kar and I moved north along the road behind the fishermen's huts, away from the Akkadian encampment.

\*\*\*

My abrupt treatment of Gibantis was once against my nature but after visiting such a perfect place, so much hatred consumed me in the old world of new Akkadia. These feelings were forgiven and vanquished when I stepped foot inside Laures' home. She looked at me through her blind eyes and told me I was complete.

'Kar,' she said, 'Kar has more challenges ahead. You, Arman, have answered your call.' She spoke like Salarn in a woman's shell and told me that my mare also had a peaceful breath of contentment. In respectful silence, Kar and I listened as she described Gibantis' latest painting. When her fingers rested on the spot where we stood like giants on the island's shore, she smiled. 'This must be you Kar and look at Arman, he is so tall he could not stand in my home.'

As I listened to her blind appreciation of the painting, my thoughts still lingered on my treatment of Gibantis and I feared what retribution might be raged against this family if their involvement in our quest was ever made known. Wevan had spoken of the sabotage that delayed the boats; however, the army's lingering presence indicated that not all was well and justice was still being sought.

'I feel you cowering in your sandals, Arman,' said Laures.

'I regret my words to Gibantis at the end of our voyage.' I told her, choosing to leave out the details. 'He fulfilled his duty yet he tried to deceive us.'

'You do not need to be afraid, Arman, for I know your voice is honest. Let Gibantis make sense of a lesson learnt late. Tomorrow, I will visit him at his boat and give him five fish. Five fish for the dead.'

'He was noble to our cause,' defended Kar, 'No one else could have taken us to the island.'

'He was what you wanted him to be,' I explained to the young Guardian, 'And played his part only so long as he thought necessary.'

'Then you have both learnt a lesson,' said Laures, 'for it is only in recount that lessons are completed.'

'My recount is still be to come,' sighed Kar. 'I know not what to tell Yanereu or Senea.'

'I can tell the story,' I said, hoping to allay Kar's concerns. 'Pled is as it was and they are safe with Stanf Warriors between them and the sea.'

'Go in peace Guardians,' blessed Laures. 'Share my

love with my young sister, Yanereu. Tell her I never planned to leave her when Gibantis took me with him on his boat. Tell her I'm happy in Zidon. We are both where we need to be.'

\*\*\*

Kar and I never spoke of what had happened in Zidon and Pled on our ride home to the East. It was a long and often silent journey through the mountains and across the deserts to the river valley. We ferried across the Euphrates outside Mari and headed north between the rivers to Khorsabad, avoiding Assur and Nineveh. After crossing the Tigris, I think we both felt a weight lifting from our shoulders. Kar began speaking more freely.

'There is someone I want you to meet,' he said as we breached the ravines cradling the new road east and followed behind a caravan heading towards the Desert City, Bit-Bunakki.

'I know Badbe, Kar. I even stayed at his home on one visit.'

'Not Badbe,' said Kar, screwing his face up, 'his daughter.'

'Ah, the beautiful Anava,' I remarked.

'I am sure she has found a worthy man by now. I wished it could have been me.'

'She has always held a fondness for Guardian men. Do not deny yourself of love so readily.

'I have already counted myself amiss. Maybe in another life?'

'The time is now, Kar, and nothing else matters more than what you do in the moment. Surely you know this by now?'

'I seem to know it too well. Anava seems always in good spirit and my life would only trouble her.' He spoke like a defeated man but held his head high, always looking to the horizon. His coverall that was cloud white and stiff on his broad shoulders when he entered Assur was now stained from a mix of mud and blood that had been rinsed by the sea. It looked comfortable against his golden skin.

'It seems your life is the problem. You should change that.'

'I cannot, for there is too much I need to do.'

'What do you need to do that is more important?'

'I would never take her from her father or home and I am needed at the tower.'

'Look at the size of this city, Kar,' I pointed ahead as we approached Bit-Bunakki. 'The buildings keep growing in size. Soon this road will lead to a new gate and a second wall will need to be constructed. And look at the soldiers assembling on the road near the traders' camp. There must be three hundred or more. The only reason the Guardians still exist is because we had eyes and ears this side of the mountains. Gentuk heard of the army moving east and he and Tahnas rescued your father and I in time. Now, if Gentuk and the others have returned to the tower, we are once more blind to the outside world. A Guardian posted at an Akkadian stronghold like this city would be more beneficial than any number on a scout ride each morn.'

Kar looked at me, his lips tucked. 'Maybe I am afraid to admit to her how I feel.' He untied his hair and pulled it apart where it was stuck and clumped in thick knots. 'She is the most beautiful woman I have ever seen and I was a frightened boy walking in Salarn's shadow last time we met.'

'I will help her see the new you.' It would not be hard. Kar did not look like a boy anymore. Fair hair, only noticeable in the light of sun, was growing next to his ears, on his lip and the tip of his chin. And even though his face looked young, his green eyes and the creases around them told of a long life. 'Nothing like a good story to tie two hearts together.'

Kar's cheeks filled with blood and he turned his smile from me as we led our horses from the road and entered the traders' camp. Our diversion from the road avoided contact with the marching soldiers. Kar's eyes kept returning to the city gates, probably hoping to sight his desert princess again. I let him be with his thoughts as we wandered our horses in search of a place to rest on the dune side that overlooked the city.

From a high position in the camp, I tried to count the number of soldiers marching back and forth along the stretch of road in front of the city walls. 'I suppose you have to give them something to do. Did I say three hundred? It's twice that count from above.'

Kar nodded and pointed to a space ahead. He had spotted a rare clearing in the occupied camp.

'This will do.' I hopped from my mare's back and stroked her neck, thanking her for the ride.

The trader camped next to our spot at the top of the dune welcomed our arrival. 'This is the best view of Bit-Bunakki.' He was seated and only raised his head on his neck to look upon the happenings below. 'Be warned, the night winds will take your tent if you stake it too high.'

'Did you have a tent?' I asked.

He pointed with his thumb behind his head. 'Lost to the sand. Now I have your horses to block some wind tonight.'

'Our horses won't be left to stand in the wind. I appreciate your advice.'

'Are you trading from Nineveh?' asked the trader who looked like a Ninevite in his long white tunic and matching headdress.

'My friend will answer all your questions,' I said, and smiled at Kar as I handed him my rein and walked away.

Kar stayed with the mares as I strolled through the camp in search of a rewarding meal. Every meal since leaving Zidon had comprised of either salted meat or dry barley bread. When I smelt the flesh of a boar cooking, my eyes watered. I might have traded my sword for just a taste. Its skin was already charred to a crisp and as I watched the northern trader cut the first leg, saliva ran free from my gaping jaw.

'You cannot eat it from there,' said the trader, breaking my dreamy stare. He sat on a small wooden stool before the hot coals of a fire; slowly turning the boar on a pole balanced between two smooth stone rests. The smell of the meat, the way he was cooking it and his vest made from boar hide, all hinted that this man was the only merchant worth dealing with for such an offering.

'One cut, whatever you can give me,' I requested.

'How about this leg?' he asked.

'For that I will give you a silver shekel and bother

you no more.'

'A gracious offering.'

I could not have thanked the man enough and his family took pleasure in my overwhelming gratitude. His wife pointed to the city and then to me and was most probably telling her daughter why they camped outside. On the slopes overlooking the city from the south, they met men who knew the worth of a boar and needed it more. For a shekel, I could have secured the whole animal. I did not need the whole animal. I did not even let him wrap the leg and with the help of my sleeves to prevent scalding my hands, I carried it naked to Kar, savouring its scent and shielding it from passers-by.

Kar was waiting patiently when I returned, holding the reins to both mares. He turned abruptly from my approach, drawn to the presence of another man.

'Tuley,' he called out over the crowds' ceaseless din.

Tuley was placing a bucket for horses tied outside a hut, halfway down the dune, closer to the road. He gestured to Kar that he had heard him and made his way closer with one of his buckets still filled.

Kar acknowledged the meal I had returned with and I waited no longer to take my first bite. The meat was tender and the juice spilled unguarded, burning my lips and trickling through my beard. I had no hand spare to wipe my mouth clean and cared not for my appearance. The sweet taste of hide basted with honey was most welcome and I was not trying to satisfy anyone apart from myself, or so it was until she appeared behind Tuley.

Tuley placed the bucket of water near the mares. 'What happened in Pled?'

'They are at peace,' answered Kar, crouching and holding the bucket still for the mares. 'I wish you could have seen them, Tuley. Life in Pled is more peaceful than life in the village and they have their own Guardians. I worried for you when—'

'Kar,' shrieked Anava, recognising him from a distance. She hitched her dress and ran our way, weaving between the traders and stalls that blocked her path. Tuley was also in the way and she ducked his spread arm to hug Kar like everything was right again. Her face nestled against his neck, partly covered by his long hair, and she let it rest as she hugged him ever tighter. The last time I saw Anava, her hair was cut short like a boy. Now it reached past her shoulders and was plaited in parts like the hair of Guardian women, like Kar's hair.

'I told her all I knew,' said Tuley. He turned to face me when he got no reaction from Anava or Kar. 'What have you found, Arman?' he asked with a grin.

'A rewarding meal.' I quickly scavenged a piece of cloth from my pack and let the leg of boar rest. The heat from the meat was burning my hands. 'A reward after a long journey,' I continued, standing and wiping my mouth clean with my sleeve.

'You must tell me more about what you saw in Pled,' said Tuley.

'It is a place best left alone, Tuley. What happened at the port of Zidon after we left is what still eludes me. And how you made it here to the Desert City.'

'A story I have only shared with Anava and her

father,' said Tuley, and he waited for Anava to look his way. 'After sabotaging the fleet, I went in search of peace.'

Anava leant back from Kar and looked at me with her head tilted. 'Arman, the Always Travelling Guardian of the East,' she addressed me. 'I was thinking I would never see any of you again. You were a young man with a short beard when I last saw you.'

'We do not live that far from your city, Anava.' I glanced at Kar and understood his quiet disposition in Anava's presence. 'You should visit one day.'

'I do not need to anymore,' she said, tucking her bottom lip and dipping her head.

'Anava and I are to be wed,' announced Tuley. 'I have found a life I could never have imagined with a woman so beautiful that this desert home is always held to the splendour of setting sun.' He stepped forwards and pulled her close with his massive arms.

My mouth hung open as they embraced and joined their lips. I glanced at Kar, saddened that his heart's desire was now lost and so suddenly.

Kar stepped to my side, staring at the two of them, his jaw also gaping for a moment until it was snapped shut and he averted his stare to the city beyond. A single tear rolled down his cheek and mixed with lines of sweat on his soiled face. He wiped his cheek and looked at his hand. His hand started to tremble.

He had not shaken like this when we confronted the Akkadian and Assurian soldiers in Assur, nor when Stanf Warriors surrounded us in Pled. There was no defence against this attack. There was nothing Kar could do in the moment to lessen the blow. He had received a god's spear straight to his heart. I drew my stare back to Tuley and Anava. At least if I did the talking, he might have time to recover before I tried to console him later. 'A beautiful woman is a fitting reward for your battles in Assur and Zidon. Peace, love, a good home, you have it all, Tuley,' I blessed.

Anava looked at Kar and then at me when she did not gain his attention. 'Father says that if he ever begat a son he would be as strong and tall as Tuley.' Anava, tried to conduct herself decently, playfully pushing back Tuley's grasping arms. 'Badbe wishes to visit your home one day.'

'How go the days for Badbe?' I asked.

'He is happy,' answered Tuley.

'He has never been happier,' added Anava, pushing her hair from her face as a strong breeze rained sand on the camp. 'The Akkadians respect his influence on trade and, with the road east to Borujerd now half complete, new merchants, carrying unseen goods, arrive each day. The only—'

'They do not need to hear any more,' interrupted Tuley.

Anava was confused and looked at Kar and then me in consideration.

I displayed my palms and implored she continue.

'We were saddened to hear of the loss of Salarn. I am still in mourning and—'

'No,' groaned Kar. He braced his hands on his knees and began swallowing repetitively.

Tuley pulled Anava back to his side as she took a step towards Kar.

'Tell us what you know, Anava,' I requested. 'This

is the first Kar and I have heard of Salarn's passing.'

'Boroe of the Harmin Village brought the news only days before Tuley's arrival,' she continued. 'I feel that Salarn wanted us to meet. Salarn is looking out for me even from heaven. You may remember my father's words, Kar?' said Anava, trying to gain the young Guardian's attention. 'When I first met you, my father said that life without Guardians is fast becoming the new way but it will never be the right way. To have one by my side has made my life whole.'

For a long while no one spoke and Anava jittered. Tuley draped his large arm across her shoulders and held her close.

'How of that servant at your home? Has he learnt to smile yet?' I asked, trying to alleviate the tense mood.

'He has, Arman,' Anava tried to say with a smile. 'Father had his workers build a new home for Farserai. Near the eastern wall it is and he now returns home every night to be with his family. With a Guardian in our service, every chore seems effortless. Farserai praises Tuley many times each day. He is a changed man.'

'I am glad for both your father and Farserai though I confess Salarn's passing has taken me by surprise. I thought him immortal like a God.'

'I could not bring myself to believe for many days. I thought of all of the stories he shared that I will hear no more.' Anava's eyes swelled. 'Boroe told us that the last of the Harmins watched Salarn ride away. He said Salarn smiled at them before he left and that he was heading to the Karun Gorge.'

Kar glanced at Anava. His eyes were also wet. He

turned away and ran his fingers through his hair until they got stuck.

I had learnt the importance of the Karun to Salarn from Kar and so I also knew that the young Guardian understood why our elder had chosen to die there.

'I am sorry to be the bearer of this news,' said Anava. She slinked beneath Tuley's heavy arm and reached out to hug Kar once more.

He blocked her approach with an extended palm. 'I do not need to be comforted, Anava. I am not a boy and I no longer need a master. I shared his fall.'

'His fall?' questioned Tuley.

'Like the Pledians, Tuley,' I answered for Kar, 'and your last night in Zidon. Some stories need time to rest before they are told.'

Anava whispered her wishes to Tuley and he spoke for her.

'We would offer you a meal at our home tonight though it appears you have already made preparations,' he said, gesturing at the leg of boar resting nearby. 'Maybe we could have Badbe visit you later?'

'No visit is required,' I assured. 'More water for the horses would be appreciated.'

Tuley collected his empty bucket. 'I will see it is done.'

'It was good to see you both again,' said Anava, looking to catch Kar's eyes.

'I am happy for you, Anava,' Kar told his princess. He stood upright and took a deep breath.

'Kar,' she sighed, 'you can leave every story behind so long as you smile when I see you.'

'I vowed I wouldn't cry in your presence again.'

He wobbled on his feet as he turned and stumbled past me though the soft sand at the peak of the camp.

'He needs time alone,' I said when Kar disappeared over the rise and into the desert on the other side. 'He spent more time with Salarn than any other man I know.'

Tuley nodded. 'I'll return with water for the horses.'

'I hope you both visit more often,' said Anava. She looked back many times on her return to the city.

# 10

# The Real World

*Scribed by Kar.*

As soon as I had breached the peak of the traders' camp, I dropped to my hands and knees and threw up. I watched my vomit soak into the sand before my face. My body convulsed and I spat what remained in my throat. I took many deep breaths before standing. My sandals sunk and hot sand slid between my toes.

Word of Salarn's passing did not seem real and it hurt more coming from Anava. Like me, she knew Salarn as a friend. I remembered the last story he had shared in her presence. He had told her about his return to the tower in the woods. The message of the tale was that parting can cause sorrow but it also helps us remember our time together. I wished that Anava's word of Salarn's final parting allowed me a chance to share with her my memories of the nights I had spent with him on the roof of the tower. Instead of resisting the urge to vomit, I could have voiced a timely tale. That is what Salarn would have done. That is what a Guardian should have done.

I continued to swallow the spittle gathering in my mouth, fighting the urge to throw up again. In an attempt to distract myself from my sickness, I stared at sand drifting east across a plateau of stone. The sun burned on one side of my face and, to the east, my shadow stretched the length of eleven horses. My gut churned. I placed my hand on my shoulder, remembering my tattoo. 'Eleven arrows,' I said aloud. My voice repeated in my head. Elkin had given Salarn eleven arrows before we crossed the desert to the Harmin Village. Near to where I stood this day, Samor of the Harmin Village had told me his version of the story of my tattoo. In the real world, my placement this day finally made sense. I understood Salarn's greater plan.

Salarn took me west to Bit-Bunakki, the Desert City, on my first journey. More than sharing a glimpse of the real world beyond my sheltered life in the East, he introduced me to Elkin and led me to the Karun Gorge. It was Elkin who encouraged me to cross many horizons so that I understood my purpose. Salarn encouraged me to head west to Pled, even though he understood why the Pledians would not leave. He knew they would not leave because they were complete. The Pledians never wanted to travel east. This message was confused in translation. The Pledian's wanted to be with their god, Salarn, in his passing. They wanted to form a new people by sharing their daughter of Pled, Yanereu, with the Guardians of the East. Salarn sent me west so that I might cross all the horizons he had before he was summoned home. Now, in my return home, I had learnt of his passing. I did not need to be told that he had travelled to the Karun. Salarn had told me that when he was ready to die, he would return to the Karun. He had departed whilst I was away and before my return so that his end and my beginning would meet.

I collapsed backwards into the hot sand of the steep dune. Before my stare I could only see desert. *One desert crossing is enough*, I remembered Elkin saying before Salarn and I had departed his cave at the base of the western frontier of the Zagros Mountains. That advice was for Salarn. I had the strength of eleven arrows to make many crossings. This eve, all I need do was inform Arman of my plan.

Arman was sharing his meal with the trader who had lost his tent when I stepped over the peak of the dune.

'Kar, come join our feast,' said Arman, noticing me immediately.

I stepped and slid my way through the soft sand until I was seated next to him. The two mares blocked my view of the city. Arman, or maybe it was Tuley, had secured a post in my absence.

'I have saved you some of the boar's skin,' said Arman. 'You will eat well when you are ready.'

I pointed at the mares. 'They block our view of the city.'

Arman laughed and filled his mouth with a slice of meat. 'I like what I see here.' He handed me a cut of meat that looked crisp on one side. 'Let your eyes rest, Kar.'

I bit into the chunk of meat and remembered tasting lizard.

'Is that the best thing you've ever tasted?' asked Arman.

'I can't return home with you,' I replied.

Arman shook his body and groaned, like one does to stay awake or fight off the cold. 'I thought you might say that.'

'I understand where I must go and I must go alone.'

'Say no more, Kar,' said Arman.

I was not sure if he wished to hear no more or was halting me from saying more in the presence of the northern trader sharing our meal.

Arman stared at the mares that blocked our view of the city. 'Before you travel west again, there is a man you must meet in Borujerd. He is, at least he was, a changed man.' Arman handed me another cut of meat. 'I will return east but you do not have to fight alone.'

*Do not fight alone if you do not have to*, were words my father shared with me when he found me fighting imaginary foes in the woods. I had told my father that day that when I left the East, I wanted to be ready to enter the Bull's Burrow. He had clutched my hand with all his remaining strength to show his support.

# 11

# A God's Game

*Scribed by Unbetum, The Guardian Who Will Not Die. The Tower.*

Lagesh and I had only ridden midway through the woods towards the plains, though still I returned exhausted. My injuries had healed only well enough to leave me feeling like a tired, old man. Chaotic dreams, filled with fire and smoke, interrupted my sleep at night and during the day I was only half awake. I showed the young Guardian, Lagesh, how to pluck a bird. 'Keep the feathers for stuffing cushions,' I told him.

With shaky hands, I lit two candles from the torch at the bottom of the stairs and trudged up the steps to Salarn's study. I placed the candles on the stone bench and slumped back on a rickety chair, made from twisted vines, in the corner of the room. At first the other Guardians were concerned about my time spent here alone. Now it was just accepted practice. I had been granted the peace of time alone that I sought though, since Salarn's departure, such an absence from association with others had also become troubling. Salarn had never blessed me as the new elder and even the tattoo that once marked me as a Guardian now sat on the

186

shelf next to me, gathering dust. I needed time alone as much as I needed my ears to be open to shared new ideas.

I understood Salarn's departure and I knew what he wanted to say when he showed me his painting before leaving. We had shared the role of raising Kar, if only briefly, and now, once more, it was my duty. He had not needed to speak that night because most of what he wanted to say he had already inscribed on his last tablet. I lifted the tablet from the lower shelf next to my chair and rested it on my lap. I followed his words with my fingertip, feeling each indent in the hardened clay.

Kar, he named as the young scribe with arrows for fingers and the Tree he named as a stem, a single branch that had found its way to the surface. He called me the Last and only spoke of himself as the Man. As the Man, he explained that the end was the beginning. The closer he got the more he forgot, until he was ready to start again with a vacant mind. It was Kar's duty to find meaning in such a quest and my responsibility to ensure such discipline was never challenged. My burden, like Salarn's and my son's, was to be shared, though with who was never mentioned in his last tablet.

Salarn's tablets were not numbered, though I could tell their age by title and symbol. The stars of The Bull always had their place in the northern sky and this was depicted on the back of each tablet, in relation to the placement and shape of the moon as it snaked its rise and fall through the seasons. I read Salarn's last tablet first though, strangely, I found more meaning in the first tablet he had scribed, the story he had shared across the land before we had even called ourselves Guardians. The night he had followed Pardensai into the woods, he had learnt something that he deemed a secret not destined for his ears. The part the Man played was also the meaning of life. Some call it a gift, whilst others may describe it as a burden. I am torn between the two names, for to accept such a challenge without choice is hardly a favour.

The Tree was full of life but, to make itself known as something greater to Pardensai, it dropped its leaves until it was a skeleton that was silent and moved no more. Salarn realised in his youth that one day he too would stop moving and, unless immersed in water, remain still and lifeless for many years to come. The next morning he had told Pardensai that he was going to find something that lived forever and never changed. Pardensai stated that this was a noble but fruitless quest, to which Salarn responded, 'Fruitless is life without possibility.' His father then told him that change is the fruit of life. They parted company without a further exchange of words. Pardensai never spoke again. When Salarn returned from Pled, he spoke of everything except Pled and what saw him return.

After reading Salarn's tablets, I found strange comfort in my son's scribed tablets. Salarn had shared many stories with Kar. Revealing more of life's mysteries than Verian had thought he could share with the rest of us, Salarn had spoken to Kar of destiny and new passage. Despite their lengthy and deep conversations, neither Kar nor Salarn offered hope for a better future, other than one governed by uncertainty. My planned writings were once full of hope. I wanted to write of the day I first noticed Kinsufa. Her story, inclusive of mine, I thought, would be given quiet voice and sanctuary in the shelves of the village school. The convergence of the East and West stole that opportunity and, after Kar showed me the tree, I began questioning, for the first time, my true purpose in life. My relationship with Kinsufa and the birth of our son, Kar, embroiled us all in a greater quest. We played a god's game.

Now, like Salarn before me, I could do no more than speak in circles. If I wanted to tell that the birds nest at night, I must also write that the trees breathe by day. With the effort required to fight on with arrows in my side, I stood from my chair and approached the stone bench. The new tablets I had shaped were resting in a pan of water. One tablet sat next to them, wrapped in damp cloth. I unfolded the cloth and picked up a thin blade. My hand trembled and I took a deep breath as I pressed another shape into the clay. Each word I scribed strengthened my grip.

I told that the story began one way only to finish ready to start again. There was no need to hear the end because it was much like the beginning: thinking I was always of the last God-King, Gilgamesh. Gilgamesh made his name and his city, Uruk, great and Ishtar loved him. Along came the wild man Enkidu and gone were the days of compassion. Strength resided over all and the majestic city, Uruk, was laid to waste. Enkidu's time on Earth came to an end and Gilgamesh went in search of answers to quell his loss of a friend, his only honourable rival. The God-King's questions were answered and a great song was written to honour his final resolve. Sense of all that had been and would be revealed was preached to all citizens. It was told that Utnapishtim held the secret to eternal life and he, by the Tree of Life, revealed all to Gilgamesh. The moon then snaked its course through the night's sky until a new God-King, purveyed to be the strength of heaven walking as man, took his place. Sargon has now also gained the favour of the Gods, according to his people and this, by my scribing hand, signs the next end. The end and new beginning overlap like a tide change once more.

I stopped writing to find my place in such a fold and visualised my son, Kar, riding like a new man. Maybe life would be better for the Guardians if I stopped looking back for meaning and just listened. There was a knock at the door and I placed my tablet down, almost complete.

It was Fankisi at the door requesting a wet tablet on which she could scribe. I gave her one freshly shaped for my long story, appreciative of the interruption. Change, even as simple as a knock at the door, was what life was all about. It is the greater changes that are harder to understand. The hairs on my arms stood upright as I returned to the shelf to find again the first story Salarn put to clay. I carried it to the stone bench and placed it in front of one of the candles. The wedged groves of each word looked deeper beneath the flame light. I read aloud the last line at the bottom of the tablet. *'I understand,' whispered the man. 'My tower, now complete, is no longer mine.'* Pardensai's words, scribed by Salarn, finally made sense to my ears. The tower was always meant to be an offering.

I only needed to share one more short verse. My hand shook as I guided it to the clay. Many gods may favour Sargon but I knew there was one that loved the Guardians. She called Pardensai south and sent Salarn west. From the roof of the tower, she beckoned my son to her side. Kar led me to her and I heard her cry. I knew what I must do and, until then, I would rest and write no more. Mother Ki's life on Earth was in my hands. Kar's quest into the Bull's burrow, whilst noble, would be fruitless if he fought alone.

# 12

# We Share Your Quest

*Scribed by Fankisi, The Curious. The Tower.*

A spotted cat, playfully stalking the children at the edge of the clearing, announced Salarn's return. That is what I thought when our eyes met. The cat had not come to hurt the children. Like me it was just observing. Curious, with luminous, unblinking eyes, the rarely sighted creature wanted to be a part of what was happening and was even more curious rather than alarmed when the first screams of labour sounded from Yanereu's room. Parbi pointed me away from the woods towards the southern window and his troubled expression left me wanting to hug him as a complete explanation for the screams of pain. Cihnah, unaware of the cat's presence though knowledgeable of what was happening in the tower where her mother Yisbin was, told Parbi that their play should continue. Parbi's distraction was short-lived and he resumed his role as the dressmaker in the girls' game. The spotted cat disappeared into the woods as silently as it had appeared and Meera, the youngest girl, told Parbi what regal dressings were required as her older sister acted out the role of a princess. Cihnah based her character on Yanereu with the addition of her mother's ideals. Together, her representation of a princess was quiet yet stately, just like the spotted cat.

Outside of playtime, Cihnah, like her mother, struggled to accept a sheltered existence. They were not prepared for a world accustomed to turning its face anew or waking to the same few faces each day. The Akkadian empire had changed every facet of their existence, yet, for Yisbin and her two daughters, life at the tower was still perceived as a temporary imposition. When they sat together plaiting each other's hair, Yisbin would tell her daughters of rich travellers visiting Susa. She filled her daughters' minds with visions of splendour awaiting their return to the South.

Yisbin was born in Susa, daughter to the regal dressmaker. Janfas, the only son of Arcobon, caught her eye when he travelled to her city on his first journey. She was a child and played with a doll near the spindle as her father told Janfas where he must travel alone. He was to deliver ten lengths of cloth to the Pharaoh and then draw him maps that led the way back to Susa. When Janfas returned from Egypt heavy with gold, Yisbin was dressed in the same cloth he had carried west and filled it with sumptuous bosom. He wed her with the high priest's blessing before escorting her to the Guardian village to meet his father, Arcobon, and the rest of the Guardians.

Another celebration was held in the village circle before the couple returned to Susa. Janfas continued procuring enviable trade relations with the Egyptians. I was a girl when Yisbin left and married with a child to Tahnas when we met again where the village once stood. By her father's advice, Yisbin had travelled from Susa with her two daughters ahead of the Akkadian occupation. The reason, he confessed, was that the city brought her ill fortune, though he may have heard already that Sargon's army was heading east. Her husband, Janfas, had died shortly after the birth of her youngest daughter, Meera. It was a simple cut to the leg that never healed that took him from the world at a young age. Yisbin told me that Susa asked too much of her husband and that Janfas would have lived forever if they had returned to the Guardian village sooner. Unbetum told her how Arcobon died protecting the village and no longer was she so sure. None of us knew then that Susa was burning as we spoke. Lan and Gentuk had buried the Guardians and Tahnas and the young Harmin, Boroe, had carted the rotting Akkadian bodies east and dumped them closer to the Kavir Desert.

'We all have to start again,' Unbetum told the women and children who watched on that day.

'Even me?' Cihnah had asked.

'No, young one,' shielded Unbetum, 'You are free to carry on just the way you are.'

Yisbin heard these words too and refused to change her ways. Just like when her will sufficed, she had helped her father cut fabric, sometimes she would sew for Jamine or help turn soil. She never found herself alone and always looked to others to shape her days up to a point of her liking. Yisbin was inside the southern window of the tower, hopefully helping Yanereu through the strain of childbirth and I was outside watching over her daughters and my own boy during her excusable absence. I had chosen my place on this special day.

Birthing was an ordeal I could not brave again, even as a bystander. Parbi was worth every effort though I was not one to tell another mother it would be all right. If not for Tahnas' arrival during my labour in Borujerd, Parbi may have never been born. I needed Tahnas by my side. I did not need him to say anything, just his presence. I felt lifeless at the end of every push and so was Tahnas. My husband would do anything for me, though on the noon of Parbi's birth he was weak. Seeing those limits in such a strong man only made me love him more. Looking up from my tablet, I saw him returning to me from the stables. The injury he had suffered in the west kept him from venturing too far from the tower; however, unlike Unbetum, it had not dampened his spirit. Tahnas found simple duties to fulfil his day and led the discussions at mealtime. He was a voice for our new elder. It was only when they heard progress reports concerning the construction of Lagesh's watchtower that the old friends shared sorrow in their inability to play a more active role.

'I am feeling stronger,' Tahnas told me as he knelt in the soft grass next to where I sat with a tablet in my lap. His chest and one shoulder were wrapped tight with a bandage to protect his wound and prevent movement of his arm.

'Then so am I,' I said, reaching up to stroke his face.

He watched the children as I continued to scribe. 'Unbetum is more quiet now than before we left for the West,' he said without turning his face from the children's game. 'Now that he is our elder I cannot talk to him as I used to. The truth is, only now that he is our elder, do I find reason to question him.'

'It is the Tree that consumes his thoughts,' I told Tahnas. 'I know this because he still shares most of his words with Lagesh who has also been there.'

'Pardensai's grave?'

'No, the tree that spoke to Pardensai.'

'It's real?' he questioned me, only turning his head slightly.

'Kar took Lagesh there and every meal since he has not stopped talking of a watchtower as high as the tower.'

Tahnas chuckled knowingly. 'They would be nearing that height today. When the nest is completed, a Guardian will be able to see over the woods to the tower and an army approaching from the north could be spotted a day's march away.'

'Would you take me to the tree one day?' I asked, unable to forget the night Kar and Lagesh returned late, soaked through from the rain and joyous.

'I think Kar was wise to take Lagesh there.'

'It was Kar who also took Unbetum to the tree,' I informed Tahnas.

'Of course,' he chuckled as he eased himself up from his knees. 'That answers many of my most troubling questions.'

'You do know that Kar has put his first journey to tablet now?'

Tahnas laughed so loud that the children stopped playing and looked our way. He leant close on one knee and kissed me on the cheek. 'Happenings in the East would elude me if not for you. Keep writing, Fankisi,

I am going to rest now.'

'Maybe when you have read his first story we can find the time to visit the Tree ourselves?'

'You want to visit a tree?' He laughed again. 'We are surrounded by trees.'

'Why does he laugh?' asked Cihnah as Meera and Parbi abandoned the game and approached.

'I laugh because I am happy, Princess Cihnah,' he said, bowing humbly before the young girl adorned in regal attire. 'Keep playing and let Fankisi keep scribing.'

Parbi continued to stumble closer with Meera, holding his hand.

Tahnas knelt again. 'Do my eyes betray me? I had a son and he wears ribbons in his hair. Shall I put a tattoo on your shoulder, Meera?'

Meera let go of Parbi's hand and ran from the threat.

Parbi stumbled on and Tahnas caught him beneath his chubby arm before he fell.

My husband and son were everything to me and I did not want for a tree or anything else that would change my life with them. Tahnas turned Parbi and he crawled through the grass to my side. Cihnah retrieved him so that she could continue her game.

Tahnas met with Unbetum at the tower door and the injured men braced their good arms together. I watched Tahnas wiggle his waist in my direction signing that Yanereu had given birth to a boy. I had thought she might ever since sighting the spotted cat.

The men building the watchtower returned earlier than normal, dusty and tired from their day's work.

Tahnas and Unbetum walked to meet them at the stable, noticing as I did that Lagesh was not with them. I knew where the young Guardian had gone and was more concerned with whether the men continued to speak of larger concerns when the women were not listening. Unbetum's presence, however, assured me of a truthful and complete response from Tahnas when I was sure to question him later.

A baby is born, men return from work and the children grow disinterested in their game. As the observer of such events, I find myself seeking summary. All that I have seen throughout my life is only enough to leave me begging for more. My idle thoughts have me think of life in the village when I was young, my dreams take me back to Borujerd and my future concerns a tree I have not seen that somehow compels me to be ready for action. I will leave this tablet in Salarn's study for Unbetum to read. *Read this Unbetum*, I write in conclusion, *and tell me before it is too late, why a tree has you question your own worth? Most of all I remember your look during the first harvest at the tower and know that ever since you have only grown quieter. You need to know that we share your silent quest, whatever it may be. When we cut our second harvest, that is now fat with seed, will I find you watching from the tower door or will it be my own husband sitting, come that day, on the stool he placed for you?'*

# 13

# Uk-Ban's Answer

*Scribed by Lagesh.*

This was the first night I sat at the men's end of the table. Already, I missed my place next to Na-ten. All I could see was part of her shadow cast by the wall mounted torches that surrounded us. I wished I could call her close and tell her that everything I planned was for her. Unbetum sat at the head of the table, where Salarn once sat, and Tahnas and Lan were seated closest to him, opposite each other. My father sat next to Tahnas and I sat next to my father, across the table from my brother and Delari, the trader. The long table that stretched towards the throne was empty apart from three candles and our clay cups.

Unbetum's chair screeched against the stone floor as he stood in his place. He wore a shoulder fur and his arm was not bandaged for the first time since our retreat to the tower. Battle scars marred his chest and gut. His beard was shaped like the tip of a broad sword. 'Now that more Guardians have returned, Lagesh can take my place on the roof of the tower,' he announced, intending this posting to be a reward.

My brother, Senea, prompted me with a nod and I told Unbetum that I wanted to build a watchtower where the village once stood.

'You have spoken about a watchtower in the plains often, Lagesh,' recollected Unbetum. 'I put your plan to the table.'

Around me, I saw the men, including the old, bony man, Uk-Ban, nodding agreeably.

My father grabbed my hand and thumped the table. 'I would like to bring to mention Lagesh's eleventh harvest that fast approaches.'

Tahnas's father, Lan, acknowledged that choosing the noblest moment in my father's life since the birth of Senea would be difficult.

'Indeed, there are many brave acts to choose from,' supported my father as if speaking of another man. I could see a smile in his eyes that did not reach his lips.

'Maybe the time he told the women of Nineveh that I was escorting a Princess,' joked my brother.

'That may seem funny to you now, Senea,' said Tahnas. 'Soon you will be a father and learn that a simple conferment offered in timely manner can save many from pointless heartache.'

'His words might have chased away more potential wives though I think Gentuk was just bragging,' laughed Lan, his baldhead reflecting light and drawing attention to his corner of the table.

'I was protecting my son and his betrothed from any unnecessary embarrassment,' explained my father, standing defensively. 'At least three young women were stowing jealous eyes upon Yanereu from each side of the campfire. I spoke for her on Senea's behalf.'

Unbetum reminded the men that the construction of my watchtower, not my initiation ceremony, was the main agenda.

'Do all agree with Lagesh's plan to build a watch-tower?' asked Tahnas, and the men, including Delari and Uk-Ban, beat their hands against the table.

'We also agree,' said Fankisi, speaking on behalf of the silent women and children gathered at the table.

'Then it is unanimous. We will start at dawn and call it also our scout ride,' said Lan. He raised his cup and when Unbetum lifted his cup, we all followed. Lan was the oldest Guardian now and the only Guardian who partook in the building of the tower in which we sat.

***

Lan had returned from the west a changed man. More than attributing his changed nature to his tales of the medicine man in Kalhu that he had shared, I could only speculate as to what happenings had reinvigorated his thirst for life. He was now a man of the gods and questioned the taking of any life. We dropped twelve trees to begin constructing my watchtower and he sprinkled each and their stumps with water before we rolled them towards the village. When I asked him why such process was necessary, he told me that the trees had no say in their future though, like us, made passage to new existence. Similarly, when the men questioned me about what birthed my plans to build a watchtower, I answered, 'Life will be different for us and our future is dependent on things done today.'

We had planned to dig the foundations to a depth

twice the height of a man. At one and a half lengths, our holes filled with water.

'This does not have to impede the tower's height,' said Lan. 'All we have to do is set the support posts further apart.'

*\*\*\**

After seven days with my father, Lan, Delari, Uk-Ban and myself working from dawn to near dusk, we had planted four long pine trunks where the western village gate once stood.

'That is a monument to the Guardians if nothing else,' praised my father as he stood back in the long grass to admire our work.

'I assure you both that it will be more,' said Lan. He faced me and pointed over my head towards the woods. 'I was your brother's age when our fathers and your father's father built the tower in the woods. Can you picture me with hair like Senea?'

I could because when Lan wrapped his head to protect it from the sun, the strands of hair at the base of his skull and around his ears still showed.

'This tower will be taller and fit its purpose,' continued Lan, looking up at our work completed so far. 'Some men dug and moved stone as others built a frame for the tower. At the end of the day, we would also gather and admire our progress.'

'I remember walking into the tower before it had a roof,' said my father. 'And I would have been your age, Lagesh. During the day I helped the women draw water and carry it to the men. Everyone helped in their own way.'

'We could make it stronger,' suggested Uk-Ban, 'if

we planted a tree at each of these posts.'

'How would this work?' questioned my father.

'The young trees would find water on every side of the posts and the freshly dug soil would soon have them wrap their roots around the planted posts.'

'We still have to go higher,' I told them. 'This height again.'

'I agree,' said Lan. 'The distance between our corner posts will allow. We can brace it tomorrow and then we need find a way to lift and secure the next posts to the top of the supports.'

'I know how that can be done,' said Uk-Ban, walking to one side of the support posts and pointing at an area of squashed grass. 'We need to build a weighted lifting device here.'

'We will do all that is necessary,' envisaged Lan. 'If it means a second tower is half completed in the process, then that is the way and we will plant new trees at the footings to each so that one day, if new passage sees me return, my village will be in the same place it once stood and a part of the woods that helped build it.'

'And we will call this watch Lagesh's Eye in my son's honour,' decided my father. He placed a hand on my shoulder and pointed towards the Zagros Mountains like we were already sharing a view from the top.

With the corner posts erected, we returned to the tower in time for the evening meal.

***

Questions regarding our progress came from all at the table before we were even seated. Fankisi wanted to know how long it would take to complete and the children, probably like my father when he was a boy, wanted to see it as it already stood. Unbetum requested that we all appreciate a moment of silence in honour of those who had died with the village and Salarn's passing before we voiced ourselves further. The moment seemed like forever before he turned to me and signed I should speak first.

'We have only placed the corner posts. Uk-Ban knows how to build it higher.'

Uk-Ban, possibly older than Lan, our oldest Guardian, was filled with ideas, eager to contribute and difficult to silence once he started talking. His skinny arms were strong and he did not tire. Like a dog, he was present as we felled a tree and already waiting where it was to be placed.

'Tell them, Uk-Ban,' encouraged Lan from the far side of the table.

The man from Catal-Huyuk stood on his stool to demonstrate. 'It was how my ancestors raised and lowered crates of obsidian from the mountains; just like your scales only we used them to control balance. We can use a similar technique to build your watchtower. All we need do is to secure supporting beams each step of the climb and make sure someone is there to clamp its rest with strong rope. Lagesh, I am certain, is nimble enough for such task."

'A precise procedure and more risky than Uk-Ban makes it sound,' raised Tahnas.

'It will challenge us,' added Lan.

'We will plan each move carefully, Tahnas,' assured my father. 'Uk-Ban will know best if the weight is in our favour."

'So who is in charge when you are working?' Tahnas questioned me, for he had remained at the tower with Unbetum and my brother, Senea, when we left each morning to continue construction.

'We all are, depending on the task at hand,' replied my father. 'We are building the tower as Lagesh envisioned. Taller than the tower we are seated in it will be.'

'And I will alert them before anything topples,' said Uk-Ban as he leant his weight to one side of his stool and braced for a planned fall as it gave way.

Unbetum did not join in the laughter, even though he was not against our plans. He looked at those smiling and laughing, admiring, I thought, the chance to see us full of life. His gaze, however, turned to a stare when our eyes met. We stared back at each other long enough for the others to notice.

'Are you thinking about Lagesh's eleventh harvest now?' questioned Tahnas, making me break eye contact.

'No,' answered Unbetum, 'I am thinking much further ahead, even though my mind is trapped in the past.' Sweeping his gaze across those seated at the table, I think he pondered the vision that had encouraged me to build the watchtower and shared his thoughts. 'At least twice our number left the Northern Sea and followed Pardensai south to build our late village. Once it had taken form and with the men venturing out as Guardians, new people soon arrived to call it home. Now we find ourselves still recovering from the loss of what once was, with Guardians still out searching for those taken west and rescuing others along the way. I see a pattern in this plight that eludes time and once more contradicts sensibility. Even so, I discover familiar meaning in the arduous tasks we are now presented with and, as your elder, I vouch that everything we do now pulls us from shadow and will see our children's children playing in view of the mountains once more. It starts with a watchtower and a home for one family beneath. Soon there will be a lake that never runs dry, surrounded by many huts and crops as far as the eye can see. There will never be another village wall though, for a wall will keep us trapped and anyone set on getting in will find it easier than our escape.'

No Guardian spoke in response to Unbetum's vision and, like the night Salarn returned with Kar from the Karun River, the women ushered the children away early for bed. Fankisi was the only woman who remained at the table and Unbetum smiled at her and me before he rose and dismissed himself. Only Uk-Ban spoke before we cleared the table.

'When I set out from my home in the north, I only had one place and person I needed to find,' said the man from Catal-Huyuk. He was still thin but he did not look starved or as filthy as he was when he arrived at the tower with the others. 'I travelled east with Guardians to find my new God. I have found him and I see him in many forms every day. Count me as the first to join you as a new arrival in your new village. Like Unbetum, I can already see it complete.'

# 14

# The Eleventh Harvest

*Scribed by Tahnas, The Guardian of the West.*
*The Tower.*

I have fought barbarians, bandits, soldiers and every other kind of crazed man who thought drawing a sword against me would settle their woes. From north of Bit-Bunakki to south of Agade I have protected enough gold, garments and grain to weigh down a fleet of ships. After countless seasons spent braving the cold, crossing deserts without shelter and never once letting my guard down, a single bronze bolt left me village bound. That bolt was destined to hit my shoulder and I would not have changed its course even if I could. I am where I need to be.

The lush grass surrounding the tower is kept short of our knees by the grazing horses and from my seated position I can see all the way to the woods that circle me in every direction. I read Kar's story aloud to my playful son, Parbi, as the women and older children cut grain. Those working pass by frequently to and from the tower door with loaded baskets. They overhear only parts of the story, much like Parbi who is often distracted by the grazing horses, the shifting light of the sun or my face when it tires. When Jamine calls rest breaks, the women and children gather in front of me and I return to the beginning of a verse and share more of Kar's story. My beautiful wife, Fankisi, has read the tablets before me yet still she listens with interest. Cradling Parbi in her arms she nestles her cheek against his and leans back and smiles when he squirms.

\*\*\*

On the third day of harvest I finish reading and, deep in thought, stroll towards Fankisi.

She lowers her sickle and brushes sweat from her brow.

'I have finished reading,' I tell her. 'I was thinking that Parbi and I could now help sow the next crop behind you.'

'Tell me first what you thought of his story.'

'It was a challenging journey for one so young,' I reply in reflection. 'Understandable, therefore, that he was short for words long after his return. Still, it was amusing seeing him bow to us before he went to bed. Amusing also that he mentioned this in his retelling.'

Fankisi shakes her head. 'Kar knew you laughed at him. I too would have avoided association with you in the days that followed.'

'Until we lay together at night?' I tried to amuse her.

'Do you forget sleeping on the floor?' Fankisi snarls, dropping her sickle and cupping Parbi's ears. 'You shunned Kar. Admit it, Tahnas. His reasons for silence should be clear to you and still you find it entertaining.'

'It is my own ignorance that I laugh at too,' I respond, smiling at Parbi. Lifting her hands from his ears, I look at her and confess, 'Never since the day Parbi was born have I felt more fulfilled. I know Kar now through his writings and, more than anything, I know that we have no reason for anger or regret. Kar might never learn what happened to his mother or gain the love of Anava in the Desert City; however, he has found himself and that is one of the greatest quests. As for me, I do not need to spend a morning in heaven nor sit beneath a god-like tree to find meaning in this changing world. You, Fankisi, little Parbi, and Naten, our new daughter, who still admires me with the look of a bemused stranger, make me happier and more complete than any other blessing could.' I kiss Fankisi, tasting her sweat and bend to hoist Parbi to my strong shoulder. 'I have not forgotten your request,' I add. 'When time allows we will seek out the tree and make sense of it ourselves.'

'Do not work him too hard, Parbi,' Fankisi says jokingly as we walk towards Jamine.

'Finally come to help have you?' Jamine scoffs.

'Not me, I thought Parbi could help you,' I say with a smile.

She sighs with dissatisfaction before looking up at me again.

'I too plan to help,' I admit, sensing no room for amusement in her tired gaze.

'Oh,' she sounds gratefully. 'Just like the last harvest, it seems the heavens are in time with the first stem cut. This time I plan to have the seeds for our next harvest sowed before we bid retreat.'

I help Jamine sow seeds and keep up with the other women and children still gathering in front of us. As Jamine predicted, rain begins to fall as the last loads of grain are carted inside. The women return to help us sow and we are also joined by the men as they return from building the watchtower. We all work as fast as we can to fill the furrows with seed, happily knowing that the rain will bind our work and allow time for rest on the morrow.

'I did not expect to find you working,' says Gentuk, not looking up upon the rain that stretches and mattes his greying hair over his ears and cheeks.

'The sooner this harvest is complete, the sooner your boy becomes a man.'

'The time when the two can be named apart is coming to an end Tahnas. What boy in the history of man has told his elders what is supposed of him—a watchtower.'

'You must be proud, Gentuk.'

'I am proud, Tahnas, and I am thankful more than anything that you helped his mother arrive in time for his special day. What you did in Mari, your rescue mission, is one of the greatest Guardian tales I have ever told.'

The morning I carried Belline from the drinking hut was a joyous moment for all the Guardians and, like today's task, it was not an endeavour completed alone. 'I needed you at the entrance to the Mari markets that day,' I tell Gentuk. 'We all needed Arman and the others to escape Assur.' Today the sky is dark in all directions and water falls heavily as we sow the final seeds. We are soaked through by the time the last handful of seeds were scattered though once more many hands have finished what was started. And I, like so many before me, have scribed my first tablet.

# 15

# The Silent Quest

*Scribed by Tahnas, The Guardian of the West.*
*The Tower.*

Lagesh went on his first scout ride the morning before his initiation as a man. His father, Gentuk, accompanied him and they returned with a large boar. It was also the first day the men stopped working on their construction of the watchtower. The ladders, climbing a frame twice the height of a pine, were left idle for a day and outside the tower door we assembled and spoke quietly amongst each other. I, like the other Guardian men and Fankisi who pressed me for my opinion, believed we knew already the tattoo that would soon penetrate the newly declared man's shoulder. The final decision was Unbetum's prerogative. On the roof of the tower, on the eve of the initiation, Unbetum, my father, and I, had shared many stories relating to Gentuk. The day Gentuk came to the rescue of so many Guardians, following the sacking of the village, seemed the most poignant tale. Unbetum and my family, now including Parbi and Naten, would not be back at the tower if not for Gentuk.

\*\*\*

Keeping to tradition, only four Guardians and Lagesh, still considered a boy, entered the tower to meet our new elder. Gentuk closed the door to the morning light. Unbetum had the torches lit either side of the throne and he walked forwards to meet us. He bowed in respect of Lan, Senea and myself before leading Lagesh to the throne. Gentuk joined us and together we stood where the creep of the torchlight ended. We stood in respectful silence for the deeds of our own fathers. My thoughts, however, had me thinking of Kar again, and the night, now almost three harvests ago, when he bowed before excusing himself from the table. It was not right of me to shun him. Salarn that night, and later Fankisi, my own wife, made that very clear to me. Only after reading Kar's story did I understand his actions and what made him different to the rest of us. We were all different, every man woman and child, and our differences were our strengths. Such inherent qualities allowed us to survive Sargon's attack on the East and still we had the power to stand against him again.

\*\*\*

Gentuk led Lagesh out of the tower and they were met by applause. Delari and Uk-Ban approached the newly declared man first and offered him a gift. Lagesh was unwilling at first to accept the side bow and told Delari that he should keep it. He knew it was precious to Delari and he had his own bow.

'I will keep my side bow, Lagesh,' said Delari. 'This one, Uk-Ban and I built from the same wood as your watchtower."

Lagesh held it like he was nursing a baby and

smiled with delight. 'I will treasure this gift until the day I die.'

Unbetum then asked that I silence the crowd before he spoke. He had told my father and I last night that he wanted Lagesh's initiation as a man to be a celebration not another lesson for the youth. 'Lagesh needs his conviction confirmed not tested,' Unbetum had said and both my father and I had agreed.

Guardian men, new and old, faced a world suddenly oppressed to our engagement. The new Guardians, however, Senea, Kar and now Lagesh, were finding their own ways to include themselves in a seemingly godless future that was fast overwritten by rules of sovereignty to the crown of man. Our last lessons in life were sure to come from them. 'Please be silent so that our elder's words are heard,' I requested and then stepped back next to Fankisi as Unbetum stepped forwards amongst the circle of men, women and children.

His voice sounded clearly amongst the silenced small gathering. 'Today is a special day in many ways and I want to take this opportunity to say everything that needs immediate voice. Let me begin by announcing that Lagesh is now officially a Guardian man.' Unbetum paused and smiled at Lagesh as the gathering of new and old Guardians clapped their hands against their sides. 'When I cut Lagesh's shoulder, the realisation that I am now officially your elder opened my eyes. Uk-Ban of Catal-Huyuk, Delari of many homes and Messim from Mari, join us as Guardians in the first Guardian initiation ever conducted and also to be celebrated at the tower. In the village days what happened today would be largely a secretive event. I want it to be a celebration. It should be different, for life in this world, in the East and West, has changed for us all. You did not need to be present the day the village was sacked to know what was lost or appreciate our efforts to sustain existence as a people unique. As I said at the table the other night, Lagesh's watchtower is a new beginning to which we are all bearing witness. In similar anticipation we will have to wait many days to view what picture has been cut and coloured beneath his bandaged shoulder. We must wait to see with our eyes but just as Lagesh can see his tower complete, I can explain his tattoo already. Lagesh's mark of a Guardian represents a noble moment in his father's life. It depicts the day his father, Gentuk, met Fankisi in Borujerd and escorted Naten to a hiding place on the road east. Gentuk then returned to meet Tahnas and escorted a Borujerdian caravan to the palace gates. Later the same day, Gentuk led Tahnas, Naten and Fankisi with their new-born towards our village to confront the Akkadians. Gentuk with the help of Tahnas and the Harmin named Boroe, saved Arman, Jamine and myself from possible death or a life in slavery. How, you may ask, did I shape so many glorifying moments into one tattoo? I answer that I cut Lagesh's shoulder and filled it with more paint than I have ever seen in a single tattoo. The first tattoo that I have been honoured with scribing as your elder is also the largest and most detailed.'

Gentuk laughed proudly and held his son's hand. 'I await its reveal.' He contained his laughter when he realised Unbetum had more to say.

'Two nights ago,' continued Unbetum, 'I retired to Salarn's study after the evening meal and found a freshly scribed tablet waiting for me. The tablet told me that you share my silent quest and so, today, I will voice it aloud for you all to hear.' He glanced at Fankisi standing next to me and then at nobody, his stare close yet distant. 'My silence began with the loss of my wife, Kinsufa, to the West and festered with my exposure to a strange tree. Let it be known that the tree I speak of is the same tree that saw Salarn absent the day his father, made new passage. It is the tree that silenced Pardensai. It is the tree that led our fathers and their fathers to build a tower of stone.' Unbetum let these words resonate as he walked from the tower door towards grass not shadowed by the sun's rise over the woods. He held his arms to the sky. 'Salarn's last written words were, "When Nammu rises with the boil and the skies shelter beneath the smoke, Ishtar will reach for a saving hand and I will be there, naked and beaming. I will take her hand in mine and not let go for her abundant love is uncompromised and our future together unwritten. Together we live, separated we only survive, as one we experience our potential." You may all have different feelings for the Goddess of Love, Wisdom and War but let me tell you what she means to me. Ishtar is the essence of every woman. It is the desire of man to be loved by her and the inherent feebleness of our nature that has us fight for her. If we learn such cause, then as Guardians we will experience that which Salarn deems our potential. The Guardians will live longer than Ki, the Mother God, naked and beaming with each new day like the sun itself. My days of silence will seem like an instant, for the quest to save what we love is eternal. Look at what we have today, not what we had in days past. Mother Ki has provided for our future. Safe in the woods we are until we rebuild the village.'

The Guardians, new and old, clapped their hands against their sides again. Unbetum's words were full of hope and they were welcomed after the seasons he had spent mostly keeping to himself since surviving the loss of the village.

He stilled our applause with a gently raised palm. 'That is not my last confession today,' Unbetum revealed with a smile. 'We have not run dry of honey wine. I saw it my duty to keep a few pots hidden for a day like this. Find a mug my friends and let us make Lagesh's eleventh harvest a day to remember.'

Like all was well again, we celebrated beneath the high sun. We did not need a village circle or procured victory to unite us, just wine, song and dance. Uk-Ban and Delari carried the pots of honey wine from Salarn's study to the tower door and Gentuk found a mug for each man and woman. Too long we had waited for the instilled joy provided by the women's voices. Belline and Jamine began singing and the men, myself included, finally spoke unguarded once more. Gentuk filled the first mug for Lagesh and happily handed it to my father when he saw that his son was distracted. Lagesh and Naten danced together in the grass outside the tower door, displaying more than just friendship. He pulled her close between spins and their cheeks rested against each other. Yanereu and Senea shared cradle of their new-born son and the babe stared almost knowingly at the increasingly friendly faces of those drawn to his fragile lure.

With an abundant supply of wine and starved of such festivity, it was not long before we were all talking, singing or moving about in easily forgotten unison. Unbetum and I were laughing together about our time in Khorsabad and how we had unintentionally encouraged dealings with a desired woman. She had seemed in need of food and company. The type of company she sought, had surprised us both.

Cihnah shrieked, as she and her sister came running towards the tower from the western edge of the clearing. The sun was now lowering in the west and it was difficult to see what chased them our way through the stretching shadow of tall pines.

As quickly as the festivity was born, all joy was sucked from the air and the carousing ended at a peak.

'What happened?' screamed Yisbin as she ran to meet her daughters.

'Something is in the woods,' said Cihnah.

Meera clutched her mother around her waist.

The Guardian men quickly grouped near the stable, where the trees shadowed our eyes from the setting sun. Lagesh pulled himself from Naten's embrace to fetch his bow. Delari and Uk-Ban extinguished a smoking pipe and joined us. I watched as they loaded their side bows and stood ready. We could hear the crunch of dry pine needles as a horse was ridden fast in our direction.

'It is only one rider,' I told the men assembled.

Unbetum turned his back on the woods. 'There is only one rider we can hear,' he said warily. 'Delari and Uk-Ban, move to the other sides of the tower to keep watch and listen for any other signs of approach.'

'What is your battle cry?' asked Uk-Ban, before he turned to leave.

'Call Guardians and retreat to the tower door if

you have to,' replied Unbetum and he immediately turned his attention to Lagesh as the young Guardian approached with his bow. 'I hope your arm is still strong, Lagesh. Draw an arrow ready. Senea, I need you to return to the women and children at the tower. Get them inside and protect the door.' Unbetum then adjusted the two throwing blades on his belt so that he was able to draw them with speed.

The sound of the rider's approach grew louder and Gentuk started sweeping his long sword and limbering up his wrists. Next to him, my father, Lan, drew his broad sword and pointed it towards the approaching rider who was still out of sight.

'Follow my aim with your arrow, Lagesh,' instructed my father. 'Be patient in releasing for it may be a friend or a foe.'

'And look for armour on the rider and steed.' I was only carrying a single throwing blade and felt the pressure placed on Lagesh when I heard him exhale heavily before tensing his bow. I was fidgety after trying to switch from a state of festiveness to one of high alert. Gentuk was also noticeably distressed and was unable to hold his sword still. Any moment now the steed would exit the woods. I saw Unbetum turn to account for Delari and Uk-Ban's positions before he turned back in time to see the rider breach the clearing.

Launching into a full gallop as soon as he left the woods, Arman rode his mare towards us with a hand held high to signal he was a friend. Kicking up dirt, he pulled his mare to a stop a pace in front of us and bellowed, 'The Akkadians are coming to finish what they started.'

Unbetum took charge. 'Keep the women and children inside, Senea. Lagesh, make your way to the roof and report what you see.'

Arman stayed mounted. 'Follow me north and see their number for yourselves.'

'Is it not best that we stay hidden?' questioned my father.

'No,' said Unbetum. 'Lagesh's watchtower is not complete yet it is sign enough that life remains. It is also a construction that could not have been completed by one or two alone. We must fight or risk losing everything.'

'How many?' Gentuk asked Arman, with his sword still gripped firmly.

Arman shook his head regretfully. 'More than last time.'

'Then it's a pointless fight,' declared Gentuk, glancing first at Unbetum and then at me.

'Maybe not,' informed Arman, 'Kar, for one, is already raising our chances.'

Unbetum stared intently at Arman, long enough for us all to begin predicting what question he was about to ask or what order he was about to give. 'How long before they arrive?' he finally asked.

'Two hundred on foot and another hundred riders were assembled for departure the morning we left Bit-Bunakki,' informed Arman. He brushed sweat from his eyes and tightened his rein when his mare began to dance. 'They march to Borujerd and from there, through the mountains to their stronghold. When they arrive in the East, those already assembled will move between the woods and the mountains towards our village.'

'They will find my son's watchtower under construction and look to the woods to find us,' said Gentuk. He started waving his sword about frantically as
he pointed it in every other direction than where the
army were coming from. 'We have to leave now. Head
east into the desert or south to Hidalu. The army will
find us if we choose to stay hidden here at the tower.'

'Calm yourself, Gentuk,' said Lan. He stilled Gentuk's swaying sword by blocking its sweep with his
own. 'Belline is safe. The wine is making you too quick
to jump.'

Arman let his mare trot in a circle. It was more
restless than he. 'We rode fast without rest to bring
the word. As soon as a day they could be marching our
way.'

'Do tell, where is Kar? Did you make it to Pled?'
asked Unbetum.

Unbetum's questions made me question the faith
Kar and he placed in the god-like tree they frequented.
The tree, which had supposedly told Unbetum of Salarn's last ride and foretold of Guardians returning to
the plains, could not even tell him where his son was
or had been.

Arman stilled his mare's circling trot. 'Kar and I
both returned safely from Pled.' He dismounted and
rested his head against his mare's sweat-soaked neck
before turning back to face us. 'We rode through the
night,' he explained. 'You must understand that we did
not even know if any of you men escaped Assur.' Arman's eyes bulged in his reddened face and he spoke
quickly. He took a moment to look at us all and his
mouth gaped when he did not see his trader friend.
'Where's Delari?'

'Delari is here,' said Unbetum.

'Delari, Uk-Ban.' I called out, so that they might re-join us. 'Take a seat, Arman,' I said reassuringly, 'you are the first bringer of disconcerting news this day. Whatever you or Kar did in Assur allowed our escape. I can't hold a sword anymore but I survived.'

Arman looked for the faces of all those he knew still alive. He saw his trader friend, Delari, hastily heading our way from the far side of the tower.

Uk-Ban arrived first at the stable side of the tower and smiled at Arman.

Arman forced a short-lived grin to his lips. 'What is this I hear of a watchtower?' he then asked me, immediately turning to face Unbetum for an explanation.

'You almost know as much as I,' answered Unbetum. 'I am told that it is the height of two trees.'

'It is,' furthered Uk-Ban, 'though without a nest it is useless. All our work was in vain. I do not understand ...'

'I understand,' said Senea as he walked towards us from the tower with his brother, Lagesh, by his side. He held a cup of wine. 'Salarn said I would die here.'

Arman, against his nature, objected violently to these hopeless words. The hanging growth from his chin blew backwards as he stepped forwards quickly to slap Senea's cup from his hands with disgust.

I predicted his move in time and deflected his swing, though I had to use the arm I had tried to keep still since my muscle was cut to the bone in our escape from Assur. My wound was stretched apart and the pain made my eyes water. I swallowed repetitively resisting the urge to expel my bowls.

Gentuk grabbed hold of me before I fell to the ground.

Arman raised his hands to Unbetum in defence of his actions and sighed with desperation as he paced away. He bellowed at the woods.

'Arman,' I called after him, still held by Gentuk.

'What Tahnas?' He turned abruptly to face me. 'How could you think I was going to hit him?'

'I knew you were not going to hit him. You were attempting to knock his cup of wine from his hands. Gentuk and I have drunk the most. Take a swipe at one of us if you question our festiveness on this day.'

Arman shook his head slowly. 'I think we should all have a drink for Kar. He is attempting to recruit the support of the Valley Bandits as we speak.'

'No,' objected Senea, 'he does not even know if the ones we saw were of the same tribe.'

'He knows what he is doing,' confirmed Lagesh, looking westward.

Senea groaned and raised his arms. 'How do you know that?' he questioned his younger brother. 'Like your tower, is it because you had a dream beneath a tree whilst he was there? Did you see in your dream that a wooden watchtower would have us need to abandon a stone tower?'

Lagesh shook his head. 'It was not a dream, brother. A vision is truth not yet made real.'

'Guardians,' yelled Unbetum, unnerving himself more than the others in raising his voice. 'Forget yourselves. Forget the tree. Forget the tower. I vouch that you will all share Mother Ki's blessings and inherent sickness before this fight is over. What unites us is our will to survive and the shared belief that even a God-King bent on world domination can be defied.'

'I hear you, Unbetum,' supported my father and next to him Uk-Ban raised an empty mug.

'And did you ever think that I would not,' said Fankisi, drawing our attention as she walked towards us from the tower. 'Men, Gods, you are alike,' she said pointing us out as if we were trying to hide. 'You both keep secrets and never can you accept defeat even when your adversary is a hundred-fold your number and clad in armour. Why not share another drink together? After all, it will be fate not ill judgement that procures our demise.' She walked past me and stood so close to Unbetum that he had to lean back so that he might still maintain eye contact. 'If the tree cannot save us today then why did you keep it secret? Why did you not share it with the rest of us before it was too late?'

Unbetum met her cold stare and she began trembling all over, or was that me still supported by Gentuk, sick with pain from the wound on my shoulder that was torn apart once more by my own exertion. I could not be sure.

The silence festered until Senea stepped forwards and offered what remained in his cup to Arman. Lan held him back.

'What has become of us?' questioned Arman. 'I want that drink and I deserve it. Let us not quarrel pointlessly anymore. Do not hold him back Lan. Let me taste the wine I attempted to waste. Let Fankisi scold me for ignoring her and let Unbetum trouble further in his role as village elder during such times.'

Senea offered his cup to Arman and the burly man

snatched it, poured it down his throat and belched immediately. Leaning back and taking a deep breath he then restrained himself from rejecting it straight away. He was exhausted after his fast ride and had probably gone without food or rest for a day or more.

'They walk among us, Gentuk,' Arman continued after giving the wine a chance to settle. He gave Gentuk a supportive nod. 'It was the Wrath of the Gods you once spoke of that saw our lives spared in Assur.' Arman turned to face Senea who had planned to be with Kar and he on this journey. 'In Pled we met a man who was abrupt to the ways of gods yet at the same time, so knowing of their presence that he was calm in the face of immanent annihilation. We need to think more like the man named Ronses.'

'I see these men everyday now,' sang Uk-Ban with his thin arms spread wide.

'I am sure you do,' supported Arman. 'But no one, not even Kar who spoke often of the tree and was by my side every step of the way from Assur to the far shore and back again, could tell in advance that the Pledians already had a Guardian of their own. Protected by gods I believe we travelled there and returned safely so that we might face this day complete.' Arman walked towards me, knelt and looked me in the eye. 'Forgive me, Tahnas, my friend.'

'I hurt myself, Arman,' I said and signalled Gentuk that I could stand on my own.

Arman walked towards Fankisi and Unbetum and stood between them before finishing what he had to say. 'Everything we do finds reason though often we do not understand how at the time. You must forgive Unbetum for the moment, Fankisi, and forgive me for unintentionally disabling your husband further. And thank you, Senea, for sharing your drink. It may be that our existence as Guardians is about to end. It will not be without reason. A visit to the tree may help us feel complete in the moment. That is not the fulfilment I long for. My life has been saved many times so that I might return this day and it is for the same reason that Kar did not return with me. We have a battle to win and I have only one question that requires answer. Do we ride north to meet Sargon's army or do we wait for them to cross our plains once more?'

Our eyes fell upon Unbetum and Fankisi signalled her support by stepping past Arman and gently bracing our new elder's crippled arm.

'Face the Akkadian army held by the repute of Ishtar and every Guardian who has made passage,' Unbetum answered. 'Let the blind disciples of Sargon not see Guardians protecting a tower but vengeful demons, mere apparitions of defiance as you whittle their numbers each step of their march. Know you must that the mother of all Gods requests such deliverance. My humble voice and the echo of Mother Ki's hereafter shall be sounded through the strength of countless kings to come. When this fight is over only one true God shall remain. Ride out to meet them Guardians as I ride the opposite way for final counsel.'

# 16

# Vision

*Scribed by Enheduanna, Priestess of Ur.*
*Eshnunna, Akkadia.*

B y name I am known as the daughter of King Sargon, though it is my birthing mother I thank most
for guiding me with certainty in addressing the people
of Akkadia. I am humbled by my mother's instilled
wisdom, not the position handed to me by my father
and its bestowed sovereignty, for one thought blessed
with superiority by birth right alone is quickly under-
mined. It was by the Goddess Ishtar's favour that our
family grew strong. My father's sacking of Susa and the
sea trade cities was not to be challenged. As a family
we were unconquerable. Together with the strength of
my father, the wisdom of my mother and I acting as a
voice for them both and besetting the worship of his
growing empire upon Ishtar, The Supreme Goddess,
we have built the largest empire the world has ever
known. So, it is with stilled regret that I turn my scribing hand to completing the Guardians' chronicle.

Let me make poignant or further bizarre my involvement in the Guardians' defiance by sharing the
voice of the unfamiliar presence that too often now

appears before me like a spectre shaped of water in my dreams. *The fight for life against tyranny or calling oneself subject to unholy governance can only be sustained with a loud voice. The loudest voice is many saying the same thing at the same time.* I know the voice only to be that of one no longer walking this earth, for no being with a beating heart could penetrate the sanctuary of my temple home and enter my mind whilst I slept. And no living being could convince me that the word of even an entire city could outweigh that of my gods. These words are, without doubt, a warning from the other side. Too often they wake me from sleep and leave me questioning whether I too am subject to unholy governance. If I were to ever learn the true bearing of my impact upon the Akkadian Empire, I had to listen to more than just my mother and the High Priests.

In watching Derahmus, the first liege officer once in control of the North-eastern Frontier, address the Court of Agade; I began to understand the spectre's repeated phrase. Derahmus, despite knowing that his confession would not be welcomed, chose to return to Agade and speak the truth. He spoke of a disruption caused by a boy at the port of Assur. A few days later the port of Zidon was left in a state of mayhem. Would more soon risk their lives in a futile stand for their beliefs? What would I learn if I ventured beyond the white washed walls of the buildings surrounding my temple home?

I sided with the deserting soldier's cause and, accompanied by Derahmus, finally saw it time to expose myself to the world beyond the ruling cities between the rivers. That is how I heard of the Guardians and

Gutians by name, though how was I to know that in my secretive and short lived abandonment of post that my mother would lose her voice and my father be challenged for the first time? I write that it is because the Guardians of the East bid homage greater than worship to Ishtar, the Goddess supreme. I believe they have the strength to challenge my father because they fight in her name rather than for her expected blessings. This is their story, though, ultimately it impacts the fate of man for all time to come. The three men who entered Zidon together at the beginning of my recount have now gone separate ways. It was, however, the happenings in Zidon that shaped their fates and Kar, like many Guardians before him, never made it home. His story travelled by way of campfire tale to Eshnunna. In Eshnunna, where we stayed with Derahmus's family—his wife and two boys—the Gutians were not strangers. The Gutians were the people who once called the lands east of Eshnunna and south to Elam their home. Kar's name and many a Gutian name were remembered because this tale mentioned a king and that king was not my father.

***

It was like his form materialised amongst the trees. In a deep valley between the Zagros' peaks, east of Akkadia, fires were burning, the children were playing and the men were expected home soon, hopefully with a fresh kill before darkness took hold. An elderly woman sat alone at the edge of the clearing, next to a small fire. She fanned her hands above smoking clay pots laid out on a fur and chanted the almost forgotten words of the people first to call the mountains home. A younger woman passing nearby noticed him first and she stilled herself mid-step. Like she was dreaming, she choked on her words and stumbled onto her hands and knees in attempt to flee, spilling a basket of freshly picked berries. She looked back, hoping it was just a dream. There he stood, silent and menacing by foreign con-texture alone. More frightening than the tall, bladed weapon he held, was his almost fragile and unguarded stature. If he was large, or even decorated with war paint or armour, she might have mustered the courage to scream in immediate defence. Something about this man waned her usual defences and instead she cowered towards the first hut without a voice to call warning in advance.

'Eteri?' cried out another woman, noticing her friend's distress, 'what is wrong?' Eteri rushed inside the closest hut without responding, so she looked about until she sighted the threat herself. 'Children,' she screamed, 'leave your play and hurry inside.'

The elderly woman, seated at the edge of the clear-ing, stilled her hands above her smoking clay pots and also looked about in search of what had startled the women. Unlike the younger women, her reaction to a stranger's unannounced presence in their home was not restricted by fear. She slid her fur from beneath her pots and began bellowing strange words as she paced towards him. She flapped her fur about in an effort to dispel his presence.

More frightened women and children emerged from the valley growth and gathered with those first alerted. Others, in the confusion, raised their heads in view of the spectacle, resigned to venturing no further than the comfort of their own huts.

'Be gone, be gone,' chanted the elderly lady with wrinkles deep enough to clamp a stray finger. 'Leave us evil spirit. Return whence you came.' When the elderly woman saw that the flapping of her fur also moved his hair, she grew more convinced in her efforts to disperse the evil presence. She shook her grey mane and beat the fur more rapidly the closer she got until finally she was upon him and the fur came down and stuck on his blade.

Kar pulled it from her grip as he turned his staff to the ground and allowed it to slide loose. He then stood erect and motionless again with his staff complementing his pose.

The old woman stumbled backwards, bracing her dangling breast.

Kar stood silent and as unimposing as he could.

The old woman backed slowly away and gradually quickened her retreat to the closest hut.

He never intended to scare the valley bandits. Even introducing himself, without another man present, could prove detrimental to his cause. Kar wanted to unite them with the Guardians for together he believed they could deter the western assault. His patience was tested as night fell and only the dying coals of the old woman's fire lit the village. It became difficult for the women and children to even tell if he was still there. The moon eventually graced the cloudy sky above and each time its face was fully revealed and the clearing was illuminated, Kar heard the muffled cries of a scared people alerted once more to his lingering presence. He did not expect his task to be easy though he had hoped they would grow more accustomed to his presence with time. In reflection, he actually questioned why he had spent his life pursuing such fanciful attainments.

Preferable to Kar would have been returning to his home with the other man who entered Zidon and joining him in recruiting their own people. That is what he would have done if he still thought as he did as a child. In truth, it was what he dreamed of doing even as a young man except that in his imaginings he wanted to face the Akkadian army alone. He did not have to live life long as a man before it seemed that his thoughts based on acquired knowledge were leading him down a path more often void of free choice and increasingly indifferent to his ideals. Some say he might have visited the Gutian village in the valley to sacrifice his life.

Long before the valley bandits reached the clearing, Kar detected the light of their torches cutting through gaps in the growth. They were as silent as he in their return and appeared single file from the trees to his south. The moment they reached the clearing, they broke formation and those wielding torches made haste to light the fires that should have been ablaze for their return. Barely visible to Kar, the bandits not carrying light positioned themselves strategically about their village. Kar heard the women tell of his presence without leaving the security of their huts and it was not long before several fires were lit and raging to life. Slowly the veil of night was lifted by growing flames and the bandits waited for Kar's position to be revealed.

Kar turned his head slowly to face the bandit standing closest. He recognised the thin-waisted man. The last time Kar had entered the valley, this man was armed with flint blades. Kar watched him carefully,

convinced the bandit would swing before questioning his presence. The bandit must have felt Kar's eyes
upon him for he turned suddenly with his sword raised
long before the clearing was fully lit. He shrieked
with alarm as he thrust his sword forwards, making
Kar break stance. Before Kar had a chance to disable
his known adversary, another bandit sprung upon him
from behind. The Guardian stooped below a menacing
swing and was soon surrounded by five more bandits,
also prepared to attack before asking questions. Kar
deflected three blades and bunted one of the bandits
swiftly in the head with the blunt end of his staff before one of them managed to land a strike. A flap of
flesh, complete with hair, was lifted from Kar's skull
and tossed aside by a circling blade. This enraged Kar
and for a moment he forgot all reason for venturing
into the bandits' home. He swung his staff low, cutting
the ankle of one bandit and sweeping two more from
their feet. The blunt, though weighted, end of his staff
then crushed another bandit's face before he drew it
close and deflected the next attack.

'Stop,' cried one of the bandits, yet to engage. His
advice was ignored as more of armed men surrounded
Kar, hollering and swinging their weapons high and
low.

Kar disarmed the next two bandits who attacked
him with the force of his strike alone. He had regained
his composure, though in attempting to defend himself
without taking lives, he was unable to avoid all blows.
Most of his left ear and more of his scalp was severed
by one strike that made it past his guard. As he charged
forwards to escape the bandits' group attack, another
blade sliced his side. Kar stole quick glances about the

village until he sighted a point of fortification.

Pursued by the bandits, Kar retreated to a sheltered space between the meeting corners of two huts. He held his hands wide, signalling surrender, hoping that they would desist from their onslaught long enough for him to explain the reason for his intrusion. The Guardian was bleeding from more cuts than he remembered receiving as a menacing crowd of bandits, numbering at least fifty, some say one hundred, formed before him. Distant war cries signalled that even more were on their way to what Kar thought was the only bandit village in the valley.

Those surrounding Kar formed a path wide enough for the approach of a lone figure. This man held authority over the others and was seemingly intent on addressing Kar personally. He was short, though with muscular arms gripping a weapon in each hand, he was not to be looked down on. Like the men who parted for him, he was painted with mud and wore an assembly of animal bones for armour. He pointed his short sword at Kar from one hand and raised a club high above his head in his trailing arm. The wooden club he held was a dark red and smooth like stones in a stream. Like Kar's staff, the bandit's club had a blade inserted at one end. The club's blade was shaped like the beak of a bird and emphasised by painted eyes either side. He kept his sword still and pointed at Kar as he attempted to betray the Guardian's attention with his club's swaying eyes.

'I came in peace,' Kar told the short bandit. 'I knew, though, that this would be a strange concept to your kind.'

'Our kind?' questioned the bandit, jerking his club

forwards and withdrawing it quickly in an attempt to startle Kar.

Kar remained perfectly still, though the blood now coursing down his face and splattered across his chest also made the young Guardian look ready for battle to the end. 'Your kind,' repeated Kar. 'I name you bandits for the livelihood of others is your prey. The lives of many merchants and travellers who might have brought prosper to the East have been wasted. Is it not because of men like you that the East is now regarded as savage?' Kar did not expect the bandits to be so fluent in his tongue and already he wished that he taken the time to choose better words.

'Who are you to say such things? Our people have watched your village of strangers grow. We have watched you invite more people to the East. It is your people that told the West what lay beyond the mountains. It is the same breed of man that follows you in search of reward without offering.'

*I knew this to be true because I had seen the Guardians' painted tablets.* They were maps of the East and West. The tablets were shelved in my father's library in Agade long before the second conquest of the East was underway. Kar was the one who was spoken of most in the countless tales shared between Elam and Akkadia. He was the man that stood taller than a horse in some accounts and was younger than ten harvests in the next retelling of the same story. Thus, I imagined him young and tall. I thought his eyes green like trees and his skin dark like bark, much like the wild man Enkidu. And, if I'd learnt anything from the countless retellings of the Epic of Gilgamesh, it was that your greatest foe could be your best friend. King Gilgamesh fought Enkidu in the streets of Uruk. But the God King's real battle, the battle they fought together, was against Humbaba, the demon in the woods. When the people spoke of Kar, I thought of Enkidu. I imagined a powerful man. I imagined a man who never had a mother to groom his hair or clean his skin. I imagined a man who was destined to become a friend of my father and, maybe this time, without the need to battle.

'You speak of the Guardians as if we are foe,' said Kar, blinking and tossing his head to disperse gathered blood from his eye. 'Only now am I aware that your numbers outweigh us twenty fold. Why is it, that if we bring such trouble to your land, you have never raised opposition?'

'This is our land,' replied the bandit, circling his club to identify the out of sight boundaries he spoke of beyond the tree line. 'Men, or as you call us bandits, secure our homeland, not walls. More successful they seem to be. It is the way of your people, not the Gutians, that the West seeks to end.'

'You are right,' admitted Kar. 'Still, any lesson learned will be fruitless if you wait like the Guardians for Akkadia to knock on your valley's door. You can take my life this night or gain me as an ally. As spokesman for the Guardians, I request the service of your warriors and warn that if the Akkadians' advance is not halted this time then this valley will be the last eastern stronghold and one sure to fall to a similar assault in due course.'

The bandit's spokesman signalled another to approach with a wave of his bird-headed club. 'Harnsek, tell the Guardian why we see their presence as no different to any other western invasion.'

Kar recognised Harnsek as the young man he had sighted on many a scout ride.

'I cannot say father,' said Harnsek. He turned to face those standing behind and called for Omah.'

'I can answer,' announced Omah, pushing through the crowd of men until he was standing in front of Kar. 'This is the man who left his kill for us. He once rode with the white-bearded man. One day he took our gold, leaving nothing.'

'Is that your way?' questioned Kar. 'Did you expect me to arrive today with offerings of food and drink? Yes, we took your gold. What would you have thought if we had left it and ignored the trap you baited in our absence?'

'Do you think of us as fools, Guardian?' asked the bandit's spokesman, now identified by Kar as Harnsek's father, though not yet confirmed as an elder.

'I do not think this.' Kar wiped blood from his brow. 'All I see is a hundred unknown faces, waiting for and reliant on our final exchange of words,' he answered. 'Was the gold not left in good will? Was I wrong in thinking that the Gutians were men of reason? Please tell me the gold was not bait for man, like rotting meat is for a boar?'

The bandits surrounding Kar, apart from those with whom he had already shared words, laughed at his questions. Their laugh, however, would be better described as a cackle for they rejoiced in his suffering as stray insults and threats like, 'Man beast,' and 'Cut him down,' were sounded unidentifiably and repeated only in more descriptive ways amongst their numbers.

Omah, one of the two who had led Kar to thinking

that the bandits could be sided with, also taunted him. 'He speaks of give and take like it is below him. He leaves a boar and we give gold. He offers nothing and asks for our lives.'

Kar lowered his staff and laughed with them. His involvement in their amusement made them silent once more. 'I repeat, that it is my own life I offer.' Blood flowed down Kar's arm from his head and gathered between his fingers. 'Tempted by Harnsek's generous offering of gold and misjudging it as a sign of peace, I have been lured like an animal in reach of your strike. Do not forget though that I am a Guardian and do not wander haplessly into harm's way.' He touched the wounds on his scalp and felt skin and blood where he once had hair. 'My life is yours for the taking though think more opportunely about the knowledge I have presented you with. Whether you decide to fight with us or not, the Guardians will face Akkadia on the morrow. The armour and weapons of fallen soldiers and the resulting riderless steeds could be yours. I only ask that you spare my life tonight so that I may be of further assistance to both you and my people. Mocking me or fighting me until the sun rises is pointless.'

'Nothing you offer is reliant on your life, Guardian,' replied the Gutian wielding the bird-headed club and short sword. He stepped between Omah and Harnsek and readied both weapons to strike.

'There you are wrong,' said a familiar voice that startled Kar more than another threat against his life could have.

Omah and Harnsek stepped backwards and the spokesman lowered his bird-headed club as once more the bandits shuffled to allow another to approach.

Kar recognised the old man's baldhead, glowing red in the firelight. 'Elkin,' he exclaimed as an old friend emerged from the crowd.

'You know this Guardian?' the Gutian spokesman questioned Elkin.

'I know him, Damir, but like you I am also concerned by his presence.'

'I had to come,' Kar tried to explain. 'I thought I would find allies here. With Salarn gone I am reliant on my own judgement.'

'And what of my advice?' enquired Elkin. 'I told you to search the horizons yet here I find you in one of the few places without a horizon in sight. Are you still seeking answers ahead of time? Did your quest for understanding end with your elder?'

Kar wobbled on his feet and steadied himself with his staff. It was hard for him to think clearly, with a throbbing head that coursed blood down his side and a hundred eyes watching. The Bandit's spokesman, Damir, also made him nervous. He still stood close enough to strike and Kar had lowered his guard. Ignoring as best he could these distractions, the young Guardian attempted to justify greater reason for his arrival in the valley. 'I crossed many horizons before arriving here,' he began. 'In Pled, I met your brother, Ronses,' Kar told Elkin. 'I am not seeking my end. If anything, I believe my quest for understanding has only heightened since Salarn made passage.'

'That is hopeful word you share,' declared Elkin. 'Why not therefore share your true vision with the Gutians?'

'Speak it, Guardian,' demanded Omah.

'I have already told you,' said Kar.

'No, you told us we must fight or suffer the same fate as the Guardians,' argued Damir.

'You did not share a vision, Kar,' agreed Harnsek. 'You only incited fear and that is why my people are still troubled by your presence.'

Kar looked at Elkin and saw the old man's lips thin with a smile. 'Let me begin again,' requested Kar, wiping more blood from his brow with his arm. 'I have not even returned home yet from my journey west where we confronted an Akkadian army in Assur and followed another to The Great Sea ready for another fight. The West is ruled by Akkadia.'

'Stop talking, Kar,' said Elkin, stepping to his side and holding a cloth to the wound on his head. 'This is not the time for stories. Tell the Gutians why, after all you have seen, they should involve themselves in a war not of their own? That is the vision you have not shared.'

*I wished that Elkin had not stopped Kar from talking at this moment.* If he had been allowed to continue, the tale of Kar and the Gutians might have revealed the true face of Kar. Derahmus and I might have learnt if he was the one who sunk a vessel in Assur and sabotaged the Akkadian fleet in Zidon. Yet each retelling of the tale continued the same way with Kar pondering what could be his final words.

Kar studied Elkin's tired gaze and noticed that he was not smiling anymore. He clasped the cloth to his bleeding head and stepped past him to address the Gutians once more. He knew this would be his last chance and that a weapon could not save him if his words did not turn favour. 'The last time Akkadia visited the East I hid in the woods until they were gone. If every Guardian had fled or hid, the Akkadians would have never left. They would not have burnt our village to the ground because they could have claimed it without effort. Akkadians would be your neighbours already if things had happened that way. This is the understanding I should have shared with you. In time everything comes to bear. Akkadia now returns to cut a thorn from their side, though it is more than vengeance and desired proclamation that sees them return. Sargon will not stop until his empire spans to the last horizon in all directions. Roads through the mountains and claim on your home he will seek next. The Guardians no longer have a village, so maybe we should stay hidden like you, though for how long? Spare my life and I will face Akkadia on the morrow. They will be defeated but I will never return home to celebrate victory. When the battle is over I will head west through your mountains and north to Borujerd. There I will tell all that the Akkadians were defeated in the East and recruit support. I will begin a journey towards the capital, Agade. Before my life is over, I will face the King of Akkadia. This I have seen in a vision. Without a tree in sight, in a place that overlooks the Southern Sea, my vision ends as everything turns white.' Kar took a deep breath. He stood silent and unarmed before the Gutian bandits, awaiting their response.

There was commotion amongst their ranks and a bandit three paces from Kar, called for his scalp.

Damir raised his bird-headed club, ordering silence. Lowering his club, Damir stepped towards Kar and whispered, 'I like your vision.'

Kar glanced over his shoulder and saw that Elkin had dipped his head in thought. 'Will you join with the Guardians for this next fight?' Kar asked Damir.

'I will tell your story to our King,' answered Damir. 'Our King will decide your fate and our fight.'

*Our King.* I remembered staring at Derahmus when this part of the tale was first shared with us. It was a startling revelation and each retelling ended the same way, *our King will decide.* The King they referred to was not Sargon. They did not speak of my father.

# 17

# The New Commander

*Scribed by Enheduanna, Priestess of Ur.*
*The Palace of Sanam-Shimut, Susa.*

I believe it was through an inseparable allegiance to his soldiers, rather than regard for my demand that Derahmus escorted me beyond Eshnunna and through the Zagros Mountains to Susa. Sanam-Shimut, once King of the Elamites, took pleasure in offering us sanctuary in his decimated palace when Derahmus named me as the daughter of Sharru-Kin. Sanam-Shimut still had the ear of his people and I promised him a voice.

The tablet bearers that made passage to Agade via Susa shared their reports of happenings in the East. Sanam-Shimut often asked me to repeat the story told, after the tablet bearers had left his palace with Akkadian guards. Derahmus paced in circles during the reading of tablets. He lifted his head like a thrusted sword when the report of a tablet bearer mentioned a name he knew, an opportunity for attack, or a new threat. He told me more of a fight than I could hardly imagine. Any embellishments to the Akkadian reports are thus owed to Derahmus as much as my scribing hand.

\*\*\*

In Borujerd, Izdubar had received an official order from the King's court in Agade. The tablet bearers who returned to Agade via Susa, recounted the same story of his reaction. Each had scribed that Izdubar's olive eyes widened with excitement as the clay envelope was cracked open and the tablet was read to him.

Derahmus was right when he stated that only the King himself could object to governance granted by a first liege officer. Izdubar had now gained Sargon's support as well. The new commander's first order from Sargon was no small ask. He was to fortify a stronghold on the eastern side of the Zagros Mountains and establish a secure trade route west through the mountains to Bit-Bunakki. Izdubar was not prepared to fail in his first mission. I recount that he listened objectively to the soldiers who had travelled east beyond the mountains three seasons prior, before offering rewards that were now credible by his rank to ensure they would be by his side. Izdubar led his army south guided also by a detailed map and fully aware that it was more than ordinary barbarians he may have to face in battle.

\*\*\*

It is told that the ground trembled and the trees at the edge of the woods shook as the cavalry unit, numbering two hundred, travelled south. Behind them followed two hundred soldiers on foot and a caravan consisting of twelve wagons with four guards appointed to each. The cavalry never advanced too far clear of the wagons that held their stores and, tightly grouped, they maintained a steady pace towards their destination. The course of one rider, though, was unpredictable.

Izdubar cut a meandering course, even between his own ranks at times, guiding the caravan that followed along a path far from the woods and as free of sudden rises and falls as possible. He was enjoying every moment of the journey to battle. In Mari, he had willingly accepted the post of Commander of the North-eastern Frontier from the previous commander, Derahmus. At the time, Izdubar believed that such an offering was temporary and would only last until a longer-serving officer staked his claim. Before he even had a chance to boast his position, or celebrate his promoted status, Izdubar had led his battalion to the North-eastern Frontier of Akkadia.

Izdubar consulted further with one of the experienced soldiers making the journey when they reached the spot where it had all gone wrong three seasons prior.

'On our return to the west, we set camp in that nest between the joining cliffs,' reminisced an Akkadian soldier named Subberest. 'It was only the senior officers who stayed up late drinking that night. I don't believe that it was their carousing that left us open to the ambush. They were torturing one of the prisoners and he was louder than all of them put together. That is what allowed the barbarians to assassinate the guards and get so close.'

'We will not make the same mistake,' vowed Izdubar. 'From now on, I want you to refer to them by their name now known to us. The barbarians we speak of are called Guardians. Our duty to the King is to bring an end to their defiance.'

'I apologise, Izdubar.'

'No need to apologise if you understand what I am

saying.'

'I understand,' replied Subberest. 'In the Bit-Bu-nakki drinking hut I witnessed a Guardian old enough to have died twice, kill, without blinking an eye, the strongest soldier to ever fight for Akkadia. Before committing to this conquest, I prepared myself to face men even stronger and know that even a moment of distraction could be my last.'

'Even now in addressing me above committing your ears to unsighted danger at the tree line or in the long grass ahead?'

Subberest shook his head and Izdubar realised that the soldier could have been insulted by his comment as he had extremely large ears framing his scarred face. 'I have been distracted,' the soldier replied.

'I will distract you from duty no longer,' said Izdubar as he held back his long, brown hair and slid on a bronze helmet. 'Sharpen your wits once more by riding ahead two hundred paces before circling back. I want you to repeat this action until we set camp at dusk.'

Izdubar looked upwards at the foothills of the Zagros Mountains to his west and across at Balih Woods to his east. Through a corridor of imposing barriers the Akkadian army travelled. He asked that Gemat accompany Subberest on the scout rides ahead. Izdubar respected Gemat because he had learnt that they were both born in Mari and had both spent time digging water furrows before the war. Gemat, a soldier with arms as strong as legs, had spoken against his Commander in Zidon. This betrayal and the soldier's thin, dark eyes made Izdubar wary. Izdubar wanted this man on his side and saw appointing him higher duty as a means to encourage his allegiance. Gemat and Subber-est repeated a scouting manoeuvre close to the woods and even into the foothills several times before the army set camp between the mountains and the woods.

According to their clay map, a map drawn by the Guardians and claimed when the Akkadians last visited these lands, they were only a thousand paces short of the mountain pass. The cavalry could have easily reached the Guardian village before dark, though Izdubar had a different plan. Without a doubt, his main objective was to face the Guardians in battle. However, in view of also establishing a trade route through the mountains, in part detailed by the map already in his possession, he had decided against over committing his troops too soon. He set camp where he was most exposed to the sight of others. He intended to use this perceived dis-advantage to his avail by ensuring his defence was kept on high alert. Izdubar had made it the principal duty of several guards following the wagons, to collect any dry logs or branches they stumbled upon. Five days after he had given the command, it all made sense. The Akkadians built and lit massive fires surrounding them at a distance before returning to their camp that was lost to darkness as night closed over. Izdubar did not rely solely on the cover of darkness; the tents were pitched in a circle surrounding the horses for their protection and behind each soldier, who sat on guard where the light of the surrounding fires ended, another soldier was posted closer to camp. Izdubar made fur-ther use of the fires by ordering scouts at random to ride wide of the flames to pre-empt any staged assault from one direction that could breach their sanctuary of darkness.

It may have been that no defence was adequate against Guardians ready to fight, though it was also arguable that Izdubar should have aimed to reach the open plains before setting camp that night. Either way, it was likely that blood would be spilled before dawn, for only a stealth assault by the Guardians could make up for their lack of numbers.

# 18

# In the Grass Passage

*Scribed by Arman,*
*The Always Travelling Guardian.*

Each Guardian who had paced through the woods, following the Akkadians' advance until they set camp, was compelled by individual motive to kill, more than any belief in rebuilding a stable home. Driven by vengeance we fought in the name of Ishtar, the Goddess of War, and all the Guardians who had died before us. Even Lan, the eldest Guardian, who had returned from the West with a new found sense of peace, knew that he would only see his wife, Jamine, again if his blade was coated in the blood of a hundred Akkadians. He laid all blame on his son's absence from this fight on the Akkadians. I too wished Tahnas was with us for this fight and cursed the Akkadians for raging war once more. I did not blame myself for disabling the man further.

A few hundred paces from where Lan, Gentuk, Senea and Lagesh contemplated what could be their last fight—a first for Lagesh—I was sided once more with my trader friend, Delari, and our new acquaintance, Uk-Ban. We, also believing that thoughts of days to come were best left unspoken, were positioned in between the woods and the mountains as a first line of attack. Our plan was to lure soldiers into following us towards the woods, where the Guardians in wait could launch an ambush.

The soldiers' last scout ride ahead of the cavalries' advance only fell short of us hidden in the long grass by a horse's length. The battle would have commenced before dark if they had ridden our way again. Instead, we were allowed the time to devise a new plan of attack while the Akkadians built their boundary fires. Upon deciding on a changed course of action, we waited patiently until night had truly arrived. Under the cover of darkness, I returned to the woods to consult with the other Guardians.

*** 

Delari and Uk-Ban experienced more close calls with random scouts in my absence and the boundary fires shed more light on the surrounds than we had expected. We could see the guards posted beyond the fires and deemed it only safe to assume that their vision could also reach us. For fear of being detected in retreat, Delari and Uk-Ban maintained their position. It happened that the first scout to ride beyond the fires pulled his armoured stead to a standstill just in front of them. The second scout, thankfully, rode east towards the woods before returning the same way. The third scout to emerge without warning from the Akkadians' camp rode straight past Delari and Uk-Ban before circling behind them and retreating just as quickly. He almost trampled me in his return to camp.

'Do we move,' whispered Uk-Ban as he raised his

head from hiding.

'We are not positioned well,' said Delari. 'Where is Arman?'

From the grass, ten paces from my friends, I mimicked a birdcall to signal my return. When I had the attention of their eyes, I raised four of my fingers and lowered them. Delari and Uk-Ban nodded in response. Flames from the closest boundary fire, fifty paces to our north, reached as high as a pine. The fires surrounded the camp in all directions and prevented a stealth approach. The Guardians waiting in the woods had agreed that we had to strike first. We had to break the soldiers' fortification. Lan, Gentuk, Senea and Lagesh were each armed with their own side bow. It was the first time they would use the new weapons. Uk-Ban had to complete the construction of three more that very morn whilst the Guardian men and women shaped an arsenal of wooden bolts.

Delari, Uk-Ban and I prepared our own side bows by drawing bolts tight and securing our levers. We did not have the protection of the woods and had to be ready to fight like apparitions in the night.

'They prepare to ride again,' warned Delari.

On the eastern side of the Akkadian camp, between the boundary fires and the tents surrounding the secured horses, five mounted soldiers were assembled in a row. Next to them was a mounted Akkadian Commander in his bronze helmet and breastplate. The mounted soldiers looked ready to ride east this time. I had to lure their attention from the woods to allow the other Guardians an opportunity to position themselves. And if they were already positioned in the grass between the woods and the fire, I had to strike now before they were exposed.

I crept towards the guard standing beyond the closest boundary fire in the south. His head turned slowly from side to side, silhouetted by the raging fire behind. Twenty paces from him, where light from the fire licked the grass in front of me, I raised my side bow slowly. I took aim.

The guard heard the snap of the tensed tendon releasing the bolt. He would have seen a slim shadow racing towards his face. A spurt of gore erupted from his skull and he collapsed. He did not have time to cry out but his death was noticed. Through the leaping flames, I saw movement in the camp and soldiers hollered, alerting all to the attack.

I looked towards the Akkadian Commander and his row of five riders. With a stiff arm, he commanded them to ride south. They rode behind the boundary fire closest to me and appeared the other side still riding in unison. Between two fires they rode south to where Delari and Uk-Ban waited in the grass.

I looked to the woods and saw Lan standing in the grass. His side bow was aimed high. Like the first bronze bolt released by Lan, more made of wood fell silently from the sky upon the camp, destined to either hit or startle a target.

# 19

# New Morrow's Eve

*Scribed by Enheduanna, Priestess of Ur.*
*The Palace of Sanam-Shimut, Susa.*

In the darkened Akkadian camp, Izdubar readied more scouts to ride and allowed those who had participated already to retire for the night. Izdubar's next move was to send a scout out in each direction at the same time. He waited for their safe return before commencing a change in guard. Izdubar was mindful that an attack launched against him under the cover of darkness would defy his strength in numbers. The new Commander of the North-eastern Frontier had one final defence measure at his disposal and that was his most accomplished soldiers whom he had allowed rest since they first set camp. He woke these soldiers after the change in guard was completed without incident. He woke them just in time.

It was a guard posted closest to the camp that sounded the alarm first. The breach in the defence was raised from the south. Izdubar sent his finest five soldiers to combat this threat and readied the rest of his troops to defence against predicted ambush from every other direction. Unfortunately, for Izdubar, the horses that his defence was staged around became his downfall. The unsettling cry of a horse stuck deep by a descending bronze bolt made the surrounding steeds revolt. Reins snapped and tents were trampled as the horses fled from the source of fear. Even Izdubar's stallion reared up and tried to buck him from mount before he had a chance to respond. 'Contain the horses,' he bellowed and the soldiers closest to the surrounding fires took hold of flaming logs and branches in an effort to prevent the escape of the riderless horses.

Every attempt Izdubar had made to secure his camp till morning had turned against him and he felt defeated until he sighted two of his finest soldiers returning triumphantly from the south. More disturbing than the indescribable cry of a wounded horse was the sound that escaped the lips of the man held aloft between the soldiers returning on horseback. The man's feet kicked pointlessly out of reach of the ground for he was suspended by the grip of the soldiers either side, assisted by leather restraints also secured to their saddles. Caden of Eshnunna and Zaid of Agade carried him this way until they were inside the ring of boundary fires. Ghani, Abda and Faraj, farmers turned soldier from Sippar, who had fought for Derahmus before the change in command, maintained a stagnated defensive structure south of the camp.

Izdubar commanded all idle soldiers to secure any horse they could and take mount. This was not a simple request for even though many horses had been blocked from escape they were still unsettled. He relayed a further order to protect the supply wagons at all cost. Upon issuing this command the still newly appointed Commander of the North-eastern Frontier realised that he was of better use to the will of Akkadia as a soldier. He found himself short of the patience required to be a leader. He was a man accustomed to playing his individual part well. It was frustrating for him to watch less disciplined soldiers act on his behalf. He wanted to be fighting alongside the five men he knew best and procuring more immediate results. Upon witnessing his friend, Abda of Sippar, fall to a bolt released from the surrounding darkness he ignored his greater responsibility and rode south.

After being released, the captive was not quick to stand. His arms had been pulled apart with such intense strain that they dangled loose of his shoulders as he staggered awkwardly to his feet.

Ghani and Faraj, the only southern defensive force, held their side bows ready. They released their bolts when they noticed movement in the grass. Before they had a chance to reload, a Guardian sprinted towards them from the boundary fire behind. The Guardian's side bow was armed and he released a bolt mid-step as he bounded through the grass. Faraj was removed from his mount. Unlike arrows, the bolts released from these new weapons accomplished immediate death upon meeting the desired target.

Izdubar, still at a small distance to those he sought to join, pulled his steed to an abrupt halt and took aim with his own side bow. The Guardian dropped out of sight into the long grass before he had a chance to release a bolt. The commander kept his eyes fixed to the grass folding before the man's crawl though, unlike his most respected soldiers, now only numbering three, Izdubar resisted pulling the lever until he had clear sight of his adversary. The Guardian's movement through the grass, noticeable in the light of the closest fire, soon slowed. Nearby, the captive still staggered about. Despite the man's presumable suffering, he voiced no further cries of pain.

Caden, Zaid, Ghani and Izdubar continued to ignore the captive's threatless presence in lure of the enabled man so close yet out of sight. This was the type of patience to which Izdubar was accustomed. The lever on his side bow was already pressed salute to the point of release. He floated his aim over the swaying grass tops. All he required was a glimpse of skin to confirm he was not repeating the mistake that had seen two of his respected five retire early.

***

Guardians positioned east of the camp continued with their silent assault from the cover of the woods. It was a merciless attack made possible by Izdubar's decision to stage his defence around what he sought to protect most—the horses and supply wagons. Derahmus told me during my scribing that he would have positioned his camp in a line between the woods and the foothills and spread the defence between four main camps. I listened to him but did not alter the official account of events. I only acknowledge in my combined account the possibility of different strategies and rely on his advice in the naming of particular soldiers not identified by the tablet bearers sent south to Susa. Derahmus had fought with many of the men before and when the tablets spoke of a soldier without notable rank making a stand, he told me the man was Jemat of Mari.

With their leader otherwise engaged and the remaining soldiers lacking the initiative to send representatives beyond the boundary fires in search of the enemy, their numbers slowly dwindled. More startled horses fled from the deadly rain of wooden bolts yet the Akkadians, who were witnessing fellow soldiers drop all around them, stayed bunched. It was a newly recruited soldier who had spent most of his life digging irrigation channels in Mari that finally took charge. He was telling the mounted soldier next to him that they would not last till dawn if they did not ride out when he witnessed a descending bolt make the man incapable of reply. A fountain of blood pumped from the man's neck as he slipped, unresponsive, from his mount. Jemat took this man's seat on the mount and separated himself from the crowded soldiers so that his words might carry more strength in his address. 'Our enemy is upon us,' he yelled, pointing beyond the fires with an arm strong enough to plough the earth. 'We must ride out to meet them or we will die waiting for them to be revealed with the light of new day.' His words were given justice when he rode on without waiting for another to be by his side. Before he had reached the closest boundary fire several more mounted soldiers had decided to follow his brave advance.

Jemat, the irrigator turned soldier, found himself alone in the deceiving light beyond the eastern boundary fires. In front of him the woods could be concealing an entire army in the black hollows and the sound of his own movement made it impossible to detect the presence of another close by in the grass that swayed a trickery of shadow. He turned his steed to the north and galloped that way in the hope of unsettling any unsighted attackers. The mounted Akkadians who followed him outside also chose to ride fast. Nearing a boundary fire to the north, between the woods and the camp, Izdubar slowed to a trot and glanced back over his shoulder. Between him and the Akkadians, still riding fast in his direction, a sole figure made haste on foot towards the woods.

'Cut off his retreat,' yelled Jemat.

Jemat must have ridden right past the man though with another eight soldiers riding a similar track north, the Guardian did not seem content to stay hidden. On foot his escape was not fast enough. The mounted soldiers circled the lone man short of the woods and closed in on him.

Jemat was anticipating their engagement when a sound close by drew his attention. He turned to see a shadow of a man disappear into the grass beyond the fire burning closest. Instead of pursuing the man, he returned closer to the camp and signalled more Akkadians his way. His commander's defensive structure had not worked because though the camp was lost to darkness, this very darkness had become the Guardians' ally. Jemat could see this clearly from a distance and, when more soldiers had gathered before him, he relayed new orders. 'They are attacking from the woods,' Jemat told them. 'We must control their advance and their retreat by lighting the grass between. Take branches already burning from this fire and spread light closer to the woods. All archers need to assemble on this front.'

# 20

# He Was a Trader

*Scribed by Arman,*
*The Always Travelling Guardian.*

Delari rolled onto his back and stared up at the sky. Foremost in his gaze would have been his side bow, armed with the last bolt he carried. Maybe he thought of our efforts in Nineveh to secure these weapons and keep them from Akkadian hands. 'Why?' he questioned any god that might be listening. 'Is it because you are restrained like man from action, or is it because your strength allows for so much neglect?' I'm sure the trader asked such defining questions because he thought it might be his last opportunity. Delari, like me, had been outplayed by the deceptive approach of five mounted soldiers. They had approached as far as the boundary fire in unison before, one at a time, they advanced further, widening their spread under the watchful eye of the rest of their unit. We were not given an opportune moment to escape from or attack the advancing riders until it was too late. Uk-Ban became a prisoner of war in an attempt to stay hidden and I followed the Akkadians back to camp in an effort to save the last descendant of Catal-Huyuk.

I don't think Delari expected an answer. I wished I could have shared another birdcall or one word to let him know I was listening. He only waited a moment to receive an answer. He adjusted his grip on his weapon and stood in the grass that concealed his position. Before the hot fire that rippled the light, three mounted soldiers had their aim already devoted in my direction. The trader took aim at one before detecting the presence of another. Delari turned to face the Akkadian Commander and they aimed their side bows at the same time.

Delari collapsed backwards, lifted from his feet by a bronze bolt that caved in his chest. The Commander, in receipt of the bolt released by the trader, was knocked off his steed and landed flat on his back from a height. The bolt that emerged from both sides of the commander's shoulder was popped from his body with the impact and twirled once in the air above the grass before falling to rest.

One of the mounted soldiers stalking me in the grass averted his aim and rode to his commander's side.

I still saw two soldiers vigilant to my end. Only moving my hands, I adjusted my aim to the closest soldier and pulled the lever. Tensed tendon launched the wooden bolt and it cracked open the soldier's face below his nose. I rolled to the side to avoid the other soldier's attack. A bronze bolt split the grass and brushed my beard. As he rushed to reload his side bow, I drew a throwing blade. Standing from the grass, I thrust the blade. It twirled once before the tip connected with his leather breastplate and the handle smacked his chin. The Akkadian's beard did little to soften the impact.

The soldier was startled and his half-drawn bolt

was released and propelled into the neck of his steed. It reared before falling to one side and dropping the Akkadian into the grass.

I drew my sword and advanced.

The soldier trotting his steed towards his fallen commander turned on me. I raised my side bow as I stepped away. It was not loaded but he did not know this. When the soldier on horseback returned his attention to his fallen commander, I ducked beneath the grass. I retreated to the woods in the hope of fighting again.

# 21

# Light Before Dawn

*Scribed by Enheduanna, Priestess of Ur.*
*The Palace of Sanam-Shimut, Susa.*

Zaid of Agade ducked for cover behind his collapsed horse and, when he stood with his side bow tensed, the Guardian had disappeared. He strained his eyes to the light beyond the boundary fire and sighted a glimpse of the Guardian's movement. 'He's retreating.'

'Forget him,' said Caden, with his side bow ready as he rode to where he had seen Izdubar fall from his mount.

*****

On the eastern side of the camp, the grass that separated the army from the woods was ablaze. Jemat had ordered the lighting of this uncontrolled fire and he ordered the archers to assemble on this front. The archers, mimicking the attack of the Guardians, aimed their long bows high and released their arrows into the sky so they might descend upon the edge of the woods. Still removed from the orders of a controlling officer, Jemat saw it his duty to take this command.

With his newly staged defence to his liking, he went in search of Izdubar, accompanied by two first liege officers. They found the commander where he had fallen. By Izdubar's side were the last two of the commander's most respected five soldiers, Caden and Zaid.

Caden's eyes were wet with sweat or tears and his voice trembled, 'Kneel close so that you might hear his last words,' he said to those gathered.

Izdubar coughed blood and his bladder popped and wheezed as he released all the wasted food he was carrying. 'You must continue this conquest without me. I appoint this man, Caden, the new commanding officer.' Izdubar took a strained breath and coughed more blood. 'Rest only by day from now on. At dawn ride...' Izdubar coughed once more before his mouth filled with gore and his eyes drew blank.

'At dawn we take the fight to them,' finished Caden. He took a deep breath and stepped away to expel his guts. He wiped his mouth with his sleeve. 'Embarrassing is our loss to so few,' he said as he straightened. He walked back towards the fallen commander. 'Vengeance will be our resolve.' Caden knelt and dipped a finger into the previous leader's mouth. He tasted Izdubar's blood.

This was not a known ritual amongst Akkadian ranks and for a moment all were silent.

'We have pushed them back,' told one of the first liege officers, breaking the uncomfortable silence. 'Jemat made the decisions necessary in Izdubar's absence.'

'Then by your word I appoint him second in command,' said Caden.

Jemat's dark eyes widened with astonishment and he extended his arm to help Caden to his feet.

According to Derahmus, Zaid was one of Izdubar's most respected soldiers and if anyone could have gathered insult from Jemat's appointment as second in command, it was he. Zaid still looked mournfully at Izdubar's lifeless body as he stroked his long, chin beard. He might have been checking if his chin bone was broken by the Guardian's throwing blade.

Jemat watched him carefully, looking for any signs that he felt betrayed for not gaining the offering of second in command.

'I hope that none of you are adverse to my appointment before you as Commander of the North-eastern Frontier,' said Caden to the four Akkadians gathered by his side. 'Let it be shared knowledge the grounds under which this transfer of power was conducted. Together I believe that the five of us can ensure our eastern campaign is successful. Just as you have testified in Jemat's name,' he told the first liege officer who reported on Jemat's defensive strategies, 'I will speak favourably of us all when we return honourably west.'

In separate decrees, Jemat, Zaid and the two unidentified first liege officers exclaimed, 'Hail, Sharru Kin.'

Caden knelt again and rested his palm on Izdubar's forehead. He gently wiped down, closing the fallen leader's eyes. From the ground nearby he picked up Izdubar's bronze helmet and held it aloft, 'Hail, Sharru Kin.'

# 22

# Dawn

*Scribed by Arman,*
*The Always Travelling Guardian.*

I don't know how I would have announced that Lan and Delari had died to the Guardians. Thankfully, Lagesh had volunteered for the cold task because he had seen Lan die in his sight. Delari had died only paces from me but I did not challenge his offer.

Lagesh did not rest before he returned to our new position in the light of early morn. He secured his mare next to the other horses and walked on to where we—Gentuk, Senea and I—stood at the edge of the woods, south of Salarn's tower. It looked like fog was creeping across the plains at the foot of the mountains but it was smoke from the smouldering grass fire.

Gentuk welcomed the return of his youngest son. 'I need your encouragement, Lagesh. Tell me again your vision of horned beasts grazing free in these lands. The Akkadian army is still strong and they will be here before the sun has fully risen.'

'My vision is strong and so I believe in Kar's,' replied Lagesh.

From the cover of the woods, we looked upon a half-completed watchtower. Uk-Ban was to be in control of raising the tower to the next level.

I saw an effort to rebuild and was reminded of more than the loss of Delari and Lan as I looked upon the place where our village once stood. 'Do you bring word from the Guardians at the tower,' I asked Lagesh.

'When I announced Lan's death, Jamine collapsed to the floor,' he said. 'Tahnas could do no more than stare upwards and yell.'

I waited for Lagesh to look my way. 'Did you tell them about Delari and Uk-Ban?'

'I told Unbetum. He was the only one still listening. I told him that Delari had taken the life of the Akkadian commanding officer by forfeiting his own and I told him that Uk-Ban refused to speak to the Akkadians despite his arms hanging loose of his shoulders.'

'We should have followed Unbetum's advice,' I said with regret. I punched the pine next to me with my fist. The tree did not move but some of its bark stayed planted in my bleeding knuckles. 'Mere apparitions he told us to be. Clear in sight, I allowed myself to be. Delari deserved a better fate.'

'Delari is sure to be rewarded in new passage,' promised Gentuk. He looked old in the shaded light at the edge of the woods. It accentuated his bulging eyes from lack of sleep and the slow creep of grey hairs amongst his short-cut hair. 'Today, I propose we follow our new elder's advice intently. Four warriors we are with countless defence amongst the trees. Only here do we stand a chance. We must fight beneath the trees, lest the lives lost already and those we protect be wasted.'

Lagesh startled. 'Uk-Ban, I see him beneath the watchtower.'

The young Guardian was not experiencing a vision. We knew of Uk-Ban's presence.

'He could be by our side,' explained Senea, grabbing his brother by the arm. 'They released him and we could not stop him from walking that way. I think he believes he will not be harmed so long as he remains in the presence of your incomplete tower. The way I see it, he plans to die there.'

'We must call him back,' said Lagesh, pointing across the grass towards Uk-Ban stumbling about beneath the legs of the watchtower.

'We tried to,' I informed, Lagesh. 'The sky is cast in gloom. Even the Gods mourn waking to this day.'

'We can't leave him alone,' decided Lagesh, stepping closer to the edge of the woods. 'His pain must have altered his judgement.'

'It's his choice to be where he is,' confirmed Gentuk. 'We must decide where we will be when the Akkadians arrive.'

I reached out and grabbed Lagesh's wrist before he ventured any closer to the edge of the woods. 'If Uk-Ban survives this battle, I will ensure he is made a Guardian. As Senea said, Uk-Ban could be by our side. He did not come to us because he is protecting our position. The Akkadians let him walk. Know that Akkadian scouts are sure to be watching his every movement. They want us to go to him. They want him to lure us from the trees.'

# 23

# Into the Plains

*Scribed by Enheduanna, Priestess of Ur.*
*The Palace of Sanam-Shimut, Susa.*

B etween the woods and the mountains the army emerged into the long grass of the plains like a shadow in the creeping fog of morning light. Smoke from the burning grass filled the sky in the northwest. The cavalry force was still at least one hundred strong and more than one hundred soldiers marched on foot at the rear, escorting the supply wagons. Led by Caden, a stern looking man with a pronounced jaw and curly, dark hair that was shaved to his scalp around his ears, the Akkadians' plan was simple. They would destroy what remained of the Guardian village and fortify a camp in the open plains before high sun. Come dusk they planned to be rested and ready, this time, to secure their position through the night on high alert. Positioned beyond the range of an arrow from the woods, the guardians of these lands would have to leave cover to launch an attack and their retreat in such a case would be preventable.

Next to Caden, rode Zaid, the only other surviving soldier that was regarded as one of Izdubar's finest warriors. Jemat, and the two remaining officers rode two rows behind. The Akkadians were sharing stories relating to previous encounters with Guardians when they sighted the watchtower upon entering the plains.

Caden held his arm high and signalled those following to assemble.

The officers left Jemat's side and rode the length of the army, confirming Caden's command.

Jemat trotted his horse to the front line and stopped it next to Caden. 'I can ride ahead and check if it is safe to proceed towards the tower,' he told his new commander.

'No, Jemat, I want you by my side.' Caden turned to the soldier he knew best and ordered Zaid to select ten riders and scout ahead. 'Make it clear that they are not to engage. I want them to return to account for the positions and numbers of any enemy force lying in wait. I repeat, they are not to engage.' Like many of the soldiers, Caden used to spend his days working in the fields. That life was long forgotten. He had played a part in the conquering four cities and countless strongholds since enlisting as a soldier beneath Derahmus. War was his game now and he planned to not only defeat the Guardians but also make his name the one that was praised when word of their victory reached his King's ears. 'Pass on the word,' Caden told the first phase of cavalry, 'we will advance slowly but surely until the scouts return.' Caden slid on Izdubar's bronze helmet and tightened the leather strap beneath his chin.

# 24

# The Will of Ishtar

*Scribed by Arman,*
*The Always Travelling Guardian.*

Ten armoured steeds rode towards the watchtower ahead of the army. When they were at an equal distance to the tower, I left the woods and rode out to meet them. I carried my side bow and Gentuk's and planned to take down two of the riders before I retreated to cover. We hoped that the Akkadian riders would follow me to where Gentuk, Senea and Lagesh lay in wait.

I reached the watchtower before them and the Akkadian riders separated in what I saw as an attempt to surround me and prevent my retreat. Uk-Ban cheered for me and I felt guilty for abandoning him so soon. I turned my mare towards the woods and away from the riders who had peeled off in my direction.

One rider gained on me and I released a bolt mid-gallop. It narrowly missed its target. I slowed my mare's gait to try again.

Like startled deer on the hunt, the Akkadian riders turned and bounded away through the grass, returning together to the rest of their herd.

Our plan to slowly dwindle the Akkadians' numbers and along with that, their morale, was always going to be difficult. I now feared the worst after seeing the riders adopt such a defensive stance. Luring the Akkadians into closed confines warfare in the woods was our only hopeful strategy. The army's scouts now knew from which direction we attacked and if they advanced as one force it was sure to be a one-sided fight. I held my open position between the watchtower and the woods as I watched the scouts re-join the front line of their offensive. I imagined the pre-emptive victory talk that would follow.

Gentuk called to me from the woods and I took a moment to find buried hope before returning. I struggled to find it. Laures, the blind woman in Zidon, had told me that I was complete. I had heard it as a complement though now I saw it as a prediction of my end. Kar had more to do, she had said. My role was completed. Maybe I should have joined Uk-Ban beneath the tower and packed a pipe for us both. I returned towards the woods when I saw the three other Guardians walking out to meet me. It was hard to keep my head upright. I did not want them to see the defeat in my eyes. Their eyes, however, were not looking at me. They had ventured from the woods for a clearer view west.

'I knew it,' proclaimed Lagesh. 'It is the will of Ishtar. It will be as Unbetum spoke.'

'We saw them move,' Gentuk told me.

'Saw who move?' I questioned, as I also looked westward towards the army advancing our way through the smoke.

# 25

# Hidden in Plains' Light

*Scribed by Enheduanna, Priestess of Ur.*
*The Palace of Sanam-Shimut, Susa.*

Caden was encouraged by the scouts' report and praised them for avoiding the Guardians' desperate attempt at ambush. 'We will fortify at the watchtower under construction,' he bellowed in an attempt to be heard by all his men. He might have been heard by the first two rows of riders. The army stretched from the base of the foothills and into the open plains. 'We will make necessary preparations to defend ourselves against repeated attacks through the night and begin staged assaults upon those who dwell in the woods on the morrow. When we return to Akkadia, we will be known as the men who claimed the East. Today we fortify, tomorrow we stake claim on these lands.'

Down the sides of the assembled army the officers rode and repeated the commander's message.

An almighty cheer sounded amongst the ranks and the army began advancing again, first the cavalry and then the soldiers on foot. Before the supply wagons were rolling once more, a soldier fell to a descending arrow. Frightened by the surprise attack, the soldiers lagged behind the advancing cavalry. The officers riding the flanks of their advance turned in time to witness a rain of arrows descending from the foothills. They were exposed in the open plains.

'Do not group. Follow the horsemen to the watchtower,' ordered one of the first liege officers.

The soldiers ran from the rain of arrows, though many could not escape fast enough.

Before Caden had a chance to react to this assault, a horde of barbarians stood in view from amongst the grass to the south and loosed arrows at the cavalry unit from the side.

An arrow deflected off Caden's helmet as he heaved on his rein and turned his horse. 'Maintain a course for the tower and keep your distance from the woods,' he ordered as he watched many a rider fall from mount. 'Lead them Jemat,' he then told his second in command before riding in aid of the supply wagons at the rear.

Following the descent of a second rain of arrows, a horde of barbarians charged forwards from the cover of a dry creek bed. These barbarians positioned themselves closer to the supply wagons in the open plains and drew taut their arrows.

Caden's attempt to ready archers came too late. Half of them fell before they had a chance to load an arrow. Surviving soldiers pursued the cavalry east only to encounter the barbarians' side assault. Left with less than ten archers and no more than twenty guards to protect the eight supply wagons, Caden was almost ready to abandon them. He stole a stare east in view of his cavalry unit and saw that they had assembled near the half-completed watchtower without further incident. 'To the woods,' he ordered the men steering the wagons. 'Move towards the woods.'

***

Alone once more in command of the majority, Jemat made another defining decision. 'I must stay,' he told those assembled. 'Half our number must return to protect the supply wagons.'

'I will go. Who is with me?' yelled Zaid. As he rode forth, fifty other willing horsemen joined him in his return to protect the supply wagons.

Jemat turned back to face those who remained. 'Keep watch in all directions,' he told them. 'Those with bows should have them ready.' He watched the riders follow his command. Once a man who dug furrows from dawn to dusk, he was now second in command of the North-eastern Frontier. He let his gaze climb to the top of the uncompleted watchtower. He imagined the view it was intended for as he surveyed the neighbouring woods to the north, the mountains looming in the west and the open plains in every other line of sight. Jemat acknowledged in his tablet sent south that this was land worth fighting for and concluded in reflection that it was men like himself, men who broke the mould in offering themselves further, that made Sargon great. All the riches Jemat dreamed of relied upon returning triumphant. He accounted for twenty-three riders still by his side. Five of these men and two of the horses had been wounded by arrows. He decided it best not to engage any more of these men in battle for the moment. If a cavalry unit numbering fifty could not turn favour then Sharru-kin himself had underestimated the resistance. As Jemat reflected on the events that had led him so far East he noticed a pillar of green smoke rising above the trees in the woods.

'Jemat ... Apologies, my liege,' called one of the soldiers who had acted as a scout prior to the ambush. 'What shall we do with this man?' asked the soldier, pointing beneath the watchtower.

'Let him be. He cannot hurt anyone with his disabled arms.'

'What is he doing?' asked another soldier as a group of riders gathered around the legs of the watchtower.

Jemat ignored the rising smoke for a moment and trotted closer to see what they spoke of.

On the ground, between the legs of the watchtower knelt the old man that had been captured on the previous night. At first glance he appeared to be praying. His shoulders were swollen blue and this impeded the use of his arms. When he lifted his face from the dirt, Jemat realised that he was attempting to draw or write something with his nose.

'What does he write?' Jemat questioned his men.

'I cannot read,' answered the one who had summoned his presence and the gathered riders also shook their heads.

'Can anyone read?' Jemat called out to the rest of the cavalry unit positioned in the grass surrounding the watchtower. He beckoned those who signalled that they could to approach as the injured man continued to scrape words into the dirt with his nose. 'I feel more foolish than this man with dirt on his nose,' said Jemat. 'Twenty-three men we are and only three of us can read.'

'It is not that you cannot read my liege,' began one of the cavalrymen who had answered Jemat's call, 'his etchings make no sense. Crazed the man must be. A day too long he has lived.'

'I care not what makes sense. Tell me what he is he drawing with his face?'

'My name is Subberest, Jemat, and last night I made scout rides at the same time as you. I saw this man brought nigh to death. Stretched by his limbs between two horses he was. That is why he draws with—'

'I know of his injuries, Subberest.' Jemat pointed at the ground. 'Does the man scribe in another language? I see words.'

'I can read three of his words,' interrupted another soldier.

'What are they?' questioned Jemat as he once more surveyed his surrounds in view of another ambush, and glanced back again at the smoke pillar growing darker over the woods.

'God, Garden, Man,' answered the only other soldier fluent in written word who had not already offered his opinion on the crudely scribed words in the earth.

'Yes, that is what he scribes with his nose,' agreed Subberest.

'It could just be that this man is doing all he can to still his pain,' Jemat told the men gathered, now numbering nine by his immediate side at the foot of the watchtower. 'It could be his final prayer.'

'Or a final curse,' suggested Subberest, pointing to the four Guardians now approaching in their direction from the cover of the woods. 'I fought here three harvests ago. We thought we had killed them all. We must kill them all this time.'

'Explain your words now lest they never be known,' Jemat threatened the old man on his knees between the tower's supports.

The man, considered a barbarian or Guardian in same voice, lifted his dusted face from the ground. 'Tell me, Jemat,' he began, 'how well do you know the god who has led you my way?'

Jemat turned to inspect the progress of the four men advancing from the woods before staring more distantly upon the battle still raging closer to the mountains, near the edge of the woods. Behind Jemat, at twenty paces from the incomplete tower, the rest of the cavalry unit, still in his command, were positioned in a defensive arc. 'I know my God, my King, more than I thought possible,' Jemat eventually answered with confidence. 'Rain, Sun and Shelter Gods I once worshipped in Mari to no avail. I thought I was void of a god's influence upon riding east. In consideration of your address, it was indeed Sargon's influence that led me this way. I know his desires as if they are my own. God or not, it is Sargon who will bless my life with riches and status. How well does one know any god apart from thankfulness for the blessings they bestow?'

'Incumbent in your words is my testimony,' said the old man. Droplets of soiled sweat gathered and dropped from his face as he looked up at Jemat. 'In the Garden of the Gods that you unknowingly decimate, you realise your potential. Your God's strength has been shared with you and will continue to be shared. Strike me down in view of your God if you are so sure of your purpose.'

'Allow me Jemat. It would be my honour,' announced Subberest, his scarred face glowing red in the morning sun.

'Stand back,' ordered Jemat, for he saw Subberest as too eager to be known as an unquestioning disciple of Sargon and he felt that some sort of deception was at work. 'Look about you. This man's allies wait at a distance. Let us not hasten their next move.'

'What do you propose?' asked Subberest, his sword still ready to strike.

'Hope, or pray if you like, that Caden wins his battle. My orders were to assemble here at this watch and for us to keep our distance from the woods. Already I have deviated from that simple command in dispatching reinforcements.'

The soldiers present looked at one another and shared their concern through many silent glances.

'Do not let yourselves think that I have been swayed by this lowly man's talk of gods,' Jemat told them. 'Our strength is speed on horseback. That is why we are still here,' he explained as more of the cavalry unit at his disposal approached from where they were positioned defensively around the half-completed tower. 'If Caden and the rest of the army falls, we must be ready for defeat though surrender we will not. Sharru-Kin must be made aware of what happened here. Therefore, I propose that we take defensive measures to prevent ambush and allow for unhindered retreat.'

'And what of this savage?' questioned Subberest.

'This savage,' answered Jemat, 'can write three more words than most of us. Without the need to be shackled he makes for a perfect prisoner. As for his four friends,' Jemat continued, 'so long as they advance no further, we will not engage.'

'The last time I was here, we shackled all prisoners and—'

'I have heard enough from you, Subberest,' shouted Jemat. 'Last time is not this time.' Jemat considered the previous night's ambush and ordered the riders gathered at the tower, apart from the three who could read, to return to their defensive positions. On the side of the watchtower closest the woods he posted eight riders, twice the number of Guardians he could see. He ordered the others to space themselves in the shape of an arrow tip, pointing south. He had one of the soldiers on the eastern defensive side loose an arrow to judge a safe distance and they stagnated their defensive line in view of its fall. When all was to his liking, he returned to the watchtower and tethered his horse to one of the support posts. Two of the soldiers who could read were waiting for their next order. 'Where is Subberest?' Jemat asked these soldiers.

'He said he was needed in the defence,' answered one.

Jemat took a deep breath and exhaled. 'Then it will be only you two, who take word west. Prepare your horses and fill your water bladders. You will ride south to Hidalu and make your way west via Susa. I, Jemat of Mari, will stay to the end.'

The soldiers began preparing for the ride by removing the heavy, leather armour from the flanks of their horses.

Jemat watched the elderly man drawing with his nose for a while. He was about to say something to the man when he realised that he too was being watched. Near the support post on the opposite corner there was a stack of thin pine trunks that were stripped of their branches and ready for the next stage of construction.

Subberest leant against the stack, staring back at him.

Jemat walked his way, stepping wide of the old man who was on his knees with his face to the ground.

Subberest patted the log next to him. 'Take a seat. You need your strength.'

'Every other soldier is on guard duty or fighting for their life and you feel it is time to rest.'

'Someone has to watch the prisoner. Sit down and share my view for a moment.'

Jemat glanced about and noticed some sense in the soldier's position. He sat down next to him.

'We can see our prisoner and our men posted to the south and east.' Subberest leant forwards and aimed his point in line with the lay of the logs. We can see the guard who stands directly in front of the Guardians. It is strategic that they do not see us all.'

'What of Caden and his battle to our west? Do we rest blind to their fight?'

'Stand and look west. You will just tire your eyes to a battle that cannot be judged from such distance. Look at those you can see and notice how they look at each other. You will know when you are needed. Do you see how your soldiers keep looking to those on guard either side of them? They are scared.'

'We think alike, Subberest. I regret raising my

voice to you earlier.'

Subberest smiled and tapped one of his large ears. 'You should listen when you cannot see. Do you know who taught me that?'

'Was it Derahmus?'

'It was Derahmus but he learnt this from the Guardians. Before you shouted your orders, I wanted to tell you that our first campaign east ended poorly because we took prisoners. Once more we hold a Guardian and they want him back.'

Jemat looked through the grass at the old man and then tilted his nose to the sky. 'Do you smell it?'

'Smell what?' asked Subberest.

'A fire burns deep in the woods. Too large to be a camp fire, it could be a smoke signal for the barbarians.'

'I saw it. Is it needed? Your grass fire would have been seen as far north as our fort.'

The two riders announced that they were ready to depart.

Jemat stood and looked again at the pillar of smoke, as dark as a pine trunk, that grew above the woods. He lowered his stare to the eight riders positioned between the Guardians and the half-completed watchtower. The Akkadians tempted the Guardians to engage by rousing their horses and then quickly restraining them. Slowly the horsemen edged forwards into the measured arrow range. Jemat turned to his two riders. 'Be sure to mention my fire and the one not lit by Akkadians.'

# 26

# To Live or Die

*Scribed by Arman,*
*The Always Travelling Guardian.*

I was the only Guardian on horseback. Gentuk and his two sons had wandered from the woods for a better view of what their eyes failed to fathom—the valley bandits attacking the Akkadians. We were fifty paces from the woods and it was another hundred paces to the eight mounted Akkadians positioned between Lagesh's tower and us. We faced our foe without the safety of the woods or the shelter of night. The morning sun only warmed one side of me. My numbed fingers gripped the handle of my side bow like they were my toes.

'If you are confident of your aim, let a bolt fly,' said Gentuk as he loaded a bolt in the side bow I had returned to him.

Lagesh added his advice. 'Wait for one of them to be distracted and take him down like you would a grazing deer.'

I glared down at them from my mount. 'All it takes is one of the herd to spot me and a bolt true to target will be wasted,' I summoned a reserved smile. 'I never told you about my time with Tuley, did I?'

'Tuley's lone fight in Zidon or his union with Anava?' questioned Senea with a sigh and the slightest turn of his head. 'You mentioned both many times last night.'

'There are those tales,' I said, 'but did I tell that I tattooed him again myself. In his father's name and Arcobon's it was cut. Kar agreed that the sacred offering could not be withheld any longer.'

Gentuk smiled. He looked warm in his thick tunic and the grey streaks in his hair shone like silver. 'I hope I get a chance to see your work, Arman.'

'Yes. If I had not blessed Tuley with such courage, he might have been here this day.' I strained my eyes open. My memories were making me tired and there was more I needed to do before I died. 'When I was young, I thought my tattoo only gave me strength at sea. The strength to endure all one day and be ready to do it again the next is the meaning I learnt late.' I looked down at Senea and Lagesh. 'Do not be too quick to name yourself to a cause not fully understood, young Guardians.'

'Wise words, Arman,' praised Gentuk. 'Lagesh, my son, I pray your true calling is many harvests away. Here in the plains you must live not die. Just as I sent word of Akkadians moving east three harvests ago, your greatest work will not need a sword. I foresee a tattoo of a completed tower on your first boy's shoulder.'

'I see that too,' I said, scratching my beard beneath my chin. 'Your first boy will be able to see over the woods and beyond the plains from your tower. He will predict the movement of deer and know of rain before the clouds assemble.'

'Unlike me,' said Senea with his eyes fixed on the mounted soldier positioned directly in front of the tower. 'Here I am told I will live and die.'

I turned my aim on the mounted soldier caught in Senea's stare, and the Akkadian lowered his bow to his side. 'Do not accept an end so willingly, Senea,' I said, admiring the stance of the Guardians standing next to me. Senea stood in front of his father with his long sword drawn. Lagesh looked as wild as Kar did before he had to replace his shoulder fur with a coverall in our journey west. 'I thought our fight was in vain this morn. Look at us now. We stand in sight of our enemy. There is more we can do. Tuley and I dressed as Akkadians in Zidon and I still have my costume. I could wear it to get close to them.'

'I don't think you'll need to,' said Gentuk. He looked west towards the supply wagons that had retreated to the edge of the woods.

The bandits, whom I'm certain were summoned to duty by Kar, had surrounded the wagons and they pursued fleeing soldiers and mounted Akkadians through the drifting smoke of the grass fire and into the woods. 'I'm wasted here,' I declared.

'Do not avert your aim, Arman,' said Gentuk.

'I must.' I switched control of my side bow to my weak arm as I reached my sword arm down and beckoned Gentuk's hand.

Gentuk handed his loaded weapon to Lagesh before he grabbed my arm and climbed onto my mare behind me.

'Maintain our stance as long as you can,' I told him. 'You are needed here. If I leave now, I can get between the Akkadians and the tower and turn those fleeing back to the plains.'

Gentuk took my side bow and readied his aim as I dismounted. 'Will you take my mare?'

'I accept the exchange. Far from our foe I will leave her tethered.'

'I will go with you, Arman,' said Senea.

'Stay with me, Senea' said Gentuk, his head jerking to his son's backwards step.

I watched an Akkadian trot his horse in a circle and Gentuk adjusted his aim.

The Akkadian stilled his steed and the standoff continued.

Senea approached his father. 'I mean not to abandon you. Akkadians have entered the woods. If we do not flush them out, the tower will never be safe.'

Gentuk, with his side bow still raised, lowered a hand and Senea held it. 'Salarn told a story once of a lost traveller living outside Khorsabad when it was still a village,' said Gentuk. 'The lost man snuck inside at night to pilfer from their stores and watch their women sleep.' Gentuk squeezed his eldest boy's hand. 'I asked you to stay for my own protection but you know what you must do. Lagesh and I will retreat on shared mount if we must. I only ask to see you before the moon.'

'I'll return with light to see your face.' Senea slid his hand from his father's grip and stepped towards his brother. He placed his hand on the loaded side bow Lagesh held. 'Be ready to hand this to father and mount quickly.'

I began walking towards the woods. It was hard to slow my pace to such an amble. I had run more in the last few days than I had in all the seasons before. The warmth now on my chilled side was encouragement. I wriggled my numbed fingers. Behind me, I heard Senea's hastened steps through the grass. 'Step slow, Senea,' I said without turning my head. 'We don't want the Akkadians to care for our departure.'

'Will we ride to the tower first?'

'We will ride fast that way to ensure we are ahead of the Akkadians retreat and then return to find them.'

*** 

When we tethered the horses deep in the woods, I thought again of Senea's question. Green smoke mixed with the morning light and stirred between the pine trunks with each gust of wind that penetrated the woods. Hollers of pain called us west yet a cracking sound, as loud as a bough breaking, had me turn my ears in the direction of the tower. Was it a trickery of sound? If Senea had even opened his mouth to speak at this moment, I would have committed to a retreat to the tower.

He stowed his side bow on the mount of Kar's stallion, Har Man. Senea's mare was still in Kar's care. At least she was when I parted company with him in the mountains.

I liked that Senea left his side bow behind. It was a sign that he wanted to fight as a Guardian with his weapon of choice. I knew this feeling. When Kar and I faced the Stanf Warriors in Pled and all seemed to be going against us, I had one last desire. I wanted to swing my sword again.

We headed west, bounding through the under-growth and only when I was committed to the run could I name the sound I had heard at the point of retreat to the tower. It was the sound of twigs and branches giving light to the larger log of a fire.

I fell twice as I tried to avoid fallen pinecones and duck low branches. Senea also fell when he slid on pine needles delicately coating a raised root. The obstacles we faced were well known to us but rarely did we move with such pace through the woods. Even my memories of running into the woods to avoid scribing lessons with Verian felt as unfamiliar as a dream. I slid to a stop behind a trunk when I heard a distant scream.

Senea stopped behind a tree ten paces from me. He pointed southwest.

I crouched beneath the drifting smoke and peered through the labyrinth of pine trunks. We were closer to the mountains, somewhere between Salarn's tower and the plains.

'Over here,' said Senea.

I looked at him. He was not calling to me. His voice sounded different. He'd adopted an Akkadian accent.

Hidden behind a thick trunk, Senea only held out his hand to wave someone closer.

I rotated on my haunches and peered out from the other side of the trunk that hid me.

From behind a low thicket of red berry bushes, forty paces closer to the plains in the south, two men raised their heads. One wore a leather archer's helmet.

I leant back behind the tree and slowly slid my

sword from its sheath. A flap of skin, still attached to strands of dark hair, fell at my feet and dried blood made my bronze blade appear as dark as pine bark. Some fresh gore would make it easier to clean. I rested my head back against the pine's trunk and listened. Two, three, six, seven, I counted the movement of different men. Nine. I looked to my side and watched Senea draw his sword. Like mine, it needed a clean.

He stood with his back to a pine and held his sword upright in his grip, like a reflection of the tree's reach to the canopy.

'Where are you?' questioned an Akkadian and this soldier was not the one closest to Senea and me. The squish of pine needles revealed the closer creeping step of four more Akkadians on the other side of the pine at my back.

I could have surprised them sooner with a battle cry, in the hope this would turn them to the plains. But they knew what waited for them there. They had fled from the plains. If I'd announced myself any sooner, they would have fortified at the red berry bush thicket or dispersed in different directions. Senea's call had drawn them out of hiding and left them grouped. It was our turn to reveal ourselves and we had to reveal ourselves as vengeful demons, mere apparitions of defiance. That was Unbetum's advice and now was the time. My only wish was that Kar was with us for this fight. I wanted to see my young friend swing his staff in the woods.

Senea tipped his upright sword to the east.

I nodded and tipped mine to the west.

Senea hollered like a bandit as he ran east and hid

behind the next tree.

The feet of at least ten men shifted.

I rolled my weight around the trunk that had kept me hidden and swung my sword at shoulder height towards the closest soldier. It severed his head at the back of his neck. His legs surrendered beneath him and I saw more faces. The wide eyes of an Akkadian archer met the next sweep of my blade. With gore from his broken face still trailing from my sword, I stepped to the side and blocked a strike from an Akkadian with a bronze helmet and breastplate.

The archer, behind the armoured Akkadian, flexed his bow.

I sliced at his gloved hand that steadied the arrow's tip and his arrow was propelled upwards through the branches. Before I could turn, the Akkadian in the bronze helmet, surely an officer, drove his blade at my chest. His blade scraped against mine all the way to the hilt. I stepped to the side and swung my sword in a full circle to fend the immediate strike of two other soldiers.

The soldiers stepped away defensively and the officer was upon me again with his long sword ready to thrust.

A shriek of pain from the archer behind him stole his attention.

Senea had cut the archer from his spine to his gut and, like a darting bird, he had disappeared again amongst the trees.

I remained exposed, unable to retreat from the repeated strikes of two soldiers and an officer. My broad sword bunted their blades aside as I stepped backwards.

One, three, two, I found a pattern in their strikes. My foot felt the arch of a root and then my back pressed against the pine that had kept me hidden for a moment before this fight. One, three, I counted again and chose the moment to attack.

My bronze blade cut the first soldier's throat. With my arms and shoulders committed to the swing, it continued its sweep towards the next soldier's face. Through the second soldier's cheek my blade swung, shattering his teeth. His face lurched to the assault as my trusted bronze weapon continued towards the officer's neck. My shoulder faced the officer as my blade completed its strike and his long bronze blade was raised to meet mine.

I predicted his blade surrendering as the weight behind my swing maintained its path to his exposed throat between his bronze helmet and breastplate. Our eyes met for an instant as our weapons clashed. There was a flash of light and a sound even more startling. My blade snapped. My gripped hands kept swinging. I tried to brace my foot against a root. My foot slid. There was another snapping sound as the muscles on my inner thighs gave way to my splayed legs. Left in my grip was a sword with a blade the length of its hilt.

The officer stumbled before turning to face me again. He raised his long sword above his shoulders.

Sitting on my bottom, I raised my broken weapon.

He paused.

Senea dashed through the drifting smoke behind him and took the life of the soldier with shattered teeth.

The officer brought his sword down upon me.

I parried it to one side and it cut my shoulder, and sliced bark from the pine with its tip.

He readied himself to strike again with it held horizontally in his grip.

Behind him, four more soldiers approached. Behind these soldiers, mounted Akkadians trotted my way from the red berry thicket. I felt I only had the strength to block his sweep once more. My hands were committed to this defence and I don't think I could have stood without them. The pain from the torn muscles in my legs filled my mouth with spittle and convulsed my gut.

'Are you a Guardian?' asked the officer. His face was shadowed with light piercing the canopy only illuminating his bronze helmet as he stood over me.

I swallowed before I could speak. 'I am.'

He almost looked away as Senea attacked the soldiers behind.

Senea cut the arm of one soldier before the rest pursued him back to the tree he had attacked from.

The officer's legs tensed and he swung his blade at me.

I met his blade's sweep with my broken weapon and leant to one side to save my head.

His blade passed over me and as he stiffened his arm to strike again, an arrow deflected off his helmet. He turned.

I lifted myself with a groan. If my broken sword was a finger's length longer, I could have cut him down at his legs. I didn't have my throwing blades but I had a blade that could be thrown.

The officer pointed his sword towards the plains

and the Akkadians approaching on horseback hastened their trot.

Dark figures stalked them through the stirring smoke and mottled light.

An arrow met with the officer's breastplate and fell to the ground.

He turned to face me.

I thrust my broken sword at his face.

He fell upon me. His face was spurting blood from his nose and his cracked jaw tried to speak into my ear as it collapsed with a crunch on my shoulder.

I lifted him from me so that I could withdraw my broken blade from his face.

The mounted Akkadians were upon me. Leading them was another bronze helmeted officer. His steed's flanks, chest and head were covered with leather amour. The officer's body and head were protected by bronze. He raised his sword by his side, as his steed's trot became a fast canter. The mounted Akkadians behind him followed his lead and hastened their trot as they raised their swords.

Soaked in the previous officer's blood, my broken sword sailed smoothly from my fingers. It rotated once before its broken tip met the stretched leg of the officer's steed.

The horse collapsed forwards in its canter and, not understanding what had happened, the officer tried to stay mounted. The riders following him, cantered past me, either side of the pine at my back.

Bellowing with pain, the horse hurled its head upwards as it fell on one flank and slid through the woods' bedding of pine needles.

The slide must have almost twisted the officer's trapped leg from his hip before the steed came to a stop between my spread legs. The officer still held his sword and he pointed it at me.

I thrust my head away from its reach and hit it against the trunk of the pine behind. Once more, there was only a finger length of blade required. The tip of his sword tickled my nose and the head of his steed knocked in my lap. I rested my hand on the horse's jaw. 'Be calm. We will go together to our next life.'

The horse, with her snout to mine, bared her teeth and whinnied.

The officer tried again to cut me with his out-reached sword. He convulsed his body that was trapped by one leg beneath his steed.

Without a weapon and braced against the tree by the fallen steed, I could only think of my end. What would Delari say if he was with me now? Would he tell me that with my legs still attached I could stand? Would my trader friend remind me of my tattoo's meaning or welcome me joining him in new passage?

The officer, trapped beneath his fallen horse, stabbed his blade with an agonising groan and pierced my cheek as I turned my head.

'Use your strength to end your steed's pain,' I told him, stilling its head.

The weight of the horse's head fell limp in my lap and I looked upon a valley bandit readying the tension on another arrow. He stood near the horse's legs. Blackened by mud, he looked like death's shadow. I turned my stare back to the Akkadian trapped beneath his steed.

Another valley bandit, also dressed in mud, and with a white streak of paint across his face, had a bronze sword pressed to the officer's throat. His foot pinned the trapped man's sword to the ground. The bandit faced me. 'Do you have a name?'

'Arman,' I told him.

'Do you have a name?' the bandit asked the officer. His blade was still pressed against the Akkadian's throat.

'Do you have a name?' the Akkadian questioned back, defiantly. His bronze helmet had twisted on his face and he stared at the bandit through one large eye.

'I have a name,' said the bandit with the white streaked face. 'It is one you will never hear.'

'Wait,' the trapped Akkadian yelled. 'Know my name is Caden. I am the commanding officer. I ask that you surrender me or my body to my army so that they may take me home.'

'My name is Omah,' said the bandit.

Caden turned his head and the press of the bandit's sword followed. 'Are you a Guardian?'

'A Guardian?' Omah looked at me. He planted his other foot on Caden's bronze helmet and pressed it back to expose the bulge in the Akkadian's neck. 'I am Gutian.'

A victory cheer sounded through the woods as the other Gutians who had chased the fleeing Akkadians arrived to see Omah cutting the commanding officer's head from his body. Those still at a distance heard the call of their tribesmen and hollered victoriously in response.

'Do you know this man?' asked Omah, lifting the

bronze helmet.

Caden's head was still held in place by his chin-strap and four arrow-wielding bandits surrounded me. 'He is an Akkadian,' I said. 'They all look the same to me.'

Omah laughed and waved his archers away with his sword.

A familiar face emerged from the woods in their departure.

'Do you know him?' asked Omah.

I nodded. 'Senea is a Guardian like me.'

Omah held the commander's head above his shoulder and hollered.

His victory cry was repeated by bandits in the woods, in the plains and through the mountains.

Senea offered his hand to help me stand.

I shook my head. 'Leave me and return to your father.'

'I'll leave you to fetch our horses,' said Senea.

Omah looked at me on the ground and Senea standing next to me with his sword lowered. He smiled and held the Akkadian's head high again. Once more his victory holler was repeated as far as the plains and the mountains to our west.

***

Senea carried me on shared mount and led Gentuk's mare to the edge of the woods, near to his brother's tower. The sun had begun its creep behind the Zagros Mountains and a hundred or more bandits, Gutians, advanced east across the plains. Gentuk and Lagesh still stood between the woods and the defensive line of mounted Akkadians separating us from the watchtower under construction.

'Your father's arm must be tired,' I said to Senea as he trotted towards them from the cover of the woods. I lost sight of the advancing Gutians in the blaze of the sun. Ahead I saw Lagesh turn and alert his father of our approach.

'We should return to the tower,' said Senea.

'I agree. There's not much left in me this day.'

Gentuk spoke to us as we trotted closer. 'I never thought I would say it,' he said with a breath of astonishment in his voice.

'Say it father,' beckoned Lagesh, making his father release a restrained laugh.

'A horde of bandits approach us from the west. They are many and we are four.'

'Are we afraid?' I asked as Senea stilled Kar's stallion.

'I am shaking,' admitted Gentuk, 'though it is not fear that consumes me.'

'Stay mindful, Guardians,' I alerted. 'The Akkadians may retreat to the trees. You have held them to position all day, Gentuk. We cannot risk that hold now.'

'What do you see, Arman?' inquired Gentuk.

From behind Senea's shoulder, I saw the same restless row of mounted Akkadians in front of Lagesh's tower. Through the blinding light of the setting sun, I saw the steady approach of Gutians. 'Our east is undefended but we are the only ones preventing an escape into the woods. The valley bandits advance in an increasingly wide arc making Akkadian retreat in our direction, most likely.'

'Why are the soldiers not already retreating?' asked Lagesh.

'A good question,' I answered.

Senea turned and looked past me towards the woods. He gripped my chin with his fingers and turned my head to share his view.

A thick plume of smoke rose above the woods from where the tower was.

'What are they doing?' Lagesh asked with mounting concern. He looked towards his watchtower in the plains and the Akkadians grouping beneath. The defensive line of mounted Akkadians had also retreated.

Gentuk studied the twisted expression on his youngest son's face before looking at me for an explanation. His stare focussed on the plume of smoke behind.

Senea pushed my hand from his shoulder and lifted his leg so that he could slide from mount.

Without his support, I collapsed on the stallion's neck. My legs were incapable of holding me upright. I took a moment to gain the strength to push myself upright again. With my head resting on the mare's neck, I saw Senea lock the tension on a bolt in his side bow. He fastened a strip of leather to the bow's wooden handle and strapped it to his back.

The Gutians slowed their advance through the grass and a disconcerting holler replaced their victory cry.

Senea saw his younger brother fall to his knees in front of him. He rushed to his side and forcibly turned Lagesh's head to face him. 'Is this part of your vision?'

Tears spilled from Lagesh's eyes and he released a

painful moan.

When Senea stepped past his brother, I did not think to call him back. I lifted my head so that I could see where he went.

After taking twenty paces closer to the watchtower through the grass, Senea turned to face the woods again. 'How?' he cried out. 'I am a fool for leaving your side again, Yanereu,' he cursed himself.

I lifted myself on my mount and turned to gaze upon smoke towering into the sky. Senea and Yanereu were both far from home when they first met in Ebla. She told him, in their first meeting, the few words she had learnt in preparation. Yanereu had told Senea that her people wanted to be one with the Guardians. Against his will Senea was not able to complete his quest to rescue the Pledians. It was with much resentment that he was forced to return east before the quest was complete. More attentive to Delari's words of advice he therefore should have been. Delari had told him in Nineveh that his Princess was not safe because he was not by her side. And Salarn's last words predicted his fall in the East. He turned his back on the woods and paced towards the half-completed watchtower.

'I wish my last stand could have been made in view of my princess and baby boy,' he cried.

By the time Gentuk and I could manage a moment to avert our stare from the hypnotic smoke plume, Senea was only paces from the watchtower.

Gentuk grabbed hold of my hand and placed it on the rein.

In a state of indescribable bliss I froze. Gentuk must have felt it too because his hand on mine went limp. I watched Senea approach the watchtower.

'Can you feel it?' Gentuk asked me.

'I feel her,' I answered. 'It is like a final hug. All her troubles are mine now.'

'Look at my boy,' admired Gentuk.

'He shows no fear,' I mused. Carrying me, Kar's stallion trotted after the displaced Guardian.

Senea walked past a stack of pine trunks and between the supports of the half-completed watchtower. He looked down at Uk-Ban as he passed but said nothing. Senea strode towards the Akkadians now cowering together as one force on the southern side of the watchtower. 'Take my blood for I am nothing without her,' he yelled.

The mounted Akkadians circled their steeds before him, neither advancing nor retreating.

Uk-Ban called the lone Guardian to a halt. 'Senea, surrender as I have.'

Senea turned his attention from the twenty horsemen he was calling to duel. He looked back at Uk-Ban and drew his sword.

Uk-Ban, the last descendent of Catal-Huyuk, stumbled to his feet beneath the supports of the watchtower led by two Akkadians on foot.

One of these Akkadian soldiers, who had a scarred face and large ears, was quick in placing himself before the other. He drew his sword on Senea before the Guardian had made sense of their ambush. The wide sweep of his sword cut Senea's tunic and drew blood from his chest. The Akkadian swung his sword back for a finishing blow and this time Senea blocked its strike front on.

'Stand back, Subberest,' ordered the other Akkadian.

Subberest ignored the order, confident of victory. 'I have killed a Guardian before, Jemat.' He pushed hard against the sword that had deflected his finishing blow and a test of strength ensued. When Subberest felt that the Guardian was committed, he dropped to his knees, aiming to cut Senea's legs with a low swing of his blade.

Senea leapt over the man and his trailing blade removed the Akkadian's scalp. He landed awkwardly and rolled back onto his feet. When he turned in his stand between the legs of the watchtower, he realised too late how close he was now to the other Akkadian.

Jemat stabbed at him and, if not for Uk-Ban standing between at the crucial moment, Senea would have felt the blade's bite.

With arms incapable of clutching himself in agony, Uk-Ban could only scream as Jemat's sword sliced down his bony chest between the open front of his hide vest. The bladed tip withdrew back through a gaping gash and Uk-Ban fell to the ground. The force of his impact with the ground pushed his guts from his body.

Senea slid the loaded side bow he carried from where it was slung on his back and aimed it at Jemat. He stepped towards him and encountered Subberest again.

The over-confident Akkadian was unable to see through the blood that lapped down over his brow despite continuous attempts to wipe it clear.

Senea stuck him half-heartedly three times with his sword before pushing him aside with his foot in his advance towards Jemat.

'Retreat. Return west,' Jemat ordered the surviving cavalry. 'Tell our King what happened here. Tell our King that I, Jemat, second in command of the North-eastern Frontier stayed and kept fighting.'

It was a disorganised departure as the horsemen rode east and others west before regrouping and challenging the seemingly thin barbarian numbers, preventing escape to the south. Previously unsighted Gutians appeared before them and Jemat could have only counted the unhindered escape of three before his own safety required attention.

Senea pointed his blood-coated sword at Subberest and tilted the aim of his side bow to Jemat's head.

Subberest, already slowly dying, begged for forgiveness. 'I have a family. Spare my life,' he pleaded. His scarred face was not recognisable beneath the sheeting blood from his scalp.

Jemat stepped back defensively.

'Swing your sword,' screamed Senea. He lowered his loaded side bow and let it hang in its sling. 'I have never seen eyes as dark as yours.' He stared deep into Jemat's eyes as the Akkadian stepped away. 'My best friend once tried to tell me that your King was a god,' he told Jemat, pointing his sword to emphasise his message. 'Pray he was not right, for a mockery of such title you make today. You took my princess's life and for that I will cut out your heart and watch it dry beneath the desert sun.'

'Let me speak first of my new God,' pleaded Jemat.

Senea shifted his sword towards Subberest and watched the soldier drop to his knees. The soldier's hands were still clutching the bleeding flap of his scalp that dangled near his ear.

'I do not know of the princess you speak of,' said Jemat, 'though hear me when I say that a woman worth fighting for, or a pillar of smoke that stops an advancing army, is cause enough.' Jemat knelt before Senea's sword. 'My life is nothing to you. To your God though, or upon your victory fire I can become part of the new garden. See me as a weed or dry soil if nothing more. Take my life with more reason than vengeance. Listen to your God's dying wish.'

Senea pointed his sword west. 'What do you know of the Gods? Do you think that the savages who surround us, and cry at the sky, are my kinsmen? Did you realise before leaving the West that you were destined to face a Guardian.'

'No. I know. I know nothing anymore,' stuttered Jemat. He let his sword rest on the ground where he knelt and pointed at the sky above the woods.

Senea lowered his pointed blade to Subberest's face. 'What about you, bleeding man? Did you think your God would reward you for slaughtering savages? Did you think Ishtar would bed you in victory?'

Subberest spread his blood-coated palms in surrender.

Senea paced back and forth in front of the Akkadians on their knees. 'Yanereu is sure to be a prisoner, for not even an Akkadian could strike down one so beautiful. I will exchange you men for her or inflict all necessary evil should our exchange not be agreed upon.'

Jemat bent even lower so that his face was pressed

into the dirt and pointed frantically at the thickening pillar of smoke.

Senea brought his swaying sword to rest. He looked over Jemat's head to the woods and the smoke rising from where the Guardian tower stood. The smoke was thick and the colour of shrubs that grow where there is no light. It hung low over the woods' canopy and sent a single shaft high into the sky like the desperate reach of one drowning beneath. Where the smoke reached its highest point, it billowed into the shape of a face.

'A woman?' Senea shouted. 'Not Yanereu,' he declared. 'Why do I feel so light?' When Senea looked back at the Akkadians kneeling before him, Jemat had reclaimed his sword. In a state of bemusement Senea was not able to raise his own blade fast enough in defence.

Jemat stood quickly with his sword thrusting forwards.

Senea closed his eyes and felt nothing.

Jemat lurched in his strike before falling face down. A bronze bolt stemmed from his spine.

Gentuk trotted my mare closer and aimed his other side bow.

'No, father' said Senea in defence of Subberest. 'He has surrendered and denounced his false God. Let him die slowly and have time to reflect.'

Gentuk lowered his aim and climbed from mount.

'Where is Lagesh?' asked Senea, looking about to sight his younger brother.

'He is returning to the tower,' I told Senea as I looked down at Uk-Ban, my head resting on the mare's thick neck. 'We will wait for them here.'

'Them?' questioned Senea. 'Who do you think has survived?'

I lifted my head and faced Senea. 'Did you not ride out in view of a God's face finally revealed for all to see?'

'Did you see her face, Senea?' furthered Gentuk.

'All I could see was her face,' replied Senea. 'I must return to her.'

'Senea,' yelled Gentuk, gripping his son's sword arm. 'You will wait here until the god has made passage. Forgive me for letting you advance alone for I thought you understood what you were doing.'

When Gentuk released Senea's arm, the young Guardian lashed out with anger, slashing the grass before him and startling Kar's stallion.

I flopped onto Har Man's neck before I could brace myself. 'Stanf,' I whispered.

Har Man's ear twitched towards my dangling head and he stilled his hooves.

The only surviving Akkadian stood and faced Senea with his palms outright in a continued display of surrender. 'I too thought you knew,' said Subberest with blood coating his face and dripping from his chin. 'We were defeated before your God. The Akkadians are not responsible for killing your princess.'

'No one has killed your princess, Senea.' Gentuk knelt next to Uk-Ban.

'As your father instructed, we will wait here for the Guardians to arrive,' I told Senea. 'Pray with me for the Mother God, Ki.'

Senea watched his father close Uk Ban's lifeless eyes.

The Gutians continued in their advance towards the watchtower and that is where Senea stood, at a loss as to where he should be. Once more he looked upon the pillar of smoke rising from the woods. 'Yanereu, seek me out once more and I vow never to leave your side again,' he pleaded.

# 27

# As Promised

*Scribed by Kar.*

High above the watchtower and above the Gutians advancing towards those sheltered beneath, flew a bird as dark as night. It turned northward towards the woods and circled those looting the supply wagons before soaring across the open plains towards six men at the bottom of the rise of a foothill of the Zagros Mountains. Elkin extended his arm and Karun landed gracefully.

'Does it bring news?' asked Damir, the leading chieftain of the Gutians.

'What do you think?' replied Elkin. 'It is a bird. It does not say much.'

The two other Gutian chieftains present seemed disappointed.

'The bird of night only carries bad news,' Harnsek, son of Damir, told them. 'Will our victory fire burn tonight without the presence of the one who it is owed?' He faced me with his brow raised questioningly.

'I hear you, Damir. It is my time to depart.' I pointed to the bird and it stepped along Elkin's stretched arm towards my hand. 'The bird has a name. He is called Karun.'

'We will not hold you to your promise,' confided Harnsek, 'not after all that has happened.'

'I am held despite.' I touched my neck and felt how cool it was with my hair now cut short. I touched what remained of my left ear and flinched to the pain. I looked at the weapons in the hands of the men next to me. My weapon of choice was not in my hand. I had not seen my staff since my fight with the Gutians. It was needed where I was going and I missed it more than my hair. 'I will let it be known that it is the Gutians who protect the East. The West will learn from me that one's neighbours are their closest allies, not their greatest foes. Never too soon will they understand a loss as grand as that of Mother Ki.'

Harnsek, Elkin and three Gutian chieftains bowed their heads to me.

I began my next, long journey by first walking up the hill and away from the plains and all those I knew.

'The women will have supplies waiting for your journey, Kar,' Harnsek called out before I disappeared amongst the trees.

I looked back. 'I hope they have my staff.'

Elkin turned concernedly to those by his side. 'There is nothing stopping any of you from going with him or delaying his departure so that another Guardian might consult him first,' he advised the gathered chieftains.

'We have made necessary arrangements,' Damir responded on behalf of the Gutians. He raised his bird headed club and hollered a victory cry.

Across the plains and through the woods Gutians repeated his call.

Elkin tilted his arm to the sky and Karun flapped his wings and flew east towards the smoke from the Guardian tower. 'I will go with you, Kar,' he said.

I waited as Elkin walked slowly up the hill. He walked steadily but he looked older than Salarn and, until two nights ago, I did not think he ventured from his cave other than to set a boar trap. 'How far will you go with me?' I asked as he approached.

'Let us first see what the Gutians have prepared for you.'

We walked on, following a path through the trees, south of the Guardians' regular passage through the mountains. I saw the place where Harnsek and Omah had stepped from the trees to watch me uncover my boar trap. Senea had ridiculed me for leaving the animal that would have fed us. Harnsek later claimed the boar and left gold. From this high vantage point I looked back once more at where I had lived in the open plains and then later in the neighbouring woods. As the sun fell in the west it illuminated the green, smoke-filled sky. Two fires burned in Balih Woods. The smoke rising from my sacred tree gathered with the plume billowing into the sky from the Guardian tower.

Elkin stood next to me, sharing the view. 'Salarn spoke of this day. Do you know who did the deed?'

'My father, Unbetum,' I replied, not knowing how he had arranged for both fires to burn at the same time.

Elkin nodded. 'The Gutians will attribute your name to this spectacle. Your name, Kar, will travel before you.' He turned and stared north along the shadowed mountain range. 'You said you would travel to Borujerd first.'

'In Borujerd I can announce defeat of the Akkadian army from where they departed. And Arman told me there is a man there, maybe more than one, who will support my quest.' I looked at Elkin and thought of his brother, Ronses. 'My final destination is the place you were born. How would you make passage to the Island of Kings?'

Elkin's lips thinned with a smile. 'I know that heading south from the mouth of the Euphrates is an unnecessary long and perilous crossing of the Southern Sea. Remember your Guardian maps and know that there are better points of departure.'

The maps were etched in my memory and, more than that, I knew the way to the Southern Sea via the night sky. From the roof of the Guardian tower, my mind had travelled that way each time I had recounted the course to Salarn. The sky had become as familiar as a face.

Elkin tapped my arm and tilted his baldhead towards a Gutian woman waiting amongst the trees behind us. 'They await your return, Kar.'

She walked ahead and we followed her up the foothill and between the trees and down into the valley on the other side.

The vision I had received at the tree had ended when I faced the Southern Sea, so I did not know if I would ever see my homeland again. I did not need to know. In the real world that Salarn had showed me, only necessary thoughts were realised. My thoughts were focused on my journey to Borujerd and how I, looking like a battle-battered boy, could convince others to join me. The white tunic I had acquired on the boat to Assur was now brown with dried blood. I would need new clothes to enter a city without drawing unwanted attention. More than a replacement tunic, I thought of a costume that might help convince others to join me in my quest to fight a God King. Arman had left me all the Guardian silver we carried and I knew its worth. In the cities I could use some of the silver to acquire goods required in the next city in my travels. City after city, I planned to travel south, using the proceeds of trade to recruit those necessary for my final fight.

The Gutian woman led Elkin and I to the door of a tall hut in their village in the tree engulfed valley. A large fire burned in the clearing between the huts and, above us, the treetops swayed in the last light of day. She signalled for us to enter the tall hut before stepping back amongst the other women and children gathered outside.

Nearby, I could see the grouping of huts where the Gutians had surrounded me. The sight made me think of my many wounds and I reached for my ear that hurt the most.

A Gutian woman grabbed my arm. 'Do not touch.'

I let her lower my arm.

'Let it heal,' she said. 'Before you enter the land of sand we will bathe your wounds again and wrap your head.'

I looked at the woman and remembered her face among many. Soon after I had shared my vision with the Gutians, I had collapsed. As vague as a dream, I remembered being in a smoke-filled hut. Many Gutian women were surrounding me and when I went to stand, I could not. I had begged my arms and legs to move. My mouth had opened to shout and no words had come out. My next memory was waking near a smouldering fire. For a moment, I thought I was in Elkin's cave. I was still wearing my hide shorts and my sandals were placed beneath a rack where my tunic was drying. It had been washed but this had only mixed the blood and soil stains into a consistent brown colour.

'Kar,' said Elkin, 'we should not make the King wait.'

*The King?* A shiver of excitement mixed with fear coursed through me. *Why does the Gutian King want my personal audience?* I thought I had completed a necessary deed in uniting our tribes to a cause but I feared it might go the way of my first trade with the Gutians. When I had not returned with another offer in exchange for the gold left by Harnsek and Omah, I had offended the Gutians. I looked at the Gutian women and children standing outside the hut. Many averted their eyes. There were smiles in the eyes of those who did not look away and, held upright in the hands of a women wearing a red dress, was my staff. 'I'll need that back soon,' I told her.

Elkin held the flap on the door aside.

I looked back at the woman in the red dress and observed that all the women were wearing dresses. They looked dressed and assembled for an occasion. I entered the tall hut and Elkin followed me inside. Two candles burned at shoulder height at the far end of the hut, twenty paces away.

'Welcome, Kar.'

The voice surrounded me like an echo in the Guardian tower. I closed my eyes and opened them slowly, adjusting them to the darkness. The shapes of men standing against the walls on both sides of the hut were revealed. 'Who speaks to me?' I asked, with my ears—ear and a half—focused on the man closest the door.

'We do,' the voice from the front of the hut repeated until the man I was facing replied at the same time as the man standing behind me.

I turned to Elkin and he stepped away from me, disappearing into the shadows. The hut smelt like rotten meat. Like the vile alley I had ridden through to escape Assur, it made vomit rise in my throat. I felt the fate of the Guardians and the future of the East and West weighing upon me as I stepped towards the candles burning at the far end of the tall hut. I was so focussed on standing proud that I did not see what lay at my feet. My toe bent backwards in my sandal and I stumbled.

A man standing against the wall snorted and this made others laugh.

I crouched and felt what had caused me to trip. It was as hard and as heavy as a rock.

'Quiet,' said the King and I heard his command repeated by the men standing against the walls. 'Be silent,' he shouted.

'Be...' began one man before he silenced himself.

I stood to attention. My toe ached. I welcomed

the pain as a distraction from my other battle wounds.

The candles at the end of the hut seemed to float towards me. Two men carried them and they stopped when the flames were held, uncomfortably close, either side of my face.

I could see their faces too. Like the first Gutians I had encountered in the valley, they were painted black with mud and one of these men wore a necklace of bird skulls. The light from the candles, so close to my eyes, prevented me from seeing further in front. I heard the Gutian King speak to me but I could not see him.

'I know the name, Kar. It means warrior. You entered our village alone, my people tell me.' The King's voice had the rasp of an old man and I could tell he was seated as I heard his wooden chair creak as he raised his voice to the roof. 'Can a warrior defeat the God King?'

It was if his question was a directed at the gods, so I did not respond. I stared his way through the light surrounding my face.

'I know you speak, Guardian,' said the King. 'Tell me how you will bring the Bull down?'

I rested my hand on my tattooed shoulder. Whilst I could not see him, I was sure he was looking at me. 'A Guardian does not know of defeat if it is a fight he must make,' I told the Gutian King. He had referred to Sargon as the Bull and that strengthened my resolve. 'I vowed that I would I fight Sargon, the Bull of Heaven walking as a man.' I leant into the light of the candles. 'Mother Ki approved of my vow and, the vision she shared with me, I have shared with your people. Her strength is with us all now, for that is the way if a god dies on earth.'

'Do you need her strength, Kar?' he asked, his voice now aimed at me.

'Like my own mother, who was also taken by Sargon's war with the world, Ki guides my life.' I paused to steady my trembling voice. 'Death gives reason to life. Sargon, the Bull, will have no say in my fate. My quest is Mother Ki's last request.'

The King's chair creaked as he leant forwards or maybe he even stood for a moment in his darkened end of the hut. 'Remember the importance of each step in your journey or you will fall before your stand against the Bull. Look beneath your feet, Guardian.'

I nodded and heard his chair creak again. If not for one of the Gutians next to me lowering their candle, I might have missed the immediacy of the King's message. The candlelight revealed hide-wrapped parcels at my feet. Most of the parcels were as wide and as tall as my spread palm. I crouched and peeled the hide from the solid object that had caused my stumble when I had approached the King. Gold glistened in the candlelight. I turned to face the Gutian King.

'Twelve Gutian Maidens will travel with you,' he said. 'If you are defeated in your quest to fight the Bull, you will have still spread our word and people across the land. Word of you travelling to Akkadia with these maidens will be shared before you.'

I stood and so did the Gutian who was lighting the hide-wrapped gold at my feet. 'I did not plan to announce my travels so boldly,' I told the King. 'In Borujerd, I hoped to announce the defeat in discussing my want to travel west. In Nineveh, I planned to announce the defeat in my need to travel south to Assur. If all know of my journey, it will surely end before it is complete.'

The King chuckled. The Gutians standing against the walls of the hut remained silent. 'Elkin,' said the King, 'tell Kar why he must travel this way.'

I turned towards the entrance to the hut and sighted a resemblance of movement as Elkin stepped away from the wall.

'Kar, my young friend, you know that everything happens for a reason. Salarn was the greatest man I ever knew but even he could not have completed this task without the defeat of an army, the death of Mother Ki and Gutian gold paving the way. You are responsible for all these things.'

'And what of the maidens?' I questioned Elkin. 'Why can I not travel alone to Borujerd and recruit only those crucial to my quest?'

Elkin stepped towards me. 'The maidens are crucial. If a man cannot be swayed by gold or offer of a maiden, they will sign an end to your quest.'

I faced Elkin's baldhead that reflected light off the candles as he stepped closer. 'Now that you know what the Gutians offer, how far will you travel with me?'

Elkin stepped into the light. 'Convince the Port Guard of Eridu to let you sail beyond his port and I will see that many follow you to the island. Like the maidens, making it past this port is crucial. Eridu is the southern gateway to Akkadia and the home of Enki. He is the pattern maker.' Elkin placed his hand on my shoulder. 'Change the guard at this port and a new pattern of life will be weaved.

# 28

# Twelve Maidens

*Scribed by Kar.*

I felt like I was a trader and the Gutian maidens my Guardians on the journey north to Borujerd. They treated and wrapped my wounds morning and night. When we rested during high sun, they shared tales and spoke of the new lives they could lead in the West. As we followed the Zagros Mountains north, on the western side of the range, the Gutians not on our journey had a task of their own. They were to spread word of our journey with the people of Eshnunna. It was hoped that by the time we made passage south towards the cities between the rivers, absolute allegiance to the King would be broken by talk of change. Whether word of our uprising would aid our plight or be our undoing, was unknown. I dared not predict the outcome of something so far from my control as the shared opinion of people.

Borujerd and the tales of Guardians who had frequented the city were familiar to me but I had never visited the city myself. We arrived at the city as the sun was lowering in the west. The steep slopes of the Zagros Mountains were covered with snow yet at their base, the foothills formed a barren, sand-swept edge to the desert. The foothills gave way to farming land. Beyond the farming land, small huts surrounded an outer city wall. Inside the city wall, stone buildings occupied every space apart from a wide, straight lane that led to an even higher inner-city wall. Unlike Bit-Bunakki, Borujerd, from wall to wall, was a city planned around its centrepiece, the Palace of Lord Vanekebek.

The Gutian maidens assembled next to me on their horses as I observed the city from the last foothill. I pointed at the palace and drew my finger towards me, following the lane to the city's main gateway. The path of my finger curved slightly to the west as I pointed the way through the expanse of small huts and farming land to where the road to Bit-Bunakki continued into the desert. 'You have escorted me safely to our first destination,' I thanked the maidens. 'I will find us place to rest tonight.'

For twenty days I had followed the Gutian maidens in the ride north. They followed me as we trotted along a lane between millet fields towards the farmers' huts outside the city wall. I stopped many times to speak with farmers in the fields. 'Do you know Maken the Farmer?' I asked them. Maken was the father of Naten, the beautiful fair-skinned girl adopted by Fankisi and Tahnas. He was not the man I had travelled to Borujerd to meet but I had to start somewhere. If Maken's wife still worked in the palace kitchen, she might also know of the movement of the palace guards.

Each farmer I met seemed to be guiding me a step closer to Maken's home until I realised we were on a path to the city's main gate. All of the huts looked the same and I remembered being lost in my own village at night when I was child. Maybe I had misheard the farmers' directions. I led the maidens back to a well amongst the farmers' huts and suggested that they re-fill their water skins as they waited for me. Leading a procession of maidens through farmers' huts was not the attention I required at this point in the journey. Many of the farmers were yet to return from the fields. It was strangely quiet.

'Are you looking for someone?' asked a thin man wearing a soiled tunic. Two men, both carrying long-handled shovels, stood behind him like personal guards.

I climbed from my mount and approached them unarmed. 'I am looking for Maken the Farmer.'

'Why are you looking for him?' asked the thin man.

'I am a friend of Arman and Delari.'

'The traders,' said one of the men holding a shovel.

'I know who they are,' said the thin man, glancing over his shoulder. He turned back to face me. 'Why does a friend of Arman and Delari look for Maken?'

'In hope that he might offer us place to camp this night.'

'Follow me.'

I unstrapped my staff from my mount and sig-nalled one of the maidens, Olles, to accompany me. Of all the maidens, she was the one who stayed closest to me in the ride north.

Olles took a thin rod from another maiden before she stepped to my side.

'Wait for us here,' I told the other maidens. I trusted that they would be safe as a group. Wary I remained as in the camps I knew that men were always looking for something.

The thin man, accompanied by his shovel-wielding guards, led us away from the well and between mud brick huts that all looked the same. We passed by Borujerdian farmers returning home and activity could be heard inside some of the huts. The scent of cooking food and smoke in the air suggested a normal end to the day.

The thin man looked back at us following. 'The long stick she carries, is that a weapon?'

'Against lizards in the desert it is.' The immensity of the Zagros Mountains and the stretch of the city wall made it difficult gain a sense of direction. They loomed around us no matter how far we walked. I relied upon the setting sun to recall my path back to the well. The shadows stretched in one direction. When the men began to circle our path northward, back to the well, I noticed. I stopped following. 'Are we close to his home.'

The thin man waved for me to follow and his guards looked at each other.

I saw their hands tighten their grip on their shovels.

'Maken's hut is here,' the thin man told me, pointing to a hut out of sight beyond the next hut in our turn.

I walked towards him and the two men with their harmless looking weapons followed either side of me.

'This is Maken's hut,' said the thin man, as he walked towards a medium-sized hut that looked the same as many we had passed. He looked around and picked up a wooden carving of a soldier from the dirt. His eyes studied the toy for a moment and he rubbed it clean with his already soiled tunic. 'Broken sword,' he said as he tossed the carved toy aside. 'Maken is probably still in the fields. You should wait here.'

'His wife would be home,' I said. According to Fankisi, Maken's wife worked in the kitchen. Things might have changed since but I wanted to check if this thin man did know the woman. 'Can you call out for her?'

'You can call for her,' said the thin man. 'It's you who wants her attention.'

'Naten,' I called out. 'Naten, are you home?' I did not expect a response.

The thin man tipped his head to one of the men holding a shovel.

I twisted my staff behind my back and knocked the head of the man next to me. Before he collapsed, I twirled my staff over my head and tapped the top of the other man's skull before he could swing his shovel. 'Stay, I want to talk with you,' I said to the thin man as his friends collapsed either side of me.

He ran.

The Gutian maiden, Olles, leant her weight on her rod and attached a tendon. She drew an arrow from her quiver and flexed it in her bow.

The thin man looked back as she released the arrow.

It sliced through the air, narrowly missing his shoulder.

He pointed and laughed.

Olles drew another arrow taught.

'Let him go,' I told her when I saw farming people appear behind. When I turned to check on the other men, a boy saw me and his feet slid as he turned quickly and sprinted away. 'Bring the other maidens,' I told Olles. 'You should be safe. I think the men made me as a Guardian.' I found a coil of rope and a strip of leather outside one of the huts and I began tying the men by their ankles, knees, hands and throats.

One of them woke before I was finished and I threatened to kill him if he moved or made a sound.

Olles would have walked against the flow of most heading my way towards their huts for soon after her departure, farming folk arrived in numbers.

I walked around a few huts until I was part of the crowd first to find the men tied together.

'Cut us free,' yelled one of the men.

'Why are you tied?' asked a farmer.

'We found a thief,' said one of the men.

'Why would a thief tie you up?' laughed a farmer.

The questions and ridiculous answers continued until one of the men said that he would tell the truth. The man tied to him by the throat, hit his head against his. The other man retaliated.

My throat tie did not allow for their heads to withdraw more than a space of a nose. Their head thrusts, whilst strained and unsettling, could continue to dawn if they were not released. I moved about the crowd listening to their response and waiting to see if anyone would cut them free. When I was convinced that the taunts would continue, I circled wide of the happening and watched my maidens' approach. The approach of guards into an unlit camp at dusk would be alerted by flame. I was convinced that the farmers would deal with the matter.'

'These are the women responsible,' yelled the thin man, stealing a place in the crowd. 'They are Guardians. Check their arms.'

I moved my way towards the thin man as he signalled the crowd towards the Gutian maidens. If he did anything to try and hurt them I was prepared to strike.

Olles's dress was sleeveless and she turned her head to look at her arms. The other maidens, whose dresses allowed, also displayed their arms.

The crowd's attention returned to the men tied together and the thin man made his way through the crowd towards his accomplices.

One man stayed close to the maidens. He was tall and reminded me of Senea with his boyish beard. Something about the maidens held his curiosity. I thought it might just be their beauty until I saw his head nodding slightly as he looked at the horses. He was counting. There were thirteen horses and only twelve maidens.

He turned and looked at the farmers in the crowd. Most had their backs turned. Our eyes met. I waited to see if he would run or call for help.

His mouth opened slightly and his look of surprise turned to a smile.

I looked down at my brown tunic, a stained mess of dirt and blood. Surely I looked like a farmer just in from the fields more than a Guardian. My head was wrapped with a scarf, so he could not see that I was injured.

He approached me cautiously.

I looked away and acted like I was more interested in the spectacle of the two men tied together.

The young man stood next to me.

I glanced at him and smiled.

'Is this your work?' he asked me.

'They are tied together and flip like fish on the ground.'

'My name is Fitsbin.'

I sighed with relief. 'My name is Kar. I should have looked for you as soon as I arrived.' Fitsbin's father, Behrant, was the man Arman had stayed with each time he visited Borujerd.

'Do you have a place to stay?'

'We are in need.'

'Follow me,' he said. 'Unless you want to keep watching.'

I nodded. 'Olles,' I said as I walked past her, 'follow us but do not all leave at once.'

The groans of the men I had tied together could be heard a hundred steps away. Farmers returning from the fields continued to head towards the disturbance. Others seemed content to go about their lives as normal, washing their faces and building fires.

'You knew I was a Guardian,' I said to Fitsbin.

'I know the faces of the farmers. It has been a while since I've seen a Guardian or even heard their name mentioned. I didn't know you were a Guardian. I hoped you were.' Fitsbin looked at me as he continued to lead me through the farmers' camp. 'How is Arman?'

I frowned as I thought how to respond. 'In the East, the Guardians defeated the Akkadians but I do not know who survived.'

'He would have,' said Fitsbin, 'or he would have taken many Akkadians with him to his grave.'

\*\*\*

Fitsbin lifted the entrance flap to his father's hut and informed him that I had arrived. The maidens secured the horses behind the hut. Fitsbin waited for them and offered to bathe their feet. I remembered when Badbe's servant had bathed my feet when I visited his home in Bit-Bunakki with Salarn. The maidens accepted Fitsbin's offer as nervously as I had when I was first introduced to the custom. I watched them sit on logs before a fireplace and hitch their dresses as I poured water from a jug into a dish and washed my own feet.

'You do not need to wait for me,' said Fitsbin. He tossed me a cloth. 'My father is eager to meet you and learn the reason for your visit.'

I parted the flap at the door.

'Leave it open, so I might see your face,' said Behrant. He lay on a fur with his back propped up by cushions.

I tied the entrance flap to one side of the doorway and then stepped further inside.

'I see you now. Come closer, so I might see your tattoo.'

I approached and lifted my sleeve.

'I know your father, Unbetum. The Guardians have shared many tales with me. Tell me yours, Kar.' He coughed and pointed to a jug of water.

I poured some into a mug and handed it to him as I knelt by his side. His hands shook as he reached for it and so I helped him hold it and take a sip.

When he was settled again, I told him what had happened in the East and the reason for my visit. 'I want to make a trade in the city markets. Arman has told me that there is a palace guard I should meet,' I explained.

'Do you wish to trade or just use trade to meet this guard?' asked Behrant.

'I wish to continue trading as we make our way south. Without goods to trade, I cannot pass as a trader.'

Behrant laughed and this made him cough again. He pointed through the door. 'You might be seen as a slave trader, accompanied by so many women.'

I smiled. 'I hope they can travel with me all the way to the Island of Kings.'

Behrant leant back and stared at the thatched roof. 'I think I know the guard that Arman wants for you to meet. The palace guards always visit the city markets at dawn to be the first to make offer in trades. You should arrange a trade with a seller tonight. Speak with my son. He is always watching those who enter and leave the city.' Behrant closed his eyes. 'Travel safe, young Guardian. I hope I am still alive when word of what happened in the South is shared in the North.'

I thanked Behrant and closed the entrance flap as I stepped outside.

Fitsbin had finished bathing the maidens' feet. He pointed to a stool opposite the large logs where they sat. 'Rest, Kar. Olles tells me that you have travelled a long way to be here.'

I sat on the stool next to Fitsbin. 'Your father tells

me that you might know some of the traders who are here in the city.'

Fitsbin started listing the names he knew and explaining what they traded.

'Kanripu, I know that name,' I said.

'Few do not know his name. Kanripu controls trade as far south as Agade. He was once an Akkadian officer.'

I felt my heartbeat quicken. 'Could you introduce me to Kanripu?'

'I can take you to him,' said Fitsbin. 'I can't convince him to trade with you.'

***

Fitsbin, Olles and I entered Borujerd through the main gate. Borujerdian guards stood to one side of the entrance to the city. They watched those entering and leaving but they did not interfere with anyone's passage. There was no reason to treat us any differently as we travelled unarmed. I carried an offering wrapped in a fur. The sun had gone down but there was still light in the sky.

We made our way down the wide lane that eventually led to the palace in the city centre. Many walked the lane, led camels or pulled carts to and from the main gate or out and through the many passages to other parts of the city. We passed another gathering of Borujerdian guards before Fitsbin led us west down a passage.

Fitsbin pointed ahead to a two-storey, stone building with a wide wooden door. 'That is where he stays when he comes to Borujerd to trade.'

'Wait with Fitsbin,' I told Olles.

Fitsbin took Olles hand and walked her to the centre of the lane outside Kanripu's home. It was dark between the tall, stone buildings but where Fitsbin stood it showed that he was not attempting to hide.

I knocked against the heavy wooden door.

'If he is not home, I know somewhere else we might find him,' said Fitsbin.

I looked up. There were no windows in the stone building. I was about to knock again when I heard movement inside. The door's brace was lifted and the door opened inward.

A tall man with dark skin stepped onto the threshold. He looked past me at Fitsbin and Olles and then each way along the lane. His hair was cut short around his ears and his face was shaved. 'I was not expecting any visitors this eve.'

'Kanripu, my name is Kar and I have travelled a long way to meet you.'

'How far? Long for some is short for others,' he laughed at his own joke. Behind him a freestanding candelabra lit the room. It was filled with stacks of leather and rolls of fur and hide. Seated on one of the stacks of leather was a young woman with raven-coloured hair. Kanripu followed my eyes over his shoulder. 'Were you here to meet me or my daughter?'

I raised my fur-wrapped offering. 'I have travelled from a valley in the Zagros Mountains, east of the Diyale River.'

The smile on Kanripu's face straightened. 'That is a long way.' He took the fur-wrapped bundle from my hands.

His daughter slid down from the stack of leather and approached behind her father. She peered past him, over his arm, as he unwrapped the fur.

'More than trade with you, I wish for you to travel with me to Agade and beyond.'

'Why do you think I would be interested?' he asked.

Kanripu had not dismissed my offer. I could tell he was interested by his repeated glances at my offering and the way he looked me in the eye without judging me on my appearance in a stained tunic. 'A man who travels between Agade and Borujerd to trade is not a regular man. You are like the Guardians of the East who once moved between the cities, helping traders along the way, and only ever calling one place home.'

'Tell me where I call home, Kar?'

'I mean not to tell you who I think you are other than with my humble praise.'

Kanripu nodded and his daughter clutched his arm, listening expectantly.

'My friend outside, Fitsbin, tells me you were once an officer in Agade, so imagine Agade is your home and you trade that far south because it allows you to return home.' I glanced at his daughter's grip on his arm. 'Like me, I think you are more than a trader.' I looked him in the eyes. 'You travel so far because you have seen the greater world and prefer the life beyond city gates. You want your daughter to see this world too.'

Kanripu hummed his lips and glanced once more at my offering. 'I know Fitsbin and his father. Who is the woman by his side?'

'Her name is Olles. She is a Gutian maiden. I travel with twelve Gutian maidens.'

'And you wish to go beyond Agade?' he asked.

'There is an island in the Southern Sea. I travel there to fight the King.'

Kanripu's daughter exhaled, drawing our attention.

'I'm sorry,' she said, stepping away.

'Come back, Hija,' Kanripu said to his daughter. He handed her my offering and her arms bent in taking its weight. 'We have much to discuss.' He guided me inside with his arm and then called for Fitsbin and Olles.

I was yet to meet the palace guard that Arman had suggested I seek out. Maybe, it was meant to be that I find Kanripu first. Everything happens for a reason, even if we do not understand why at the time. I felt like the best plan for fighting a God-King was being discovered in action.

There were no tables or stools in Kanripu's Borujerdian home. Hija returned to her seat on a stack of leather. Olles followed me across the room and sat next to me on a pile of furs. Fitsbin stood and sat in a few different spots, never comfortable in being still for too long.

Kanripu paced as he spoke, only leaning momentarily against the wall or a stack of leather before his pacing continued. Once an Akkadian officer of Agade, he told me that I was right about his new life. 'I am not a disciple of a King who stops trade between cities and I know of others who feel the same way. We should meet with them. You were wise to meet with me.'

# 29

# Island of Kings

*Scribed by Enheduanna, Priestess of Ur.*

I leant against a statue that was shaped in my father's image. It had the body of a bull and wings large enough that one could imagine the creature taking flight. If it did not wear his head, it would have been viewed a monster. On each side of the highest landing, on the steep steps leading up to the massive white stone gazebo, these creatures stood testament to my father's prowess.

The citizens of Dilmun loved my father, or so I thought, for he had shared more wealth and leniency in his governance here than he had even in his Capital, Agade. To reach Dilmun from the mouth of the Euphrates River, he crossed lethal water, seas that only the Great Gilgamesh and the Sun God had chartered before him. He ventured to this island in search of the immortality that Gilgamesh was denied. His people between the rivers believed him to be away visiting the Gods when he made lengthy stays on this island. The counsel he sought was instead that of fellow kings. Behind the drapes, tied to the circling white-stone pillars of the gazebo, they met regularly for an orgy of food, drink and sex. The height of the gazebo above the Southern Sea allowed cool winds to fan their sanctuary as they indulged their desires for days on end.

'Are you being tended for in your stroll, High Priestess?'

I turned and smiled courteously at Derahmus. His long brown hair swayed gently behind his broad shoulders as he walked down the first flight of steps from the gazebo. The morning light glistened on his polished bronze breastplate—a gift from the High Priest Amar Sudra. We had visited Amar Sudra in his temple in Agade after returning from the East. An opportunity to speak with my father or mother is what I desperately sought. Unfortunately, they, including my father's new bride, had travelled to Nippur two days before our arrival. I spoke with Amar Sudra instead. Without revealing my want for Kar and my father to become allies without the need to battle, I spoke of the Akkadian defeat in the East and the reported death of Mother Ki. He seemed grateful to hear my report and thanked Derahmus as well by gifting him the bronze breastplate. It was not the response I expected. Amar Sudra's graciousness surprised me. For a while, I felt relieved to be back in Akkadia. 'Loyal Derahmus, how wrong this all is.'

'Can I bring you anything?' he asked, always respectful in never inquiring upon my personal thoughts.

'You can afford me your company.'

He stood with me on the highest landing and shared my view from between the stone sentinels. From this height, the edges of the island could be viewed in most directions. The stairs were ten paces wide and the two landings allowed room for noble folk to gather for celebrations and special announcements. Twenty steps below was the next landing and it was a further fifty steps to the ground. This is where the Akkadian soldiers gathered and protected the King's sanctuary.

When the kings feasted, the people on these shores also celebrated. Secretive, the visiting kings' affairs remained for such reward. Only the soldiers who would live out their days on these shores, barkeeps and stall owners tended to regular duty on such days. Beneath us, many of the citizens had gathered for a street performance, sure to be another rendition of one of my father's countless conquests. I guessed this one would be about the lion he had slain in his first visit to the Land of Kush. Did the actors know that behind me in the gazebo, Negusa Nagast, The Second, King of Kings and ruler of the Upper Nile Valley, the man who had hosted my father's stay, lay on a sealed bed of feathers whilst being hand fed olives by a naked maiden? Did the actors who retold my father's subduing of the lands west of Ebla, earlier this morn, know that the former King of Zidon was also behind the drapes, drunk to a point of indiscretion?

'I will escort you closer if you wish to watch,' offered Derahmus.

'Is that supposed to be a lion?' I asked, pointing to the monstrous head being twirled about on poles by two of the performers.

'I believe it is, my Priestess. Though I have only seen paintings of lions, I do not think they have horns.'

'Or are as large,' I added.

'Kar of the East may be that large,' said Derahmus, immediately regretting voicing himself so freely.

'What do you mean, Derahmus?' I questioned him.

'My grandest apologies, High Priestess.' He hung his head.

'Do not apologise, Derahmus. I asked you what you meant when you said Kar may be that large?'

He only half straightened his head, averting his eyes. 'I cannot forget what we were told in Eshnunna and was reported in Susa.'

'Neither can I, Derahmus. Correct me if I am wrong. The story was that Gutians faithful to the Guardians defeated your army and that Mother Ki burned for all to see. We cannot believe all campfire tales or we would never sleep from the horror.'

Derahmus raised his head and looked me in the eye. 'My Priestess, we heard more than campfire tales.'

I knew what I had heard but I wanted Derahmus to voice himself. In the East, when I was not clothed as a Priestess, he had been forthright with his words.

'Akkadian scroll bearers and soldiers lucky to reach Susa alive reported Akkadian defeat in the East,' he continued. 'You wanted to meet Kar. Is that not why we consulted Amar Sudra upon our return? Did you not tell the High Priest—'

When I touched his bare arm, he stopped speaking and dipped his head. I placed my hand under his chin and lifted his face. 'You can look at me, Derahmus.'

He looked at me and down and up the steps to see if anyone was watching. A Priestess was not to be touched by a man and thus a priestess should not touch a man. This rule was broken numerous times when I travelled east with Derahmus. He had helped me mount when we had to ride. In Eshnunna, he had held my hand and led me to his home. His eldest son had washed my feet.

'I still want to meet Kar,' I told him. 'The tale I cannot fathom is the death of Mother Ki. The tablet bearer described it as a face in the smoke that gave all pause.'

'That was an Akkadian tablet bearer's report, not a campfire tale,' said Derahmus. He looked at my hands. 'You should hold your hands by your side, Priestess. Raised hands will gain attention from the people.' He looked down the steps at the gathering watching the play.

'Tell me, Derahmus, who do you believe Kar to be? Was it desperate imagining that allowed me to think of him as anything but an enemy of the throne?'

Derahmus closed his eyes for a moment. 'I thought that Kar was a name given to their rebellion until I heard the tale of Kar and the Gutians. Now, I think I sighted Kar from a distance.' Derahmus looked past me as he recalled the day. 'A boy on a pilgrimage had distracted my soldiers as a man with a shaved head and muscles like a bull commanded a ship to sail from the Port of Assur. I thought my bronze bolt ended him.' Derahmus took a step away from me. 'On our return to Agade from the East, a farming man described Kar as beardless with short hair. Could it be the same man that I saw in Assur?' he asked me. 'You said you felt something too, the day my army was defeated.'

'I felt...' I did not have to answer Derahmus. He was my servant. Then I remembered why I had defended him in the Court of Agade. He was a man of truth. Derahmus had safely escorted me into the world not seen or heard from temple steps. I owed him my opinion and I wanted to hear more of his before I spoke to my father or mother. 'I ventured far from home with you, Derahmus, and learned more in those forty days than I have in all my schooling in the temple. How lowly the people think of my father, I did not know. Those who gather when I speak at my Temple in Ur and the people of this island appear allegiant.'

Derahmus shook his head. 'They are obliging for fear of death. Your father's decree is a final verdict even if he is not present. The people here in Dilmun, like those in the outer states of Zidonia and Elam, will rejoice at any disruption to your father's rule. In Zidon they smiled courteously at my approach and laughed as I walked on.'

'The tiresome schedule of the travelling merchants and farmers we met was hardly imaginable for I knew not of a life where one works to eat and eats to work. And their tales of Kar on our return, as enchanting as god tales shared by Amar Sudra, teased my remaining sensibility.' I held my dress to my side as the wind swirled around the high steps leading to the gazebo. 'That a lone man of savage origins, accompanied by twelve maidens, sought to take down my father with his own sword, I thought laughable.'

'Not a sword, a bladed staff, High Priestess.' Derahmus looked past me again but this time it was as if he had seen something behind my back.

I glanced behind and saw nothing. 'They were fanciful tales, Derahmus, still ones worth scribing, do you agree?'

Derahmus looked at me. The wind on the steps lifted his brown hair around his face like the mane of a lion. 'I have seen the staff carried by Kar.'

'Where?' The light hairs on my arms stood to attention even though I was warm and enjoying the morning light.

Derahmus nodded to himself and then at me. 'I saw him and he saw me. I gave him permission to move on.' Derahmus gritted his teeth and sucked air.

'Calm yourself,' I told him, 'and tell me more.'

Derahmus clutched the hilt of his sword. 'He was a boy. He was a tall boy. I let him enter Assur.'

'What else do you remember about him?'

Derahmus tittered and then sighed. 'I failed your father when I allowed him permission to enter the city.'

'Tell me,' I urged, 'was his skin dark like bark and his eyes as green as trees?' My own voice trembled and the wind felt colder against my back.

Derahmus stilled his hands by his side. His cheeks twitched.

'Only I need know that you have met Kar. I did not come here to witness my father's debauchery. Our stay on the island should be an opportunity to talk with my parents and, when this play is done, I will begin by sharing reports of Akkadian defeat in the East and the death of Mother Ki with my mother. I wish Amar Sudra could be here before the morrow.'

'My opinion is all I can offer you, High Priestess, and I would rather bite off my tongue than speak words that may not be true.'

'Now that my mother speaks no more, I can only trust in you,' I assured Derahmus. 'I have never spoken more openly to any other, even my maidens. You showed me what it was like to be treated as a regular woman in our journey and, though it was a worthy request, you never asked that I bid you leave to stay with your family when I requested we travel on to Susa.'

Derahmus lowered his head and turned from me. He paced back and forth on the landing between the statues manning each side of the stairs. When he looked up at the gazebo, the white drapes were fluttering in the breeze. He stopped and stared that way. The delicate pluck of a harp could be heard. After allowing himself time to postulate his opinion he faced me. 'I believe a boy named Kar, not just a namesake, seeks your father's end. His eyes are green and his skin, like mine, has spent its days in the sun. Adorned like a king himself he will be, for the people in Eshnunna speak so highly of him. Twelve maidens, as told by many in our return to the West, will accompany him. Access to your father's sanctuaries he may even be granted until the riches he carries are spent. He may also be made privy to confidential knowledge in his dealings with court officials. Your father's calendar of upcoming events that require his presence may be revealed. He might already know of this secret island for in the tale of Kar and the Gutians many mention his fight ending in view of the Southern Sea.' Derahmus stopped suddenly, in time with a final pluck of the harp. He waited for the music to recommence before continuing. 'As for your father's new bride, all I can say is that she is respectful of your mother.' He leant close to me. 'They were standing together inside when I left to check on you. Trust in their silence for they advise your father. I fought for your father and never saw myself as a disciple of Amar Sudra. You do not need his blessing to make your decisions.'

'You have enlightened my thinking once more,

Derahmus.' I placed my hand on his cheek. 'Unlike
the spectre that visits me in my dreams, your explanation is concise. Know that I mention your name many
times in my stories. I let the reader know that the previous Commander of the North-eastern Frontier is by
my side. The people should know your name, Derahmus. The Akkadians, like me, deserve to know what
happened in the West and East. Beginning with your
arrival in Zidon and based upon tales told in the East
and the reports shared with us by Sanam-Shimut in
Susa, true testimony of these happenings I can sancti-
fy. Unholy, my father will claim my endeavours to be.
Unholy, I regret to say, may be his decree if he ignores
the plight of so many.'

'I live to serve you, Enheduanna,' promised Derahmus, referring to me for the first time by my birthing
name. 'You must keep your writings secret until they
are complete,' he then warned. 'Your creed surmounts
all others as High Priestess. Indifferent or even greater
punishment you would bear should word of your secret scripture be divulged too soon. Hence, we should
speak no longer on the matter.'

I nodded in agreement. 'Amar Sudra stated before
the Court of Agade that he would give me a new name
come the Feast of Ishtar. Have you heard any news of
his arrival?'

Derahmus stepped away from me and huffed, further demonstrating his dislike for the man who would
have persecuted him without my intervention. 'The
Akkadian fleet left the Port of Dilmun two days ago at
dawn. They should be commencing the return voyage
soon. Amar Sudra will be here in time for the Feast of
Ishtar.'

'For all my teachings and lectures, through all my years spent in tutorage by the wisest governors, through godless harvests and dark moons, I have learnt nothing quite the like of what now—'

'High Priestess,' interrupted Derahmus.

I turned and cut short my ramblings. Were they ramblings, or did Derahmus truly believe that my word was important? Guilt subdued my ego as I faced Derahmus and the woman who had ventured outside the gazebo and down the steps without my notice.

Derahmus lowered himself and extended his arm. 'Enheduanna, allow me to introduce you to Ankhnesmenre. She is the—'

'I know who she is,' I said, transfixed by her long lashes and wide painted eyes. 'Ankhnesmenre, my apologies that he did not say your name correctly.'

'Ankhnesmenre is a name that must be sung,' explained the Egyptian princess as she stepped delicately down the steps, hitching her long, thin gown.

'Let me help you,' offered Derahmus as he bounded up the steps to her side.

She clutched his hand and leant close to him like each step down was another slippery stone in a perilous creek crossing.

I had time to watch more of the street performance before they finally reached the landing, twenty steps below the gazebo. 'I am glad you both arrived safely.'

'I think it was worthy of me to venture down to you and share your view for a few moments,' replied Ankhnesmenre, gracefully waving her hand about as if she were admiring my home. 'It would be nicer if we spoke inside where there is food, drink and servants to fan this heat of day.'

'I disagree, Ankhnesmenre. I appreciate visiting new lands. It is written that here is where the Sun first rose. Have you also read this?'

'Oh,' exclaimed Ankhnesmenre, 'I did not realise you were out here celebrating the Sun and new lands.'

The Egyptian princess was insulting me through masked words. Each time she looked at me she would cast her eyes down over my body and smile boastfully. She was judging me on the dress I wore and the way I held myself. I tried to keep smiling courteously and maintain a hospitable charade. 'It is the Feast of Ishtar that saw me travel to this island,' I said and pointed north across the sea towards Akkadia. 'This street performance does not interest me. I prefer it though to being trapped inside and surrounded by the smell of strangers.'

'They will always be strangers if you do not make time to meet them,' Ankhnesmenre told me. 'I have a nice dress you could wear and whilst your chest looks like a man's we could use cloth and a gown as a deception.'

'As a deception for what purpose?' I questioned her.

Derahmus stood at the end of the landing and feigned that he did not hear our words.

'Young priestess,' she addressed me, gesturing for Derahmus to look my way, 'you look like you have just woken from slumber. You wear no face paint to hide the blood flowing below your pale skin and your shoulders droop like you are about to surrender.'

I straightened my back and shoulders. 'Is this more

to your liking?'

Ankhnesmenre laughed and encouraged Derahmus to laugh as well. 'Nothing about you is to my liking.'

Derahmus stepped closer from the far side of the landing.

She glanced at him and then pointed at me. 'I find pale skin repulsive and though your hair is tied immaculately to your headdress it only accentuates your pink face and round eyes.'

'I think you look beautiful today, Ankhnesmenre,' I replied with a smile. 'Did you visit me today so that we might compare our beauty?'

Her eyes tightened. 'You must know now that the most private agendas of a king are only disclosed to those with whom he lays. I heard you speak of your father's demise and feel this should be mentioned in his present company.'

'I spoke nothing of the sort,' I said in defence. 'Honest counsel regarding worst predicament is all I asked of my faithful guard. Everything I know of will be shared with my father.'

'Not everything,' she said with a devious smile. 'Come with me,' Ankhnesmenre requested, signalling Derahmus to follow and waving me onwards just as casually.

We walked halfway down the next flight of steps to a point almost as close to the gathered crowds as the gazebo above. At the bottom of the last flight of steps, were eight guards. Before the fleet of ships left for Akkadia there were three-fold this number. I was wary of venturing so close though Derahmus reassured me with his confident stance. The actors in the street performance were nearing their surprise climax, the moment where the lion lurches to life once more before realising that sharing his soul with my father is the only way to live forever. Before the play had chance to conclude, the crowd was distracted by our presence.

Ankhnesmenre bent down in praise of those who had noticed our approach. With her new son, Merenre, now suckling a servant's breast she was free to boast her enlarged bosom and flirt with the crowd. 'Have I distracted you from the play?' she asked as she fanned her hands around her body, cupped her breasts and lifted her dress as she twirled.

Derahmus directed my attention to the soldiers who were now forced to batter some of the men in their over eager progression too close to the steps.

'Why do you tease them like that?' I questioned the Egyptian princess. 'The men on these shores do not need encouragement to resort to savage ways.'

'We do Enheduanna. We still need our savageness. My husband Pepi, though you must call him Nefersahor, beds my younger sister as we speak. How can I just watch when the reward of food and wine, not a new prince for me, is all he offers? Tend I will to the young boy he has given me but I will not forgo the earthly pleasures of a woman in the process.'

'By earthly pleasures do you mean bearing a child to more than one man?' I asked her, unafraid of the knowledge she held against me.

'No, Enheduanna.' She clutched my wrist. 'Clearly you are still a virgin and know not what happens to a woman after they give birth.' With eyes like a cat stalking prey she faced Derahmus. 'This man is wasted in your duty.'

I found myself unable to speak to such blatantly voiced claims and signalled Derahmus to step to my side.

'I heard you speak like someone I wanted to talk to,' she whispered to me as she cradled Derahmus' arm. 'Wrong I must have been. I overheard you speak of defiance yet those words must have been no more than a child's complaint for I could not stand with a woman who does not even attract men. Enjoy the rest of the street performance, priestess.'

I held my hand out to Derahmus in the hope he might prove her wrong.

He turned from me. 'To one so young I am not attracted,' he said, averting his eyes. He unstrapped his bronze breastplate and held it out.

When I did not take hold of it, he let if fall onto the steps.

The Egyptian princess let her eyes wander from his muscular chest and down further past his sculpted stomach to where his waist was wrapped with a well-oiled hind skirt.

'Have your way with him,' I said with disgust. 'After all, that is what we are here for.'

'It seems he does not need your permission, Enheduanna,' boasted Ankhnesmenre. She fluttered her painted eyes and raised her arms from her dress so that it rejoiced in the wind.

Derahmus pointed to a landing on the far side of the outer gazebo and both he and the Egyptian princess smiled flirtatiously at each other as they strode up the steps with joined arms. Her slight stumbles on the even steps were a ploy to clutch him and giggle like a young girl.

I hoped that Derahmus was protecting me. Maybe he was taking her out of sight to fill her glass with wine until she forgot what she thought she heard. It was more likely that he, like those in the Gazebo, was about to satisfy his earthly pleasures. Even my personal maidens, like the viziers loyal to the Egyptian King, showed their true selves here. I travelled to this island for the Feast of Ishtar and now I cared not what the God of Beauty and Wisdom offered. I wanted to tell my mother that the East believed Mother Ki was dead. The Mother God, Ki, is dead and a disciple of hers travels this way for the blood of my father. I wanted her to tell me that Nanna, the Moon God, would have warned me if this were true or that savages were prone to exaggeration. In response I would have told her that Nanna only shared her words. I did not believe in Nanna anymore. I wanted to watch my father's expression carefully as she shared my report. Would he laugh, rage or fall silent? Instead, now more than ever, I felt the need to reread my doctrine in view of discrepancies. I thought it best to return home to my sanctuary in Ur where I could hide from the public for an entire harvest if I desired. There I could quietly await the coming of Kar.

My exposure to the ways of man had left me confused and, the further I was from my temple the more I began to think like Ankhnesmenre. I was beginning to think more like a princess than a priestess. No man would dare share a greeting with me in my temple, yet clothed as a mere peasant woman in the wild country, men had flocked to my side. A shameful existence it was that I pondered, though should I be numbered first amongst Kar's maidens I would accept. Cast the others aside, I would say to him before requesting a horse to carry us away from city walls and temples. My father would have to agree, even in my mother's silence, for he would know that foregoing an alliance with his would-be conqueror would be detrimental to his rule. Maybe, like Derahmus, I would face the Akkadian court. Indifferent or even greater punishment I would face for my betrayal than would be dealt upon a regular woman.

Fanciful was my every pondering that saw me indulging in life like Ankhnesmenre and young maidens. The Egyptian princess was right about a few things. My skin was pale, my breasts were small and I never wore paint on my face. I hung my shoulders during the day because at night I would spend so long leaning backwards looking at the moon. I lied when I told Ankhnesmenre that the play did not interest me. I wanted to be much closer and feel the jostle of the crowd. No conquest by my name would ever incite a new play. I saw the usefulness of my body on earth as no more than a vessel for my mind and scribing hand. I was envious of her body. She saw only my body.

# 30

# The Slave Trader

*Scribed by Etes Pomarous, of Uruk,*
*Port Master in Eridu.*

No one arrives or leaves the Port of Eridu without my knowledge. Situated at the mouth to the Euphrates River, the Port of Eridu is the most southern port in the Akkadian Empire and the oldest. As the Port Master, it is my duty to record all exchanges and account for every happening at this portal to the Empire. I am a scribe, a counter and a gatekeeper.

It was at this port, twenty days before the Feast of Ishtar, that I met the slave trader, Kar. He was young, like the many women he offered for sale. It was his bright, green eyes that revealed his age. He stepped across a boarding plank onto the wharf with his head covered by a fur hood and a green cloth tied so that it draped from the bridge of his nose. A thin, mauve cape was fastened to the shoulder straps of his hide vest and it fluttered in a gentle warm breeze sweeping the River Valley. Under his vest he wore a white, short-sleeved tunic and in his hand he held a smooth wooden staff with hide wrapped around the upright end. Accompanying Kar and his slaves, was an Akkadian officer and another wearing a blue cape. Four Akkadian soldiers stayed on their vessel. By tell of the mast's flag, that was red with a painted silhouette of Sargon's head in profile, the vessel they docked in had sailed south from the Port of Agade. It was nearing dusk and the other boats tied to the dock were ready loaded for a return trip to Uruk at first light.

I approached the newly docked vessel with my regular accompaniment of four soldiers. Kar waited for me with one officer standing by his side and the other a step in front, ready to greet me. The officer standing in front had dark skin and wore a red cape that was secured by two brooches. The silver brooch, in the shape of an eight-pointed star, signed that he was an officer of the Court of Agade. I did not recognise the blue crescent shaped brooch. On the deck of the boat they had departed from, a crowd of young women mingled freely, unlike slaves would. They were not shackled and were helping themselves freely to a barrel of beer that was fastened to the mast. Four soldiers stood watch on deck and resisted the temptation to drink or carouse with the young women whilst on duty. 'Welcome to Eridu,' I greeted the officer standing closest. 'What brings you our way this day?'

'This is Kar,' the officer informed me, gesturing behind at the supposed slave trader and foregoing introducing himself first. 'He has gathered a fine selection of northern maidens and we are escorting them to Dilmun for the Feast of Ishtar.'

I was about to tell him that sailing beyond this point was forbidden when Kar addressed me personally.

'Are you wed, soldier?' he asked. His voice was

friendly and his stance relaxed.

'Not yet, I have a bride in waiting,' I told him, looking past the green cloth covering most of his face into his eyes of the same colour.

'Maybe a slave to help you build this new life might interest you.' He gestured at me with one hand and then held out his staff and signalled the maidens on the boat to look my way.

A maiden with long black hair was the first to stop carousing and take interest. Her light blue dress and thin, sparkling silver bracelets showed off her smooth brown skin. She smiled at me and then dipped her head.

'What do you ask for in exchange for a slave?' I questioned him.

'We require your permission to continue south and another accompaniment of four soldiers to replace these men.'

'I cannot give you that permission, nor do I have soldiers at my disposal,' I replied without need for consideration. 'This is my post and—'

Kar raised his hand dismissingly. 'I know you do not deal in soldiers, friend,' he chuckled and his eyes showed that he was smiling as he waved his arm in the direction of the many docked vessels. 'You are a port master. Your duty is to oversee the arrivals and departures from these wharves. I know this; however, we need to depart soon and a change of guard is required as the four soldiers enlisted by the officers by my side have been on duty since dawn and they have never before travelled this far south.'

I turned my gaze from Kar to the officer standing

closest. 'Officers of Agade should know that sailing beyond this point is forbidden at such a time,' I told him. 'The Feast of Ishtar approaches.' The merriness of the maidens and the silence of the two officers concerned me. The slave trader's masked face also made me cautious and I was not convinced of their motives.

'What is your name, port guard?' asked the officer wearing the red cape fastened by brooches. His bronze breastplate and his helmet, both polished to a shine, signalled him to be a highly ranked officer though this deception had been tried before. If they were infiltrators and this was a seized vessel, then it was my duty to alert the tower guards and bring them to justice.

'My name is Etes Pomarous, of Uruk. I'm not a guard. I'm the Port Master,' I told the officer. 'What is your title?' I questioned him in my response.

'Etes,' he greeted me with a tilt of his head, 'I am Kanripu Shorlah, of Agade, an officer of the Court of Agade. Find one man amongst your Akkadian ranks in this city whom has served in Agade and he will vouch for my name, I assure you.'

'I do not doubt your name, Kanripu Shorlah, of Agade. It is that you ask me to go against orders that has me hesitate in accommodating your needs,' and I glanced over my shoulder to check that my accompaniment of soldiers were also remaining dutiful. I found them distracted by the maidens on the boat and realised that they had probably not heard a single word of our exchange.

'They are rightfully distracted, Etes,' said Kanripu, his smile and eyes wide. 'The maidens on this boat are destined to serve kings and priests. They are not ordinary slaves.' Kanripu extended his arm and rested it on the slave trader's shoulder. 'Kar's stay in Agade was hosted by the High Priest, Amar Sudra, and it is by the High Priest's order that we travel to Dilmun.'

I looked concernedly at Kar and then at each of the officers. The officer wearing a blue cape—a short man—seemed to have one eye on me and one on the boat at the same time. 'What you ask of me is beyond my power. If your voyage is being conducted under special authority, you will need to take the matter before the court because it goes against Sargon's law.'

Kanripu looked Kar's way for approval before saying more and the slave trader nodded obligingly. 'This river flows to a cove in the Southern Sea.' Kanripu pointed south and waited until I looked that way. 'We want to board a vessel there and sail unhindered to the shores of Dilmun. You have the knowledge and authority to allow this.'

Before I had a chance to respond, Kar told me more.

'This boat will attract attention at the cove and the price of these women in gold is enough to turn even a wealthy sea merchant into a bandit. We need your help to complete the journey.'

'Do you see the guard towers watching over this port?' I asked Kar and the officers. I pointed one-by-one at each of the four towers. 'The guards also know that no boat is allowed to sail beyond this point. I do not have the authority to let you sail on and even if I did—'

Again I was drawn to silence by Kar's raised palm. 'Allow me a moment to consult with the officers,' he requested and he waited for me to signal approval.

Kanripu and the short officer, who was also dressed in a full uniform with a bronze breastplate, turned to face the slave trader. They discussed their plans without fear of me listening.

Kanripu pointed towards the city, 'If we are not granted higher approval then our voyage is sure to be halted once more as we sail closer to the sea. Etes would know where the next Akkadian stronghold is.' Kanripu glanced my way but did not seek my confirmation.

Kar rested his hand on Kanripu's shoulder, 'Then this is where you and I must part company.'

The officer put his hand on the slave trader's and nodded respectfully. 'I would have gone with you all the way to Dilmun.'

'I believe you would have,' Kar said sincerely. 'Your work is here now. The scroll must make it to the right hands. Do not expect the same level of support as was shown in Sippar, Agade and Uruk. The Court of Eridu would have heard of Sargon's defeat in the East yet their memories of the highlanders' siege of the cities between the rivers before his rule would not be as strong. The cities of Eridu and Ur were spared from the war with the Elamites and their allegiance to Sargon will not wane to fear.'

Kanripu squeezed Kar's hand and closed his eyes briefly. It was as if he needed to draw strength from the slave trader for what he was about to do.

I ordered my guards to be ready and rested my hand on my sword hilt, fearing the worst. It was Kar's and the officer's softly spoken words without attempt to hide their agenda that had me delay in alerting the tower guards.

'Let the scroll talk for you,' Kar advised Kanripu. 'Do not try to be the spokesperson for the message it sends. If they are averse to the High Priest's plans then they will not be any more understanding of your words. They will send representatives north to his court in Agade. I suggest that you travel with them and, when opportunity allows, take your family north to Nineveh. Nineveh is where I first announced Sargon's imminent defeat. You have witnessed yourself the number of attempts to take my life since arriving in Agade. There are supporters of Sargon who will outlive the King himself. In Nineveh you stand the greatest chance of starting a new life.'

Kanripu released Kar's hand and stood erect, taking a deep breath. 'Izad, fetch the scroll for me,' he requested of the other officer.

Izad trotted down the wharf on his short legs and across the boarding plank, disappearing amongst the tapestry of colour from the many maidens' flowing dresses.

Again, I signalled my accompaniment of guards to attention before turning back to face Kar and Kanripu. 'What is your new plan?' I asked in Izad's absence.

Kanripu looked at me for a long while before answering. It did not look like he was judging me as much as he was trying to find the right words to explain his task. 'I suggest you take a slave, Etes, before the offer is revoked. We carry a scroll that bears the name of twenty officers stationed between Nineveh and Agade. The final seal is that of the High Priest of Agade, Amar Sudra, on behalf of the King's court.'

'What message does it send?' I asked and Kanripu looked like he was he was going to reveal its contents when a distant rumble of thunder in the east distracted us both. I looked to the darkened sky above the city on the east bank and then at two of the four guard towers that faced the full fury of the setting sun. The guards in these towers could not see me. They would not see the wharf until there was only coloured sky left in the west.

Izad bounded down the wharf and handed a papyrus scroll to Kanripu.

Kanripu displayed the scroll's wax seal, angling it to the last light of day.

I had seen Amar Sudra's seal many times before. Only two days ago, it was his seal that was broken when a first liege officer read that the Feast of Ishtar was to be celebrated on the night of new moon and that all river travel was to only course north on the Euphrates for twenty days before and after the celebration. The scroll Kanripu held was from the High Priest and its seal was only to be broken upon delivery to another high priest, first liege officer, or the King.

A shriek from one of the maidens put Kanripu on edge. He turned his attention to the boat, holding the scroll protectively behind his back. Laughter soon followed and he realised that it was a false alarm. 'I will take this scroll to Enki's Temple and deliver it personally to your High Priest,' he told me in a low voice. 'There is a rising in the East and the end of Sharru-Kin is near.' He looked cautiously about at roused boatmen gathering on the decks of nearby vessels before continuing. 'When the King's boats return west from the Southern Sea, a new order will be in place. In Uruk, Agade and Sippur, talk of this change is already rampant in the streets.'

In Eridu there had been no such talk of revolt. 'What can I do?' I asked. I hoped to keep them held at port until the change of guard. Only the masts' flags gathered light from the setting sun. Soon, all four guard towers would have unblinded sight of the wharf.

'Kar has already told you what we need,' replied Kanripu, still talking softly. 'We have four soldiers that need to be replaced and we need your permission to continue.'

Kar stepped closer. 'Can you do this?'

I sighed heavily and took a moment to judge the tower guards' line of sight. Something was not right about these men and their plans and as the Port Master it was my duty to control all river traffic south to the sea and north to Uruk. My four port guards were now suddenly more interested in my decision than the many beautiful maidens that continued to mingle on the deck of the boat nearby and tease them with quick flirtatious smiles and giggles. On the decks of the other docked vessels, sea merchants and fishermen that had been lulled to attention by the maidens' festivities, watched on closely and quietly. The darkening sky in the east grumbled. Enki's Temple, the highest point in the city, glowed like gold as the sun set.

'Etes,' barked the slave trader as he tapped my head with his wooden staff and withdrew its reach before I even saw it move. 'Twenty nights from now is the Feast of Ishtar. If we do not arrive in time for this celebration, Sargon and his fellow Kings will still believe the Gods favour him. There is talk he will unite with the King of Kush. Do you know what this will mean?'

I shook my head and glared at him. 'I do not know what it will mean. There is order in this city. The message you carry defies the rule of Sharru-Kin.' From behind my breastplate, I drew a red cloth and held it above my head. The cloth fluttered in my grip.

'He has alerted the tower guards,' Kanripu told Kar. 'They will send for reinforcements.'

'Listen to me carefully, Etes,' requested Kar. 'More than a change in power looms over Akkadia. The allegiance between Akkadia and Kush will only prove strong whilst both empires are strong. When Akkadia falls to the might of savage Gutians and the re-united forces of Elam, the allegiance will be broken.'

I listened to Kar, confident that my four guards would soon be replaced by tenfold the number.

'Negusa Nagast, the ruler of the Upper Nile Valley, will pounce like a lion and turn the heartland of Akkadia into the far east of the largest empire the world has ever seen.' Kar displayed his palm as a gesture of honesty. 'Amar Sudra, the High Priest of Agade, understands this fate if we wait for Sharru-Kin to return. Only I, accompanied by these maidens, can breach the island sanctuary and tell the truth in time. New rule can appease the hatred felt for Akkadia by our eastern neighbours. Akkadian forces pressing the boundaries of Zidonia and Kush can be allowed to withdraw and as a result, the western states can also be appeased. We can save Akkadia.'

I rubbed my head, where Kar had struck me with his staff without even drawing the notice of my guards. The quick tap had taken me by surprise. Now I felt a dull pain. I touched my head and looked at my fingers. There was no blood. I addressed Kar. 'This is the last stronghold on the Euphrates and my decisions must be made in the name of the Empire. Sargon's law is final.

I will not assist you. Do I need to repeat ...'

Kar nodded and Kanripu smiled at him.

I felt like tearing out my tongue, for in confirming my stance, I had unintentionally revealed the lack of Akkadian defence if they sailed beyond my port.

'You men,' said Kar, boldly addressing my soldiers like they were his own. 'If you travel with us to Dilmun, I would offer each of you a maiden that is willing to suit with you. You will have a new life on a new shore.'

'They will have nothing of your offer.' I faced my guards. 'You will be returning to your homes at the change of guard.'

The row of four looked at each other, not me, in making their decision. When one took a step, the rest followed.

'Return to your positions,' I shouted.

Kanripu stepped aside and hurried them down the wharf.

'The penalty for desertion is death,' I threatened them.

They glanced back but not one sought approval from me as their superior as they eagerly approached the docked vessel. My threat was ignored. A different maiden welcomed each soldier aboard and a moment later they were one with the festive crowd.

I drew my sword and, in my other hand, I waved my red cloth above my head to alert the tower guards to the desertion.

Izad, the short officer, who was yet to speak, stood behind me and raised his sword above his head. He waved it from side-to-side.

I turned my blade on him. 'Do you mock me?'

He lowered his blade to meet mine. 'Do I not assist you in alerting the tower guards?'

Izad's lizard eyes, always looking in different directions, made me nervous. I watched Kar brace arms with Kanripu as I stepped back against a mooring post with my sword still raised.

Kanripu walked on alone down the wharf towards the empty market square.

Until the change of guard, I too was alone. Never had I witnessed insubordination amongst Akkadian ranks. And the ease with which my guards had revolted was unheard of. I, like all living Akkadians, only knew life under Sargon's rule. Sargon was more than our King; he was Sharru-Kin, the true King. He was the King of Akkadia when I was born and a life spent in his servitude was the only life I could imagine. 'What, in any gods' name, saw you turn on our King?' I asked Izad.

Izad did not say a word. He pointed to the top of the guard tower closest to the entry to the wharf.

I followed his pointed finger because his eyes seemed to be looking at different towers. The guards in the closest tower had their bows drawn and aimed at Kanripu as he entered the square. 'All I need do is lower my hand and they will release their arrows,' I said, reminding them of the power I still held over the happenings at my port.

'Izad was once like you,' said Kar.

We both turned to face him.

'I did not know you then,' Kar told Izad. 'Allegiant to the Lord of Borujerd, you were.'

Izad stooped his head.

Kar shook his head. 'Do not look back on those days, Izad. Remember the end of day when you met Arman.' Kar glanced west across the river and then looked at me. 'It must have been about this time. The sun was leaving the sky and the city never looked farther away.'

Izad nodded and looked up at me. 'I was a head guard. I will be a Guardian.'

Once more I felt insignificant in the play of events. It seemed I was only useful to these men's cause so long as I did not go against it by ordering the tower guards to release their arrows. The thought of doing just that entered my mind as Kanripu walked into the centre of the square. All I had to do was raise my right hand to the tower guards and then drop the same hand in the direction of the lone officer. Greater than the High Priest of Agade and unchanged by the opinion of any number of deserting officers, was my allegiance to my King. My hand trembled by my side and I think Kar noticed this.

'Life will be the same for many under new rule,' he said.

I turned to face the slave trader and twice I tried to say something. Lost for words I just stuttered, 'I ... you ...'

Kar reached between his face and his hood and untied the green cloth that draped over his nose. He pulled it loose and tucked it under his leather vest. Though he was not a large man, his every movement made tight muscles bulge on his thin arms.

I expected his face to be heavily scarred. He looked

friendly and even younger than his eyes alone told me. Younger than most of the maidens he escorted, he may have been. Next to his left eye was the only visible scar and the thin skin was still pale, telling that it was a recent injury. The scar ran out of sight into the shadows of his fur hood and I pondered if it was from one of the attempts on his life that he had mentioned to Kanripu. I wondered what other scars his hood covered.

Kar looked at me inquisitively and I almost apologised for turning away when I heard a small battalion of riders enter the port's square from the city. There were forty mounted soldiers in the battalion and each wore full armour. Leading them was Hajuom, a gallant and strong, commanding officer of Eridu. Hajuom controlled Akkadian forces near the city centre by night and I was convinced therefore that word had been sent his way via a scout from one of the guard towers. I felt embarrassed, that he, as my commanding officer, was needed to take charge of these unusual happenings. But my report to the High Priest of Eridu at the Temple of Enki would be completed as usual. The only additions to my scribed parchment would be mention of the desertion of my four guards on the ground and my attempts to relay the law of Sargon.

The sun had now moved past the horizon and the sky above the port was dark with orange light only reaching the highest clouds in the east above the shadowed city below. Eridu, and its massive stone Temple of Enki, was soon lost to darkness. Water sloshed against the docked vessels in the port and, on the decks of each, sea merchants and fishermen continued to gather silently to watch the spectacle of at least twenty maidens and my four undisciplined soldiers carousing freely.

The battalion of Akkadian soldiers assembled in front of Kanripu and waited as Hajuom lit a torch. Hajuom handed the torch to one of the riders who made his way around the square lighting more. The slave trader's vessel lit up at the same time as the soldiers dutiful to Kar placed flaming torches in clasps attached to the bow and next to the boarding plank.

From a distance, I could not hear what Kanripu told Hajuom and the battalion gathered in the Port's square. Kanripu showed them the sealed scroll and it was not long before Hajuom ordered his riders to dismount.

Kar stepped to my side. 'Is your allegiance to your King greater than your allegiance to your bride to be?'

'I am dutiful to both and never before have I been asked to divide my devotion,' I answered with conviction and watched the slave trader's face carefully for any late reveal that might sign him as a foe.

Kar smiled at me. It was a warm smile. He tilted his head and looked admiringly at the first stars to shimmer in the darkening sky.

I could not break from staring at him as I pondered how a slave trader ended up being escorted by an officer of the Court of Agade to my port.

'Do you see those two stars?' he asked, and paused as if he knew my gaze was upon him. Kar pointed between the stars and aimed his finger north. 'They will guide you and your bride to a safe land. If I were you, I would ride to her side this night and ask her to start a new life with you far from this river valley of war. Much as I have advised Kanripu, I tell you that only north of Sippur will you find lasting peace.'

'Should I take your advice, how would I provide for my bride? I am a Port Master.'

Kar looked down from the stars. He rested a hand gently on my shoulder and turned me towards his boat. 'Hija,' he called out. 'Hija, join us.'

I searched the deck with my eyes, hoping to sight the dark-haired maiden wearing the blue dress.

'Many soldiers and officers have asked me for advice on what they shall do next,' Kar told me, standing so close that his words were almost my own. 'You must learn to provide for yourself or help others plant seed. Maybe you, like the Guardians of the East, could see to it you work to protect the goods of merchants as they are transported by river between the cities. You could live a life unconstrained by city walls and duty to a man you have never met.'

I opened my mouth to tell Kar that I had seen my King. He was right though. I had never met the King. From the port end of the wharf, I had seen Sargon standing on the deck of a vessel as it sailed south. At least, I had thought I had seen Sargon. The man I saw was larger than an ordinary man and his beard was plaited. The excitement of this possible sighting had skewed my judgement. Before my exhilaration had settled, I had boasted of my sighting to all those I met on my return from the port that eve. It was only when I recounted the story to my father, the Port Master of Eridu before me, that I was given pause. My father asked me that night if I had seen Sargon's eyes. I had not. I had only seen a large man of regal stature from a distance.

'The maiden, Hija, is from Assur,' continued Kar. 'She is a gentle woman who can sew, farm and cut meat. She could help you start a new life with your bride and in return you could set her free when the time comes.'

Kar continued to tell me all he knew of this woman as she stepped across the boarding plank with another maiden and waited with her eyes downcast. 'Her father is a leather trader and her mother a seamstress. They work out of the same stall in the market square of Agade. They raised her well and she partook in the bidding for her sale. Twenty silver shekels I offered ...'

I watched Hija twirl a lock of her dark hair around her finger as Kar spoke to me. Her head was dipped to my stare and whenever our eyes met she averted them quickly. The way her dark skin contrasted with her silver bracelets and the light-coloured cloth that draped delicately over her lean frame, captivated me. She was very beautiful yet I did not look at her with the eyes of a lover. I had a bride and this young maiden looked like someone we could share our home with. Kar's idea of guiding boats between the ports as a new occupation also appealed to me. While I was away from home it would be comforting to know that my wife had a maiden to run errands, mend clothes and prepare meals. For a moment I was consumed by fanciful thoughts and missed hearing some of Kar's words. 'Did you say twenty silver shekels?'

'There should be no price on a person's life.'

'Strange words coming from a slave trader.'

'Would you treat her as a slave? No maiden will leave my care other than by her own choice.' Kar turned to face Hija and called her closer.

'Do not make her,' I told him when I saw that Hija was afraid to leave the side of her friend.

'I can tell that you are a good man, Etes. Dutiful to a failed king you are though still a good man.' Kar turned suddenly to face the port square and raised his staff high in the air.

I looked the same way and saw that Hajuom, the officer in charge of the battalion, had his hands raised to signal my attention. When Hajuom saw that I was looking his way he pointed to Kanripu and raised his arm four times in quick controlled motions. Hajuom then swayed his arm to symbolise the sea and pointed south. Following this signal, he pointed both arms to the south to sign that this course was allowed.

'You may travel south from this port tonight,' I told Kar, 'and you can tell Hija that I already have a bride and that her service for two seasons is all I will ask of her.' I was quick to confirm my acceptance of Kar's offer at this point, half expecting it to be revoked now that permission beyond my control had been granted.

'I will have Izad confirm that with a contract. Her service to you for two seasons will be in return for duty already completed on your part. Do you agree?'

'I agree,' I told Kar, welcoming an offer that might have gone to Hajuom if I delayed my acceptance.

Izad sheathed his sword and returned to their boat.

I looked at Kar and behind him at Hija. 'Why do you willingly offer me a maiden when leave from the port has already been granted?'

'You are the Port Master, and it is from your port that I wish to sail south,' Kar answered. He signalled

Hija to approach and called for the soldiers who had travelled with him from Agade, to disembark. He raised his staff and pointed them towards Kanripu who stood waiting in the port's square that was now bright with the light of many flaming torches. 'Let it be known that we wish to leave before the moon has fully risen,' he told the departing soldiers. Kar faced me. 'Treat Hija well and heed my earlier advice, Etes. Make this your last night of duty under Sargon.'

I watched Kar return to his boat. Whilst I had fancied the idea of a life spent travelling between ports, I knew to which port I would return on the morrow. I was a Port Master, like my father before me.

*** 

An almost full-faced moon beamed down on the maiden, Hija, and I as we watched Kar's boat cast off from the wharf into the turbulent, easterly current of the Euphrates River. She smiled and I smirked at his departure. I knew that his single-sailed vessel would not last a day in the Southern Sea.

Hajuom, accompanied by his battalion, rode from the port towards the Temple of Enki. They would deliver the scroll to the high priest. Four guards had replaced my deserters. They stood at the end of the wharf; noticeable only by the torches they held. The maiden, Hija, and I walked towards them. Each creaking plank beneath our step was another whine from Sargon. Life without Sargon was hard to fathom and many this night had heard or seen the happenings that led to a boat being granted leave to travel south against his law. I was not convinced that Sharru-Kin's reign was over and I felt I had only faltered in revealing that

Eridu was the last stronghold on the Euphrates. My re-count to the Court of Eridu did not have to reveal that detail. I had remained dutiful but even a Port Master of my standing would be held responsible should the contents of the scroll not support the overarching power of Sargon's law. My guards' desertion could sign that I did not have the power necessary to command a port. A plank creaked painfully beneath my feet as I turned back to face Kar's vessel disappearing into the dark mouth of the river. The choice to leave the city tonight or face trial for treason was weighted in my mind.

'Can we join my father now?' said Hija.

I raised my brow to her request stated like an order. 'If we ever travel via Agade, I will allow you to see him.'

She shook her head and pointed to the port's square, 'My father is waiting for us now.'

Kanripu stood in the square brandishing a flaming torch that glistened light off his bronze breastplate and brooches. I looked above him to the guard tower nests and saw no guards manning their posts.

'Kar will fight Sargon and win,' declared Hija as she tried to walk me towards the square.

I pulled my hand from hers and cast my eyes across the graveyard of sail-drawn masts. On the horizon, I noticed the flickering lights from boats sailing our way from the north.

'That is the might of Akkadia heading our way,' Hija alerted me, showing no concern or resignation for her part in the act of deception. 'They come for our heads and those you let sail onwards.'

I held my hands away from her clasping reach and looked once more at her father, the man who appeared to be an officer of Agade. Behind him, the faces of the four new port guards were visible in the torchlight. I stepped backwards. The guards at the end of the wharf were the ones that had departed Kar's boat.

'Come back to me, Etes,' begged Hija. 'We need to leave.'

I shook my head. 'You deceived me. You all defy Sharru-Kin.'

Hija reached again for my hand. 'It was not all deception. My father is still considered an officer and the High Priest, Amur Sudra, allowed for our journey to your port,' she explained.

'If the High Priest allowed this, why does he send an Akkadian army south in your vessel's wake?'

Hija displayed her palms. 'If Kar fails, Amar Sudra will not. The High Priest will either be known as the one who came to the rescue of his King or the one to maintain power when he announces the new king. Our fate need not be aligned with them. Let us collect your bride and leave this city tonight.'

'Tell me Hija, if that is your true name, were the maidens all slaves?'

'All of them were rightfully paid for with Guardian silver or Gutian gold, including myself. I am your servant, Etes. You have the contract approved by Izad. I will farewell my father and stay by your side if that be your wish.'

'So your father is not an officer? Is your mother a seamstress?'

'My mother is a seamstress in Agade. My father,

once an officer of Agade, controls the trade of leather in the north and between the rivers.'

I glanced once more at the lights of the boats on the northern horizon before hastily stepping back to Hija's side and grabbing her hand. 'Not by my will is my duty now to my bride over my King,' I told her. 'I hope Kar and your father are wrong, for life in Eridu is good for most citizens and it was the strength of Sargon that made it so.'

Hija leant in front of me and tried to look me in the eye. 'You are doing the right thing, Etes.'

I stared past Hija at her father as we walked his way. 'They will not make it to Dilmun. Your reed boat is not seaworthy and, even if it leaves the cove, it will encounter the fleet returning from Dilmun to escort Amar Sudra to the island. All those you travelled with will die in a sea that only gods and kings like Sargon can traverse.'

Hija laughed and reefed her hand from my hold. Her once innocent and coy demeanour was gone and she stood tall and menacing in my gaze. 'Only a fool or a king with something to prove would cross that sea from the cove. Kar only needs to sail to the cove.'

I was not sure if it was Hija's voice or her words that captivated me. Maybe I was captivated by fear, for I no longer had guards by my side or watching me from above. Even the traders and fishermen had retired after the earlier commotion. I jolted from my state of confusion as light from Kanripu's torch breached my face.

'We must move on, Hija' said Kanripu.

Hija stepped to her father's side and held out her hand to me.

'Why do you care about me?' I asked and looked through the flickering flame at their faces wavering in the light.

'You are a deserter like us now,' she explained, 'an enemy of the King. No one can trust a deserter, so do I have my father kill you or do we take you to your bride and have her tell you to wake up?'

'Her home is close to the Temple of Enki.'

'I will escort you via her home,' offered Kanripu. 'I can take you and her family north beyond Agade to safety or as far as you wish to travel.' He prompted me to walk on with a wave of his torch.

I stood still. 'Does Kar plan to ambush Amar Sudra at the cove?'

Kanripu pointed north to the lights of the boats heading our way. 'When Amar Sudra sets sail for Dilmun from the mouth of the river beyond this port, Kar will already be three day's ride ahead of him to the south. Just as your King gained maps to his land in the east, Kar has gained maps from those born where the sun first rose. Kar has blessed our lives and I will return the favour by escorting you north. We leave now.'

Hija grabbed my hand and pulled me into my next steps.

'We must not delay,' advised Kanripu as he paced ahead and extinguished the flaming torch by stabbing it into a barrel of fish guts at the end of the wharf. 'Lead the way to your home, Etes.'

I hastened my step as we walked through the dark, empty port.

Hija squeezed my hand tight and after that it was I who held hers.

# 31

# Steps to the Kings

*Scribed by Enheduanna, Priestess of Ur.*

B eyond the last drinking hut that sat near the steep
road to the Port of Dilmun, I saw a large sailboat
arrive from the west. This boat flew the flag of Akkadia yet it had not travelled from Akkadia, unless it
had got swept far off course. From a distance, I could
not see clearly the occupants though I could detect the
vibrant colour of many maidens' dresses. My perceived
noble servant, Derahmus, was probably fornicating
with the Egyptian Queen when I called out his name.
So startling was my shriek that Negusa Nagast, The
Second King of Kings, spread the drapes of the gazebo
and sprung forwards into the sunlight with his sword
held high. 'Be gone ill demons,' I think he cried out,
though he may have said, 'Adore my heavens.' Truth be
told, I did not care what words the drunken, Ethiopian
King voiced in all his naked glory. Naked maidens and
Akkadian soldiers, apparently intoxicated by the way
they carried themselves, followed him out. The soldiers
playfully wrestled with the King until they had control
of his sword and they carried him back inside to the
squealing pleasure of the naked maidens. Again, I was

alone on the steps leading up to the gazebo. I decided then and there that I had devoted myself enough to my father's growing empire. If this were to be the beginning of his fall then I would be the one to hear first what was to come. The priestess I was last high moon would have fled up the steps to shelter. She would have hidden from the mere thought of change. Whilst the thought of change still scared me, I was more frightened of not sighting Kar with my own eyes. I needed to see him stand before me in the light of day. He was the proof I needed for doubting my devotion to Nanna and allegiance to my father's empire.

The play ended as I predicted with the Lion lurching to life and I smiled to myself as I walked down the steps to meet the man who parted the crowds, leading twelve women my way. Arriving at ground level, near to the people of Dilmun gathered for the street performance, I grew nervous. I unclipped the button that secured a finger-length blade in a sheath sewn to the side of my dress.

The soldiers guarding the gazebo steps were alerted to my presence. They were unaware of the vessel I had seen arrive at the dock from the west. Surrounded by citizens of Dilmun and Akkadian soldiers, my view of the man leading the procession of women towards the gazebo was blocked. I could not be sure it was Kar. I had heard about the eastern warrior via the recounts of locals in Eshnunna and from many others as we returned to the West. They all told me, without knowing that Sargon was my father, that the warrior had only one enemy and one destination. To fight my father as an equal was his only desire. Laughable I had deemed this plan to be. My father was never alone and only the

High Priests knew his calendar of events. Kar's quest to fight my father seemed weighted against him and I never supposed, until Derahmus had shared his insight, that Kar might find my father here, separated by the sea from the true might of his armies.

It only took one man to notice my presence for all to be made aware.

'Enheduanna, the Priestess has joined us,' announced one of the play's actors.

An army of eyes swung my way and the crowd jostled as men and women moved closer to the bottom of the steps, overwhelming the guards with their sudden advance.

'Stand back,' I screamed, knowing my words would only further my condemnation, for only a priestess without heavenly support would show such fear. I did not care for the people's opinion so long as I was myself when Kar arrived. Thankfully, many of the men present had their own women to hold them back. The dirty farming man who pulled on my braid felt my knuckles in his eye socket. My hand throbbed as I drew it back to my chest. I stuck the fat man who ripped at my dress with my finger length blade. The sight of blood on my own blade made me quiver with excitement. I wished it had connected with his heart, though it had only cut his shielding hand. The smear of blood on my own blade was more arousing than the pump of blood from a sacrificed lamb. My fear and excitement were inseparable. I felt removed from my body, controlled by all I hated in this world.

The eight armoured guards formed a protective arch around me and forced the crowd back from the steps.

I looked up at the gazebo, hoping to sight Derahmus running to my aid. Despite the noise raised by this debacle not even one soldier, Akkadian, Egyptian or Ethiopian, stuck their head out in enquiry. Every one of them was indulging themselves, even my noble servants.

'High Priestess you are not safe here,' alerted one of the guards, directing me back up the steps with a wave of his broad sword.

'I am safer with you than with your drunken soldiers atop these steps.'

He bit his lip to avoid saying any more and turned back to face the rowdy crowd.

From behind his shoulders I watched as the people of Dilmun parted to form an aisle that led to the steps to the gazebo. Like a new play was about to commence, the crowd became less vocal. I glanced up at the gazebo again. Did Derahmus think he was protecting me from Ankhnesmenre by servicing her desires? Anything she may have overheard us talking about on the top landing was about to be proved. Would he therefore view his choice to abandon me foolish in hindsight? Maybe the chance to bed an Egyptian Queen in his otherwise mundane existence in my servitude, he felt owed.

The crowd closest the bottom of the steps shuffled about and whispered to each other as the occupants of the boat I had spotted from a distance arrived.

The head guard took a defining step into the path of those advancing. 'That is close enough,' he warned the man who arrived followed by a procession of twelve young women. 'State your name and business here.'

For the first time since I had sighted the boat's arrival from a distance, doubt concerning who this man truly was entered my mind. He was accompanied by maidens and held a staff; that he was a slave trader escorting these women to the gazebo now seemed more likely. The citizens who Derahmus and I spoke with in Eshnunna described Kar as a fearless looking man with captivating eyes and long brown hair. I watched this man remove his fur hood and catch his heel awkwardly on his mauve cape as he bowed to the head guard. His head was shaved to the scalp and revealed deep scars. The deepest scar began on his cheek and had removed half his ear as it circled around to the top of his scalp. He was even younger than me and hardly looked strong enough to challenge the head guard, let alone my father. But he was tall, carried a staff and his skin had spent many days in the sun, just as Derahmus had described the boy he had allowed to enter Assur.

He straightened and held his staff firmly at his side. 'I am Kar, a Guardian of the East and I have come for your King.'

My whole body quivered but the citizens of Dilmun who overheard his announcement laughed boisterously. Many must have thought it part of the street performance for the actors remained on stage and directed the crowd's attention to the bottom of the steps.

'You do not speak like it is counsel you seek,' the head guard replied, with his broad sword raised. 'Return whence you came before I am forced to strike.'

Kar began to casually untie the hide on the end of his staff. 'Only the King must face judgement today,' he said in a disconcerting, soft voice.

'I will not hear any more of your threats,' yelled the head guard and he tapped his sword against his bronze helmet. This signalled the other guards to be on high alert. 'Turn and walk away now or it will be you who is judged.'

'Wait,' I blurted.

The head guard was stupefied by my command and turned his head so quickly that he had to straighten his helmet. 'Do you know this man, High Priestess?'

'I know of him,' I replied, 'if it is counsel he seeks.'

'I do not believe it is, High Priestess.'

'Is it counsel with my father you seek, Kar?' I asked him directly.

To the guards' raised swords he was unresponsive; however, confessing that the man he sought was my father captured his attention. The young man turned his contemplative gaze from the blade fastened to his staff and our eyes met. They were the greenest eyes I'd ever seen. They shone like palm fronds in the afternoon sun and were more captivating than any I had seen before. They were the eyes I had heard about—eyes like the wild man Enkidu—and I wanted to know him.

'Let him pass so that I may speak with him,' I ordered the guards.

'I shall not, High Priestess,' protested the head guard. 'My duty is to protect Sharru-Kin with my life. Even your word is subject to his.' He turned to make sure the other guards also understood to whom foremost their duty resided.

Kar called his party of maidens close and their private conversation was a further insult to the head guard.

'I will say it once more and that will be the extent of my tolerance,' he said to Kar's turned back. 'Walk away or I will—'

Eight of the twelve maidens approached with cloth-wrapped offerings.

'My name is Silda, daughter of Ashipa of Nineveh,' said the beautiful maiden who stood before the head guard. 'This is yours so long as you leave and fight no more on these shores.'

I stepped closer and watched as the head guard spread the cloth covering the maiden's offering.

'It is a gold mug,' he startled.

'And you should take it and start a new life on the far shore,' advised the maiden, Silda. Her fine cloth dress was sunset orange and in the breeze it rippled like the flames of a fire. Only missing a regal head-dress, her dark hair was braided and coiled into a high bun like my own hair. She smiled at the head guard and he lowered his sword to his waist.

The other seven guards also had maidens standing in front of them with similar gifts.

This morn, before I had spoken with Derahmus, I had thought Akkadian soldiers dutiful to death in the name of my father's Empire. Now I knew they, like the people I met in Eshnunna, to only be obliging for fear of death or lack of greater offer. A gold mug was a grand offer.

'Are we going to accept?' asked the guard closest to the stage.

The head guard heard these words of desertion and raised his sword. 'Maintain your stance, soldier,' he shouted.

At the top of the steps, outside the gazebo, a drunken assembly of soldiers was now forming. I could not sight Derahmus or any of the kings amongst their numbers.

The head guard also turned and inspected this gathering. 'You should retreat up the steps, High Priestess.'

Such an idea I had already abandoned. Amongst the people I would learn the truth. I stepped past the head guard and extended my hand to Kar. 'The offer of gold is not required. I have wished to speak with Kar since I first heard of his quest.'

Kar looked past my extended hand at the blade I still held in my other hand.

'I was protecting myself,' I explained as I returned the finger-length blade to its sheath and extended my hand again.

'Priestess,' said the head guard, 'if you allow him to walk the sacred steps, I will not challenge him again. Have him surrender his weapon.'

I looked at the head guard and the other seven guards protecting the steps. In front of each of them stood one of Kar's maidens. The offer presented to each of these guards was the same, a gold mug. The gold in each mug would be enough for them to buy land, servants and food for many harvests. It made me think of the farming people in Eshnunna and the trials of their daily work. What the gold could not buy was surely the soldiers greatest concern. The penalty for desertion was death and my father could claim ownership of any possession of a deserter. They would have to flee into the savage lands where crops, homes and people are not protected by the gods or soldiers of Akkadia. But, maybe, more than the mugs' worth in gold was what the offering of a cup symbolised.

Kar did not reach for my hand. He stood still with his staff by his side. Like a shepherd watching his herd, he appeared attentive but strangely calm considering his placement before eight sword-wielding Akkadians. When the bronze blade on his staff caught the light of the high sun, I was reminded again of his intent.

I lowered my hand and clutched my dress at my side. 'Kar, will you surrender your weapon?' I asked him.

Kar glanced at me and returned his stare to the head guard. He might have only heard his name over the voices from the crowd.

The crowd that had formed an aisle for Kar and his procession of maidens to approach the steps had since closed the gap. Whilst the people were no longer forcing themselves upon the steps, they were more vocal as they tried to see and understand the reason behind this strange party's visit.

'Priestess,' said the head guard, 'let me end this.' His feet were braced and his sword was raised.

Silda stepped away from him, her hands still extending her offer of a gold mug.

'There is no need to battle,' I told the head guard. But Derahmus was wrong about the soldiers' allegiance to my father. Kar had announced that he had come to fight the King and the guards remained dutiful despite the temptation of gold. I could not convince my own ears of this confrontation proceeding another way. Kar's maidens and I might have been the only ones who hoped for peaceful compromise. My hands scrunched and twisted my dress at my side.

The head guard ordered Silda to stand aside.

The butt of Kar's staff lifted from the ground and the muscles on his arm tensed.

'Stop,' I shouted as I stepped between Kar and the head guard. 'My father fears no man. I welcome him to join me on the steps. There is no need to battle.'

The people gasped as I took Kar's hand in mine.

I turned to lead Kar to the steps and the head guard stood in my path.

He faced me, his eyes shadowed by his helmet. 'I cannot fight him whilst you hold his hand,' he said. 'Lower your blades,' he ordered the other guards. He stepped aside and waved my way to the steps with his sword. When I stepped past him, he faced the maiden in the orange dress. 'I accept, Silda. May I be so bold as to request that you be included in the offer?'

The other guards smiled at each other, seemingly thankful for his decision, until he said more.

'We will only take one gold mug to share,' stated the head guard. 'We leave the rest for the people of Dilmun.' He pointed his sword ahead of his advance into the crowd and the rest of the guards delayed only for a moment before following their leader's controlled exit.

The soldiers at the top of the steps watched on as the eight guards in charge of protecting the gazebo abandoned their posts, accompanied by Silda, one of Kar's twelve maidens.

I thought I had prevented a battle by aiding Kar's advance. The eyes of the crowd told me otherwise. The guards, with their more than modest bounty, were allowed passage. A greater offering of seven golden mugs remained.

As the eight guards disappeared amongst the crowd, Kar pulled his hand from mine and called for his eleven maidens to follow him up the steps.

Unlike the day Gilgamesh battled Enridu in the streets of Uruk, I still hoped that blood on my finger-length blade might be the only blood that was spilled this day. 'Kar,' I called out as I hitched my dress and followed him up the steps. 'Let me tell my father why you are here. He might listen to me.'

The crowd surged into the space occupied by the guards but none dared to venture onto the steps.

Kar, standing not much higher than the actors on their stage, addressed the sea of faces before him. 'Citizens of Dilmun, you dwell where the sun blossomed in the sky first.' He raised his staff to the sky and turned it so that its bronze blade caught the light of the sun.

I'm not sure if it was the light reflecting from his blade or the sight of a stranger on the sacred steps that gained the people's attention. They stilled themselves enough that his voice was carried by the wind.

'Ancestors you are to a god who offered you free will,' he bellowed. 'Be the pattern makers of Enki. Make our father god, Anu, proud in his return. The choice to live as always or become something greater is now upon you. Eleven maidens wait for eleven men to ensure their safe passage from this island. Each maiden still carries a gold mug. You can drink a new life on the far shore. People of Dilmun,' he shouted, 'stand with me against the tyrant king, Sargon. Fight with me in the name of the mother of all gods, Ki. This is the final wish of Mother Ki who burnt for many to see.

She gave her life so that I would arrive here this day. Today I will show you the strength we all have when it is a fight we must make.' Pointing his staff to the top of the stairs, Kar announced, 'God or man, I will fight Sargon this day.'

The crowd raged. Like the high waves of the Southern Sea, they looked ready to spill onto the steps. There were shouts for blood to be drawn and fights broke out as people were pushed from their feet. Others stared upwards with gaping mouths. An actor on the stage repeated Kar's message. It received cheers from some and shouts of condemnation from others. A rock, thrown by someone in the crowd, connected with the actor's head. All the performers quickly departed from the stage.

The eleven maidens followed Kar further up the steps. As I contemplated following, I felt a strong hand grip mine. 'Derahmus, you abandoned me,' my voice quaked.

'For your own protection, Enheduanna,' he explained whilst leading me up the steps to where the maidens had gathered on the first landing.

'And what of your Egyptian lover?' I asked, still angered by his abandonment.

'A story for another day and maybe not for your innocent ears,' he said with a snake's smile. 'Stay close to my side for we stand with the enemy.'

'It is Kar. I bid him entry to the steps.'

'I know, Enheduanna. Your father also knows he is here. Soon more soldiers will follow my path out the back entrance of the gazebo and we will be trapped with the enemy.'

At the top of the steps was a rabble of drunken Akkadian soldiers, numbering at least twenty. Their drunkenness was not a weakness. The soldiers often drunk beer and fought each other when not on duty or before a battle. Next to them, on the Southern Sea side of the gazebo's outer ring, stood Negusa Nagast's personal guards.

Kar positioned himself on the landing between this defensive force and the anxious maidens who waited near Derahmus and I on the landing below.

Might there have been men supportive of Kar's cause, they were too slow in presenting themselves for duty. An Akkadian defensive force, matching that standing before Kar, had made their way out the back entrance of the gazebo and was assembling at the bottom of the steps. Several of these Akkadians saw it their first duty to light the signal fires that would warn others on the island of the siege.

The maidens grew increasingly nervous though Kar spoke as though their plight was not compromised. 'I am here for Sargon's head and no other,' he told the Akkadians barring his pass to the gazebo.

The soldiers looked at each other and laughed like he was joking.

Kar dipped his head and, though I could not see his face, he seemed to be laughing with them. I thought of the story I had scribed in Eshnunna. When surrounded by Gutians, I was told he smiled.

He lifted his head to face those guarding the gazebo. 'If Sargon is the God-King you believe him to be, why is he in need of your protection? Have him face me alone on these steps for all to see,' Kar told the soldiers as he unhooked his mauve cape and let it fall at his feet. 'Is he too frightened to even show his face?'

The soldiers surrounding the gazebo could not see that Kar had a blade sheathed behind his back and a bronze bolt fastened to a side bow.

Derahmus stepped from my side and I quickly grabbed him before he alerted the soldiers.

'Protect me Derahmus. Let the soldiers deal with Kar.'

Derahmus pulled his arm from my grip. 'On equal ground they said Kar would face the King. I will not stand idle as your father is assassinated.'

'He will not do that,' I assured him, swallowing my own doubt.

'Know that in listening to you now I am forgoing any chance at a full pardon.'

'If my father falls you will not need a pardon, Derahmus.'

'My duty is foremost to you, Enheduanna,' he confirmed and stepped back to my side. 'You know we are alike?' He smirked. 'We both offered Kar passage.'

Kar turned his back on the Akkadians guarding the gazebo when he heard the guards below begin their advance up the stairs towards the maidens gathered on the first landing.

Derahmus tried to halt their advance; however, like the guards who manned the entrance to the stairs before them, they seemed only dutiful to my father. Wearing a leather skirt, and nothing that distinguished him as an Akkadian, Derahmus was ignored. He clasped my hand between his hard palms and tilted his head to his bronze breastplate. It rested ten steps above where we stood on the lower landing. 'I should retrieve my armour. I'll only leave you for a moment.'

Derahmus bounded up the steps and I looked beyond him at Kar.

Kar rotated his loaded weapon from his back.

On the top step, an Akkadian archer knelt with his bow flexed.

Kar released a bronze bolt without the need to flex tendon.

The bolt removed the top of the archer's head, splattering blood on the white curtains of the gazebo. As the archer collapsed, the arrow he had drawn taut was released.

I screamed words I could never write as I fell to my hands and knees.

Derahmus looked at me as my head lifted from my stumble. He tumbled down the steps with an arrow through his neck. Void of life, his contorted body came to rest next to me.

If he had been wearing his bronze breastplate, the arrow would have still struck his neck. It was my offering of passage to Kar, not his, that had allowed this. I shrieked at the sky and clawed my nails into the stone landing. My nails bent, broke and bled.

The soldiers advancing up the steps paused and looked at me astonished, as if they had never heard so many references to the gods in one outcry. Before they took their next step, a parting curtain at the gazebo drew all's attention.

I looked up with spittle stringing from my mouth. My father had finally showed his face.

He parted the blood-splattered white cloth that

hung at the entrance to the gazebo and stepped between his soldiers. Over his sparkling silver, regal-silk gown he had fastened a bronze breastplate. His tightly plaited beard rested against the breastplate as he stared down the steps at Kar. Twice the size of his adversary my father was. Shadowed by thick brows of hair, his eyes looked like the hollows of a skull from a distance. In his left arm he held a long sword, the length of an ordinary man and his muscles strained not as he pointed it towards Kar. 'A noble to my throne and respected amongst gods will be the soldier who brings me this savage's head,' he announced, standing taller than all, in front of the gazebo.

Kar drew a blade from behind his back and aimed it at my father threateningly before thrusting it at the first soldier to advance down the steps towards him.

The blade caught the Akkadian guard in the stomach and the guard dropped his sword as he bent over with pain and fell awkwardly down the rest of the steps to the landing. Still alive, the guard lifted his head and bellowed with agony.

Kar bunted him with the blunt end of his staff and the last sound from this guard was his skull cracking between the force of Kar's strike and the stone it met.

Twelve Akkadian soldiers continued their advance upwards towards the gazebo and Kar's eleven maidens shuffled from their path to the Southern Sea side of the landing.

That was when the first man of Dilmun presented himself. Brandishing a short sword he launched an attack on one of the four guards still manning the entrance to the steps below. There was a huge cheer from the crowd gathered closest the steps. He was not successful, though the moment he fell another picked up his weapon and continued the assault.

On the steps above, Kar fought alone. Four at a time, the soldiers attacked and it was impossible for Kar, despite the deadliness of his strike, to take them all down with immediacy.

An Akkadian soldier re-gathered his sword after his first attempt and charged back at Kar from behind.

With a flick of his staff, Kar lifted his mauve cape from the landing and tossed it at the Akkadian. Before the Akkadian could peel it from his face, Kar kicked him in the chest and the soldier sailed backwards down the steps, bones cracking with each tumble he took.

Four more Akkadians descended on Kar from the gazebo.

Kar stuck his bladed staff into two of the fast-advancing soldiers before rotating it underarm and cutting the face of the Akkadian who stepped wide and tried to attack from the side.

No longer could I doubt the stories I had heard in Eshnunna. Kar fought with the strength of ten men on the awkward footing of the steps. Only an arrow released without his notice could bring him down. I did not want this bloodshed. 'Speak with him, father,' I screamed as I got to my feet. 'Remember Enkidu, the wild man. Make a friend of your foe.'

Shouts and cheers from the crowd muffled my cry.

The Akkadian soldiers who were making their way up the steps to confront Kar did not venture past the first landing. From this defensive position, they watched Kar slice, stab and in every other way, break open the bodies of their fellow soldiers. Blood from the fallen gathered and began to trickle down the stone steps.

One of the advancing soldiers abandoned duty and fled back down the fifty steps.

This encouraged another citizen of Dilmun to stand with Kar. He slipped past the guards protecting the entry to the steps carrying a sickle.

The fleeing Akkadian tried to step wide of the man ascending the steps but his retreat was not allowed. Forced to the edge of the steps where there was a sheer drop onto the cliffs below, he swung his sword.

The man from Dilmun blocked the deserting soldier's sword with his farming sickle and then brought the sickle's point down on the soldier's head.

That is what I wanted to do when the dirty man had ripped at my dress. I wanted to stab my blade in his heart and let him know whom he challenged. Kar had told the people of Dilmun that they had this strength if it was a fight they must make. I wanted this strength or at least the strength of voice to gain my father's ear.

At the bottom of the steps, more men stepped from the crowd with any form of weapon they could gather. The Akkadian guards fought them back. Frightened maidens and viziers to the foreign kings filled the outer ring of the gazebo as the battle ensued on the steps between them and the populace of Dilmun below. The white cloth drapes at the entrance to the gazebo were pulled open and behind my father stood Negusa Nagast, Pepi the Egyptian King and their respective queens. Negusa and Pepi offered their personal guards to the fight. As quickly as the drapes were parted, they were closed. My father was the only king who remained outside. I imagined Ankhnesmenre fleeing down the back steps to the gazebo ahead of her young son. If any of the party of kings, queens, princesses, viziers and maidens still sought refuge in the gazebo, there were only twelve fighting men left to protect them.

The crowd was wild. Families fled, shielding their children with protective arms. A man stood upon the actors' stage, inciting the crowd's rage. More joined him on the platform. Those who remained gathered at the bottom of the steps applauded those who ventured towards the gazebo. Cheers erupted when a citizen of Dilmun reached the first landing.

My father watched as Kar duelled the previous four soldiers he had ordered to descend before commanding anymore to attack.

Kar was struck on his side as he battled two sol-diers across the highest landing. He eventually cut them down and swept his blade back defensively at the soldier attacking from behind. Another Akkadian solider launched at him and Kar bent low and hoisted him up under a wing of one of the monstrous statues manning the steps. The stone tip of the wing cracked the soldier's spine. Kar rolled away and let the soldier's lifeless body fall with a slap.

The remaining soldier sliced Kar's leg above his knee and Kar stumbled backwards off the landing and down five steps before he re-gathered his footing. He paused to wipe blood from his eyes.

The now confident Akkadian, who had cut Kar's leg, bounded down the stairs with his sword aimed like a spear.

Kar blocked his blade and rotated his staff around so that the blunt end connected under the soldier's chin. Dazed by this strike the Akkadian was now at Kar's mercy and none was shown. Kar drove his blade into the soldier's chest and forced him off the side of the steps.

The soldier screamed with pain until his body was heard smacking against the stone cliff below.

Kar's assembly of frightened maidens still huddled to one side of the landing and when the first few men reached their side they begged to be taken away. They knelt and offered their gold mugs. I wanted to be taken away too but I needed the attention of Kar or my father to allow this. Derahmus's lifeless eyes begged for me to do more. In Susa, he had told me how he would have commanded the Akkadian assault on the East. He never spoke of ending the fighting.

At the top of the steps my father still had twelve soldiers in his control, counting the Egyptian and Ethiopian guards.

The men of Dilmun, and a woman, who had made it to the first landing, staged their support for Kar and committed themselves to the fight. Some were only armed with sickles, hoes and other farming tools. The woman wore a leather apron, like a metal worker, and carried a short-handled axe in one hand and a dagger in the other. Despite the weapon they had been in possession of, or been handed, they all looked ready for battle. They had already proved themselves capable of fighting by defeating the Akkadians guarding the base of the steps and ascending to the first landing. Apart from quick glances at each other and behind, they kept their eyes focused on the soldiers above.

A young man, amongst them, signalled his enthusiasm by raising the sword that had once belonged to
the first to join Kar.

An outburst of applause came from the crowd.
Whether the wide spread appreciation was for the ac-
complishment of the daring Dilmunians or just for the
sake of spectacle was not clear. Voices called out for
the King's head to be taken and others still cried out
for blood.

'Spill blood, take hearts and heads,' chanted the
group of men and women who had occupied the stage.

A citizen of Dilmun filled every space as far away
as the drinking hut that sat atop the steep traverse to
the port and I saw no indication of Akkadian support
arriving from anywhere on the island

My father took his first step down the stairs and
signalled the citizens of Dilmun to be silent with a
raised sword. This only roused the crowd more.

The men, and the woman wielding a weapon in
both hands, also called for the crowd below to be still.

Kar raised his staff above his head.

A chant for blood continued from those gathered
on the stage. They got their wish when the wooden
structure collapsed beneath their weight. Wails of pain
ensued but once more the wind could be heard as it
swept around the heights of the massive gazebo and
stirred the seas surrounding the island. Most of the
crowd had stilled. The collapse of the stage might have
reminded them of gods' play.

I looked up at my father, questioning whether he
could have summoned the collapse.

'You are a strong warrior,' my father said in praise

of Kar, 'and an honourable stand you have made.'

The crowd became vocal again as my father, King Sargon, stepped slowly down the stairs between many scattered bodies to the highest landing.

Whilst shared words on the highest landing did not reach the ears of the people gathered, they were witnessing a rare public appearance of their King. The face depicted on statues and on silver shekels was revealed in the light of day. His presence, even to me, was captivating. In the last three harvests, I had only stood in his company once and on that occasion had only spoken with him through my mother. I thought he saw me standing below but he might have been looking past me at the maidens.

My father addressed Kar who stood ten steps below him, between the two landings. 'I must warn you, young man, that if you continue this fight you will be condemning yourself and the people you have enlisted to certain death.'

'Death is certain for us,' yelled the woman wielding a weapon in each hand. 'Do you bleed?'

My father signalled her silence with a raised palm. The crowd was not silenced. He faced Kar. 'Superior in battle to the average soldier you have already proved yourself to be. Summoned a sleeping king you have. Take your glorious story and leave with your new following before my reinforcements from the port arrive. Live to fight me another day on familiar shore.'

'I did not cross endless horizons only to surrender,' stated Kar. He wiped blood from his face and flicked his wrist to toss it aside.

I looked over the people's heads and down towards

the distant port. Kar had disembarked from his vessel and walked to the steps of the gazebo only accompanied by his maidens. Whatever had allowed for his advance to go unchallenged was still at play. There would be no reinforcements. The crowd, despite the lack of guards, remained grouped at the bottom of the steps. Maybe the impaling of one in the stage's collapse had sent a message to all about challenging a king or a god. The people of Dilmun stood to attention like the citizens of Ur had when I last read a hymn from the steps to Nanna's Temple. There was civility enough for my father to hear the reason for Kar's arrival. I hoped Kar would tell my father of Ki's death or the defeat of my father's army in the East.

Kar stood on the steps between the two landings and pointed his staff at Sargon. 'I judge you not worthy to be King and call you to duel.'

'No, tell him why you travelled here,' I yelled, taking a step towards Kar from the landing below. 'Father, let Kar tell you what happened in the East.'

My father smiled. I knew he was looking at me this time and I recognised his deception. He stepped to the edge of the landing with his sword lowered at his side. 'I asked you, young man, what you saw upon arriving on this island? Was it not people celebrating life?' My father pointed over the mass of people gathered below. 'You interrupted a private gathering of kings. You sucked all festiveness from the air. To call me to duel whilst I entertain is an insult. The sword I carry is mere jewellery.' He pointed the largest sword I'd ever seen at Kar. 'You, on the other hand, are equipped for war and deceived the people by disguising yourself as a slave merchant.'

'Admit the truth, Sargon,' challenged Kar, pausing to wipe the blood trickling down his forehead and into his eyes. 'I caught you off guard. A God would not be caught off guard and that makes you a man like the rest of us.' Turning to address the people of Dilmun, Kar forgot that the Gods are best known for their trickery.

My father ordered all the men he controlled to attack with a slight wave of his hand and behind him, an Ethiopian guard steadied himself to release an arrow.

The Dilmunians, who had made it to the first landing, alerted Kar to the attack and began their climb up the steps.

To the sound of my scream and many more from the crowd below, the Ethiopian's arrow was released and stuck in Kar's waist as he twirled his staff in a desperate attempt to deflect its course. The Guardian was struck for the second time in an effort to fend off three strikes at once.

More soldiers bounded down the steps and surrounded him.

With blood coating his side and still flowing from his forehead, Kar removed the swords from two of the Egyptian guards' hands and left them easy prey for his new recruits. He then swung his staff full circle in an effort to divide the staged assault. As he drew his staff back defensively, my father sprung upon him with a sword assuredly not just aesthetic in quality. It sounded like Kar's staff cracked beneath its weighted swing, though in one piece it remained. Twice Kar parried my father's heavy long sword before an Akkadian soldier found his way behind the Guardian's defence.

Two blades sliced the soldier's legs before he could

strike. The woman of Dilmun ascended the stairs. She turned her axe and dagger on another Akkadian attacking from the side. A man of Dilmun hacked open the soldier's throat, almost removing his head, with the sickle he wielded.

Looking up, Kar saw my father lunge at him from above. The Guardian rolled to the side and my father found himself below him on the steps. Still on one knee Kar's staff swung at my father's head and cracked his skull. Kar tried to stand and his injured leg failed him. He collapsed onto his hands and knees.

No blood spilled from my father's head though when he rocked on his feet and fell onto his back next to Kar, it was clear that he had been injured.

The Guardian thrust his bladed staff.

My father turned his head to see Kar's blade nestled against his throat, only short of drawing blood. He released his grip of his sword in surrender.

The men, and the woman, of Dilmun kept fighting until the last Egyptian guard and the two surviving Ethiopians retreated up the steps and hid behind their cowering kings. The white curtain at the front of the gazebo had been torn down. My mother stood with my father's new bride. Ankhnesmenre's painted face looked paler than the moon as she huddled against her husband.

'Do not kill him,' I yelled. 'Take me, Kar. I will leave with you.'

Kar glanced at me. Another voice stole his attention.

'You must not kill him, Kar,' repeated my father's new bride as she walked down the steps from the gazebo, accompanied by my mother. 'He has only done what the Gods commanded.'

Kar kept his blade pressed to my father's neck. 'I do not understand,' he said, his voice trembling more than the grip on his staff. 'This fight was for you.'

'And thankful I am to see your face one more time,' she said, her golden hair lifting from her shoulders in the breeze. 'A god the people here will call you, though to me you will always be my little man. You will understand when this is all over and we are free from burden in heaven.'

My mother smiled and nodded in agreement of my father's new bride's chosen words.

Kar was not convinced. He hollered like one immersed in battle before withdrawing his bladed staff from my father's neck, and even then he held it close, ready in the hope the King would attempt to continue the fight.

The people of Dilmun gathered quietly at the bottom of the steps. They were in a state of bemusement though most knew now that what was happening was not another street performance.

'I have been defeated,' my father announced, still lying on his back. 'Humble once more before my Goddess, Ishtar, I am.'

'Your work here is done, Kar,' said my father's new bride. Her green dress, a colour I had never seen in cloth before, hung weightlessly from thin straps on her shoulders. She stretched her hand towards Kar. Around her wrist was a shell bracelet. 'Before you leave, let me hold you one last time.'

Kar struggled in getting to his feet and before he

collapsed I ran up the steps to his side. I lifted his arm around my shoulder and held him half aloft as my mother and my father's new bride approached.

My mother hitched her dress and used a layer of silk to wipe Kar's eyes and forehead clear of blood. She stepped back respectfully.

My father's new bride, a woman whom Derahmus had described as beautiful beyond words, helped me lift Kar to his feet. She kissed him gently all over his face and whispered, 'Walk to heaven a victorious man. Wait for me there with my true love, Unbetum.'

Kar tried to smile at her with tears in his eyes. He then pushed against me and signalled that he could stand by himself. With the help of his staff he turned from the gazebo and hobbled down the stairs past my father to the first landing. There he looked upon the faces of the huddled group of maidens he had led to this faraway land.

One of the young women, like my mother, saw the need to tend to his wounds and raised cloth from her dress as she strode towards him.

Kar stopped her short with a raised palm and signalled his maidens to care for the people of Dilmun who had rallied against the Akkadians.

Many of the brave men of Dilmun had also suffered injuries and now that the fight was over, they noticed their own blood. The woman, who had fought with Kar, sat and placed her blood-coated weapons on the step next to her. She untied her hair, leant back and let it dance in the wind. Like the Sun had chosen one, an ethereal glow painted her face.

Kar removed the feathers from the end of the arrow that had pierced his side and pulled it through the wound. He clasped his side with a green cloth and continued down the steps to where the crowd formed an aisle leading away from the gazebo towards the port.

The maidens were quick in finding suitors amongst the men who had fought their way to the first landing. The four young women who did not find a man on the steps only had to widen their gaze to see that at the bottom of the steps there were many more to choose from. Amongst these men were some closer in age to the young maidens and they were being offered by their parents who had assumedly held their sons back from fighting a seemingly unwinnable battle. Only one of Kar's maidens remained on the steps and she sat with the woman from Dilmun. They seemed prepared to happily wait for whatever came next. Neither of them looked back at the King lying on his back amongst dismembered limbs and lifeless bodies.

The aisle formed for Kar remained open for the exit of the maidens and their suitors. One painful step at a time Kar hobbled further away from the gazebo.

There was no applause for what had happened, just respectful silence and some whisperings of admiration, attempted explanation and confusion. Those who thought they were witnessing just another spectacle of entertainment in the day's events were surely left the most baffled.

'What are you waiting for Enheduanna?' asked Ankhnesmenre, startling me once more with her sudden approach. 'How many good men must fall into your lap before you choose one worthy?' Black lines streaked her cheeks from tears fallen from her painted eyes.

I turned to face my mother and, as though she had sent Ankhnesmenre to counsel me, she smiled agreeably. Next to my mother stood my father's new bride. Tears filled her eyes and spilled down her cheeks as she watched Kar walk away.

Alone, on the highest landing, stood my father with a look of unbearable defeat upon his face. He would not look me in the eye. Not even my mother dared approach him.

My father was a God-King and a mortal had defeated him. Soon Amar-Sudra would arrive to bear witness. Regardless of his arrival, the people would turn. The shock that held the people would not last. I knelt next to Derahmus on the first landing and closed his eyes. Before the crowd reoccupied the aisle, or sieged upwards to the gazebo, I decided to follow after Kar. I descended the steps and hitched my dress so that I could run like I had never needed to before.

# 32

# All Goes White

*Scribed by Enheduanna, Priestess of Ur.*

The soldiers manning the Port of Dilmun had made it to the crest of the steep cliffs and there they had assembled at a distance to the gazebo under siege. It was more than a coincidence that opposite their fortified position was the largest drinking hut on the island. As I ran past them, down the wide street, I noticed that ordinary folk oddly separated the soldiers' ranks and that drink was already being consumed in a festive manner. It was not until many hid a mug behind their back and paused from conversation to salute me, that I realised I had run all this way still wearing my regal headdress. I stopped running, short of breath, and pulled desperately upon my headdress to remove what exposed me as the daughter of the King. It was secured with my own hair and my effort to pull it free was in vain.

On the road between the Akkadian soldiers' camp and the drinking hut I had stopped and, when my repeated efforts only loosened my headdress, I surrendered to leaving it in place a while longer. Men I did not know were edging their way closer and I had never spoken to a man without another by my side. I was about to bid a swift retreat when a lady of Dilmun came to my rescue.

'Keep your thumbing hands away from her, Ozil,' warned the table servant to a man approaching me from behind.

He looked at me with distressed eyes and I turned away quickly before he sensed my own fears.

The table servant placed the drinks she had carried outside down on the ground, signalling the waiting men to help themselves. They smiled at the old lady as she pushed me to my knees and started to untie my headdress.

The man she had referred to as Ozil had ventured dangerously close to me in my moment of distraction, though, according to the table servant who now helped me remove my headdress, he was not to be feared.

'Ozil would have protected you until help arrived. He smells trouble like a dog. Every fight, every fire or leaking barrel, he's there. All men you must treat like dogs. Scold them when they misbehave and only reward them when necessary, otherwise they will be jumping at your side all day or sniffing where they do not belong.'

'Do you know why the soldiers gather here?' I asked with my head stooped as she untied my headdress.

'Blame me, Princess,' she bent to say. 'They mingled here for a while and I offered them drink. I told them they were best off watching before advancing further. Those four, over there, seem newly acquainted with their maidens and needed no encouragement.

Right I was, I believe.' She put her hands either side of my face and lifted my head. 'Look at me, tending to a princess with my rough hands.'

'I am a priestess not a princess,' I said in a defiant yet quiet voice. 'My life is devoted to Nanna, our moon God, not my father.'

She pushed my head down to untie the last few braids holding my headdress in place. 'Why do you run then child? Is your god not in your service this day?' She pulled the headdress loose and I looked up at her.

'I chase after a man I may never see again.'

She smiled, the hairs on her upper lip glistening in the sun. 'He went that way, Priestess,' the old woman told me. She pointed away from the steep road that led down to the port. In her spare hand she held my headdress.

'You lie. The island has only cliffs that drop to the sea in that direction.'

'Oh child, you do not know what a lie is until you have suffered as a result. I tell the truth. Despite your origins you are more innocent than my own daughters. Chase him to the cliffs. Show the man your love, Priestess. Make his last combat be a choice to die alone or in your arms.'

I shifted my gaze from the steep traversing road down to the port to the rarely tread ground that expanded east to the other side of the island's narrow peninsula.

'Why do you hesitate?' she asked me. 'Fast in pursuit you were until you stopped to deal with this hindrance. Look and you can see that even the soldiers are curious to know what the young Priestess will do next.'

Without looking, I felt their eyes upon me. 'I am not regretful for doubting you, woman. My headdress is yours to keep and should by chance your words be deceptive, then I will suffer as a result and learn the true essence of a lie. Maybe my whole life is a lie. I have spent my life recounting messages from the Gods. Do you know —'

'Stand back, Ozil. That goes for all of you. If any of you men even breath upon this lady, I will have my father block the barrels.' After this outburst she returned her attention to me and apologised with a forced smile for the men's behaviour.

'I do not even know your name,' I told her, sensing a reason to continue our conversation.

'Is my name as important as the man who hobbles further away?'

'No, it is not,' I admitted, 'though too many a quest I have heard of goes wrong in trusting a stranger.'

'Then trust your own judgement, Priestess. I could call myself by any name.'

The table attendant's supplied response made the unmapped course towards the cliffs on the far side of the peninsula the most promising path to pursue in the hope of seeing Kar once more. I gazed upon the hazardous path ahead for a long while. I was waiting for Nanna or another god to offer me the necessary advice to commit. My mother had lost her voice and Nanna had only ever spoken to me through her. News that Mother Ki had died during my father's last eastern conquest justified my concerns. The mother God had made the sky in the east turn green as she made new passage and word of the battle that had taken place beyond the Zagros Mountains had been spoken about as far away as Agade before I even left for Dilmun. My whole world was changing and I was conflicted. I ran all this way so that I may be the one to bathe Kar's wounds. Only Kar could tell me whether my father was a God and who his new bride was. I needed to understand why my true mother lost her voice and still respected my father's new bride. I wanted to be able to explain to the people who frequented my temple and all of Akkadia a reason for this madness.

I opened my eyes and imagined an ideal future. More than imagine, I prayed, envisaged and lusted for one event, one event that would make sense of all to come and all that had been. Kar and I had to join as one. As priestess of the Moon God, Nanna, and he, a warrior of the Earth, strong enough to challenge a King, our child could continue the fight. I would find Kar no longer carrying a weapon other than the staff that held him postulate. The leather breastplate and Akkadian tunic that had covered his hardened, war-battered body would lie on the ground at his feet. Cast aside it would have been, as easily as the gold that bid him command of twelve maidens. Susceptible to the cold touch of wind he would be.

'Look that way until the sun falls and you will be no closer to him, Priestess. Let me see you on your way.' The life-hardened, old lady slapped aside a man standing too close, and picked up the only remaining mug from the tray of drinks she had placed on the ground. With the mug in one hand and my headdress in the other, she escorted me past the gathered soldiers, past the track down to the port and steered me towards the eastern side of the peninsula. When she finished the drink she carried, her participation in the hike was over. She signalled me to keep heading in the same direction east.

'I have nothing else to offer for your service,' I regrettably informed her.

'Women have to look after each other,' said the table servant as she signalled me on with a wave of her hand that held my regal headdress. 'Be careful of your footing, Priestess, and be wary in your return. Even a fool can tell that you are not a lowly woman. You are viewed like gold before many a man's eyes.'

I thanked her once more and watched her return towards the drinking hut before continuing the trek alone.

\*\*\*

My sandals were breaking at their seams and my feet slid in gathered sweat each time I took a step. I did not think I would be walking so long. The rise and fall of the hills hid the horizon in the east and I stopped many times, fearing that I may have ventured past Kar on a different route. Despite questioning my knowledge of maps that showed the island's peninsula to be narrow, and all the while growing more convinced that the lady serving drinks had misled me, I kept walking.

The sun soon warmed only my back as it began its decent. Still, I was yet to receive any encouragement from the gods or sight Kar. Maybe all the gods had abandoned their posts upon the death of Mother Ki. My every decision from now on may have to be made alone. Never before had I needed to make the decision of whether to walk further into the unknown, alone. Even on my journeys to Eshnunna and Susa, I had Derahmus to rely upon. I thought of all my dealings with the Moon God, Nanna, and realised that only my mother had made a connection. Kar and his people knew my God better than me. The Guardians had mapped Nanna's journey through the sky. I had studied their work that was stolen in my father's eastern conquest and knew it to be accurate. Maybe when a man knows the ways of a god, there is no required use for that god. Nanna might have left a long time ago and that would explain my mother's silence. It would also explain why Amar Sudra planned to give me a new name.

Only one god would still most certainly have the fortitude to be vigilant following today's trial. Ishtar, the Goddess of beauty, wisdom and war would have the strength to carry on alone. She, like me, would defy her father and law for love. Yes, I convinced myself, Ishtar is still here and she is in support of my wandering. This is why, despite my concerns, I am not afraid. This is why the revolt against my father did not continue after he surrendered to Kar. Maybe she was the reason that he surrendered to Kar. I smiled to myself and felt a strange sensation course through my weary body. My mother did not need a voice with Ishtar by her side. Nanna did not need a voice either. The new Queen of Akkadia was a God. My father had not chosen her just because she was beautiful. Maybe she had chosen to return to his side now that he had fulfilled his legacy. She had attended him in the gardens of Kish and noticed the delicate way he cut branches. It was Ishtar that made him great. 'This boy who tends the palace gardens of Kish steals my heart,' Ishtar had said when my father was a child and merely the adopted son of an irrigator.

I often asked what happened to Akki, the irrigator.

'*Remember your father, not his father,*' my mother had told me. '*Remember always that he is loved by Ishtar.*'

I remembered Ishtar's words to Akki as if I had heard them myself. '*I feel so close to him that my gaze wanders no more. Cup Bearer to the throne, I will promote him. One day all man will heed his word and I will whisper to him his intentions,*' she had said.

My conviction was strengthened by this belief. Ishtar put my father in the throne and saved him from Kar's blade this day. She whispered her intentions and silenced my mother's counsel. Strangely, she also favoured Kar by allowing him time to retreat. She even called him her son. Whilst still confused, I was no longer alone on this journey into the unknown. Ishtar, the strongest God remaining on Earth, surely blessed my quest.

***

I reached the eastern coast. A treacherous assembly of jagged, brown rock hindered hasty progress towards the steep cliffs. I had to keep going because there he was. He was sitting cross-legged with his head tilted back. From a distance, Kar looked at peace. I had to reach him before darkness made the perilous climb still between us any harder to navigate.

Between boulders that looked ready to collapse together and over scarred rock faces ripped by wind and the scorching sun, I crawled closer to the steep drop that was the edge of the island. My dress was soiled and torn, and my knees and hands were bleeding by the time I got close enough to gain Kar's attention. He must have heard a whimper of pain for as I climbed onto the rock face behind him, he asked if I required assistance.

'Are you safe, Princess?'

I did not correct him that I was a priestess. 'I followed you to offer my assistance,' I told him instead. 'It will be dark soon. Is this where you plan to spend the night?'

He tilted his head back towards the sky and I sat down nearby. I watched his eyes flicker like cricket wings and forgot the question I had planned to ask first. He wore only a loincloth and the long shadows from the setting sun made the scars on his body and baldhead look even deeper. Blood still flowed from his scalp and waist. I could not see the cut to his leg but the pool of blood he sat in signed that this also required my attention.

'Tell me, why does Sharru-Kin's daughter follow me here?'

I edged slowly closer across sharp rocks. 'Let me tend to your wounds?' I asked. He only had half an ear, so maybe he had not heard. 'I must bandage your wounds before you bleed to death. Kar, please let me help you.'

He rolled his head slowly to face me as I slid down the rock behind. 'I was only a boy when your father sent his army east the first time.'

I climbed up the next rock face towards him. 'Some would say you still are. At least three harvests younger than me you must be.'

He smiled and sighed. 'I do not feel young any-more. My body is now as broken as my mind.'

I shuffled across the smooth rock without waiting for his invitation and knelt by his side. 'I will tend to your leg first. I saw it cut by a blade.'

He closed his eyes and the smile on his face turned to a grimace of pain.

'Lean back,' I told him. He cooperated though his movement opened the wound he had clamped shut in his seated position. He did not cry out with pain, he just released a low, steady groan that seemed to have no end. 'How can you say your mind is broken?' I questioned him and hoped he would keep talking as I used my finger length blade to cut and tear strips of cloth from my dress to cover his wound.

He opened his eyes and was quiet for a long while before he answered. 'We spend so much time through-out our lives questioning our purpose and which gods, if any, we should worship. Discover those truths and you would rather talk about anything else. Held by a never agreed upon vow of continued silence, the one thing everyone wants to hear cannot be voiced and can never be written. It is as though the gods have cast a spell of secrecy or given us tongues that cannot speak their words.'

'Tell me Kar and we can change that,' I whispered, noticing as I glanced sideways that his eyes were closed once more. 'I will finish my next tablet by scribing that I, Enheduanna, am the compiler of this tablet and tell my King, my father, that something has been cre-ated that was never created before.'

'What happened this day at high sun?' he asked me, not waiting for an answer. 'Look at where our travels have led us this eve.'

I was tying the first bandage in place around Kar's leg when I felt his hand tapping at my side. I turned to face him and lifted his hand so that I might hold it in mine. 'What pains you, Kar?' I asked.

'I believe I know it all now,' he confessed. His eyes opened wide with excitement though his face was still pale. 'When to think is to know, your role becomes simple. You play your part with little enthusiasm, always reflecting on the past because you know what the future holds in store.'

'If you are trying to make the truth sound bearable to my ears, you waste your needed strength,' I warned him. I pressed his hand to the arrow wound on his side and tore more cloth from my dress. His scalp was now coated in blood and also needed immediate attention.

'The truth I have learned is that the Gods walked too long on this earth. Always strangers we were meant to be. Enlil thought starting again was the best solution yet Enki did not believe that all mankind should suffer for mistakes that the Gods' made. Hear my proclamation, Princess.'

'My name is Enheduanna, Kar, and I am a priestess not a princess.'

'Enheduanna,' he continued, 'Priestess or Princess you are the daughter of Sharru-Kin or of the Bull of Heaven as he has also been revered. Demonstrate his strength he did until once more Ishtar fastened his heavenly reins. He would not have surrendered to me otherwise. I would have rejoiced in using the last of my strength to cut your father's throat and toss him down the stairs. Still, he was defeated and now a new morrow is upon us. My father hastened its arrival and your father must have learnt at a late age what it is like to be a man. Your father will be brought nigh to death when he returns to the mainland. The long lie of destiny he will have to live with and an escape, like the one I plan to make, will not be allowed with my mother by his side. It will be age that takes your father's life. He will have to learn many a lesson late. That will be his redemption and the reason I was told to spare his life. My mother and father, unlike your parents, were allowed to live their lives and learn these lessons before duty was bestowed upon them. As for me, I have spent my whole life trying to be a man. Now that I am one, I feel ready to die.' He turned his face to mine. His eyes glowed bright green and beneath them lines tracked down his dusted face from tears already shed. 'Was it all worth it? What will consume your father's mind when he is removed of all duty and stature? Will he regret or rejoice in the lives he has taken to build his empire?'

Kar's words and the slap of my unfastened hair against my face angered me. Yet, the exhilaration of sitting alone with this wild man of the East and the growl of the sea below was strangely comforting. 'Too much blood is flowing to your head now that I have tied the cut on your leg,' I told Kar. 'Sit up for me,' I requested. I lifted him myself and shifted so that one of my legs supported his back before tearing more cloth from my barely recognisable dress.

Never had I seen so much of my body in the light of day. Shimmering white, like the paint on our temple walls, were my exposed limbs. Rested against Kar's golden skin, my legs looked strange and the dark hair between my thighs was visible. Thankfully, Kar was distracted by deeper thought. I looked at the delicate brace of my thigh on his lower back before I studied his face.

His eyes scrunched shut. 'My escape is not destined,' he said. 'I know why I found the tree and I know why others experienced visions like me.' He faced me.

I wiped dried blood from his cheeks. 'Please tell me more, Kar. You must, as my fate is entailed.' I was enthralled by his words though the absurdity and inconclusiveness of his supposed learnt truth left me unfulfilled and angered. I wanted to reintroduce Kar to my father as a changed man. Kar might have changed him and together they could achieve what no leader had before. My father's empire was immense and, with the support of Kar, lasting peace and prosperity was possible. The plight of many could be realised in greater ways. It could be an alliance as great as that of Gilgamesh and Enkidu. I would write a timely tale that could be retold to the people who dwelled in the lands my father planned to conquer. From us they would learn the art of writing and diplomacy and we would learn to accept their culture. Independent of our rule as separate and self-governed lands they would remain. New forms of dance and play would be entertained and, instead of half the Akkadian populace being dressed as soldiers, only a few would be necessary. Should the need arise, every man, woman and child of Akkadia would stand against the threat. If the strongest empire in the West could set an example like that, peace could endure. 'Do you trust that I care for you Kar?' I asked and nudged his back playfully, though it was also an attempt to see if he was still alive.

'I do not trust that you hear what I say as truth, Priestess. Guardians love to tell a tale and that is all most are interested in.'

I laughed, 'Do you think I followed you here to listen to another story? Never before have I ventured so far alone. It would be a lie though if I told you that I never imagined a day like this.' I tore another large strip of cloth from my dress and lowered it over his face. I proceeded to wrap the piece of cloth against the open wound on his scalp. 'You do not need to impress me, Kar. My presence should have told you that. Let me be your destined escape. My father, or Ishtar herself, will dispatch men to rescue me and I will ensure that your life is spared so that you might serve us all. My intended duties for you will be, in entirety, to love me, to always speak your mind, and when the time comes, plan an escape for us both together to a land without walls and temples. Is that not a more hopeful plan? Sleep from this day forth you can in my arms.'

'It is cloth from your dress,' exclaimed Kar.

'Yes, it is cloth from my dress. Be still while I tie it.'

'You do not understand,' he cried out over the sound of the sweeping winds and waves crashing against the rocks below. The blood trickling down the bridge of his nose was splayed across his cheeks as he shook his head like a dog drying itself. 'I cannot wipe my eyes clear. I am afraid to open them again.'

'Let me tie this knot and I will.'

'No,' shouted Kar, 'I must make sense first. The

vision shared with me has found end. This is the vision I experienced when I took my friend, Lagesh, to the tree.'

'The tree?' I questioned.

'The tree is ... was Mother Ki. She is the God who stayed the longest on this Earth. She found a way to stay in hope for this day.' Kar tried to stand but I held him seated by putting my leg over his. He accepted my restraint. 'Beneath her branches I had a vision,' he continued. 'After facing your father, I walked past crowds accepting of my presence to cliffs overlooking the southern seas. Before I rested here, I looked upon the sea before turning my stare to the sky. All went white. That is how my vision ended. It was the white cloth of your dress covering my eyes. All turned white when my vision ended. This is where my life starts again. The end is the beginning.'

'Are you telling me that you dreamed about me, Kar?'

'It was not a dream, Priestess. It was a vision of things to come.'

I secured the final dressing to his head before leaning around and wiping his eyes and cheeks clear of blood. 'Reward me then, Kar. Tell me the reason for our meeting this eve. The shadows are long and the sea dark and foreboding yet the sky still lights our faces.'

'I thought I was dying,' explained Kar, 'yet here I sit in the real world and my life still feels like a dream unfolding. My vision, so demanding, is already just a memory. All turned white and now I see again.'

'Look at me Kar. Show me that you see me in the real world,' I requested sternly, for his gaze was too distant even when it caught my eyes.

He turned to face me and in the light of the setting sun his wide, wild eyes were alive again. The colour had returned to his face. 'I see you, now, Priestess.' He raised his hand and caressed a lock of my hair in his fingertips. 'Twice you saved me this day. Mother Ki knew of you but we were destined to meet as strangers. It had to be this way.'

'Is Mother Ki dead?' I asked. 'How much of what I have heard is true?'

'My father burnt a beautiful tree for the whole world to see. Her dead branches smoked like wet grass and filled the sky. Light from the Kavir Desert in the east made shapes and faces in the billowing smoke, and it was so mesmerising that Akkadians and Gutians alike, stopped fighting.' Kar lifted my leg from his and twisted on his buttocks to face me. 'My father shared the strength of Mother Ki with all by burning a tree. Can you feel her life in you? Maybe you had to be there to see and smell the tree burning.'

I placed a finger on Kar's tattooed shoulder and circled it around the image of a girl standing next to a man with arrows stemming from his body. 'Is this you and me? Do you know my father's new bride? She seemed to know you.'

Kar smiled at me and lifted hair stuck to my cheek. He then lowered his hand and rested it on my thigh.

His touch took me by surprise and my entire body shuddered. I had torn most of my dress apart to bandage Kar's wounds and with my legs spread around him, parts of me that not even my maidens had seen were exposed.

'I know your father's new bride,' divulged Kar. 'In my vision, like what happened today, she appeared before your father and turned me away.' His hand left my thigh as he pointed out across the sea to where it met with the sky. 'I would not have crossed so many horizons if I knew my mother was sleeping with my greatest foe.'

'She is your mother?'

'Yes, and I know now that she too was fighting in her own way every step of my journey here.'

'Is she Ishtar? I felt like she kept me strong and helped me reach you.'

Kar's hand returned to my thigh. His other hand clutched my arm beneath my shoulder, his fingers touching his thumb around my thin arm.

I felt his strength run though me. The sensation of his hand on my thigh made me want to sit upon him.

'It is the strength of Ishtar flowing through my mother that you feel. The God may be gone, though the women and men that repeat her miracles are here to stay. I am sure my father felt her strength as he cut and burnt the tree'

'Your father murdered a God.'

'It is not murder if one asks to be killed,' Kar explained. 'My elder, Salarn, told me what the tree wanted and I was careful in telling anyone even about its existence. It is only due to Salarn's teachings that I found the tree and for me it was a place where time stood still. Salarn always spoke of the real world like it was a separate plane of existence, a place where if you understood its offerings, one could defy time. When I stood on the roof of the Guardian tower in Balih

Woods I was looking for something already. I know that now. Salarn needed me to find the tree. Unbetum, my father, was presented with the task of killing Mother Ki. I'm glad it wasn't me.'

I placed my hand on Kar's and braced it to my thigh. 'Can you tell me what you understand or is this truth still masked by a god's spell?'

Kar's smile shone through his eyes and he leant close. 'I was a puppet in their grand plans,' he said. 'I thought only of fighting your father and avenging my mother and other Guardians. But, a long time ago, my elder ventured further into the unknown than any had before and learnt that no matter how far you go, there is always more to see.' Kar released his hold on me and faced east. 'Salarn discovered the real world—people living without a king or city walls, with purpose in their stillness. The real world is all around us, priestess. Often we are just too sheltered by our own world of thought to notice its presence. In the real world you can observe change and only act when necessary. My arrival at this island today is what Salarn, my elder, spent his life completing.'

I gripped Kar's arms. 'You said, "Their grand plans." Who else do you refer to?'

'Salarn, Mother Ki, Elkin and his brother, Ronses, guided me here. They all helped orchestrate my meeting with your father. To know my mother is alive is reward enough for me. The defeat of your father will lead to a change of guard and in the east the Gutians grow strong again. For now, the Pledians are safe. My vision has ended and it was the white cloth of your dress that closed and reopened my eyes.'

The sun was now low in the west and its splendid

colour was curled and mixed on surging waves that peaked before breaking against the stone cliffs below. Soon, I feared, the spell that had united Kar and I would be broken. 'You will die here, Kar, if I do not find place for you to rest.'

'Immersed in fresh flowing water is the fastest way to ascend to new life,' proclaimed Kar. 'Submerged in the salty sea one will know not death but cradle. The satisfaction a baby knows before they open their eyes could be mine forever if I do not survive the plunge. No sight nor sound, no caress nor warmth; mere existence in a place between two worlds is my destined escape if my planned escape fails.'

Against my will, he pulled his arms from my hold and used his staff to help support his weight as he stood.

'There must be another way,' I said, wanting the moment we had spent together to last for eternity. I followed Kar towards the cliff, fearing that even a strong wind could blow me over the edge. 'We can just stay here and await what comes next,' I suggested, thinking of the woman from Dilmun who sat on the steps and placed her weapons aside.

Kar stopped a step shy of the cliff's edge. He turned and handed me his staff. 'I was taught to always go another way rather than part with my weapon of choice. Where I'm going, it's not needed.'

I looked at the sharp blade fastened to one end and felt the contours of the smooth wood in my grasp. My feet, knees and hands were bloodied and my dress was no more than a shredded piece of cloth hanging over one shoulder, barely reaching my thighs. The wind lifted my dress beneath my arms, destroying any modesty I had left. My nipples were erect and they tightened more with each gust of wind. Usually dressed with crown and well combed, my hair was now a mess of knots and coated with blood after using it to wipe my hands clean while I tended to Kar's wounds. A very different version of me, Kar must have come to know.

'Every man must have a princess and mine is a priestess,' he told me. 'With the last of my strength I must leave now and step over the edge.'

I pointed in the opposite direction, over the rocky climbs and falls that eventually led back to the drinking hut or farming land if we headed more to the south. 'If my father loves your mother, a life for us both is possible in Akkadia.'

'My soul will find cradle in the salty sea if I die in the jump.' Kar glanced at the staff in my hands before he cast his eyes over the edge at the sea surging below.

At a distance, I saw the silhouette of an Akkadian vessel heading our way along the coastline. It was the boat that Kar had arrived upon. I sighed. His distant stare as I sat with him was more than reflective. Like all men, he was still thinking of himself. He was pondering his escape. 'You should not have called me a princess or a priestess,' I told him.

'What should I have called you?'

'Amar Sudra was to rename me at the Feast of Ishtar. You should fulfil his role.'

Kar stretched his hand out to me, 'I would name you, Ishtar.'

I did not feel like a princess or a priestess anymore. Kar's words and presence made me feel like a god of love and war. These were the sensations that I had truly experienced for the first time this day.

'Should I survive the jump, I will try to find you again, Ishtar,' pledged Kar as he balanced himself on the cliff top and noted the position of the vessel sailing our way. 'I no longer have a vision to guide me, so this day I speak of might not come to be.' His face stiffened with his body as he prepared to take the dive.

'I will arrange our next meet, Kar, by pulling you from the cradle of the salty sea.' Carrying his staff, I bounded past him and leapt from the high cliff into the surging sea below. Half way through the fall I tossed the staff aside and my arms spiralled fiercely as I entered the water.

It felt like I had plunged to the bottom of the world. I swum desperately towards the surface and it just seemed further and further away. As my arms tired, I was lifted by a wave and gasped for breath. Through the foaming water I saw the cliff face and I held my hands and feet out to the impact. I was sucked back out to sea over jagged rocks before another wave battered me against the cliff.

'Grab the rope,' bellowed a siren's voice through the sea spray.

As the wave collapsed and I was pulled out to sea again, I saw the rope she spoke of amongst the sea foam. I grabbed hold and as the next wave hit, I felt my body float before I was dragged once more towards the cliff.

When my body surfaced on the other side of the wave, I saw that Kar's boat had arrived.

The maiden, Silda, pointed me out as the head guard from the gazebo steps and four farming boys from Dilmun hauled the rope and pulled me through the waves.

I heard the boat creak as its hull was flexed against rock and watched guards whom had once protected the steps to my father's sanctuary correct the sails. My hands grew weak and I wrapped my legs around the rope so that I could hold on long enough. When I was closer to the side of the boat several men held onto one man so that he could reach down and pull me from the water. Silda covered my naked body in a fur and other maidens on the crowded deck began tending to me.

'Leave us alone,' Silda ordered the mix of guards and farming men surrounding me like beggar children in the markets.

They followed her order and further orders from the boat's captain.

At the steer of the boat stood an old man with spindly legs, dark skin and a baldhead. 'Raise front sail and turn main sail due south,' he hollered with a coarse, aged voice. 'We will sail around this peninsula with pace and head for the horizon in the east.'

'His name is Elkin,' sounded a familiar voice, barely audible over the sound of crashing waves and the flap and slap of the sails as they were turned to align with the wind.

I pushed my hand against the maiden tending to my head wound and she adjusted her footing so that I could see who spoke to me from the far side of the deck.

'Elkin knows what is beyond the next horizon,' Kar called out to me, before grimacing as the bandage around his waist was pulled taut by a man with eyes wide on his face.

Between us on the deck our pooling blood met and slurred. The front sail caught the wind and lurched the vessel away from the rocks and into the open sea. A new life had begun for me. For better or worse, I had aligned with the enemy.

# 33

# Heaven Knows No End

*Scribed by Kar.*

My journey was complete and I had reached heaven alive. I crawled down a smooth rock face and let my feet dangle in the fresh water rushing through the Karun Gorge. From the highest peaks, a torrent was on its way, the swell crashing around the river's banks on its determined course. I awaited its arrival—this day had been coming for a long time. The sky grew dark as if the almighty wave blocked the sun. I stared at the cliff face at the northern entry to the gorge. The surge of water hit it like a battering ram as it rounded the last bend. It curled upwards before it collapsed with the weight of a tower upon me. Smack. My face hit the stone. Gush. My face surfaced as the rush of water continued down through the gorge. I was sodden but alive. With my hand stretched out in front of me, I tried to lift myself to my feet and that is when I awoke.

Pain tore through my body as if I was being stabbed. Water splashed against my naked skin as I sat up. A hand gripped my arm. I pulled away defensively, unable to see in the darkness.

'You are safe, Kar.'

I recognised her voice. 'Ishtar.'

'My new name is still strange to me,' she said.

'Should I call you—'

'No, I want the name. I want the name you chose for me.'

Moonlight broke through a gap in the clouds and reflected off the turbulent sea, lighting the side of her face. Like the moon, she looked pale and peaceful. 'Go back to rest, Ishtar. I need to pass water.'

She lowered her head and it became one with the uneven ground. Surrounding us on the deck were at least eight others. Their bodies and faces were wrapped in their furs. This was necessary to sleep through the crash and splash of the waves as the boat lifted and fell.

I hobbled along the side of the vessel towards the stern, never letting go of the boat's reed edge. If I relieved myself where I woke, the wind would have scattered my offering over all those who slept nearby. In line with the mast, I unwrapped my loincloth. I noticed a flickering light low in the sky and stopped what I was doing. That's not a star. I refastened my loincloth and hastened my awkward shuffle along the side of the boat.

The crack of a slackened sail in the shifting wind startled me and I regretted not passing water sooner. I turned and glimpsed a figure disappear beneath the deck though a trapdoor. At the steer end, there was no one controlling our vessel.

'Are you lost?'

The voice startled me more than the flapping sail. His silhouette appeared to be an extension of the mast, as he stood so still and thin in his lean. 'Elkin, can you see the light?' I called back. I could not tell north from south or see my own hand as I pointed. 'We are being followed by another boat.'

'They were following until our torch was extinguished by the rain.' Elkin stepped towards me in time with the boat's rock and crouched, holding onto a rope to the mast sail. 'We are also blind. I might have sailed beyond the mainland's last peninsula.'

'I will help you look for stars.'

Elkin reached out and placed a hand on my shoulder. 'You need to rest, Kar. Izad is building a new torch.'

'We should not light our position,' I warned Elkin and held on as the boat lurched in the sea. A pain in my leg shook my whole body as I balanced myself.

'Only fear the storm, Kar. Your maidens accompany the Akkadians who follow. You did promise them life on new shore, didn't you?'

I made sense of the predicament. Elkin had followed me to the island to help escort those who supported our fight. South-east of the Island of Kings, according to Guardian maps, there should have been a peninsula extending from the mainland. If we sailed beyond this, we could end up sailing to the end of the Earth. 'Thrice you have saved my life. I remember first meeting you after a sand storm. I must help you.'

'You will help me by resting.' He pointed to my head. 'Even the son of a man who wore eleven arrows is mortal. One day your count will reach eleven and there will not be a saving hand.' Elkin stood and stepped across the rocking deck to the mast.

I touched my cloth-wrapped head and could not tell if it was blood or water trickling from my scalp. Before retreating, I tried again to empty my bladder respectfully. In the darkness, with the wind twisting and lifting the waves, and the rain continuously sheeting across the deck, I was not sure how successful I was. I tied my soaked loincloth to a sail rope and edged my way back towards those sleeping beneath furs.

'Kar,' the priestess called out. Her voice sounded like a whisper competing against the shouting wind. She lifted her fur to accommodate me.

I lowered myself on my good leg and shuffled along the deck until I was wrapped beneath her fur.

The sound of the sea was silenced beneath her fur. I only heard her breathing and the sticking of her dry lips each time she opened her mouth and did not speak.

'Are we safe, Kar,' she whispered to the back of my neck.

I rolled over and placed my arm around her, feeling no cloth between my hand and her body.

She gripped me tight, sharing her warmth.

'Elkin will find a way if a way is shown.' My hand caressed her naked back and I felt her breasts press against my chest. 'I saw the vessel following,' I told her. 'They are close but until Izad lights another torch, they are blind.'

'More of your maidens are on that vessel. They could be lost at sea.'

'There was slack in our sail. Elkin waits for them. I trust that he knows these seas.'

'Do you trust the other man, Izad?'

'I do. He wants to be a Guardian.'

'He is not a Guardian?'

'I am the only Guardian on this journey.'

'So we both travel with strangers.'

It did not feel that way. Like the Gutians, each person who joined my quest felt like a Guardian who had been lost to the West. 'Is it still the same day?' I asked her.

'The sun has not risen again since we met, if that's what you mean.'

'I have felt lost since I woke.'

'You startled me when you leapt from the fur,' she said. 'I thought you might not remember me.'

'I would not have forgotten a priestess who twice saved my life in one day and then leapt into the sea.' I remembered a fleeting glimpse of her half naked body rushing past me. My plunge into the underworld soon followed. When I had looked across the deck I did not see a priestess or a princess, I saw a woman without crown. Her hair was wet and there was no paint upon her face. Unlike Anava, my princess of the Desert City, this woman's brows were thin; her skin was pale and her arms weak. In our shared darkness, held close beneath her fur, she became the source of my imagining. 'I need not go where I planned to go,' I told the priestess I had named Ishtar.'

'Where did you plan to go?'

'The Guardians might begin riding out to meet me on my return when they learn my quest is complete.'

'Then you should ride their way.'

'Two fires burned the day Mother Ki died. One would have hollowed the tower we held sacred and that worries me not for the Guardians need hide no more in

Balih Woods. Stronger the Guardians are now with the Gutians to protect us.'

'Would I be welcomed if I returned with you?'

'I can only speak for the Guardians. The Gutians do not need their gods anymore though I am certain they will still praise them. Remember their name Enheduanna, for should your neighbouring city fall raid to the Gutians, your city will be next. The Gutians will be named as a people who brook no control.'

'I don't want a city anymore, Kar.'

'New life in the East is reliant upon change in the West. A new king—'

'Likely to be my eldest brother, Rimush,' she said.

'And all that was done could be forgotten. Heaven knows no end where the beginning and end meet unchanged. Each rest for change is a glimpse of heaven. I found heaven first at the Karun Gorge. I find it again with you, lost at sea.'

'Should we settle upon solid ground, where will you go?'

'I will rest in the West. There is nowhere I need go without you.'

Ishtar, the former Akkadian Priestess was still and silent in my brace. For a long while, I could only hear her breathing. 'I will complete my last tablet. It will be finished as promised except that I will inscribe, Ishtar, instead of my former name, Enheduanna, am the compiler of this tablet. I will tell the new King that something has been created that was never created before. Will you know where to find me when my work is done?'

'I will.'

# 34

# The Eye of Lagesh

*Scribed by Lagesh.*

The East and its people are safe from King Sargon's war with the world. High in the mountains to our north, the Barbarians have carved depictions of the sun and birds into the cliffs for Enlil to feel as he sweeps by. In the mountain valleys to their south, the people we labelled bandits have swapped bones for clothes. They study Guardian maps and plan changes. Susa, the capital of Elam, is beautiful once more with its gardens in flower and the cracked stone now delicately lined with moss; a timely reminder of the capital's importance and the sacrifices made. In the hollows of the Guardian Tower, the children climb the stone throne, pretending to be kings and queens. No one older dares sit there amongst the soot-lined walls of a roofless tower.

I spend many days admiring the view west from the watchtower that I called my people to build in the open plains. Beyond the mountains is a land I do not know very well and I pray for three things. First, I pray that I have time to tell Naten and my next born child about my life with Mother Ki. Then I pray that

Kar will return one day and complete my vision. Last of all, I pray that my dream of Heaven on Earth was a vision; a vision being a truth not yet revealed.

Kar has now been gone for twelve harvests. He may not recognise me anymore. 'He rests in the west,' an old and seemingly wise visitor to our village, called Elkin, told me. Whether he is or he is journeying elsewhere is no longer my quarrel. For the Guardians, it is and has always been about the ride and sharing a journey with another. Be it a wild stallion, a fellow Guardian, a trader or even an accompaniment of maidens, the experience of the ride is in our blood and our blood will not flow full stream without such pursuit.

\*\*\*

In the vision shared with me by Mother Ki, I saw Kar from my watchtower when Naten was giving birth. The morning my daughter, Ameneh, was born, I never left my post in the watchtower. I am not sure if I felt more regret for not being by Naten's side or missed more my anticipated return of Kar.

By Kar's deeds the strength of heaven, Sargon, was brought nigh to death. The King returned to Agade, the city he founded, and before the gathered populace, he was humbled. The High Priest, Amar Sudra, announced from the temple steps that the Father God, Anu, had declared Rimush, Sargon's eldest, the new King of Akkadia. Beneath his son in the seat of power, I hope Sargon has time to reflect on what happened in the East. He would have heard of the death of Mother Ki and know that if a God dies on Earth, then that is where they must stay. Sargon, if he is a god, will not be granted the escape to new life offered to Unbetum and the other Guardians.

Unbetum, our village elder, recruited all the women and children, including my beloved Naten, to help him cart the hacked limbs of Mother Ki back to the tower. Before returning to the tower with the final load of branches secured to the back of his mare, Unbetum stacked a bundle of grain stems around Mother Ki's remaining stump and started a fire. Late, that same day, assembled outside the tower, the Guardian women and children watched Unbetum venture inside to light the greatest fire the world has ever seen. Tahnas did not need to explain to those gathered, why Unbetum never returned. The sensation released upon the Mother God's death was insatiable. It was Unbetum's choice to stay and listen until the end.

My father, Gentuk, is now our village elder and he lives with us in the new village, built on top of the village where I was born. We meet between our huts in the village circle to discuss trade agreements with the Gutians or agree upon the planting of crops. The village circle is much like it was in the old days except that all are welcomed to every gathering and meeting. Fankisi is often present at the meetings and she sits proudly with Tahnas, Parbi and Jamine, next to Gentuk. My brother, Senea, and his Princess from Pled, often sit on the other side of Gentuk. Senea never leaves her side. Arman and I are more haphazard with where we sit or stand. My duty is in the watchtower and Arman regularly travels to Dilmun. He has escorted many farming families to our new home. They are welcomed like they are part of the growing Guardian family but there will be no more Guardian men. Parbi's initiation was the last and like Kar, he trains with weapons in the morning and learns to scribe after high sun. I can foresee him travelling one day with Arman and returning with amazing stories. My vision was complete apart from Kar's return. I had seen his return in my vision and the birth of my second child approached.

When I first returned to the tree, I hoped to find it sprouting new growth. I thought that Mother Ki might have had a greater plan that saw her live to see better days. Instead, I found all the tablets from the tower stacked around a burnt stump and hardened by fire. They were assembled in a circular order and Unbetum had scribed his last words into the final tablet in the spiral.

*No one person can tell a story complete. You may be able to read minds, predict the future or even be a god though the truth is always answerable to many. A changed king, a new age, the same burden in a different form. The burden of change is not as worrisome as the knowledge that life, perceived unpredictable, finds ways to remind us of previous ill judgement. Continue to learn and share knowledge we must for the God's work is ours now. Pray to my beautiful wife Kinsufa if all fails for she is not known in heaven and we sense her not on Earth. Her path through life is not the work of gods. Kinsufa created her own destiny. That is something we all must do now.*

\*\*\*

In the distance I saw a crowd of Gutian farmers gathering near our new well. Further afield, I noticed several horses riding their way from the horizon in the south. I glanced down at the hut where Naten was soon to give birth for the second time. A boy this time, we thought it would be. 'Parbi,' I called out, when I saw him walking from the village circle to the school. I climbed down from the watchtower and met him on the ground.

'Do you want me to stand watch?' he asked eagerly.

I handed him my bow. 'Naten is my life and I was not by her side for the birth of my first child. I will not repeat that mistake again. It is high sun and I want to see my new son, maybe my next daughter, before the shadows creep. Riders approach. Be sure to alert the villagers.'

I was tempting fate, I thought to myself as I paced towards the hut where Naten was preparing to give birth. I expected Parbi to call out to me mid-climb and announce that Kar had returned. If he did not, I would feel that I had done the right thing in abandoning the watch over something more important. If he did call out, then the thought of whether that would have happened if I did not leave watch would be my mind's quarrel. Content I am in knowing that I have always been a pattern maker. I guided my people to the open plains and dug new wells. I established regular trade with the Gutians and gave them weapons. Enki, Enlil, Mother Ki and the strength of so many other old Gods now flows through us all. Only Anu left before this new life took hold. If the father God is not happy upon his return to our world, then that will be his regret, not mine. We are all his children now.

# 35

# Last God Standing

*Frederick Baker's Journal, Ottoman Empire, December 1850.*

I let the book rest in my lap. It was clear to me now why Babu, in our first meeting, had suggested the unnamed work be titled Last God Standing. If I had the time to complete my read before we embarked on this mission to Assur, I might have proposed another site. This other site would surely be the location sought by fortune hunters following in our footsteps. I watched as Victor's hands untied the lower strings of our tent and entered.

'Hot days and equally cold nights out here,' he said. 'I left the fire before Qasim started another tale.'

I held the book out to Victor. 'I've finished reading.'

'And?' he stayed on his haunches at the entrance to the tent.

'If we travelled further east we could search the woods neighbouring the Zagros Mountains for a burnt stump, remnants of a tower or any unexplained clearings.'

'You've gone mad,' said Victor. He took a swig from his hip flask before crawling further inside and handing it to me.

'I have gone mad.' I placed the book down and took a swig. 'I think of finding the cremation site of Mother Ki.'

'Mother Ki?'

'Mother Nature, the mother of all gods.'

Victor edged closer and looked me in the eye. 'You speak to me seriously.'

I tilted my eyes towards the book by my side. 'It reads that the mother God was burnt for all to see. We might find the tower first and that would be enough.'

'What tower?'

'East of the mountains there is, was, a tower. If we find it or any unexplainable clearing in the woods, this book is more than fable.'

'And what of Assur, is it not definitive proof?'

I sighed. 'It is and it's closer. Any discovery there will probably have us working for many years on the site.'

'Sleep soundly with that knowledge.' He sat next to me on his blanket and unlaced his boots. 'The cremation site of Mother Ki,' he exclaimed. 'There is plenty of God talk by the fire if you are interested. Our guide, Qasim, calls our destination, Assur, the City of God.'

I was interested in this discussion but I heeded Victor's earlier advice and decided to sleep before it got any colder.

***

Qasim was invaluable. East of Egypt, in the Ottoman Empire, everything had a price and Qasim knew when humble thanks or a monetary offer was required. He also seemed to know his way without need for a map. Outside Karbala, a city on the western bank of the Euphrates River, he met an elderly man herding goats. This man left his goats in the care of his son and returned with a camel he had borrowed from a neighbour. He led us through the holy city and towards the Euphrates River. With his help, we crossed the river with our camels on a flat barge and began a two day journey north-east to Baghdad.

'Karbala used to be referred to as God's Sanctuary and the Mountain of Victory,' Lateef told me, translating Qasim's conversation with the elderly guide as we rode behind them. 'Noah's ark settled there and the Prophet Noah and the believers who shared his ark were saved from the great flood by the almighty.'

'They say, the Prophet Noah, not Utnapishtim?' I asked as my camel strode along next to Lateef's. The hardened dirt track allowed us to ride and talk at the same time and I recalled many mentions of the flood in the Guardian manuscript. The Zidonians believed that they lived where the water first rose and the ancient God-King Gilgamesh attempted to discover the source of immortality by visiting Utnapishtim.

'Utnapishtim is the name given to the ark builder by the Sumerians and mentioned again by the Guardians. It is likely the same man.' Lateef was wearing a white keffiyeh and a black agal. The traditional headdress suited him and as it had been twenty days since we left Cairo, a thin beard now also balanced the obtrusion of his thick moustache. He listened to more of the conversation between Qasim and our guide from Karbala before turning back to face me. 'The Koran and the Bible are much the same in their recounts of the great flood. It is the practice of the differing religions that creates the greatest divide.'

I smirked, 'I have seen the divide you speak of.' Our guide from Karbala made only one modest request in exchange for his service and that was that we be silent during prayer. Yesterday, he had shouted at Victor in Arabic when Victor was telling a story during a high sun break beneath a rocky outcrop. Victor should have known to be silent. No matter where we were in the journey, and from the first day we set out from Cairo, Qasim would stop and roll out his mat at noon, in the afternoon and just after sunset. He prayed in the morning and at night too.

I appreciated his prayer times. They gave me time to rest and pray also. I prayed that my lost love, Gloria, would find happiness with Mr Johnston. I prayed that Babu and Lateef would be rewarded for their efforts and I prayed for my parent's health. I also prayed for Victor. Help Victor do what is right. I paid particular attention to the way I worded my prayers. I wanted my prayer to help Victor, not change who he was. I liked that he fancied a drink and still achieved more than most each day. I liked that he called his Bowler hat a Coke and assured all of the difference. My mother had also taught me that praying for myself was not appropriate. So, twice now, I had reached into my knapsack and touched the Guardian book on the side where the pages gathered. That was my silent prayer. It rekindled my dormant pagan beliefs in spirits and good fortune. The book was not made of wood but the pages were. I hadn't said, 'Touch wood,' aloud for many years. I'm not even sure why I felt the need to say it. Was it an effort to connect with Mother Ki or folklore that beckoned me to say such words?

In my first year at Eton College, we played tiggy after the final bell. The goal was to evade capture and make it back to the old oak tree in the centre of the courtyard between the red brick buildings. You had to say, 'Tiggy touch wood, one, two, three, home,' before the person chasing tagged you. That tree was always a safe place. As the boys ran and dodged and screamed, the tree would stand still watching over the game like an old and disciplined adult. Hopefully when I touched the book, I received that tree's timeless blessing. For whatever reason, despite my prayers, I felt the need to say, 'Touch wood.'

\*\*\*

In Baghdad, Qasim and the elderly guide left their camels in our care and approached a wharf that docked many vessels. The sun was lowering behind the city and shadows from the taller buildings stretched like fingers over the port and Tigris.

'One of us should be with them,' said Victor, as he tied his camel next to ours at an empty trough.

Lateef shook his head. 'Qasim said to wait.'

Victor looked at me.

'He said to wait.'

Victor took a sip from his hip flask. He lifted his Coke and tucked it under his arm as he splayed his long unfastened hair with his fingers.

'This looks hopeful,' I said.

'Or compromising.' Victor donned his Coke again as Qasim returned from the wharf followed by the elderly guide and five other men. 'Are you ready to protect yourself, Fred?'

My head jerked. 'No, what do you mean?'

Victor spread his jacket to reveal a curved dagger held in a leather sheath.

'You are telling me this now?'

Lateef cleared his throat.

I looked his way and he showed me the interior of his jacket. Like Victor, he had a dagger at arm's reach, except his was smaller and not curved like Victor's blade. It made me laugh. 'Your blades will not protect us in this empire.'

'Hold that thought,' said Victor as Qasim and the men following approached.

They walked past us and begun pumping water from a nearby well.

'Are you all right?' Qasim asked Lateef, glancing at Victor and me and trying to make sense of our peculiar faces.

'We are concerned about the next stage of the journey.'

Qasim waved his palms, 'No problem, Fred. I know the boat man.'

The men, who had followed Qasim up from the wharf, emptied their buckets into the dry trough where we had tied the camels. They then began to offload our stores on the bank as the camels drank.

'Why are they offloading our stores?'

Victor approached them and told them to stop.

They looked confused.

Qasim thanked the elderly guide first and then called Lateef aside to discuss a private matter.

'Good show,' said Victor, tapping the humble guide on the back and shaking his hand vigorously as he finally took a step away from the other's company.

The elderly guide, who was herding goats when we approached him in Karbala, stood motionless before me as Qasim spoke to Lateef. It was not the custom but I felt the need to bow to him. I kept my bow lowered longer than planned when I felt him patting my head and speaking in Arabic.

Qasim paused in his conversation with Lateef. 'He tells you that all sin is forgiven by one god and to pray to that god not him.'

I raised my head and thanked the man with a handshake.

'He also said that you should pray to this god or face eternal fire,' added Qasim.

I watched the man approach his camel at the trough and wave farewell with a joyous grin.

'He did not say that. Did he?' I asked, unable to imagine the gentle faced, elderly man saying something so damning. I remembered the time he shouted at Victor and returned a heartbeat later to silent prayer.

'He did say that,' confirmed Qasim. 'For three days he has watched Victor talk during prayer time, complain about the heat and food and listened to you explain hope for better treatment in the city.'

'I was silent during your prayers.'

'You were silent to gain his appeal. The English always want something. As a devout Muslim, he does all without hope of thanks or worldly possession.'

My head dipped as I contemplated the man's generosity without asking for return favour. I looked up at Qasim, 'Not all can live like this. Surely, I am not damned to hell for complaining about the heat or want for a better meal.'

'Cast a stone, Fred, I dare you,' said Victor, stepping to my side.

'What did you say?' spat Qasim. There was anger in his eyes as he paced towards Victor and me.

'I dared Fred to cast a stone if he was free of sin,' explained Victor with a smile.

Qasim stood before us. 'What do you mean by this?'

'You brought religion into this, Qasim, and I refer to John 8:7 of the holy book. Unless you can say you are free of sin, don't be stating or recounting any damnable end to my friend.'

I placed my hand on Victor's shoulder. 'The sun is going down. I suggest we respect his afternoon's Salah—his prayer time.'

Qasim closed his eyes and then opened them with a smile. 'I understand your comment, Victor. My apologies for raising my voice.'

Victor tipped his Coke hat. 'You want to tell us why these men are offloading our stores?' They had paused when Victor told them to stop but had recommenced the offload a moment later.

Lateef still stood where Qasim had called him aside. 'Our voyage up the Tigris is arranged,' he pointed to a long wooden boat with a sturdy mast.

I looked to our guide from Karbala as he walked his camel into the city. My mouth clenched and I exhaled heavily through my nose. 'Qasim, have our camels been exchanged for our trip upstream?'

Victor looked at him concernedly as well.

Bells rang throughout the city and on the docked boats and throughout the port, all found their mats and knelt to pray. We walked downstream from the port to find space to speak quietly.

\*\*\*

On a strip of sand between the reed banks of the Tigris and a twenty-foot-high clay brick wall, I asked Lateef what Qasim had told him and whether he planned to share his knowledge with Victor and me.

Victor leaned in with his ear.

'No one will take the camels upstream,' explained Lateef. 'Qasim should have spoken to us first but I think he has made a wise decision. We could waste many days waiting for a boat that carries animals.'

'Do you remember Kar's agreement with the boatman in Zidon?' I asked Lateef. 'We will need those camels for our return. This is not a one-way trip.'

'Qasim fetched a fair price. I can purchase camels for our return.' Lateef looked to the river in thought. 'You mention Kar's dealings with the boatman in Zidon but I think of the boatman who the Guardians travelled with to Assur. Our journey so far has been without incident. If we keep moving, attention will not be drawn to us. This land and its people are foreign to me also. We must trust that Qasim knows what he is doing.'

\*\*\*

The slender boat narrowly missed other vessels as it

sailed upstream on the crowded river. Our boat also felt crowded as Qasim's ego continued to clash with Victor's. When Victor lifted his Coke and waved at passers-by, he was met with disapproving glares.

'I have suggested that you should tie your hair,' said Qasim.

Victor took a step across the deck. 'I will swap my hat with you for a day.' He gestured to Qasim's blue turban and lifted his Coke. His hair fanned in the river's breeze. 'Maybe you should let your hair down. I sense some pent up anger.'

Qasim smiled. 'I am happy in my travels, Mr Ascott.'

Victor nodded and stepped back to sit next to me.

'Nothing is gained from provoking him,' I told Victor.

'He has a crocodile's smile. I've never trusted him.'

'He has served us well so far.' I remembered my first introduction to the man and his vague answer to my question about fishing. 'Maybe keep a quiet watch and avoid misjudging him.'

The character wrinkles near Victor's eyes tightened with his smile and he looked back at me for a long while without saying anything. Eventually, he nodded and turned his stare to Lateef at the bow.

Lateef was appreciating every leg of the journey. He reminded me of the Guardian, Kar, in that he was a man before his time and he struggled with his boyish appearance. Standing at the bow of a boat travelling north up the Tigris, was what Lateef had worked for in his many days reading about such adventures in journals. He cared not, in the moment, for his untameable mop of hair or the thick moustache that sat large on his thin face. He was going to places he had only read about and he did not ...

'Look, Fred,' he yelled from the bow. 'Do you see the natural battlements?'

The mountains were shaped like the top of a fortress wall and I leapt to my feet to get a better view.

'I think we will find a lot shaped this way,' said Victor as he followed me to the bow.

'Only one in such proximity to the Lower Zab River,' said Qasim, as he looked over my shoulder.

There was a settlement at the river's edge before the raised cliffs and behind the settlement was a rise in the ground that did not look natural. 'I see a tell,' I told Victor. I glanced at him and pointed towards the raised slopes to our west and tried to describe the irregularities in the gradient of the ground.

'Calm down, Fred, we don't need every man and his camel involved.'

Qasim held his turban as he lowered his head to me. 'You speak like a prophet, Fred. This is your destination. As you explained, it is another day via river to my home in Mosul.'

Victor put his hand on Qasim's shoulder. 'We've had our differences and—'

'They all leave,' yelled Lateef.

I leant over the bow and then turned back to face Qasim. He had left my side to speak to the boatman. I looked upwards, thinking that our vessel might be flying a threatening flag. The mast was un-flagged.

Qasim returned to the boat's bow. 'He does not know why the people fill the wharf.'

'Do we dock or sail by?'

Qasim stared at the wharf fast approaching. There were two boats tied and the people filled them to tipping point. On the east bank, opposite the settlement, people disembarked from a third boat.

'We dock,' Victor answered. He looked at Qasim.

Qasim nodded and relayed the instruction to the boatman.

As we neared the short wharf, I noticed that the people gathered were not alarmed but waiting patiently for the third boat to return from the other side of the river. The huts in the settlement were constructed from mud brick with reed bound roofs. I counted twenty men and women on the wharf and a similar number on each of the loaded vessels. When I turned to check on Qasim, I found him by my side. The boatman had lowered the main sail and adjusted the staysail to guide our boat to dock. We approached with pace.

Our boatman tossed a rope towards the dock and a man on the wharf threw another one back. Qasim caught it and Victor and I helped him pull it taut. We staggered backwards as the rope caught the boat.

On the wharf, a man pulled the stern of the boat close with the other rope.

I stayed on our boat as Qasim stepped onto the wharf and spoke to those gathered.

A man dressed like Qasim with a blue turban, pointed towards the higher ground on the west bank of the Tigris and explained why they were leaving.

Qasim shook his head and waved his palms at the man as he questioned him in Arabic.

Lateef stood next to me and tried to translate. 'The

soil is no good ... Qasim tells him of the City of God.'

A man wearing a white turban stepped from one of the loaded boats and approached Qasim. He yelled as he shoved Qasim and almost knocked him into the river.

'What does he say?' I asked Lateef.

'He curses and calls Qasim a thief. The other man tells Qasim to leave.'

'A thief?' I questioned Lateef and when I turned back to face the confrontation, Victor was standing between the men.

The man, who had disembarked from one of the loaded vessels, drew a blade from a sheath at his waist and yelled past Victor at Qasim.

Victor drew his curved blade from his coat and cocked his head.

Lateef continued to translate the men's words but I was only focussed on their movement. Qasim stepped back next to our boat and Victor waved his curved blade to signal the other man to leave.

The man wearing a white turban stepped back onto his boat.

'He curses,' Lateef continued with his translation. 'Qasim apologises. More cursing. He tells Qasim to stay on this shore, so that he can watch him die.'

The man who had confronted Qasim continued yelling as the loaded boats were released from the wharf.

'Anyone else want to threaten my friend?' yelled Victor. He tapped the hard brim of his hat with his blade. 'Think about it.'

I stepped onto the wharf between Victor and Qasim. 'I think you have their attention.' Before us stood twenty men all donning white kaftans and keffiyehs of varying colour, tied with black agals. I turned to the man wearing the blue turban who had helped secure our boat to dock. 'This man was saying something about the soil before you were interrupted.'

Qasim pointed over the man's head to the steep banks beyond their settlement. 'They have planted gunpowder kegs in the high ground. In the collapsed soil they plan to grow crops.'

My mouth was agape. 'Have you explained to them the significance of the city that is buried beneath?'

'I have tried. I will try again.' Qasim approached the men and they parted as a young man rushed at him.

Victor shoved Qasim aside and held his curved blade to the assailant.

The young man pointed his blade at Qasim and shouted in Arabic.

'He is a thief and man of many lies,' translated Lateef. 'No, he lies with many. He is an adulterer.'

'Which is it?' I faced Lateef before he spoke. 'I don't care.'

The third boat arrived and Victor waved a few men to approach and help it dock.

I grabbed Qasim by his arm to gain his attention. 'I have no quarrel with you. No quarrel overwrites the importance of this city.'

He nodded. 'I can stop this.'

Victor ordered the young man who had tried to attack Qasim aboard first. He signalled the others to follow.

'Curse word, curse and mention of god, another

445

curse,' translated Lateef as the white robed men walked past us and onto their boat.

When the wharf was cleared, I followed Qasim onto the bank.

'Can you see them?' he asked. He pointed at three places on the high bank.

'I see two men.'

'I see three. Ensure our boatman does not leave.'

I turned to direct Lateef and he was already on the boat. He yelled at the boatman in Arabic, surely instructing him to wait. Victor stood next to the other boat, ensuring that no one left it to fulfil any act of revenge. When I turned to face Qasim, I saw him ascending stone steps on the far side of the settlement.

'Steps,' I shouted to Victor and Lateef. 'He climbs the steps of Assur.'

'And the others descend,' Victor yelled back.

From a nook in the steep bank, I saw the man I had not sighted before leap to his feet and join the others in their descent past Qasim. 'He can't stop all three explosions,' I yelled.

Victor chased after me, wielding his curved blade. 'If you pull the wire it could explode.'

I ran up the ancient steps that I had watched Qasim ascend from a distance.

'We have to take shelter,' Qasim yelled as he bounded back down the slope above.

I pointed to the nook from which I had seen the third man raise his head.

'I can't make it in time,' yelled Qasim.

I looked at Victor and he tossed his curved dagger at me. I caught it above my head by the handle.

Victor leant over with a sigh of relief.

With his dagger in hand, I scaled across the steep bank to the nook. The ignition cord disappeared into a deep crevice. I bounded up the sheer face of the cliff and cut the cord. The loose end sizzled to an uneventful climax.

I looked across at Victor and Qasim and nodded. My nod was like a signal for the fourth and highest planted keg. A gunpowder keg we had not detected exploded on the cliff above.

Victor and Qasim raced the descending soil to the wharf.

I saw the explosion that broke apart the cliff above me and remembered the day I turned a drill in a stone twelve miles outside of Cairo. I dreamt of dying in an explosion that day. I thought that anything would be better than the relentless smoulder of the Egyptian sun. Today, the sun was blocked as earth rained down on me. Beneath my feet, I felt a tremble. The ground gave way and as gentle as a path towards the light, I was entombed in darkness. This is what it's like, I thought to myself. No sight, nor sound, just the endless cradle of the earth. I liked it. It was not as grandeur as my body being splattered high and far but there was peace in the press of the earth. It felt like the soft mouth of a giant fish had swallowed me. Like Jonah 1:17, maybe I would be in the belly of the whale for three days and three nights before being expelled safely on dry land. A glint of light brightened my tomb and I looked above as more dirt and sand fell upon me. A deep throat stretched to the speckle of light above. I wriggled my fingers and found them loose. I tried to move my feet and found them stuck. I glided my hand across my chest to my waistcoat pocket and fumbled my crushed packet of matches. There were several that had not broken.

When the dust had settled, I sniffed the air. There could be trapped methane in the ancient chamber. My nose only smelt dry earth. I struck a match against my coat and watched it ignite. It burned bright in the darkness.

'Fred,' yelled Victor through the speck of light above.

'I'm alive,' I called back. 'I'm standing in a small room. There is a painting of the sun on the wall.'

'That's good, Fred, we should have you out soon.' There was a tremble in his voice that I'd never heard before.

'Victor,' I yelled. 'Look for the cremation site.'

'I will.'

'Fred,' called out Qasim.

'Yes?'

'Can you take a closer look at the sun,' he asked.

My feet were stuck but I managed to lean closer to the wall. My match still burned. The flame was nearing my fingertips. With my spare hand I brushed dirt from the wall at the top of the sun. I kept brushing the image when I noticed more detail. The match was extinguished when it met my fingertips. I dropped it and looked above to the speckle of light at the end of the throat of dirt to my tomb. 'It's not a painting,' I yelled.

'What do you see?' Qasim called back.

'It's an engraving. The sun has feathered wings that extend outwards like an eagle in flight.' I sensed commotion above. Dirt rained down on me. 'What's happening up there?'

'Victor wants me to stay away from the hole but this is important.'

'Speak, Qasim,' I shouted.

'You are looking at a winged sun disc, a symbol for the Sun God, Assur. You have found the lost city of Assur. Do you hear me, Fred?'

I heard him but I wasn't looking at anything without a struck match. The few I had left had to be used sparingly.

'I never fished in Mosul,' Qasim continued.

'I'm still listening.'

'I was a pickpocket and saved my money to travel west and start a new life. I'm sorry I lied to you,' he confessed.

In the belly of the earth I could not have hoped for better company than that of a winged sun god—light in the dark and flight to new life. My end was another beginning, another's reason to dig a hole.

*Here lies Frederick Baker,*
*the only child of Joseph and Margaret Baker,*
*who found peace in the earth*
*beneath a shared sun.*

Like Kar's father, Unbetum, I had a story to complete before I struck my last match. 'Are you still there?' I called out.

'I'm here, Fred,' replied Qasim. 'Victor and I are both here.'

'Qasim, if I can forgive you then surely Victor and the almighty God can too.' I looked up at the small gap of light above. It crumbled in on itself.

# Ackowledgements

I dedicate the completion of the trilogy to my father, David. He crafted and strenghened my interest in history, especially, the lost, forgotten and inexplainable parts that are the essence of this epic story.

My unending thanks to Margaret Kerlin, Cathy de Vos, Peta and Sue. You have inspired my writing and I'm extremely grateful for your feedback over the years.

To Ameneh, thank you for gifting me a Farvahar wall plaque from Iran. I treaure it and respect its meaning.

Special thanks to Naomi Nixon, my new editor for Book 3. Your expertise and the time you took in familiarising yourself wiith the backstory has certainly improved the story in countless ways.

Last, but in no way least, thank you to my readers. I hope you enjoyed the journey. I'd love to read your feedback and answer any questions you might have.

# About the Author

J.P. Manning is a senior English, history and media teacher, documentary film maker and author. He lives on Queensland's Capricorn Coast. His debut novel, Eleven Arrows, was published in 2020.

In 2021, following the publication of his second novel, Enter the Bull's Burrow, he released his debut feature documentary, Last Store Standing, about the rise and demise of video rental stores around the world. This film, like his writing, embraces his love of history.

End of Morrow (2023) completes his Guardians of the East trilogy. More information about the author can be found by visiting the Lost Book Productions' website.